Dear Reader,

I hope you've enjoyed the first two entries in the Rose Cottage Sisters series. In this volume, you'll meet two more D'Angelos—high-powered attorney Ashley and tender-hearted Jo.

Though the thought of the isolation of Rose Cottage practically gives Ashley hives, her sisters convince her it's the best place to recover as her professional life unravels. Despite the family track record, which is two for two in finding love at Rose Cottage, the last thing Ashley expects to find is the perfect match while she's nursing her injured pride. Josh Madison is Ashley's exact opposite. He craves the peace and quiet, and he has a thing or two to teach Ashley about relaxation and the magic of love.

Unlike her three skeptical older sisters, Jo D'Angelo knows firsthand just how powerful a pull this place by the Chesapeake Bay can have when it comes to love. She met her first love there…and had her heart broken. But this is Rose Cottage, after all, and it definitely has enough mystique left to mend one more heart. In its cozy rooms, Jo remembers why she fell in love with Pete Catlett the first time, and he does everything in his power to see that she doesn't get away a second time.

I hope you've enjoyed sharing the enchantment of Rose Cottage and its effect on the D'Angelo sisters. The truth is, wherever we find love will forever be touched with magic in our memories.

All best,

Sheryl Woods

SHERRYL WOODS

Return to Rose Cottage

MIRA®

Recycling programs for this product may not exist in your area.

ISBN-13: 978-0-7783-2814-8

RETURN TO ROSE COTTAGE

Copyright © 2010 by MIRA Books.

The publisher acknowledges the copyright holder of the individual works as follows:

THE LAWS OF ATTRACTION
Copyright © 2005 by Sherryl Woods

FOR THE LOVE OF PETE
Copyright © 2005 by Sherryl Woods

For questions and comments about the quality of this book please contact us at Customer_eCare@Harlequin.ca.

www.MIRABooks.com

Printed in U.S.A.

CONTENTS

The Laws of Attraction

Prologue

The headline said it all: Guilty Man Freed.

Albert "Tiny" Slocum was a charming two-bit punk who'd hoodwinked his lawyer and an entire jury into believing in his innocence. It hadn't helped that the case presented against him hadn't been airtight. He walked out of the courtroom a free man with a clean slate, thanks to Ashley D'Angelo, who'd once been dubbed Boston's "savior of the innocent."

Of course, Tiny had spoiled his innocent act a bit when he'd had the audacity to turn to the jury in front of the judge and call them all suckers. That moment of pure cockiness had proved just what a psychopath he was. It had also earned him a promise from the prosecutor that he would find a way to put Tiny right back behind bars, maybe not for the crime of killing Letitia Baldwin for which he'd just been acquitted, but for some other heinous act he had already committed. There were bound to be some.

That appalling scene had also been the moment that every criminal defense attorney with a conscience dreaded. Ashley D'Angelo was no exception.

Ashley hadn't much liked three-hundred-pound Tiny,

but she *had* believed in him. He'd declared his innocence with such passion. He had a clever mind and a sharp wit that he'd used effectively to charm her into thinking he couldn't possibly be guilty of such a barbaric crime. In the course of what appeared to have started as a botched purse-snatching, elderly, frail Letitia Baldwin had been beaten nearly to death by someone in an obvious rage at finding only a few dollars in her wallet. Tiny had professed to love and respect women. His own mother had backed him up, saying he was the ideal son. Ashley, who'd built her entire reputation on defending the innocent, had been taken in.

She'd also seen all the holes in the prosecution's case. She'd spent months building a defense, but before she could spend a single second feeling triumphant over the not-guilty verdict, she'd been hit with the gut-wrenching realization that Tiny was indeed responsible for Letitia Baldwin's massive injuries. The elderly woman had later died in the emergency room, changing the charge from assault to murder.

There wasn't enough merlot in all the wine cellars in Boston to help Ashley get over that sickening image. The crime scene photos played over and over in her head, like a looping newsreel that never quit.

Later, in the dark of night, when she was lying sleepless in her fancy penthouse apartment, Ashley had finally admitted that on some level she'd known all along that she was defending a murderer—and doing it with the kind of aggressive tactics that were almost guaranteed to win an acquittal. She didn't know how to defend a client any other way, which was one reason she'd always been very, very careful about whom she chose to represent. Her firm had allowed her that latitude because she'd racked up courtroom victories and a lot of press in the process.

But even as she'd planned Tiny's defense, she'd suffered pangs of guilt. She'd been assailed by doubts. That's why she'd run to Rose Cottage before the trial had begun. It had been eating at her even then. Not that she'd wanted to say it aloud or even allow the thought to form. She'd wanted to go right on believing in Tiny, because she had to in order to live with herself. In retrospect, she knew she should have quit the case the moment she'd had that first niggling doubt, but somehow winning had become more important than anything else, and she'd known she could win.

Now that the truth was out, she was sick of the law, sick of her own ability to twist it for her client's benefit. Her self-respect was in tatters. How had her life come to this? This victory tarnished all the others, all the cases she'd been proud to win, all the cases that had earned her a full partnership at her law firm in record time.

Heartsick, she'd been locked away in her apartment for nearly twenty-four hours now, refusing to answer the phone, refusing to go to the door. She'd given a brief press conference, declaring that she was stunned after the debacle in the courtroom, then gone into hibernation to avoid the inevitable media frenzy over that disturbing courtroom spectacle.

Right now she couldn't imagine ever showing her face again, but realistically she knew that the desire to hide would eventually pass. She was a fighter by nature. She just wasn't ready for battle quite yet. She needed time to lick her wounds in private.

Unfortunately her sisters all had keys to her place, and not five minutes ago they'd arrived en masse to offer her comfort and support. Ashley appreciated the gesture, but it was wasted. She'd gotten a murderer off scot-free, and she was going to have to live with that for the rest of her life. It pretty much made a shambles out of the pride she'd always taken in her success.

"It's not your fault," her sister Jo said quietly, once they were all seated with coffee that Maggie had brewed from the gourmet beans she'd taught them all to appreciate. "You were doing your job."

"A helluva job, isn't it?" Ashley said grimly, lifting her coffee cup in a mocking toast.

"Stop it," Maggie ordered irritably.

Maggie and Melanie had driven up from Virginia the minute they'd heard what happened in the courtroom the day before. They'd picked up Jo on their way into downtown Boston. Ashley had little doubt that they'd planned this gathering down to the last detail on the ride over.

They were seated in Ashley's penthouse apartment with its expensive modern art on the walls and its sweeping panorama of the Boston skyline outside. At the moment, none of it meant a thing to Ashley, not even the loyal support of her sisters. Loyalty was a D'Angelo family trait. They would have been here for her, no matter what she'd done.

"Jo's right. You were doing your job," Melanie said emphatically. "Not everyone who says they're innocent is, not everyone who's accused is guilty, and everyone is guaranteed a right to a complete defense and a fair trial."

How often had she said exactly that? Ashley wondered. She had believed it, too, but knowing that she'd been responsible for putting a violent, totally amoral man back on the streets made her sick.

Having been validated by numerous acquittals from juries, Ashley had gotten used to believing she was always right. She'd grown comfortable looking at the law and its loopholes more intently than the crime and its victims. Maybe that was sound law and a solid defense tactic, but she was beginning to question whether it had anything at all to do with justice.

"The man made a complete fool of me," Ashley told her sisters. "How am I ever supposed to trust my own judgment again? How can anyone else? After this, if I said it was sunny, I'd expect people to check for a second opinion. And what client would want me, knowing that every jury is going to regard me with total skepticism from the outset? It's hard enough to fight the evidence in most cases without the added liability of having a controversial lawyer."

"This was one case out of how many?" Maggie asked, regarding her sister worriedly. "Stop beating yourself up. You have an excellent track record, Ashley. The papers describe you as brilliant, relentless, passionate about the law."

"Not today," Ashley retorted, gesturing toward the stack of newspapers on her coffee table. She'd read them all with a sort of morbid fascination, just as she'd watched every newscast. "Today they're asking questions about how many other criminals I've helped to set free. I have to admit, I've been wondering that myself."

Jo regarded her indignantly. She was the quietest of the D'Angelo sisters, the most sensitive, but when she felt strongly about something, she could make herself heard above their nonstop boisterous chatter.

"Do you really think for one minute that you've intentionally set out to free a bunch of criminals?" Jo demanded. "Because if you do, then you're right. You need to get out of law. You need to find some other field where your mistakes in judgment don't matter, where you can't ever be fooled by a clever client."

"I honestly don't know what I'm doing anymore," Ashley replied. Uncertainty was an unfamiliar feeling, and she didn't like it. She'd always been the D'Angelo with a sense of purpose. She was the confident big sister who protected the rest of them. She didn't like being the object of their pity. She didn't like needing them, rather than the other way around.

"A day ago I would have said I was a champion for the truth," she added. "Now I'm wondering if I'm not just a clever lawyer who's easily duped by a little charm and just the right note of righteous indignation." She stared bleakly around the room. "Look at all this fancy stuff I've accumulated because I'm good at my job. When I had to look the victim's son and daughter in the eye today and tell them I was sorry, I felt like a failure and a fraud."

Her three sisters exchanged a look, then seemed to reach some sort of silent, mutual decision.

"Okay, that's enough self-pity, Ashley. Sackcloth and ashes don't suit you. You're coming back to Virginia with us," Melanie said decisively. "A month or two at Rose Cottage is what you need. You promised Maggie you'd come back after the trial anyway. Now it'll just be for a little longer, until you get your feet back under you."

Ashley stared at her younger sister, horrified by the prospect of an entire week—much less a couple of months—away from work. Work defined her. Of course, today that definition pretty much reeked.

"No way," she said fiercely. "I know you and Maggie thrived while staying in grandmother's old cottage, but I'm not cut out for the boonies. A weekend is about as much as I can take." She scowled at Maggie. "I thought I'd made that clear."

"Hey, you're the one who's been carrying the key around with you as a talisman all these years," Maggie reminded her. "Now it's time you made use of it. Melanie's right—you need to get away. You need to think. You can try to figure out what went wrong this time and stop it from ever happening again. Or you can decide to chuck law and do something else entirely. The one thing we won't let you do is sit around and wallow in self-pity."

"As if there are a lot of other career options open to me," Ashley said bitingly. "I'm a lawyer. That's all I know how to do."

Maggie rolled her eyes. "If you were bright enough to graduate from law school with honors, you can probably find another career in which to excel, if it comes to that. You have to take this break, Ashley. You owe it to yourself. For you to overreact like this, it's obvious you're burned-out. You've been working at a breakneck pace ever since law school in order to jump on that fast track at your law firm. It's time to slow down and re-evaluate."

"I agree," Jo said, her jaw set stubbornly. "These two may only be around for a day or two to nudge you, but I'm here for the duration. And I promise I will pester you to death until you agree to take this vacation. In fact, if it were up to me, you'd take a six-month sabbatical."

When Jo, the youngest of them, made such a firm declaration, Ashley knew she was defeated. "Two weeks," she bargained, refusing to even consider as long a leave of absence as Jo was suggesting. "That's all the peace and quiet I can bear."

"Two months," the others chorused.

"Three weeks," she pleaded. "That's it. That's my limit. I'll go nuts if I have to rusticate even one second longer than that."

"Done. Three weeks it is." Maggie and Melanie exchanged a grin.

"What?" Ashley demanded, instantly suspicious of their gloating expressions.

"We were sure you'd bargain us down to a week, max," Maggie said. "You really must be losing your touch."

Ashley started to chuckle, but it came out more like a sob. Wasn't that exactly the point? She *had* lost her touch. And right this minute she couldn't imagine ever getting it back again.

1

This didn't have to be the worst thing that had ever happened to her, Ashley decided stoically as she stashed groceries into the refrigerator at Rose Cottage.

Two of her sisters and their husbands were close by, so it wouldn't be like she was isolated among strangers. She could always order cable, so she could get Court TV and CNN. She'd brought a case of her favorite wine with her from Boston, along with a year's worth of articles by some of the country's foremost lawyers. She'd even tucked a few novels into her suitcases, books centered around trials, of course.

The key was going to be planning out her days, organizing every minute so she wouldn't have time to think about what had happened in that courtroom back in Boston. Heck, that ought to be a snap. She excelled at organization. That was one reason she'd been able to maintain such a high caseload.

Dispersing those cases among the other partners for the duration of her absence had taken an entire week. She'd worked compulsively to make sure each attorney fully understood her clients' needs. She'd briefed them so thoroughly, they'd seemed a little eager to see her gone.

After that frenetic pace, after loading up the car with all the essentials she couldn't possibly live without and after the long drive, she was just starting to feel a bit of a letdown, that was all. It was to be expected. By morning she'd probably be climbing the walls...or calling the office every five minutes to make sure all the cases she'd left behind were being handled properly. She knew it wouldn't take more than a day for that to wear thin with the already exasperated lawyers she'd left in charge. She would simply have to resist the temptation.

She put her laptop on the kitchen table and placed a stack of legal pads and pens right next to it. It had taken every ounce of willpower she possessed to leave behind her law books, but there was a lot of information to be found on the internet. She'd make a few notes on her pending cases and pass them along when the time was right.

The mere sight of those familiar tools made her feel better, as if her life hadn't spun wildly out of control.

No sooner was everything in place, though, than Maggie and Melanie swept in the back door, took one look at her stash of supplies and loaded the lot into a shopping bag. They ignored every one of Ashley's heated objections.

"What the hell do the two of you think you're doing?" she demanded, trying to snatch things back as fast as they picked them up. "This is *my* house. Those are *my* things."

"Actually it's grandmother's house," Maggie reminded her.

"Don't you dare start nitpicking with me," Ashley commanded. "I will leave here."

"No, you won't," Melanie soothed. "You know this is the best possible place for you to be right now."

"And all your precious stuff will be at my place for safekeeping," Maggie promised. "You can have everything back when you leave."

"I need it now if you expect me to stay sane," Ashley protested.

"Forget it," Maggie responded. "And while we're at it, hand over your cell phone."

Ashley felt an unfamiliar hint of panic crawling up her throat. "Come on, Maggie," she pleaded. "I want that stuff. And I've got to have a cell phone. What if somebody needs to reach me?"

Maggie gave her a wry look. "Can you honestly say there's anyone back home besides Mom and Dad and Jo that you're anxious to talk to right now? As for the rest of this, you only need it when you're working."

"And you're on vacation," Melanie reminded her, even as she checked out the stack of reading material Ashley had piled up on the counter. "Sorry. This needs to go, too." She rummaged in Ashley's purse and plucked out the cell phone.

Ashley frowned at the pair of them. "What the hell am I supposed to do for three whole weeks?"

Melanie chuckled. "You're supposed to relax. I know it's a foreign concept, but you'll get the hang of it eventually."

"I can't sit here all day doing nothing," Ashley protested. "I'll go out of my freaking mind."

"We thought of that," Maggie soothed, handing over

a bag filled with videos and paperback novels. "Comedy and romance."

Fluff, nothing but fluff. Ashley moaned. "Dear God, what are you trying to do to me?"

"We're trying to get some balance in your life," Melanie said. "Of course, there's a lot to be done in the garden now. The tulip and daffodil bulbs need to be thinned, and I bought some new ones to be planted out front."

"It's fall, not spring," she reminded Melanie. "Aren't you supposed to plant things in the spring?"

"Not bulbs. They come up early, remember? Trust me, this will be good for you. A little physical work in the sun will take your mind off your problems."

"I don't do physical work," Ashley retorted, glancing at her perfectly manicured nails and trying to imagine them after gardening. She shuddered at the image.

"You go to a gym," Maggie reminded her. "In fact, you're as compulsive about that as you are about everything else. This will be even better for you. You can go for long walks. You'll be breathing in all this fresh, salty air."

"It smells like fish," Ashley retorted, determined not to take pleasure in anything just to spite her hateful sisters. How had she gone all these years without noticing how controlling and obnoxious they were?

Clearly undaunted, Melanie bit back a grin. "Not so much in the garden. You'll see. There are lots of wonderful fragrances out there. Grandmother saw to that and Mike and I recreated it just the way it was."

Defeated, Ashley sat down at the kitchen table and rested her head on her arms. "I want to go home."

"Don't whine," Maggie chided. "It's unbecoming."

Ashley's head snapped up. "You sound exactly like Mom."

"Of course, I do," Maggie said. "We all do, with a touch of Grandmother Lindsey thrown in. They were our role models. The only thing missing is the Southern accent."

Ashley thought back to the subtle lessons their grandmother had instilled in all of them on their visits to Rose Cottage. Cornelia Lindsey had been very big on manners. And, despite the fact that the D'Angelo sisters were growing up in Yankee territory, she'd wanted them to become Southern ladies. She'd taught them the importance of family and friendships, of generosity and kindness. Some of the lessons had stuck better than others.

Ashley relented. "Okay, no more whining," she promised. "But you have to get me out of here before I go stir-crazy."

"You just got here two hours ago," Melanie reminded her, looking perplexed.

"And your point is?" Ashley retorted. "In my life, that's a freaking eternity."

"Okay, okay, we'll go to lunch," Maggie soothed. "No wine with lunch, though."

Ashley stared at her. "Why the hell not?"

"Because you don't need it," Melanie said. "You'll want a clear head for all that introspection you intend to do."

"I need the wine for that." Even as she uttered the words, Ashley heard the hint of desperation in her voice and knew it was a warning. She sighed heavily. "Okay, no wine."

Once they were out of the house, Melanie and Maggie refused to let her wallow in self-pity. By the time they'd eaten a leisurely lunch and shopped for a couple of hours, Ashley had actually managed to laugh without restraint a couple times. She'd almost forgotten that this was the first of what promised to be way too many unstructured, unfulfilling days. When she remembered that, she shuddered.

Back at Rose Cottage, Maggie gave her a fierce hug. "You're going to be fine."

"I suppose," Ashley conceded grudgingly. She didn't believe that, not for a minute.

"And we're expecting you for dinner tonight at seven," Maggie added. "I'm making all your favorites. All those dishes Mom used to make for you before you started subsisting on salads." She winked. "Play your cards right, and you can even have a glass of wine."

Ashley laughed. "Now you've made it worth my while to come over and put up with more of these invigorating, if somewhat annoying, pep talks."

Melanie patted her cheek. "Sweetie, we just want you to get yourself back on track. We promise we won't hover, but we will be around if you need us."

"I know and I'm grateful. I really am, even if I have been sounding like a total jerk." She watched them go, taking her laptop, all those articles and her legal pads. She felt a mixture of relief and fear as they disappeared from sight.

Inside, she glanced at the kitchen clock. It was only two. What on earth was she going to do for five whole hours? What had she done on all those lazy summer afternoons years ago? It finally came to her that when she and her sisters hadn't been out on the water, she'd gone into the backyard with a book in her hand. She'd gotten lost in amazing adventures in exotic locales.

Impulsively she reached into the bag that her sisters had left and withdrew a paperback without even glancing at the title or the author. Neither really mattered.

Before she could suffer a pang of regret or pick up the phone to call the cable company, she went outside to the swing facing the bay. It was wide enough for her to turn sideways and put her feet on the seat, and there was enough breeze to keep it in motion; just a slight, soothing back and forth.

She opened the book, read the first paragraph with the intention of hating it, then read the second with a more open mind. By the end of the page, she was hooked. She was reminded of the pleasure she'd felt years ago when her days had been lazy and undemanding and a good story had been all she needed to keep herself entertained for hours on end.

The best days had been the rainy ones, when she'd curled up on a chair in the living room or on the porch, book in hand, a glass of freshly squeezed lemonade beside her. She'd read incessantly, emerging only long enough for meals or to play cards or board games with her grandmother and sisters.

The satisfaction of that was coming back to her, page by page. In this book, the characters jumped off the page, the romance was steamy and the author's voice was filled with intelligence and wit. Ashley lost herself in the story.

She was stiff and cramped when she finally turned the last page. Her cheeks were unexpectedly damp with happy tears. When was the last time she'd read anything that had affected her like this? Probably before she'd gone to law school. Since then she hadn't had time for the simple pleasure of reading for entertainment.

For the very first time, Ashley saw this self-imposed banishment in a new light, as a real gift. Maybe if she went back to the girl she'd once been, to someone who was filled with hopes and dreams, she'd be able to discover where she'd slipped off track. Maybe she'd rediscover the humanity that had made her a good judge of people before she'd started to rely on cool calculation and mental agility to succeed.

Not that she intended to tell her sisters that she was beginning to see the benefits of this sabbatical. They'd gloat.

"Oh, my gosh, dinner," she muttered, glancing at her watch. It was ten minutes till seven, and she'd never even taken a shower or changed. After all her grumbling about the mere thought of being isolated, if she was late for a party, she'd never hear the end of it.

"They'll just have to take me as I am," she said, laughing at the evidence that she was already adopting a whole new attitude.

That didn't stop Ashley from grabbing her purse and car keys and tearing out of the driveway at her more accustomed frantic pace. She simply couldn't be expected to change everything about her personality overnight.

Josh felt like a rebellious twelve-year-old running away from home and unwanted responsibilities. As he neared the Chesapeake Bay, he could smell the tang of salt water in the cool September air. As he got closer to his family's longtime second home by the water, there was also a faintly fishy scent that he'd come to acquaint with summer. His mother had balanced that with a garden filled with fragrant blossoms, which were just beginning to fade as summer moved into autumn.

When he turned at last onto the final leg of the journey, a long, winding country road that led from White Stone toward Windmill Point, he spotted a dozen or so brand-new homes interspersed with the old cottages and other recently completed vacation homes. The new additions were huge, dwarfing their quaint and occasionally run-down neighbors, but large or small, they all shared the same incredible view of the Chesapeake Bay and its inlets.

He was almost to the cutoff to Idylwild, the small clapboard cottage with its neat green shutters and sweeping porch, when a fancy car being driven toward him way too fast took the turn ahead of him wide. The driver spotted him too late and tried to overcorrect. Josh cut the wheel in the opposite direction, but the crunch of metal against metal was inevitable, the contact jarring but not enough to cause injury.

He leapt out of the car in full lawyer mode, then backed up a step at the sight of the tawny-haired driver of the other car suddenly bursting into tears. At once all he could think about were broken bones and soft, bleeding skin.

"Are you okay?" he asked, leaning in the driver's window close enough to catch a faint whiff of something exotic, sexy and expensive. The combination dealt a knockout punch to his belly and put the rest of his all-too-male senses on full alert.

Brown eyes, shimmering with tears, glanced up at him, then away. Her cheeks blazed with unmistakable embarrassment. Josh studied her, trying to figure out why he felt an almost immediate connection to her, as if they'd known each other before. But that couldn't be, of course. He would have remembered any woman who looked like this. Except for the tear-streaked face, she was as sleek and polished as any of the society women he'd come to know in Richmond. The clothes were expensive, if wrinkled. Gold-and-diamond studs winked from her ears.

"I'm so sorry," she whispered. "It was my fault." She was already fumbling in her Gucci bag, apparently digging for her driver's license, car registration and insurance card. "Dammit, dammit, dammit! Why can't I ever find anything in here?"

"It's okay," Josh soothed, sensing that she was about to burst into another noisy round of sobs that would claw at his gut. "There's no rush. We're in the country. Folks around here don't get all worked up over a little fender bender. We can take care of the formalities in a minute. How about some bottled water? I just picked up a case of the stuff. It's warm, but it might help. I have a first-aid kit, too. We can take care of that scrape on your cheek."

She self-consciously touched her hand to her face, then stared at the blood with shock. She immediately turned pale.

"Hold on," Josh said. "Don't you dare faint on me. It's nothing. Just a tiny little cut." He glanced inside the car, trying to figure out if anything was broken. He couldn't see any glass that would explain the injury.

Without waiting for a reply, he ran back to his ridiculously oversize but trendy SUV, retrieved a bottle of water, some peroxide and antibiotic cream, then went back. By then, the other driver had emerged from behind the wheel, all five-ten or so of her, with narrow hips and endless legs and just enough curves to make a man's blood stir with interest.

"I'm Josh," he said when he could get his tongue untangled. He handed her the water. He poured the peroxide on a cotton ball and reached over to touch the wound, but she immediately tried to take the cotton from him.

"I'll do it," she said.

"You can't see what you're doing," he said, holding firm and cupping her chin in his other hand, then daubing the peroxide on the scrape. He bit back a grin when she winced even before he'd made contact.

"There, that wasn't so bad, was it?" he asked when he'd cleaned the wound.

She frowned at him.

"You never did say what your name is," he reminded her as he smoothed on antibiotic cream, trying not to linger on her soft-as-silk skin.

"Ashley."

He heard the unmistakable Boston accent. "Just visiting the area?"

"For three weeks," she said emphatically, as if that were two-and-a-half weeks too long. "Are you a local?"

"I like to think of myself as one," he said. Richmond

might be where he lived, but this was the home of his heart. He hadn't realized how much he'd missed it until he'd made that final turn onto this road leading to the cottage where he'd spent some of the happiest summers of his life. He'd finally felt as if all the problems that had sent him scurrying down here were falling into perspective.

"Either you are or you aren't," she said, studying him with a narrowed gaze.

Amused by her need for precision, Josh said, "I've pretty much grown up around here."

"Then you probably know the sheriff or whoever we need to call to report this," she said.

"Let's take a look and see if it's even worth reporting," he suggested. He examined first her car and then his own, concluding that they were both in need of new front bumpers and maybe a paint touch-up, but that both cars had escaped serious damage.

"Look, why don't we call this even?" he suggested.

"Because I caused it," she said, grimly determined to take responsibility. "I should deal with all the damages."

"That's why we carry insurance," he corrected. "You deal with your company. I'll deal with mine. It might not even be worth it, though. A body shop could fix things up for next to nothing."

"But I should pay whatever it costs," she insisted.

Josh couldn't seem to stop himself from suggesting, "Then have dinner with me one night while you're here. We'll pick someplace outrageously expensive, and you can buy if it'll make you feel better."

She murmured something under her breath, but finally nodded.

Josh studied her curiously. "What did you say?"

"I said you're obviously not a lawyer, or you'd be all over this, milking it for every dime you could get in damages."

He laughed. "That's just about the nicest compliment anyone's paid me in months," he said, deciding then and there that not being a lawyer for a bit suited him just fine. It wasn't that far from the truth. Wasn't that precisely why he'd come here, to figure out if he wanted to be a lawyer anymore with all that it entailed, including his expected engagement to his boss's daughter?

"Do you have a phone number, Ashley? I'll call you about dinner."

She jotted it down, but before she handed it to him, she added something else, "If you change your mind about my paying for the damage to your car, I won't fight you."

Josh glanced at the paper and saw that she'd written, "My fault. I owe you," then signed her name in the kind of illegible scrawl usually used by physicians.

"A confession?" he asked, amused. "Think it would hold up in court?"

"It would if I wanted it to," she said flatly, then lowered herself gracefully into her car, giving him one last intoxicating view of those incredibly long legs. "See you around."

"Oh, you can count on that," Josh said, fingering the piece of paper she'd given him.

He stood watching until she was out of sight, then

tucked the piece of paper into his pocket and gave it a pat. Coming home was turning out to be one of the smartest decisions he'd made in a long time.

And ironically the past couple of minutes had already given him insight into one of those important decisions he was here to consider. If he could feel this powerful tug of attraction to a woman who'd just creamed his beloved car, then the very last thing he ought to be considering was marriage to Stephanie Lockport Williams. First thing in the morning, he'd have to call and make it clear to her that despite her father's wishes, they had no future.

And right after that, he'd call the mysterious Ashley and invite her out for a crab feast. There was no better way to get to know a woman than watching her handle the messy task of picking crabs. Stephanie had flatly refused to touch the things, which should have told Josh all he needed to know months ago.

Something told him that Ashley would show no such restraint. In fact, he had a hunch she'd go after those crabs with all the passion and enthusiasm of a local. There was something wildly seductive in watching a woman hammer away at the hard shells, then delicately pick out the sweet meat and dip it in melted butter, then savor every bite. He thought of Ashley's lush lips closing around a chunk of backfin crabmeat dripping in butter, and concluded it was definitely a spectacle he could hardly wait to see.

2

"Stupid, stupid, stupid," Ashley muttered as she sat with Maggie on the porch of the farmhouse Maggie and Rick lived in a few miles from Rose Cottage. It had an orchard out back, the trees laden down with ripe apples. The sun was beginning to drop in the western sky, splashing everything with orange light. It was so serene, it should have creeped Ashley out, but she had other things on her mind, like that ridiculous accident she'd caused by driving too fast on an unfamiliar winding road. For a split second she'd lost her concentration, and that had been enough to nearly cause a tragedy. There would have been no adequate defense for it.

"What is *wrong* with me?" she asked her sister plaintively.

Maggie glanced at her husband. Both of them were fighting a grin.

"What?" Ashley demanded. "Why are you two laughing at me?"

"We're not laughing at you," Maggie rushed to assure her. "It's just that the saint is discovering she's human. It's a wonderful thing to see. I, for one, never thought it would happen. I can't wait to tell Melanie and Mike when they get here."

Ashley gave her sister a sour look. "You know, if you keep this up, you're going to make me sorry I agreed to come to Virginia for five minutes, much less three weeks," she told Maggie irritably. "I can go back to Boston first thing in the morning, you know."

"But you won't," Maggie said.

Ashley found her confidence annoying. "Oh? Why is that, Ms. Know-it-all?"

"You made a deal with us. If you break it, then we'll know you're in some sort of emotional meltdown that probably requires hospitalization."

Ashley scowled. "Not even remotely funny."

"I didn't mean it to be," Maggie assured her. "You need this sabbatical, Ashley, and one way or another we're going to see to it that you take it. Rose Cottage is much cheaper and a whole lot more pleasant than some quiet sanitarium in a tranquil setting with shrinks watching your every move." She let that image sink in, then asked, "Don't you agree?"

Ashley stared hard at her sister to see if she was joking. She didn't appear to be. "You wouldn't do that to me."

"If it was the only way to assure that you get some rest, we would," Maggie retorted emphatically. "Don't test us. That's how worried we are about you."

"Mom and Dad would never allow it," Ashley said.

"Are you so sure of that? They're worried sick, too."

"I'm not having a damn breakdown, though you could easily drive me to one," Ashley said, barely keeping a grip on her temper. The last thing she needed to do was give them ammunition to have her committed. And they *would* do it. She could see that now. There was no mistaking the resolve in Maggie's eyes.

"You're not having one *yet*," Maggie agreed. "But you're on the verge, Ashley. None of us have ever seen you strung this tight before. Everyone has their limits. What happened in court was only the final blow. You've been pushing yourself too hard for too long."

"I think we need to change the subject before you really get on my nerves," Ashley told her sister. She deliberately turned to Rick. "Do you know of a Josh around here?"

Rick looked as if he didn't really want to be drawn into the conversation, even if the subject seemed to be neutral. Ashley could hardly blame him. When he shrugged, she turned back to Maggie. "What about you? Do you know a Josh?"

"Is that the man you hit?" Maggie asked.

Ashley nodded.

"No last name?"

"He didn't offer one," Ashley said, then remembered the exchange of notes. Maybe he had written it down. "Wait. Here it is. Madison. Josh Madison."

Maggie's expression turned thoughtful. "There were some Madisons who had a summer place not far from Rose Cottage. I think Grandma knew them. Maybe he's related to them. That would certainly explain why he was on that road. Melanie and Mike might know him."

"I suppose that's possible," Ashley said. "But he said he was local."

"Maybe he is now," Rick finally chimed in. "But I don't recall the name, and I talk to a lot of people around the area. I could ask Willa-Dean next time I go to Callao for lunch. That girl knows everybody, especially the single men."

Ashley shook her head. "No need. I doubt we'll even cross paths again, unless he changes his mind about me paying for the damage to his car."

Maggie grinned. "Why so interested, Ash? Is he gorgeous? Sexy?"

"Nice," Ashley said, refusing to be drawn into a discussion of Josh Madison's appeal. *Nice* was safe. *Nice* didn't stir up hormones.

Unfortunately, Josh Madison was a bit more than nice. As rattled as she'd been by that stupid accident, she'd noted that he was sexy and gorgeous, just as her sister had guessed. Not that Ashley cared, of course. Men were the last thing on her mind these days. But accepting that didn't mean she couldn't appreciate a fine specimen when one happened to cross her path, even if this one was clearly not her type.

After all, he'd been dressed in a faded T-shirt and equally faded jeans, with boat shoes and no socks. It wasn't a look that appealed to her. She was drawn to men in designer suits and expensive imported footwear. She was drawn to men who reeked of ambition and success. Josh Madison looked…normal. Just an everyday guy. Ashley didn't do ordinary.

Not that she'd done all that well with the overly ambitious type, either. The one serious relationship in her life had been with a man every bit as driven to succeed as she was. He'd worn all the right clothes, gone to all the right places, been seen with all the right people.

But Drew Wellington turned out to have this nasty habit of lying to her, hiding things from her such as the supposedly unimportant detail that he had a high-school sweetheart back home whom he saw every chance he got. He'd also failed to mention that his old flame was pregnant with his child.

Not that he intended to marry her. She wasn't suitable, he'd tried to explain to Ashley when she'd discovered his tawdry little secret. Ashley was the woman he wanted to marry.

She wasn't sure which part of that had made her sickest, the lying or the snobbery, but the betrayal had all come flooding back to her in that courtroom a week ago when she'd realized that her ex and Tiny shared a common lack of familiarity with the truth. What was it about her that made people think they didn't have to be honest with her? Did they think she was too stupid to discover the lies, or that she wouldn't care if she did?

Either way, she definitely hadn't done so well with her one foray into love of the proper kind. Still, that didn't mean she was ready to start compromising her ideals for a man utterly lacking in style and ambition, even if that did make her into the very kind of snob she claimed to despise.

Which was unfortunate, she concluded when Melanie and Mike arrived not five minutes later with Josh Madison in tow. Her heart promptly began the kind of enthusiastic staccato rhythm she hadn't felt in years. Josh had cleaned up nicely. His hair was damp and spiked with gel, his cheeks were smooth and he'd changed into chinos and an expensive knit shirt with a designer logo emblazoned discreetly on the pocket. He was still wearing the disreputable-looking boat shoes, though, and no socks.

"Look who we found," Melanie announced cheerfully. "We ran into Josh on our way over and invited him to tag along. He's our neighbor. You guys must remember the Madison house. And Josh remembers Grandma Lindsey. Hope you don't mind, Maggie, but we didn't want to leave him on his own. I know you always cook enough for a mob."

Ashley frowned at Maggie, who was struggling unsuccessfully to contain a chuckle.

"I think it's great," Maggie enthused. "I just hope you didn't run into Josh the same way Ashley did earlier. I doubt his car could take another encounter like that."

Melanie's eyes widened as she turned from Josh to Ashley and back again. "Ashley is the person who hit you?"

Ashley turned her scowl on Josh. "Couldn't wait to spread the word, I see."

"Actually, I didn't volunteer anything. Mike noticed the dent and asked about it," he said. "Would you have wanted me to lie to him?"

She sighed at that. "Of course not."

He regarded her speculatively. "I hope it's not going to make you uncomfortable having to sit across a dinner table from me?"

Ashley frowned. He seemed to be relishing the prospect of causing her a little discomfort. "Absolutely not," she lied.

Josh grinned. "You can always think of it as that

penance you were so anxious to exact from yourself earlier," he suggested. "Though don't think tonight will get you off the hook on that *other* dinner you promised me. I'm counting on that."

Maggie and Melanie stared at them, clearly fascinated by the exchange. They were going to make way too much of this, Ashley could tell. She needed to defuse their speculation as quickly as possible.

"Whatever," she said with a very deliberate shrug of indifference. "I can stand it if you can. I'm used to uncomfortable situations."

"She's used to staring down prosecutors," Melanie explained. "She's very good at it."

Josh's grin spread. "A lawyer. I should have guessed. It explains a lot."

Normally she would have challenged him on a remark like that, but Ashley was in no mood to be drawn into the kind of passionate debate that might be misinterpreted by her sisters as some sort of chemistry. Instead, she reminded them mildly, "But right now, as I have been repeatedly told, I'm on vacation." She turned her gaze on Maggie. "By the way, I'm starved. Didn't you say something about dinner when you invited us over here, Maggie? Or was that some bait-and-switch thing?"

"See, there you are in lawyer mode again," Maggie retorted. "How are we supposed to forget if you can't?"

Ashley could see her point. "I'm working on it," she swore. "I really am." But something told her it was going to be easier said than done.

When she glanced at Josh, she caught a commiserating look in his eyes. It seemed as if he actually understood what she was going through, and that made her wonder if she'd totally misjudged him. Then again, maybe that kind of sensitivity merely went along with being nice. Neither were traits with which she had a lot of experience. Drew had been smart and savvy and sophisticated, but definitely not nice. Her male colleagues were brilliant and clever but rarely nice, and hardly ever sensitive or considerate.

"Something tells me there's a story behind that," Josh said quietly, his expression thoughtful.

"Not one we're going to get into tonight," Maggie said decisively. She turned to Ashley. "Since you're so anxious to eat, Ashley, you can help me in the kitchen. Rick, get Josh a glass of wine."

Ashley reluctantly followed her sister into the kitchen. She knew precisely what was coming, especially since Melanie was right on her heels.

"First day in town and you find yourself a keeper," Maggie taunted as she handed Ashley another place setting.

"Don't be ridiculous," Ashley retorted. "We don't know anything about him."

Melanie beamed. "That's why it's so nice that you have all this time on your hands to change that."

"Even if I were interested—and I am definitely not saying that I am—what makes you think Josh doesn't already have a girlfriend?"

"Oh, please," Maggie said. "Have you seen the way the man looks at you? It's as if he can't quite believe his luck."

"Drew used to look at me like that, too," Ashley commented wryly.

"No, he didn't," Maggie responded, her voice laced with derision. "Drew looked at you as if you were a particularly valuable possession he'd acquired along with his BMW and his Rolex."

Ashley couldn't deny Maggie's take on the past, but she rolled her eyes anyway. "Could we just get through dinner with the least amount of humiliation possible? Do not try to foist me off on Josh like some pathetic thing who needs to be entertained."

"I won't have to," Maggie said confidently. "You'll see. Josh strikes me as the kind of man who'll take things into his own hands if he gets the slightest bit of encouragement from you. Hasn't he already gotten you to agree to have dinner with him?"

"Yes, but—"

"I rest my case," Maggie said, her triumph plain.

"I am not here to encourage some man I've barely met," Ashley insisted.

"I agree with Maggie. Just open yourself up to the possibilities," Melanie pleaded. "That's all we're asking. Now go set a place for Josh, then sit down right next to it. Maggie and I will get dinner on the table."

Ashley laughed despite herself. "You two never give up, do you? Just because you landed fantastic men doesn't mean everyone has to settle down to be happy. It's possible to be single and totally fulfilled."

"Maybe," Maggie conceded with obvious skepticism, "but you can't blame us for wanting you to be as happy as we are. You nudged me and Rick together. Now it's my chance to return the favor. Melanie's, too."

"I don't consider this a favor," Ashley said, giving it one last try.

Maggie smiled serenely. "Something tells me you will," she said.

Melanie nodded in agreement, then added with a grin, "Eventually, anyway."

Josh noted that Ashley had managed to seat herself at the opposite end of the table from him, much to her sister Maggie's very evident dismay. He, on the other hand, was a little relieved. The woman overwhelmed him. He literally needed some space between them so he could catch his breath.

Besides, he hadn't made that call to Stephanie yet. It was a point of honor with him that he needed to officially break things off with her before he moved on. If Ashley were too close, he might toss aside his better judgment and try to figure out some way to crawl directly into her bed before the night was over. That kind of reckless, breakneck pace was a very bad thing, especially for a man who had supposedly taken some vacation time to make some tough decisions about his future.

He'd always been a plodder, taking things slowly, thinking them through. He'd just about thought the whole engagement thing to death, which was one reason—thankfully—that it had never happened.

The woman sitting opposite him made him want to seize the moment, which was a very scary proposition. When he'd agreed to come to dinner tonight, he'd had no idea that Ashley would be here. The hop, skip and jump of his pulse when he'd spotted her dented car in the driveway had been way too telling. He was about to throw caution to the wind. The length of the dinner table and the presence of four obviously fascinated observers were the only things standing in his way.

Well, those things and that look of distress in Ashley's amazing eyes, which had turned a golden topaz in the candlelight. She was clearly vulnerable and hurting. It evidently had something to do with her career. Since his own was likely to go up in flames as soon as he broke things off with Stephanie, he could relate to Ashley's professional uncertainty.

Brevard, Williams and Davenport was one of Richmond's premier law firms. Josh had been proud when they'd hired him straight out of law school, then promoted him quickly. But it had been increasingly evident that his future there was directly tied in to his relationship with Stephanie. If he broke up with her this weekend, he was very likely to be fired on Monday. The thought didn't terrify him nearly as much as he'd expected it to. In fact, when he could ignore the churning in his gut, it seemed to give him an amazing sense of freedom.

"You're awfully quiet," Mike said. "You sure you didn't bump your head in that accident?"

Josh shrugged off his concern. "Just thinking about how life takes a lot of unexpected twists."

Mike glanced over at Melanie, and his entire expression softened. "Indeed, it does."

"How long have the two of you been married?" Josh asked him.

"Four months."

"Long engagement?"

Mike grinned. "Hardly. We just met in March."

Josh stared at him in shock. "You seem like you've known each other forever."

"I guess that's the way it is when you meet the right woman," Mike said. "What do you think, Rick?"

Rick blinked and dragged his gaze away from his wife. "What?"

Mike chuckled. "Josh and I were discussing whirl-wind courtships."

Rick laughed. "You're definitely asking the experts. Maggie and I were together for, what, a couple of months?"

Josh's jaw dropped. "And you've been married how long?"

"About four weeks," Rick said. "The D'Angelo women don't waste a lot of time. A smart man seizes the moment when they're around."

Josh fell silent, staring at the three women at the opposite end of the table, their heads together. How had he missed it? Of course, the three women were more than just friends. They were sisters. Melanie had even said as much when she'd referred to their grandmother Lindsey earlier. He'd been fooled by the different last names or maybe by the fact that they'd all grown up into such vibrant but distinctive women.

As girls, they'd been cookie-cutter versions of each other, varying only in height. Oh, they'd been gorgeous enough to catch his attention and leave him tongue-tied, but they'd worn their hair in similar styles and dressed in variations of the same shorts and halter tops. Back then, there had been no mistaking the family resemblance. In fact, only those who knew them well could keep them straight. Josh hadn't known them at all. They'd been on the periphery of his life, a taunting reminder of what an outsider he was.

Josh studied them quizzically, then asked Mike, "Isn't there another sister?"

"Jo," he said at once. "She still lives in Boston. You knew the D'Angelo sisters, growing up?" Mike asked.

"Not really. It's more like I knew of them. We didn't exactly travel in the same circles."

"But didn't Melanie say your family knew their grandmother?" Rick asked.

"Fairly well, as a matter of fact," Josh admitted. "But you know how kids are. They find their own friends, especially in the summertime around here." Determined to move on, he asked, "How did you meet them?"

"Maggie and I met in Boston," Rick said. "I stepped in at the last minute to handle a photo shoot for her magazine. She came down here, and I followed her."

"Melanie and I met here," Mike explained. "She was staying at Rose Cottage for a bit." He grinned. "Sort of the way Ashley's staying there now for a little R & R."

Rick gave Josh a considering look, then added pointedly, "History tends to repeat itself at Rose Cottage."

Not this time, Josh thought. Not that he wasn't attracted to Ashley. He was. Not that he didn't intend to see more of her while she was here. He did.

But his life was in chaos, and something told him hers was, as well. That made it a very bad time to be thinking in other than the most immediate terms. Dinner. A few laughs. That kind of thing.

When he glanced around the table, he noticed that four pairs of eyes were regarding him way too speculatively. The only eyes that counted, however, were watching him with unmistakable wariness. Clearly, Ashley was no more inclined to be railroaded into a relationship than he was. And wasn't that all that mattered?

"Maybe you and Ashley should get together to work out a settlement for the damages from the accident," Maggie suggested without any attempt at subtlety.

"We've taken care of that," Ashley replied at once.

To his shock and dismay, a streak of totally unfamiliar perversity sliced through Josh. "I've been thinking maybe we were a little too hasty. Neither of us was thinking too clearly."

"I was thinking just fine," Ashley retorted. "I offered to pay for all the damages since it was my fault. That offer still stands."

"As a lawyer, you should know an offer like that could open you up to exorbitant demands," Josh countered. "You've admitted guilt. You couldn't possibly have been thinking clearly or you would never have done such a thing."

"I was taking responsibility for my actions," she retorted. "You turned me down." Her gaze narrowed. "Are you changing your mind? Suddenly feeling the onset of whiplash, perhaps?" she inquired tartly.

If it would keep the fire in her eyes, Josh would have prolonged the argument as long as possible, but they were being watched with total fascination by everyone else at the table. He didn't want to encourage the meddlers.

"Possibly," he equivocated, rubbing his neck. Sure enough, sparks of indignation lit her eyes.

"Well, be sure to let me know when you've made up

your mind," Ashley replied, a hint of sarcasm in her tone. "Why is it that men can never make a decision about anything?"

"Hey," Rick and Mike protested in unison. "Don't turn this into some sort of gender war and drag the rest of us into it," Mike went on.

"Uh-oh," Maggie said. "Watch your step, Ashley. You're about to unite these men in a common cause. Something tells me it won't be pretty."

"Doggone right," Josh agreed, suddenly eager to stir the pot. "Men are not the problem. We think logically and rationally."

"Oh, please," Ashley said. "What was logical or rational about letting me off the hook so easily?"

"You were clearly shaken up. I was trying to be a nice guy," Josh retorted.

"Ha!" Ashley muttered.

"Women hate that," Rick advised.

"They see it as a sign of weakness," Mike confirmed.

"Well, you can be sure I won't make that mistake again," Josh vowed. "I thought you were a reasonable woman."

"I am. You're the one behaving like an idiot. You're no more injured than I am."

He frowned at her. "You're calling me an idiot?"

"You bet I am."

As the exchange ended and her declaration hung in the air, Ashley suddenly blinked and looked embarrassed. "What just happened here?"

Maggie grinned at them. "Offhand, I'd say we just witnessed an explosion of hormones. I, for one, found it rather fascinating."

"Stimulating," Melanie added, casting a pointed look at her husband.

Before Josh could utter a desperate denial, Ashley whirled on her sisters. "Eat dirt," she muttered, then stood up. "I have to go."

Josh was way too tempted to follow her. Instead, he merely winked as she passed. "Drive safely," he murmured under his breath.

She stopped and scowled at him. He waited for her to utter the curse that was obviously on the tip of her tongue, but she fought it and won.

"Lovely seeing you again," she said sweetly. Her voice, thick with Southern syrup, nonetheless lacked sincerity.

"I'm sure we'll cross paths soon," Josh said. "Hopefully without colliding."

Though he had to admit, as he watched her walk away, that bumping into Ashley D'Angelo, literally or figuratively, was starting to make his life a whole lot livelier.

3

Fresh from his second disconcerting, intriguing encounter with Ashley D'Angelo, Josh knew he couldn't delay the inevitable talk with Stephanie for another minute. That explosion of hormones Maggie had referred to had been very real. It had been a couple of hours now, and he was still half-aroused when he thought about it. Stephanie had never had that effect on him. They'd been friends who'd understood what was expected of them and accepted that real passion wasn't part of it.

Even as he reached for the phone, he acknowledged that it was probably a conversation he should be having face-to-face. Since he didn't plan on being back in Richmond for a while, though, he wanted to get it over with now, tonight. Something told him that by morning, or at least by the time he had his next encounter with Ashley, he should be totally free from the past.

Fortunately, Stephanie was a night owl. Even though it was after eleven, he knew she'd be awake. What he hadn't expected, though, was the sound of a party in full swing in the background when she answered. She sounded carefree and happy, happier than he could recall her being in a long time. Somehow when they were together, she always seemed subdued and thoughtful.

"Steph, it's me," he said.

"Josh, sweetheart, I wasn't expecting to hear from you this late."

"Evidently." He had no idea why he couldn't seem to keep the edge out of his voice. He wasn't jealous. No, if anything, he was relieved. Maybe this odd mood he was suddenly in simply had to do with the possibility that now wasn't the best time to have this conversation, after all. "Look, you obviously have company. Maybe I should call back in the morning."

"Don't be silly. It's just a few friends kicking back on a Friday night. I'll just go into the other room, where I can hear better."

The music and laughter grew more muffled. "There. That's better," she said. "How's it going? Are you having a good time? Are you getting all that deep thinking done?"

"Some of it," he said.

"I wish you'd let me come with you. Maybe I could have helped. You've always liked bouncing ideas off of me in the past."

"Normally that's true," he said, "but not this time. I had to work this out on my own."

"You're thinking about us, aren't you?" she asked, sounding resigned but not surprised.

Josh had always known that Stephanie was smart and intuitive, but he hadn't expected her to cut right to the chase on this one. "Yes," he admitted. "I think we need to talk about where we're headed."

"Okay," she said.

"I owe you better than a conversation on the phone, but I didn't want to wait till I get back."

"Come on, Josh, just say it and get it over with," she chided.

"I know your father is counting on us announcing our engagement soon and that we've been talking about it for a long time now," he began. "But I think you and I both know that he's more enthusiastic about the idea than either of us are."

His words were greeted with silence.

"Stephanie?"

"What are you saying, Josh?" she asked.

He sucked in a deep breath and forced himself to be brutally honest. "That we're all wrong for each other, Steph. We both know it. We've been trying to make the pieces fit, but they don't. This isn't your fault, Stephanie. You're amazing. It's me. I want something else. I wish I could explain it better than that, but I can't. I only know this isn't fair to either one of us. I need to let you go, and I feel sure you'll be far happier with someone else."

"I see," she said softly.

She didn't sound half as brokenhearted as he'd feared she might. "I'm sorry," he apologized.

"No need to be," she said, sounding oddly relieved.

Josh was astounded that she was taking his announcement so well. He'd expected tears or histrionics. In fact, he'd been dreading a messy emotional scene, if only because he was throwing a monkey wrench into her father's plans for the two of them, and Stephanie was, first and foremost, a dutiful daughter who understood what was expected of her.

"Do you mean that?" he asked, still not quite believing that the breakup could go so smoothly.

"To be honest, I've seen this coming," she confessed. "It's something I should have done myself, but I've never had the courage to defy my father. I guess I owe you for making it easy."

"You're really okay with this?" he asked.

"Were you hoping I'd fight you?" she asked, sounding amused.

"No, of course not, but—"

She laughed. "No buts, darling. You're off the hook. I'm weak, not stupid. To be perfectly honest, I've known for months now that we're not a good match, not for the long term. I guess I was hoping that Daddy was right, because you are so damn nice."

Josh was getting a little tired of being nice tonight. Nice guys usually finished last. Sometimes he wondered if that wasn't why he was so uncomfortable in a courtroom. He hated going for the jugular. He preferred mediation to confrontation.

"You're probably letting me off too easy," he told her. "I doubt your father will be half as understanding. Would you like me to explain all this to him?"

"Forget about Daddy. I'll talk to him," Stephanie assured him. "I won't let him kick you out of the firm over this."

"You don't need to go to bat for me," Josh said. "I'll handle your father if I decide I want to stay on."

"*If?* You're thinking about quitting your job?" she asked, clearly far more shocked by that than by his decision to break up with her.

"Actually I am," he admitted. "But I'm trying not

to do anything hasty." He was a plodder, after all. He liked knowing that all his ducks were in a row before doing anything too drastic. It had taken his immediate and intense attraction to Ashley to get him to make this decision. Otherwise he might have drifted along indecisively for a while longer just because being with Stephanie was comfortable.

"I do love you, you know," she told him. "Just not the way you ought to be loved. And I want you to be happy."

"I want the same for you." He recalled the lively sounds of the party. "Something tells me you won't have to wait too long."

"What about you?" she said. "What kind of woman do you really want?"

An image of Ashley resurfaced for about the hundredth time since they'd met that afternoon. He wasn't about to mention it, though. He wasn't that foolish. Stephanie might be taking the breakup with a great deal of grace, but he doubted she'd like knowing that he'd found a replacement already.

"I'll let you know when I've figured that out," he promised.

She laughed. "Please do. Will you call me when you get back to Richmond?"

"Sure, if you want me to."

"I'd like us to stay friends," she told him with unmistakable sincerity. "You're the best one I ever had. I'm not sure I realized that until tonight, when you set me free."

"Then this is a good thing for both of us?" he asked, still worried a bit by her calm demeanor.

"It really is," she assured him. "Now go out there and find the woman who's really right for you, and I'll dance at your wedding."

"You're amazing," he said sincerely.

"I know," she said, laughing. "I think I'm just now figuring that out, too."

Josh hung up and sighed. Relief washed over him. That had gone a thousand times better than he'd anticipated. If only all the other decisions on his plate would go half as smoothly.

Ashley had scrubbed the kitchen floor, cleaned out the refrigerator, rearranged the cupboards and even considered the bags of bulbs that Melanie had surreptitiously left on the back steps. She might be going stir-crazy, but she wasn't quite ready for a close encounter with the garden worms just yet.

Still, it was barely midmorning, and she'd already done every single thing she could think of to do inside the house. She'd passed her limit on coffee for the morning and eaten a bran muffin and a banana, which was more than she'd usually consumed by this hour.

Normally by late morning, she'd been to the gym and had already been at her desk for hours. There was little question that exercise was what she needed now to take the edge off the stress.

Suddenly she recalled the kayak that used to be stored in what had once been a garage but was too small to accommodate anything other than the smallest of today's vehicles. She found the key to the lock and opened the creaky door. Sure enough, the kayak was still inside, along with its paddle.

Pushing aside all the boxes that had been stored around it, she finally managed to drag the kayak out. She hosed it down, then dragged it to the water's edge. She found a baseball cap on a hook in the kitchen, retrieved the paddle from the old garage, then climbed into the kayak and shoved off, praying that paddling was like riding a bicycle, something one never forgot.

At first she stayed close to shore to be sure the kayak was still seaworthy and hadn't sprung any leaks over the years. When she was finally satisfied that it wasn't going to sink and that she still had the hang of paddling it, she grew more ambitious.

The September sun was beating down on her bare shoulders and glaring off the water. She wiped the sweat off her brow and paused long enough to twist her hair into a knot on top of her head and stuff it under the cap, then began to paddle in earnest.

It took Ashley some time to find her rhythm and longer to move at a pace that provided real exercise. When her arms and shoulders started aching, she let the kayak drift, leaned back and closed her eyes. The sun felt good now that it was being tempered by a breeze. Her body felt energized and, in an odd way, lazy at the same time. Maybe this was what relaxing felt like. If so, she might be able to get used to it eventually.

A part of her immediately rebelled at the thought. She wasn't going to get used to this. She needed excitement and challenges. This was just a little break, a chance to regroup.

To prove her point, she sat up straight, grabbed the paddle and put herself into the task of rowing back to the cottage. She was not about to turn into some goalless, lazy slacker, not even here. Not even for three weeks.

Her sisters might have taken away her legal pads and her pencils, but the stores in town would have more. Suddenly it seemed vital that she get new supplies and put her nose to the grindstone. Pleasant as it was, she was wasting time out here.

Her enthusiasm waned almost as quickly as it had peaked when she realized that she had no real work to do. She was supposed to be thinking, contemplating her future, but the idea held no appeal at all. She could make lists and prioritize all she wanted to, but something told her she would only be floundering right now. Her brain really did need a break.

Well, hell, she thought, letting the paddle fall idle as tears stung her eyes. She brushed at them impatiently and took up the paddle again. Dammit, she was not going to wallow in self-pity. If she couldn't excel at law right now, then she could excel at kayaking, she decided with grim determination. Maybe the world had enough lawyers anyway…at least for a few more weeks.

His situation with Stephanie resolved, Josh had finally let his thoughts turn to Ashley. It had taken him a ridiculously long time the night before to get it straight that all three women in the room were D'Angelos and that they were the granddaughters of Mrs. Lindsey, the woman who'd been a good friend of his own grandmother.

As a kid, he'd envied the boisterous activity that went on just up the road at Rose Cottage. He'd been a bit of a nerd, far too studious for his own good, and way too much of an introvert to ask to be included in the impromptu gatherings that seemed to be going on all the time whenever the four granddaughters were in town. Besides, those four beautiful girls had drawn admirers from at least two counties. Josh hadn't stood a chance.

He'd matured a lot in the years since then, in both attitude and physique. He'd found a sport he loved—tennis—and a gym he hated but used regularly. A brilliant student, he'd gained confidence in law school, then added to it when he'd been selected for Richmond's most prestigious law firm. Beautiful women no longer intimidated him. Nor did money and power.

Knowing that he could have it all—lovely, well-connected Stephanie Lockport Williams, the money and the power—had somehow been enough. Discovering that he didn't want any of it had been the shocker.

That's why he was here, in fact, to wrestle with himself over how incredibly stupid it might be to throw it all away. He was having far fewer second thoughts today, now that the breakup with Stephanie had gone so smoothly and left him feeling so thoroughly relieved. It had made him wonder if the timing wasn't precisely right for a lot of dramatic changes in his life.

He was up at dawn, anxious to get out on the water, where he could while away the morning fishing...or pretending to. He rushed through breakfast, put away the few clothes he'd brought along, then made a quick call to his folks to let them know he was settled in.

Eventually, armed with bottled water, a sandwich, a fishing pole and bait, he headed for the bay where it lapped against the shoreline at the back of his family's property. He climbed into the seaworthy old boat at the

end of the dock and pushed off. Paddling just far enough
away from shore to sustain the pretense that he was at
sea, he dropped anchor, cast his line, then leaned back,
his old fishing hat pulled low over his eyes.

He was just settling down, content with the warmth
of the fall sun against his bare skin, when something
crashed into the boat, tilting it precariously and very
nearly sending him over the side. The splashing of icy
water all over his heated skin was as much a shock as
the collision.

Oddly enough, he wasn't all that surprised when he
peered over the bow to see Ashley with her face buried
in her hands, the paddle floating about three feet away
from her kayak.

He couldn't help chuckling at her crestfallen expression. "You know, if you wanted to see me again, all you
had to do was call. If you keep ramming into me like
this, I'm not going to have any modes of transportation
left."

"Obviously I am completely out of control on land
or sea," she said in a tone that bore an unexpected edge
of hysteria.

Josh stared at her. "Are you okay?"

"Sure. Fine," she said at once, putting on a brave
smile to prove it.

She was reasonably convincing, but Josh wasn't buying it. She might be physically fine, but there was something else going on, something that had to do with this
vacation she was taking with such obvious reluctance.
Her sisters had alluded to it last night.

"Maybe you should come aboard," he suggested, not
liking the idea of her being on the water alone when she

was obviously shaky. On closer inspection, he thought he detected traces of dried tears on her cheeks. Maybe if he focused on her turmoil, he could put off his own decisions.

"I have my kayak," she protested.

"We can tie it up to the boat." He gestured toward the paddle that was drifting rapidly away. "You won't get far without that paddle, anyway."

"Story of my life lately," she muttered, but she held out her hand to take his, then managed to gingerly climb into the rowboat. "You're very brave, you know."

"For taking you in like this?"

"Exactly. I'm obviously a danger to myself and everyone around me."

"Something tells me that's a relatively new condition," he said, keeping his gaze away from her, hoping she would feel free to tell him what was going on that had her behaving with what he suspected was uncharacteristic carelessness.

"I suppose," she conceded.

To his disappointment, she stopped right there. He decided not to press. Instead he asked, "Know how to bait a hook?"

She regarded him skeptically. "With what?"

"Shrimp."

She nodded. "That's okay, then. If you'd said worms, I'd have jumped overboard and swum home."

"Squeamish, huh?"

"No, absolutely not," she said at once, rising to the challenge with predictable indignation.

"Some sort of animal-rights stance?" he taunted.

A faint flicker of amusement lit her eyes for the first time since they'd met.

"Hardly," she said. "They're just… I guess messy describes it."

"Then I can assume you won't be cleaning any fish we catch for supper?"

"I don't expect to catch any," she said, even as she gingerly dangled the baited hook over the side of the boat, then studied the line with total concentration. After a minute, she glanced at him and asked, "Do you do this every day?"

"Every day I can. I get some of my best thinking done out here on the bay."

"You're not bored?" she asked wistfully.

Josh bit back a grin. Maybe that was the trouble with Ms. Ashley D'Angelo. She didn't know the first thing about relaxing. Even now on this beautiful fall day surrounded by some of the most glorious scenery on earth, she was obviously edgy and uptight.

He studied her intently for a minute, trying not to let his gaze linger on those endless bare legs. He certainly couldn't spot any other flaws. Maybe he could help her work on the relaxation thing.

"I'm never bored," he told her. "I like my own company."

"No significant other?"

"I've been seeing a woman," he admitted. "But I've just recently reached the conclusion that she's not significant. She's a great woman, just not right for me. We broke it off last night."

"Last night?" she asked, obviously startled.

"I called her after I got home from dinner at your sister's."

She seemed to be wrestling with that information. He waited to see if she'd ask if there was a connection, but she didn't.

After studying him with undisguised curiosity, she eventually asked, "How did you conclude that the relationship was over?"

"I was faced with fishing or cutting bait, so to speak. It was time to get married...or not. I couldn't see myself with her forever. Fortunately, as it turned out, she couldn't see that, either."

"Is there something wrong with her?"

"Absolutely not. She's beautiful, intelligent, well-connected. She'll be a dream wife for the right man."

"But not you?"

"Not me," he confirmed.

"If beautiful, intelligent and well-connected aren't right for you, then what kind of woman do you want?"

"I'm still figuring that out," he admitted. "Offhand, though, I'd have to say one who's comfortable in her own skin, someone who knows who she is and what she wants."

"And this woman isn't like that?"

"She is." He shrugged. "But the sparks weren't there. Who knows why that happens? Seems to me that love is just as mysterious as all the philosophers have claimed it is."

She seemed to deflate a little at that. If they hadn't just met, Josh would have said she was actually disappointed.

"That whole bit about being comfortable with who and what you are would definitely let me out," she said a little too brightly.

"Going through an identity crisis?" Josh asked, relieved to finally have something specific to work with to try to figure her out.

"Yes, that's exactly it."

"Welcome to the club."

"You, too?"

Josh nodded. "But I'm not going to worry about it today. Neither should you. Relax and maybe the answers will come to you when your mind's clear of all the clutter."

"Relax?" she said again, as if it were a foreign concept.

Josh chuckled. "Like this," he explained patiently. "Lean back."

He waited until she'd followed his directions. "Okay, then. Now pull the brim of your hat down low to shade your eyes."

She did that, her expression totally serious.

"Now close your eyes and concentrate on the water lapping against the side of the boat," he suggested soothingly. "Feel the sun on your skin."

She sighed. "It feels wonderful."

"There you go. It's all about getting in touch with yourself and letting everything else kind of drift away."

She followed his advice as dutifully as if her life depended on it. He might have been amused, if there had been time. Unfortunately, a fish picked that precise moment to snag Ashley's line, and the next thing he knew he had his arms around her waist and was hanging on for dear life as she tried to reel in the rockfish that was just as determined to get away.

He was all too aware of the soft, sun-kissed scent of her skin, of the way her muscles flexed as she worked the line, of the softness of her breasts against his forearm. She was strong and fiercely determined not to be beaten by a fish. In fact, he had to bite his lip to keep from chuckling at the string of curses she muttered when she seemed to be losing the battle.

Only when the rockfish was finally flopping around in a bucket of salt water onboard, did Josh finally dare to meet her gaze. "Competitive, aren't you?"

"You have no idea," she murmured.

Josh nodded slowly. The revelations were coming bit by bit, each one adding to the enigma that was Ashley D'Angelo. Things were definitely going to get very interesting before he had a complete picture of this woman who was so triumphant about landing a fish.

And if the jangling of his pulse right now was any indication, this vacation of his might not turn out to be half as relaxing as he'd imagined.

4

"That's three for me," Ashley announced triumphantly as she reeled in her third rockfish of the morning. She grinned at Josh. "And how many for you?"

He laughed, obviously not the least bit intimidated by her success. "None. I haven't had the time. I've been too busy trying to get your fish in the boat without you going overboard. You really need to curb your enthusiasm just a little. A rowboat isn't as stable as, say, a fishing pier. You can't jump around on it."

"That sounds like an excuse to me," Ashley said, enjoying goading him. He refused to take her seriously. She supposed it was that *nice* thing again. He actually seemed happy that she was doing so well and having so much fun. She couldn't recall the last time she'd been around a man who wasn't out to get the better of her. Maybe that was because most of the men she knew were prosecutors. They tended to be driven, focused and devoid of humor.

"Now what?" she asked Josh, surprisingly eager for more of the kind of lighthearted banter and entertainment he was providing. She hadn't thought about work for several hours now.

"We take them home and clean them," he said. "The person who catches them is definitely responsible for cleaning them."

"I don't think so. I've done all the hard work," she retorted. "We have these fish because of me. I think that makes it your job to clean them."

"Excellent point," he said.

"Thank you," she said modestly.

He held up his hand. "However, and this is important, you did not reel them in entirely on your own. I did help."

Ashley considered his claim. Fairness dictated that she acknowledge his role in the day's catch. "I'll give you that."

"So we clean them together."

She shook her head. "I don't think so."

"How would you suggest we divvy up the labor?"

She thought it over. "You clean 'em. I'll cook 'em. How about that?"

"Can you cook?"

She laughed. He had her there. Maggie was the cook in the family. "At least as well as you can fish," she said eventually. "I'll call Maggie. She's the professional in the kitchen. I'm sure she can coach me through it."

Of course, even as she uttered the words, Ashley knew what a bad idea it was to call her sister in on this. She'd never hear the end of it. "Better yet, I'll find a cookbook. There's bound to be one at Rose Cottage. If I could pass the bar exam, I'm sure I can follow directions. How hard can it be?"

Josh held out his hand. "Deal."

Ashley accepted his outstretched hand. "Deal," she agreed, as her pulse did a little bump and grind at the contact. Her gaze sought Josh's to see if he'd felt it, as well. With his cap pulled low over his eyes, it was impossible to read anything in his expression.

When they reached the dock at Rose Cottage, he tied up the rowboat, then stepped into the shallow water and secured her kayak.

After helping her from the boat, he picked up the bucket of fish and his cooler and headed for the house. "I'll just put these inside, then head home to get cleaned up. What time do you want to have dinner?"

"Actually I'm starved now," she admitted, surprised to find that it was true. Her stomach was actually growling. It must have something to do with the salt air and exercise. "Much as I appreciated it, that half sandwich you shared with me didn't do the trick."

"Same here. How about I come back in an hour? It shouldn't take me more than fifteen minutes to row back to my place. That'll leave plenty of time for me to shower and drive back. Anything you want me to pick up for dinner?"

Ashley thought about the contents of the refrigerator. She'd brought some things with her, and Maggie had seen to it that it was stocked with plenty of salad ingredients before her arrival. The only thing missing was dessert. Normally she was content with fresh fruit, but the first full day of her vacation seemed to call for something decadent. If nothing else, it might demonstrate that she was starting to view this time-out as something worthy of celebration, rather than as punishment.

"Would you mind going to the bakery if there's time?" she asked.

"Let me guess. You want chocolate," he said, grinning.

"The richest, gooeyest chocolate they have," she confirmed. "Brownies, cake, fudge, mousse—I'm not choosy."

"And if the bakery's closed?"

"Why would it be closed?"

"It's almost five now."

She stared at him in shock. It couldn't be. "We spent the entire day on the water doing nothing?"

He laughed. "Pretty much. You got the knack for relaxing a lot quicker than I expected you to. The nap you took filled an hour or so."

"I did not take a nap," she protested. "I merely closed my eyes for a couple of minutes."

"Whatever. Bottom line, the day has slipped away. Let me get going before any more of it slips by. I'll do my best on the chocolate thing."

She watched him go with an odd feeling in the pit of her stomach. She'd spent an entire day in the company of a man she barely knew, doing something that hadn't exactly taxed her mind, and she hadn't been bored. Not for a single second. Amazing.

She was still pondering that when she went inside and discovered the phone ringing. She debated ignoring it, but realized that would only bring her sisters rushing over here in a panic. She picked it up reluctantly.

"Where the devil have you been?" Maggie demanded at once. "I've been calling for hours. I was beginning to think you'd run back to Boston. Melanie was about to start packing so we could come after you."

"I've been fishing," she responded.

"Excuse me?"

"You know, the activity in which a person puts bait on a hook, puts the hook in the water and reels in a fish. At least that's how it's supposed to work. It turns out I'm pretty good at it. I caught three rockfish."

"Uh-huh," Maggie said, clearly stunned. "When did you learn to fish?"

"Today."

"Who taught you?"

Ah, there was that minefield she'd been dreading. "Josh," she admitted. "I sort of ran into him on the water this morning."

"Ran into him?"

"Literally," she confessed. "I took the kayak out. When I slammed into his rowboat, I lost the paddle. He took me on board his boat."

"As in kidnapped you or offered you refuge?"

"Refuge, I suppose."

"I see. You sound surprisingly upbeat for a woman who has spent the entire day in the company of a man who supposedly annoys you, doing something that you wouldn't have been caught dead doing a week ago."

"Times change."

"And your attitude toward Josh—has that changed, too?"

"I always said he was nice. He just got on my nerves last night at your place."

Maggie laughed. "Oh, this is too good. I'm picking

up Melanie and coming over. I want to hear more about this fishing excursion."

"Forget about it," Ashley said emphatically.

"Why?"

"Because Josh is coming back for dinner. I'm cooking the fish."

"You're cooking the fish?" Maggie repeated so skeptically it was insulting.

"Yes, dammit. You could help and just tell me how. It'll save me having to look up a recipe."

"Who's cleaning the fish?" Maggie asked.

"Josh."

"Thank God. For a minute, I thought the world might be coming to an end."

"Stop it. Are you going to help me out here or not, Maggie?"

"Okay, okay. You want simple or fancy?"

"What do you think?" Ashley asked wryly.

"Simple it is. Dredge the fillets in flour, salt and pepper, then fry them in about a quarter inch of oil. Make sure the oil is hot, but not too hot. You don't want to burn the fish."

Ashley jotted the instructions down, even though they seemed foolproof. "How long?"

"Till the flour is golden brown. It shouldn't take more than a couple of minutes on each side, depending on how thick the fillets are."

"And that's all there is to it?" Ashley asked, frowning at the simple directions. "You're not leaving out anything critical, so I'll wind up being totally embarrassed?"

"I would not let you humiliate yourself," Maggie

said, sounding wounded by the suggestion. "This is an easy one, Ash. You'll do fine. What else are you having?"

"Salad, and Josh said he'd pick up something for dessert."

"Chocolate?"

"Yes, if you must know."

"My, my. You don't usually lay into the chocolate until you're really, really comfortable with a man. Or under a lot of stress. Which is it, Ashley?"

"Go suck an egg. Josh is an easygoing guy. It's no big deal. It's not like it's a date or something."

"Really? Not a date? Just out of curiosity, what would you call it?"

"Dinner with a friend."

Maggie chuckled. "Delusional, but nice. Have fun, big sister."

She hung up before Ashley could reassert that her sister was way, way off base.

What was it with women and chocolate? Josh stared indecisively at the display case in the bakery. There was a chocolate layer cake, a chocolate mousse cake, two brownies with icing and walnuts, and eclairs topped with chocolate icing and filled with chocolate cream. They all looked decadent enough to him, but which one would satisfy Ashley? He had a hunch she was very particular.

"Decided yet?" the cheery young clerk asked him.

"Which is your favorite?"

She shrugged. "I like blueberry pie myself."

Obviously she was going to be no help at all. He finally gave up in frustration. "I'll take it all."

Her jaw dropped. "Are you having a party or something?"

"Not really." He was pretty sure dinner with Ashley didn't qualify as a party. He doubted she even saw it as a date.

To be honest, he hadn't quite decided what this evening was all about, either. He just knew that he'd rushed like crazy to get ready to go to Rose Cottage. Being invited there by one of the D'Angelo sisters was like a dream come true. Despite all the strides he'd made in building his self-confidence over the years, he still couldn't quite believe it. He felt like the shy, awkward boy he'd been at sixteen. He wanted to get this right.

He paid the disbelieving clerk for the boxes of desserts, then headed the few miles back to Rose Cottage.

When Ashley opened the door, he almost swallowed his tongue. She was wearing a thin robe that clung to her still damp body, revealing every intriguing shadow, every lush curve. Her hair was in damp ringlets that sprang free from some sort of scrunchy thing that was supposed to be holding it on top of her head.

"Sorry," she said, sounding frantic. "I had a phone call right after you left. It took me longer to get started in the shower than I expected. Make yourself at home. Get whatever you need in the kitchen to clean the fish. I'll be down in a minute."

She bolted for the stairs without waiting for a reply. Just as well, Josh thought, since it took him fully a minute to get the blood flowing back to his brain where it was necessary for speech.

"Clean the fish," he muttered as he set out to find the kitchen. "Just concentrate on cleaning the fish." Maybe that would drive the provocative image of Ashley in that revealing robe out of his head before she came back downstairs.

He was out back, scraping the scales from the last fish, when she finally emerged from the house. Thankfully, she was wearing loose jeans and a shapeless T-shirt, which looked as if they'd been borrowed from someone two sizes larger. Even so, she managed to stir his blood. Apparently she was going to do that no matter what she wore, he concluded. He'd just have to resign himself to it.

She'd dried her tawny hair into waves that fell to her shoulders. Her skin was clear and free of makeup, except for the faintest pink gloss on her lips. Even with all the suntan lotion she'd lathered on while they were on the water, her color was heightened to a healthy pink glow. She looked a thousand-percent better than the pale, shaken woman he'd met the day before.

"How's it coming out here?" she asked.

"Just about finished. Have you figured out how to cook them?"

"Rest easy," she said. "My sister has coached me through it. We probably won't die of food poisoning." She regarded him with apparent amusement. "By the way, why are there four bakery boxes on the kitchen table?"

He shrugged. "I couldn't make up my mind what you'd like best."

"So you bought out the place?"

"Pretty much—at least everything chocolate," he admitted. "You don't have to eat it all."

"But I probably will," she admitted with a sigh. "Chocolate is what gets me through stress."

"And you're stressed now?" he asked.

She hesitated, then regarded him with surprise. "Not right this second, no."

He grinned. "I told you there were advantages to a day in a rowboat."

"Apparently so. I haven't thought about work all day long. That's like some sort of miracle."

"Then let's keep that track record intact and get dinner on the table."

Ashley nodded at once. "Good plan. If I start to bring up anything work-related over dinner, cut me off."

Josh wasn't sure he'd be able to agree to that indefinitely, but he could for tonight. "No work. Got it."

In the kitchen, they worked side-by-side. He made the salad while she fried the fish. When the plates were ready, they sat at the kitchen table and Ashley lifted a glass of wine in a toast.

"To relaxation," she said.

"It's a wonderful thing," Josh added.

"Even if it can't last forever," she said, looking just a little sad.

"Hey, that borders on mentioning work," he scolded. "Maybe we need to have a penalty."

Competitive woman that she was, Ashley immediately seized on the idea, just as he'd known she would.

"Such as?" she asked at once.

"We each have a pot and put in a dollar for every

infraction. We're on the honor system. We have to put the money in even if the other person isn't around. At the end of the week, the one with the fewest violations gets all the money." He grinned. "And gets treated to dinner by the loser."

She considered the scheme thoughtfully, as if weighing her odds of winning. "I can do that," she said finally.

Josh doubted it, but he lifted his glass. "To relaxation," he toasted one more time.

They'd no sooner taken a sip than his cell phone rang. He could have sworn he'd left it turned off on his dresser, but apparently it had been stuck in the pocket of his jacket.

"Aren't you going to get that?" Ashley asked.

He debated the wisdom of it, then finally reached for his jacket and grabbed it out of the pocket. "Yes?"

"Have you lost your mind, Madison?"

"Mr. Williams," he said, barely containing a sigh.

"I've spoken to Stephanie," his boss said. "She tells me the two of you have called off your engagement."

Josh barely clung to his temper. "We were never engaged, sir."

"Semantics. We all knew you were headed in that direction."

"You were the only one who really believed that," Josh corrected. "Fortunately Stephanie and I realized before it was too late that it would be a mistake. Look, sir, this isn't really a good time. Perhaps we can discuss this later."

"Now's good for me," Creighton Williams insisted.

"You realize what this is going to do to your future here at Brevard, Williams and Davenport, don't you?"

"I assume it's over. If so, that's fine."

His ready acceptance of the end of his career clearly caught his boss off guard. "Now let's not be hasty, Madison. You're a good lawyer. This might get you off that fast track, but I don't want to lose you over this. Besides, Stephanie made it clear she'd be furious if I fired you. We'll work something out when you get back."

"That's very generous of you, sir, but I'll have to get back to you on that."

"What the devil are you saying?"

He finally risked a look at Ashley and noted that she was listening avidly to every word. "I'm saying that I'm on vacation. We'll discuss it another time. Thanks for calling. I mean that, sir. It was very gracious of you."

He shut the phone off completely and barely resisted the urge to toss it out the back door. He waited for the litany of questions to begin.

"Go ahead, ask," he said finally.

She grinned. "That was about work, right?"

He nodded, uncertain where she was going. It didn't seem to be in the direction he'd expected.

Ashley held up a slip of paper with little marks on it. "I counted half a dozen references to work, minimum. That's six dollars in your pot, please."

Josh fought a laugh. "You counted that conversation in our bet?"

"Of course. We had a deal. We sealed it with a toast before the phone rang."

"Oh, brother, you must be hell on wheels in a courtroom."

She grinned. "That's another one. Seven dollars."

He frowned at her. "Dammit, I was referring to *your* work, not mine."

"Did we differentiate?" she inquired sweetly.

He sighed. "No, we did not differentiate. This is going to be a lot trickier than I expected."

"Which means we should probably change the subject, even though I'm winning," Ashley conceded with a magnanimous air. "Do you know anything about baseball? I'm a Red Sox fan myself."

Josh stared at her, not entirely sure if she was serious. "Really? When was the last time you went to a baseball game?"

She faltered a bit at that. "I don't actually go to the games," she confessed eventually. "That doesn't mean I don't follow the team."

"Then you watch them on TV?"

"Not really."

"Read the sports pages?" he asked, his amusement growing.

"Okay, okay, I don't know a damn thing about baseball," she finally said. "But people in the office mention it. Obviously it's something some people care about. I thought you might be one of them. I was just trying to make conversation."

Josh grinned and held out his hand. "I'll take a dollar, please. You mentioned your office."

She stared at him with apparent dismay. "That doesn't count."

"Of course it does. Office, work, it's all the same thing."

"Oh, for heaven's sakes," she muttered, as she dug in

her purse and tossed a dollar onto the table. "I'm still winning."

"And we have a week to go. Don't get overly confident, sweetheart. It's unbecoming."

She frowned at him. "Seen any good movies lately?"

"Not a one. You?"

"No."

"Read any good books?" he asked, fully expecting her to slip up and make some reference to a law journal.

Her expression brightened. "Actually, I read a great one yesterday afternoon. It almost made me late for dinner."

"Would I like it?"

"I doubt it. It was a love story."

"Hey, I'm all in favor of love."

She regarded him with blatant skepticism. "You want to read this?"

"Sure, why not? The fish was very good, by the way. You follow directions well."

She seemed startled by the praise. Her gaze shifted to his clean plate, then to her own. "I do, don't I? Maybe I'll learn to cook while I'm here."

"I'd be happy to be your guinea pig," he offered. "I have a cast-iron stomach. I have to, given how lousy I am in the kitchen."

"Maybe Maggie could give us both lessons," she suggested. "That could be fun."

"Even relaxing," he retorted. "As long as you don't turn it into some sort of competition."

"Not everything has to be a competition with me," she insisted.

"Really? I'll bet by the time you were three, you wanted to know if your hands were the cleanest when you came to the supper table."

"I did not," she said, but there was a spark of recognition in her eyes that suggested she saw herself in his comment just the same.

Josh wondered if a woman who obviously thrived on challenges would ever be content with a slower, less stressful pace, or if she would always need to be in the thick of some battle. It was something he needed to decide about himself, as well.

He'd come down here to simplify his life, to cut through the clutter of being on the fast track and see if he wanted to get off entirely. He suspected Ashley wasn't in the same place at all. If anything, she was probably champing at the bit to get back on that fast track. It might be the kind of complication that meant they were doomed, but it was hardly something that needed to be resolved tonight.

Tonight it was enough to be with a woman who stirred his blood and kept him on his toes mentally. At some point during the evening, he'd gotten past the triumph of being invited to Rose Cottage by one of the unattainable D'Angelo sisters. Now it was all about being with a woman who intrigued him, a woman with strengths and vulnerabilities he wanted to understand, a woman whose bed he wanted to share.

When that thought cavorted through his head, he immediately slammed on the brakes. He was getting ahead of himself, way ahead of himself.

He glanced across the table and saw Ashley studying him intently. There was an unmistakable and totally unexpected hunger in her eyes. He told himself it had to be for the chocolate.

"Ready for dessert?" he asked, his voice thick and unsteady.

She nodded, her gaze never leaving his.

"Cake?"

She shook her head.

"A brownie?"

Again, that subtle shake.

Josh swallowed hard. "Eclair?"

"Not right now."

"What do you want?"

"You," she said quietly.

Amazement flooded through him. "But—"

"No questions, no doubts, unless you don't want me," she said.

"That is definitely not the issue," he admitted.

Her lips curved slightly. "Then why are you still sitting there?"

"Because I'm an idiot," he said, trying to ignore the way his pulse was racing with anticipation. He *was* a nice guy, dammit, and she was vulnerable. He would not take advantage of her.

She stared at him for an eternity. "You're saying no?"

He nodded. "I don't know what brought you down here, but having sex with me isn't the answer."

"It could be the answer tonight," she said lightly.

He smiled at that. "Indeed, it could be spectacular, but when you and I get together for the first time—and we will, Ashley—then I want it to be because it's inevitable, not because it's convenient."

Patches of red flared in her cheeks. "I'm sorry. I'm the idiot," she said, instantly stiff and unapproachable again.

"Don't you dare say that," he chided. "You have no idea how flattered I am that you suggested this or how hard it was for me to say no. We'll get around to making love, make no mistake about that."

"I'm only here for three weeks," she reminded him, as if to define the urgency.

He grinned. "Which means we still have twenty days left. Since we barely got through one without tumbling straight into your bed, I suspect we won't waste too many."

She stared at him quizzically, as if she were trying to discover if he was making fun of her. Apparently she recognized just how serious he was, because she laughed. The tension evaporated.

But Josh knew that thanks to his noble gesture, sleep was going to be a very long time coming.

5

Ashley still felt like a first-class idiot in the morning. Josh had been amazingly gracious when she'd hit on him, but she'd clearly misread all the signals. She'd thought all those sparks were going to lead to something that would help her to forget her problems. Fishing, pleasant as it had been, sure as hell wasn't going to do that. A steamy, meaningless affair might have.

Oh, well, no one died of acute humiliation. She simply wouldn't make that mistake again. For all she knew, Josh wouldn't even set foot on the grounds at Rose Cottage again, despite all those pretty words and promises.

She was still beating herself up as she lingered over her second cup of coffee when someone knocked on the kitchen door, then walked right in. She glanced up, fully expecting it to be her sisters, only to find Josh there in another pair of faded shorts and another of those equally disreputable T-shirts. He looked incredible. Her resolve to forget about an affair sizzled and died.

Without saying a word, he walked over to the table, leaned down and kissed her. The first touch of his lips on hers was a shock. She had a hunch he'd meant it to be nothing more than a casual, good-morning kind of kiss, but it set off enough heat to boil eggs. Her head was spinning, and she was pretty sure her eyes had to be crossed by the time he pulled away. If he'd been trying to prove that he'd meant what he said the night before, he'd accomplished that and then some.

"I thought you might be over here beating yourself up about trying to seduce me last night," he said as he casually turned to the coffeepot and poured himself the last cup. She'd drunk all the rest of the coffee herself.

Indignation flared at his comment, even though he'd guessed exactly right. "So what? You decided to come over and toss me a consolation prize?"

He laughed. "No, I came over to prove that you have nothing to worry about. A couple more kisses like that one and I won't be able to resist you. My noble intentions will fly right out the window."

She frowned at him. "Was that my mistake last night—not grabbing you and kissing you right off the bat?"

"You didn't make any mistakes last night," he assured her. "Aside from being a little premature." He surveyed her. "Why aren't you dressed for fishing?"

"I didn't know we were going fishing," she said, her tone still peevish. He'd thrown her completely off-kilter yet again. It was getting to be an annoying habit. The men she liked were predictable. None of them would have turned down her offer of uncomplicated sex.

And, she was forced to admit, none of them would have been back here this morning suggesting a fishing trip.

"You have something else planned?" he asked.

She shook her head.

"Then let's get a move on. Those fish won't wait forever."

She grinned despite herself. "I thought the object was to relax, that actually catching a fish didn't really matter."

"It doesn't to me," he said indifferently, then winked. "But you seem to need immediate gratification."

"Is that an insult?"

He laughed. "Nope, just an observation. We're going to work on that."

"What if I don't want to change?" she asked curiously.

"Then it will be more of a struggle than I'm expecting," he said easily. "Go, put on a swimsuit under your clothes. Maybe I'll let you race me to the dock later."

"Will you let me win?"

"Not a chance."

Ashley laughed. "Now you've really made it interesting. I'll be right back."

Upstairs, she pulled on her prim, one-piece bathing suit, then added a T-shirt, shorts and a pair of dingy sneakers she hadn't worn since college. She grabbed her cap from the day before and a bottle of suntan lotion. She hesitated in the bedroom doorway as if she were forgetting something, then realized that going fishing didn't require a tenth of the paraphernalia she took with her to work each day. It was actually a relief to go downstairs without a purse or briefcase weighing her down.

She took the keys from a peg on the wall, then announced, "I'm ready."

Josh grinned. "Love the shoes. They make a statement."

She glanced pointedly at his faded and misshapen boat shoes. "It's not as if you just stepped out of a designer shoe showroom."

"Hey, don't you dare insult these old things. They're just getting comfortable."

They'd barely stepped out the back door, still bantering, when Melanie and Maggie rounded the corner of the house. Ashley's good humor vanished in a heartbeat. She muttered a curse, ruing the day she'd ever interfered in her sisters' lives, since they now seemed to feel totally free to butt into hers.

"We heard that," Maggie scolded. "Is that any way to welcome your loving sisters who've come to check on you?"

"As if that's why you're here," she retorted. "You're here to spy."

"Which would hardly matter if you have nothing to hide," Melanie commented, her gaze on Josh. "Been here long?" she asked him.

"A few minutes," Ashley responded emphatically.

"Then this is like a second date or something," Maggie said. "Fascinating."

"It's not a date," Ashley said automatically. "We're going fishing."

"Oh, yes, fishing," Maggie repeated, amusement threading through her voice. "I forgot that doesn't count. If it did, that would actually make this the third date, since you went fishing yesterday, too, isn't that right, Josh?"

He regarded her with undisguised reluctance. "Don't ask me. I'm staying out of this one. You ladies work it out. Me, I'm not much on labels. I'm a go-with-the-flow kind of guy."

Ashley frowned at him. "You are not. Otherwise—"

He interrupted, grinning at her. "Do you really want to go there?"

Ashley sighed and shut up.

"Smart and handsome," Melanie said with approval.

"A dead man," Ashley commented, scowling at him. "You were supposed to back me up. We're not dating."

"Oh, I must have missed that memo." He dutifully turned to her sisters. "We're not dating."

"Then what are you doing?" Maggie inquired sweetly. "Besides kissing, that is?"

"Kissing?" Ashley asked. "Where would you get an idea like that?"

"The clues are everywhere," Maggie said blithely. "Those telltale traces of lipstick on Josh's face, for instance, and the fact that your lipstick is the exact same shade... What's left of it, anyway."

Ashley felt her cheeks flaming. She turned to Josh. "Have I mentioned that my sisters are a couple of obnoxious meddlers?"

"I think it's sweet," he said.

"Sweet?" she echoed incredulously. "What's sweet about them barging in here and making you uncomfortable?"

"I'm not uncomfortable."

She stared at him. He did seem perfectly at ease. She was the only one about to jump out of her skin. "Oh, forget it. I'm going fishing. The rest of you can do whatever the hell you want to do."

"Sorry, ladies," Josh said. "I think that's my cue. Have a nice day."

They were in the boat before Ashley finally risked a look into his eyes. They were sparkling with amusement.

"You thought that was funny, didn't you?" she demanded irritably.

"I don't know about funny, but it wasn't quite the big deal you want to turn it into."

"Just wait," she muttered direly. "Just you wait."

She was going to take a certain amount of perverse pleasure in watching Josh squirm when her sisters decided he was exactly the right catch and set out to reel him in for her.

Josh recalled Ashley's warning when he was sitting in a booth at a café later that afternoon with a cappuccino and the Richmond paper and he spotted Maggie and Melanie about to descend on him. They looked as thrilled as if they'd just noticed an especially plump turkey for their Thanksgiving dinner.

"Hello again," Maggie said, sliding into the booth opposite him.

Melanie slipped in beside him, so there would be no escape. "Where's Ashley?"

"I dropped her back at Rose Cottage about an hour ago."

"Catch any fish today?" Maggie asked.

"Not a one," he admitted, recalling just how frustrating that had been to Ashley. She hadn't quite gotten the knack of appreciating the process more than the outcome. She'd been very irritable when he'd left her at Rose Cottage.

Melanie laughed. "Uh-oh, that must have driven Ashley up a wall. She probably took it as a personal affront."

"Pretty much," he agreed. In fact, she'd made such a commotion, it was little wonder the fish had taken off. He hadn't had the nerve to point out to her that fish tended to flee when humans made too much racket.

Maggie's gaze narrowed. "Did that make you run for cover?"

"No, it made me run home to change into clean clothes so I could meet her here for coffee."

"Oh," Maggie said, obviously deflated.

"Do you honestly want to be here cross-examining me when she gets here?" he inquired.

The two women exchanged a look. "Probably a bad idea," Melanie admitted.

"She'll think we're spying again," Maggie agreed. "But we have our eyes on you, Madison. Don't forget that."

Josh laughed. "Not for a minute," he promised.

Maggie gave him one last considering look. "You could be good for her."

"Thank you."

"Has she told you why she's hiding out down here?"

"No."

"Make her tell you," she urged. "She needs to talk about it."

"Maybe what she needs is to put it behind her," Josh suggested. "Sometimes you can talk a thing to death."

"Nice theory, but talking things to death is how Ashley handles a crisis," Maggie informed him. "This time she's clammed up. It's not healthy."

"I don't suppose you want to share a little information with me, maybe tell me what it is I'm supposed to get her to talk about," he suggested.

"Sorry," Maggie said. "She'd kill us if we told."

"Does it have something to do with work?"

They exchanged a look, then nodded.

"Then we have a problem. She and I have agreed to avoid the subject of work at all costs. In fact we have a bet going about who can do the best job of steering clear of the topic."

"Great, that's just great," Maggie said in obvious disgust, oblivious to the suddenly frantic signals Melanie was trying to send her.

"Actually it *is* great," Ashley chimed in, startling Maggie. "Work is not a topic I care to get into with anyone right now, including the two of you. Go away." She frowned at Josh. "Didn't I warn you about them?"

"Hey, I was sitting here minding my own business and they turned up. It's not like I invited them to join us."

Maggie's expression brightened. "What a good idea! We'd love to."

"It is *not* a good idea," Ashley said emphatically. "Go away. If you don't, I will."

"Okay, fine," Maggie said as she and Melanie stood

up. "We'll leave you in Josh's capable hands." She turned to him. "Remember our advice. And forget about that stupid bet."

Ashley stood watching them until they were out the door. Then she sat down opposite him. "What advice did they give you?"

"They think I need to ask you about what drove you down here," he said. He searched her face, watching for a reaction. She managed to keep her expression totally neutral. "Do I?"

"Absolutely not. I don't want to talk about it," she said fiercely.

He sighed. "Which tells me it is exactly what we need to discuss."

She regarded him plaintively. "Why?"

"Because it's apparently the key to getting to know who you are."

"You know who I am."

"I know what you've allowed me to scc. It's all pretty superficial, Ashley."

She gave him a sour look. "Am I boring you?"

"Hardly."

"Then think of it this way—there are layers and layers yet to be peeled away. One of these days I may let you get started on that, but not now, okay?"

"You can't solve problems if you hide from them," he commented. Not that he was a sterling example of someone who paid attention to that particular advice. Wasn't he as guilty of avoiding things at the moment as she was? He hadn't given one moment's thought to his future once he'd resolved things with Stephanie. He was letting it all percolate on the back burner in the hope that things would work themselves out eventually without any effort on his part.

Ashley frowned at the unsolicited advice. "I can only learn one new trick at a time. I'm still having trouble with the relaxation thing. This other business would pretty much set me back by a month."

Josh laughed. "Okay, okay. We'll stick to relaxing for now. And speaking of that, what would you like? I could use another cappuccino. I'll go up to the counter and order."

"A cappuccino sounds good," she said. "I'll look at the paper till you get back."

It didn't take Josh more than five minutes to order their coffee and take the drinks back to the table, but something had obviously happened while he was away. Every bit of color had washed out of Ashley's face, and she was clutching a balled up chunk of newsprint in her fist.

"Ashley?" he asked, scooting into the booth next to her. "What is it?"

She shook her head, looking dazed.

Josh tried to pry the paper from her hand, but she refused to release it. He racked his brain trying to recall anything that had been in the paper that might have had this obviously devastating effect on her, but nothing came to him. Besides, she had no ties to Richmond that he knew of.

"Talk to me, sweetheart. Something's obviously upset you."

"I can't," she whispered, her voice choked. "Let me out of here. I think I'm going to be sick."

She ran from the café with Josh hard on her heels. He

caught her at the corner. She was bending over, holding her stomach, gasping for breath. He rubbed her back, murmuring soothing nonsense, until she finally shuddered and turned to him, burying her face against his shoulder. He'd never before in his life seen anyone with such a stricken look in their eyes. It made him want to kill whoever was responsible for putting it there.

"Tell me, please," he pleaded. "I can't help if I don't know what's going on."

"Can we take a break from the bet?" she asked.

Josh almost laughed that she would think of their bet at a time like this. "Okay, we're on a time-out," he assured her. "Now tell me."

She lifted her gaze to his, her expression drained. Finally she seemed to reach some sort of conclusion because she held out her hand and let him take the piece of newspaper.

Josh smoothed it out as best he could with one hand, while still keeping one arm firmly around her waist. He had a feeling she needed the contact far more than he needed to get immediate answers.

The first side of the page was nothing but part of an ad for a Richmond department store. When he turned it over, he saw that it was from a column of national news briefs. The dateline was Boston.

Freed Killer Strikes Again, the headline stated. He glanced at Ashley's face. There was guilt and shame in her expression as if she were somehow responsible.

"What do you know about this?" he asked quietly.

"I know that man," she said after what seemed like an eternity. "I represented him at his last trial for murder. I just got him off a week ago. My firm's still representing him."

Oh, dear God in heaven, Josh thought, his heart aching for her. *That* was what had brought her to Rose Cottage, the knowledge that she had helped to free a murderer. And now the man had almost killed again. Only quick police intervention had stopped him. It would devastate any lawyer, but especially one who took such evident pride in her courtroom skills. She'd obviously been duped by the man into believing in his innocence. She wouldn't be the first lawyer to be fooled, or the last, but she obviously held herself to exceedingly high standards.

"It's not your fault," he said firmly.

"Of course it is. That disgusting creature wouldn't have been back on the streets if it hadn't been for me. Maybe I didn't know he was guilty when I defended him, but I should have seen it. He would have been in jail now if I hadn't been so aggressive in that courtroom."

"Was the prosecution's case airtight?"

"No," she admitted. "The forensics evidence was sloppy as hell."

"Did you do anything unethical?"

"No."

"Did you follow the law?"

"To the letter."

"Then it wasn't your fault," he repeated. "Remember, our legal system is based on the principle that it's preferable for ten guilty people to go free than for one innocent person to be convicted. The jury is instructed not to convict if there is reasonable doubt, and it's up to the prosecutor to remove that doubt from the jurors' minds."

"Justice wasn't served," she insisted. "Not even close. I have a reputation for picking my cases very carefully. I blew this one."

Josh couldn't argue with that. He knew all too well how cases could sometimes be won or lost not on the evidence, but based on the comparative skills of the lawyers involved. It was one of the reasons he was questioning his own commitment to the law. Maybe now was the time to tell Ashley that, to commiserate with her in a way that told her he really did understand. Somehow, though, he couldn't bring himself to do it. This was about her feelings, and he didn't want to divert the conversation away from that for even a moment.

"I'm sorry," he said softly. "I know how this case must eat at you. My saying it's not your fault doesn't really help. You have to get there on your own."

"I don't know if I ever will." She eyed the article he was holding as if it were a serpent. "Especially now. I'll never be able to practice in Boston again."

"Of course you will," he said. "If that's what you want to do. Good people, honest people, innocent people, get accused of crimes, and they're going to want an attorney who fights with passion and conviction on their side. Those are the ones you'll help."

She regarded him with a sad expression. "But don't you see, Josh? I can't tell the difference."

The misery in her eyes and the hopelessness in her voice were enough to break his heart.

"Of course you can," he assured her. "It's one mistake, Ashley. That doesn't render you incompetent."

"Another person nearly died because of me," she insisted fiercely. "If the police hadn't had him under surveillance…" She shuddered at what could have happened. "I'm as guilty as Tiny Slocum."

"I know that's how you must feel, but you'll see it differently in time," he said, wondering even as he spoke if that were really true. Ashley clearly had a conscience that ran deep. It was one of the most admirable things about her. How would she ever be able to reconcile what had happened with her vision of justice? With her vision of herself?

Worse, he knew that there wasn't a damn thing he could say that would set her mind at ease.

6

"You can go now," Ashley told Josh after he'd fixed them both dinner, then sat there patiently, his gaze unrelenting, until she'd eaten almost every bite. His presence, undemanding though it was, was wearing on her nerves. Sooner or later, he was going to insist she talk about Tiny Slocum.

Right now, though, he merely grinned. "Trying to run me off before I make you finish your peas?"

"You caught me," she admitted, trying to match his light tone. "I hate peas."

He gave her a perplexed look. "Then why were there six cans of them in the cupboard?"

"Because Melanie was here first and she stocked the cupboards. She loves peas." Ashley grinned halfheartedly. "Maggie won't touch them, either. Maybe I should consider wrapping them up and giving them to Melanie for Christmas."

Even as she spoke, there was a semi-hysterical note in her voice as she realized that it was entirely possible that she could still be here at Christmas, that her firm might not want her back after all, now that her sterling reputation for being on the side of the angels had been tarnished. Her three-week break, which she'd barely become resigned to, could turn into months of unemployment and indecision.

Given that realization along with everything else, it was a miracle that she could find anything at all to joke about. Ever since she'd seen that news brief in the paper, she'd felt as if all the air had been sucked from her lungs. She hadn't said a dozen words all during dinner. It was little wonder that Josh was reluctant to leave her, even though he had to have lost respect for her, knowing how badly she'd been deluded in the Tiny Slocum case. She was sure Josh would bolt the instant he thought she was calm enough to be left alone. That would be that, the end of a budding…what? Friendship? Relationship?

She regarded him thoughtfully. "Why haven't you run for the hills by now?" Maybe the answer to that would tell her what she needed to know. Maybe it would help her to define whatever was going on between them. She liked everything in her life sorted into nice, neat cubbyholes. Up till now Josh had defied all her attempts at categorization.

But rather than giving her the direct, uncomplicated answer she'd hoped for, he regarded her blankly. "Why would I do that?"

"You've seen unmistakable evidence that I'm a terrible judge of character," she explained. "That might be okay for the average person, but it's a lousy trait for an attorney. *I* don't even have any respect for me anymore."

"Come on, Ashley. I'm not about to confuse a mistake you made with who you are," he told her. "You're a good, decent person."

"You haven't known me long enough to be sure of that," she protested, determined not to listen to anything positive when she was mired in this down-on-herself mood.

"It's *obvious*," he contradicted just as emphatically. "Otherwise this wouldn't be tearing you up the way it is. You'd chalk it up to experience and move right on."

She stared at him in shock. "How could I do that? How could anyone?"

"Attorneys do it all the time," he insisted. "They passionately defend people they know or suspect to be guilty because that's their job. You said yourself that someone at your firm took over Slocum's defense."

"You don't seem to have a very high opinion of lawyers," she observed.

"Just a realistic one, quite possibly a better one than you do at the moment," he said, then waved her off when she would have interrupted. "Let me finish."

"Fine. Go right ahead."

"Maybe a good attorney will try to encourage a plea bargain if the evidence is overwhelming, but ultimately his duty is to act in the best interest of his client, guilty or innocent, and to offer that client the competent defense that is the client's constitutional right, correct?"

"Yes," she admitted.

"You thought you were defending an innocent man. It turned out you were wrong. It's not the same thing as deliberately setting out to free a guilty man."

Ashley refused to be placated. "It feels like the same

thing. It feels as if I'm as responsible as Tiny Slocum was when he beat up yet another woman."

Josh looked her in the eye. "How do you think the jurors who acquitted him are feeling right now? Do you blame them? Do you think you duped them?"

She closed her eyes and sighed. "No, not deliberately. Tiny fooled all of us. I'm sure they're as sick at heart as I am."

"Add in the fact that the prosecutor and police messed up. Seems to me as if there's plenty of blame to go around. You don't need to take it all onto your shoulders." He scooted his chair closer and skimmed a finger along her bare arm. "And lovely shoulders they are, too. Much too lovely to have all this weight heaped on them."

Ashley shuddered at his touch. It would be so easy to allow him to distract her, just for a little while. It would be wonderful to have his mouth on hers, his hands exploring her body, to feel him inside her, to give in to sensation, to let him take her hard and fast until she came apart. It was exactly what she'd wanted last night, and it was even more appealing now.

But she wouldn't ask him to stay, not again. Her pride wouldn't allow it, even if her common sense wasn't telling her that the timing was no more right tonight than it had been the night before. If anything, it was worse. They would both know she was only using him to forget her troubles. That was a truly lousy thing to do to a man who'd been nothing but thoughtful and supportive.

She grabbed Josh's hand and pressed a kiss to his knuckles. "You should go," she said quietly. "I need some time to think about all this."

"I'm not so sure you should be alone," he said, his expression uneasy. "If you don't want me here, how about calling one of your sisters?"

She shook her head. "Maggie and Melanie have already listened to me moan and groan enough about all this. They came straight up to Boston to get me after the trial. If you think I'm in bad shape now, you should have seen me then. I was totally impossible and unreasonable. They threatened to have me committed if I didn't take some time off."

"Really? Good for them."

She frowned at him. "Don't tell me you're a proponent of the tough love approach, too."

"I'm a proponent of love in all its forms," he retorted genially. "Now let me do these dishes, and I'll get out from underfoot."

"Josh, I don't think I'm so shaken that I can't wash a few dishes. Doing something totally mundane and mindless will be good for me," she said, anxious for him to be gone before she changed her mind and threw herself at him.

"If you say so," he replied.

"Go. Do something fun and don't spend one second worrying about me. I promise I'll be here in the morning, bright-eyed and ready to go fishing."

He studied her intently for a moment, then nodded. "Okay, then, you win. I'm out of here. Call me if you change your mind and decide you need company. It doesn't matter what time it is. I'm not on any sort of schedule right now. I can be back here in a few minutes."

"I will," she promised.

He leaned down and gave her a hard kiss that stirred regret that she'd already decided to send him on his way.

"Just something else for you to think about," he teased lightly. "I don't want you wasting your whole night on useless guilt."

After he'd gone, Ashley touched her lips. It had been a helluva tactic. As stressed-out as she was about things in Boston, there was a whole lot going on right here to give her pause. One of these days she'd have to figure out why she was so attracted to a man who seemed to have an endless supply of time on his hands and no noticeable goals that she'd been able to discern.

Josh wasn't happy about leaving Ashley alone, but the stubborn set of her jaw had told him she wasn't going to give him any alternative. Better to go gracefully than add to her stress by digging in his heels and staying put. Besides, he had some thinking of his own to do. Maybe this was the perfect opportunity. Ironically the questions plaguing Ashley were not that much of a stretch from those bothering him.

Not that he'd gotten a murderer off recently. He swam in a different legal pond, mostly with the corporate barracudas. It was cutthroat law of a different kind, and he'd pretty much concluded months ago that he wasn't suited for it. He was always hired to represent one side, but he was too damn good at seeing both sides of the picture, especially in some of the high-stakes mergers and acquisitions he handled. His evenhanded judgment made it a lot harder to go for the jugular, even when that was precisely what he was being paid to do.

People who hired Brevard, Williams and Davenport could pay for the best representation available. More and more lately, Josh had wanted to be on the side of the little guy who couldn't afford the big guns. Maybe this was his chance to do just that. He had no financial obligations, no family to consider. If he was ever going to dramatically alter his income and lifestyle, now was the time.

A part of him wanted to go back to Ashley's and bat the whole idea around with her for a while. He had a hunch she would bring a unique perspective to the picture. Maybe it would even help her wrestle with her own dilemma. They could be sounding boards for each other, at least once she got over the shock of discovering that he was one of those lawyers she thought he held in such disdain.

He sighed and dismissed the idea. Ashley didn't want a sounding board right now. She wanted to hibernate and lick her wounds. He honestly couldn't blame her. He'd give her tonight to do that, but come morning, he was going to be back over there and was going to insist they talk her situation out some more, especially if she was still neck-deep in guilt.

"You look like a man with a lot on his mind." Mike startled Josh out of his reverie when he found Josh still sitting behind the wheel of his car in his driveway after he'd driven home from Ashley's.

"Just thinking about this and that," Josh said, climbing out of the car and plastering a fake smile of welcome on his face. "What are you doing here?"

"Actually I was out for a walk and saw your car turn in. I decided I'd stop by and see if you wanted a little company. Melanie and Jessie went shopping for school supplies so I'm at loose ends."

Josh grinned at the restless note in Mike's voice. "Is that what marriage does to you, makes you incapable of being on your own for a few hours?"

Mike laughed. "Pretty much. I'm still shocked by that myself." He gave Josh a speculative look. "You're on your own pretty early, too. Did Ashley kick you out?"

"She had some things she needed to think through," he said, careful not to allude to what those things were. If she didn't want her family to know, it wasn't up to him to spill the beans.

"About your relationship?" Mike prodded.

"No way. To hear her tell it, we don't have a relationship."

"I see. What's your take on that?"

Josh gave the question some serious thought. He liked her, no question about that. He was attracted to her. Definitely no question about that, either. Did they have a future? How could he possibly answer that when neither of them had a clue what they really wanted for the rest of their lives, professionally speaking, anyway? He settled for giving a reply that was honest as far as it went.

"I think that depends on how determined she is to go back to Boston," he told Mike. "There's not much chance of having a relationship with someone whose life is hundreds of miles away."

Mike didn't seem convinced. "You hear about long-distance relationships working all the time. They're tough, but it can be done if both people are committed to it."

"I think it's a little soon for either of us to be thinking about commitment. We barely know each other."

"Sometimes the whole lightning-bolt thing happens," Mike reminded him. "It happened that way for me and Melanie. Same thing with Rick and Maggie. Maybe it's the way things go with the D'Angelo women."

Josh thought of how connected he sometimes felt to Ashley, far more connected than he'd ever felt to Stephanie, despite having known Stephanie so much longer. Maybe Mike was right. Maybe time had nothing to do with love. Still, for a plodder like him, it seemed wrong to be thinking of jumping from thoughts of an eventual engagement to a certain woman one day, to a full-throttle relationship with another woman a few days later. A full-throttle affair, maybe, but he'd already vetoed that idea.

"Let's not jump the gun," he told Mike. "I don't think Ashley's in the best place to be worrying about a relationship with anyone right now."

Mike regarded him with pity. "A word of advice, don't wait for her to decide or to be in the right place. If you want her, let her know it. If you want her to stay here, then pull out the big guns and persuade her to stay. If she's anything like her sisters, this area is in her blood just as much as Boston is, but it might take a little push to help her realize that."

Josh nodded. "I'll keep that in mind. Now how about a beer?" he suggested, anxious to change the subject. "We can swap lies and gossip about everyone we know except the D'Angelo women."

Mike laughed. "Total avoidance. It's a great tactic. I used it a lot. In the end, it didn't matter. You can get those women out of your head, but it's impossible to get them out of your blood."

Josh was beginning to get that. Oddly, it didn't terrify him half as much as it should have.

It took a great deal of courage for Ashley to call Jo in Boston the minute Josh left. There were things she needed to know. If her life as she knew it was over, she needed to start making an adjustment right now. She'd have to scale down her lifestyle, find a whole new career, maybe even move to some other city.

"Slow down," she scolded herself as she dialed her sister's number. "This isn't the time for making rash decisions. Get the facts first."

Jo picked up on the fourth ring, her tone hesitant.

"Hey, it's me," Ashley said.

"Thank God. I almost didn't pick up."

"Why?"

"The media," Jo said succinctly. "They're trying to track you down. This latest beating—you have heard about it, right?"

"I've heard."

"Well, as you can imagine, it's stirred them up all over again. They want your reaction to it."

"I'm so sorry. You need to get caller ID."

"No, I don't. This will pass. How are you? How did you find out, anyway? I was hoping it hadn't made the news down there."

"There was an item in the Richmond paper," Ashley admitted. "So how bad is it? Are the papers screaming for my head?"

"Of course not," Jo said.

Unfortunately, her baby sister was a terrible liar. Ashley heard the faint hesitation in her voice.

"Come on, Jo. What are they saying? Tell the truth. If you don't, I'll just have to call the office and ask them what's going on. Something tells me they won't sugarcoat anything. I'll be lucky to have a job. They loved having me on board when I was saving the innocent and bringing in great PR for the firm, but now? I can't imagine they're happy about this."

"Okay, it's bad," Jo admitted. "But that's today. The beating just took place yesterday. Everyone's bound to be in an uproar. Things will quiet down in a few days. One paper already put some perspective on the story by asking how the prosecution and cops screwed up the first trial so badly. They've stopped focusing on you completely."

"That doesn't mean I'm off the hook, even with that paper. It just means that the prosecutor and police are dangling on the hook with me," Ashley said cynically. She bit back a sigh. "Maybe I should go back and face the music."

"Absolutely not," Jo said. "You stay right where you are. We're all agreed about that."

"Everyone in the family knows?"

"Mom and Dad do, of course. They've been getting the same calls I have."

"Dammit," Ashley muttered. "I'll call them and tell them not to answer the phone."

"No need. I think Dad's actually enjoying giving the media an earful about irresponsible reporting. You know how he is when anyone picks on one of his baby girls."

The reminder almost brought a smile to Ashley's lips. Max D'Angelo was a stereotypical overly protective Italian father. Nobody hurt one of his daughters. Heck, it was a wonder any of them had ever had a date, given the way he loomed over every male to cross the threshold. As teenagers, they had all been driven crazy by it.

Now Ashley could only be grateful for her father's innate protectiveness. He'd stand between her and an entire army of reporters and photographers, if need be.

"He's something, isn't he?" she said.

"He loves you to pieces," Jo said. "Don't worry about him and Mom, okay? They just want to be sure you're all right. They think Rose Cottage is the perfect place for you till this mess settles down. They're relieved that you're not here in the thick of it."

"Have you spoken to Maggie or Melanie?"

Jo hesitated. "Don't be furious with me. I did try to call them to let them know what had happened, so they could decide the best way to break the news to you, but neither one was home. This wasn't the kind of message I wanted to leave on a machine. I think you should tell them, though. You shouldn't be alone."

"I'm not alone. Well, I am now, but Josh was here until about a half hour ago. I sent him home."

"Josh?" Jo repeated, immediately intrigued. "Spill, big sister. Who is Josh?"

Ashley was surprised. "You mean the family grapevine has failed you? I thought surely you would have had detailed reports by now. Maggie and Melanie are certainly making a lot out of the fact that I met a man a few hours after my arrival."

"An interesting man?"

"That's one description," she conceded.

"What's a better one?"

Ashley thought about that before answering. "He's soothing," she said eventually.

"Soothing? As in boring?"

She laughed. "No, he's definitely not boring."

"Not the least bit sexy?"

"Oh, he's sexy, all right."

"Really?" Jo said with more enthusiasm. "Now it's getting interesting. Tell me more, Ashley. Are you going to follow the family tradition and fall madly in love while you're at Rose Cottage?"

"Don't be ridiculous. I have way too much on my mind to even think about a man right now."

Jo laughed. "I'm pretty sure love and passion don't require a lot of thinking. You're supposed to go with the flow. Not that I would know, of course, my own love life being what it is."

"Which is?" Ashley asked, eager to steer the subject away from her own problems.

"Not something I care to discuss," Jo said emphatically, in a way that only stirred worry that there was something she was hiding.

Even through her concern, Ashley had to admire her baby sister. No matter how complicated her life got, Jo simply dealt with it. They usually didn't know until much, much later that Jo's emotional life was in turmoil. She was quiet and steady as a rock.

"If you change your mind, I'm here," Ashley said, fully aware that she was wasting her breath.

"I know that. I know I can depend on all of you."

"You just choose not to," Ashley said.

"It's not that I wouldn't value your advice or your support," Jo said. "It just makes it more difficult to know my own mind if there's all this sisterly clamor going on around me."

"Fair enough. I suppose we could listen without offering advice," Ashley offered.

"That'll be the day," Jo said with a laugh. "Maybe one leopard could change its spots, but three? Not a chance."

"Okay, then," Ashley said briskly. "Thanks for filling me in. I'll be in touch."

"If you aren't, I'm coming down there and bringing Mom and Dad with me. We'll circle the wagons."

"Heaven forbid!" Ashley said, truly aghast at the notion.

Jo chuckled. "Thought that would provide sufficient motivation for you to call home more often. Love you."

"You, too, brat."

She hung up the phone slowly and realized she was smiling, despite everything. She might not want her family hovering, but it meant the world to know that they were there if she needed them.

7

Josh arrived at Rose Cottage by 7:00 a.m., but Melanie and Maggie had beaten him there. He spotted their cars as he crossed the backyard from the dock. Something told him that word of Ashley's latest crisis had spread despite his own attempts to keep it under wraps during Mike's visit. He was beginning to realize that the D'Angelo grapevine was an efficient means of communication. He hadn't decided yet if that was good or bad.

He tapped on the back door and walked in to find all three sisters at the kitchen table. Ashley looked as if she were under siege. She turned to him so eagerly, it made his heart skip a beat or two. He wished he could believe that welcome was specifically for him, and wouldn't have been given to anyone who'd walked in the door just then.

"Time to go?" she asked, leaping to her feet. "I'm ready."

"Not so fast, big sister," Maggie said. "Josh, perhaps you would like a cup of coffee before you go?" It wasn't really a question. She was already pouring the coffee, and the determined glint in her eyes was more command than inquiry.

Josh glanced at Ashley and caught the pleading expression in her eyes. Even though he understood and shared her sisters' well-meaning concern, he opted to side with her for now. "Sorry. No time. We have an appointment."

"With some fish," Melanie noted dryly. "I didn't know they kept date books. I imagine they won't be all that disappointed if you're a little late."

"These are very busy fish," Josh retorted, undaunted by her undisguised skepticism. "And you know what they say about early birds."

"They get the worm," Maggie responded. "Which I don't think applies in this instance." She frowned at Ashley, then relented. "Okay, go, but we're not finished with you."

"I think I got that," Ashley said, sounding resigned.

"What time will you be back?" Maggie asked Josh.

"Hard to say," he responded evasively, suspecting they would be waiting on the doorstep if he gave them a specific hour. "With this whole relaxation thing, we try not to think in terms of timetables."

Maggie rolled her eyes. "Oh, please," she scoffed. "I don't know about you, but my sister's brain is equipped with an automatic day planner. I'm relatively certain she has no idea how to turn it off."

"I've noticed," Josh admitted. "We're working on that. She's already made impressive strides. You'd be surprised." He beamed at both of them. "See you."

He stepped aside to let Ashley bolt past him. She

was halfway to the dock before he caught up with her. To his shock, she threw her arms around his neck.

"Thank you, thank you, thank you," she enthused. "Your timing was impeccable. I told them you were coming, but they didn't believe me. They thought I was just trying to get rid of them."

He grinned. "Which you were."

"Well, of course."

"I gather someone filled them in about the whole Slocum situation."

"My folks," she admitted. "Had to be, since Jo hadn't been able to reach them. She reluctantly agreed not to call again, but Mom and Dad refused to commit to silence."

"Then you have spoken to your folks since last night?"

"Yes. After I talked to Jo and found out they were being pestered by reporters, I had to call them. I was trying to convince my father to limit himself to 'no comment.'"

Josh heard the combination of frustration and amusement in her voice. "A thankless task?" he guessed.

"You have no idea," she said ruefully. "He's been using this opportunity to vent about media irresponsibility. I suppose I should be grateful. It's doubtful any reporter will call him a second time." She gave him a wistful look. "Can we table this subject till later? Maybe reinstitute the rules of our bet and keep work off-limits? I've done nothing but think about this mess all night long. I could use a break from it."

He noted the dullness in her eyes and the shadows under them.

"Absolutely," he told her. "In fact, once we anchor offshore, you can take a little nap, if you like."

She gave him a surprisingly indignant look. "You're assuming I won't be catching any fish today?"

He chuckled. "You don't even have to cast your line, unless you really want to. Remember, the object is to sort of drift along, watch the clouds roll by and relax. Fishing is just an excuse to leave all your cares behind and be out on the water on a beautiful day."

"I wish I could," she said wistfully.

"You'll get the hang of it," Josh promised. "Sometimes relaxing takes a little effort."

She frowned at him. "Isn't that an oxymoron or something?"

"I suppose it is, if you feel the need to analyze it to death."

She nodded, her expression serious. "Got it. No analyzing. No thinking. Just drifting."

"Exactly."

She settled back against the cushion he'd propped on the seat, tugged down the brim of her cap and closed her eyes. Josh watched as her tensed muscles finally began to relax. Her bare legs and arms were turning a golden brown and her cheeks had a healthy glow, even if it couldn't quite dispel the evidence of her exhaustion. Silently, he waited for her breathing to fall into a slow, steady rhythm.

Just when he thought she'd fallen asleep, she murmured, "Josh?"

"What?"

"Don't you dare catch a fish while I'm taking a break."

"Why not? It's my turn. You've caught all the others."

Her lips quirked in undisguised triumph. "Oh, right, I have, haven't I? I've caught three, and you haven't caught any."

He barely contained a laugh. "And you felt the need to remind me of that because…?"

"Knowing I'm ahead makes it easier to rest."

"Then, by all means, gloat," he replied quietly. "I can take it."

"You're a nice man," she said.

Josh sighed. There it was again. *Nice.* One of these days he was going to have to get around to showing her just how wicked he could be. Something told him that with Ashley in his arms, he could top his very best efforts to date.

The instant Ashley woke up from her nap, she peered into the bucket of salt water. "No fish?" she asked Josh, trying to keep a gloating note out of her voice. It wasn't her fault that she'd turned out to have a knack for it that he seemed to lack.

"Actually I caught five whoppers," he said. "Threw them all back."

"Yeah, right. Speaking of whoppers…"

"Hey, I did," he insisted, his expression perfectly serious. Only the twinkle in his eyes gave him away. "How was your nap?"

"Restful," she admitted.

"Good."

"What time is it? How long did I sleep?"

"A couple of hours, actually. It's almost ten. I was about to slather some more suntan lotion on you."

She grinned. "Sounds like fun," she teased, handing him the bottle. "Just pretend I'm asleep."

"But you're not. You could do it yourself."

"Come on, Josh. Go along with me here. Be daring."

He rolled his eyes. "Okay, sweetheart, you want to take risks, it's fine with me." He took the outstretched bottle, poured lotion in his palm, then told her to turn around.

Ashley jerked when the cool lotion hit her bare shoulders. In a heartbeat, though, she wasn't even aware of the lotion, only of Josh's hands on her skin. It was evident that he had no intention of making quick work of the application. He stroked slowly. He caressed. He sent goose bumps dancing across her flesh until Ashley could hardly breathe.

When his fingers dipped into the low V on her back, skimmed down her spine, then slipped just beneath the fabric of her swimsuit, she almost jumped right out of the boat. He'd turned her taunt into a torment, a seduction. She could feel her nipples beading. Warmth pooled between her thighs. She closed her eyes and sucked in a breath, aware that they were playing a very dangerous game, one he'd apparently anticipated.

"Enough?" Josh asked, his voice suspiciously thick, even though it was evident he was taunting her.

Ashley wasn't quite ready to call it quits. Somehow he'd gotten the upper hand. She wanted it back. "You forgot the front," she told him, slowly turning to face him.

His gaze locked with hers, his eyes glinting wicked sparks. "Do you really, really want me to go on?"

Swallowing hard, she nodded.

He squirted more lotion into his palm, then smoothed it across her chest. His fingers skimmed along the edge of her bathing suit, then took a sudden dip into the cleavage.

"Wouldn't want you to get burned there," he murmured, holding her gaze. "That's very tender skin."

"Uh-huh," she whispered as he shifted his attention to her arms. He seemed to be intent on the soft, pale and surprisingly sensitive underside.

"What about your legs?" he inquired eventually. "Shall I do those?"

Ashley figured she could stand it if he could. "Sure," she said, determined to play out the game she'd started.

Of course, she hadn't realized just how long he could draw out the process. He didn't miss so much as a freckle or a pore, not from the tips of her toes to the tops of her thighs. She was all but coming unglued when he finally pronounced the job done. It took everything in her not to beg him not to stop.

"Thank you," she said primly. "You were very thorough."

"Any job worth doing is worth doing well," he said, a knowing sparkle in his eyes.

She couldn't seem to make herself meet his gaze. "How safe is this water?" she asked.

"For what?"

"Swimming."

"Safe enough. Why?"

Without bothering to respond, she dove over the side of the boat. The water was colder than she'd anticipated, but it felt good against her overheated skin. She finally broke the surface gasping for air, but with her hormones back in check.

"Cool off?" Josh inquired, amusement threading through his voice.

"Sure did," she said cheerfully. "You should try it."

"No, thanks."

"Chicken?"

"You are not going to dare me to dive in there with you," he scolded.

"I just did," she corrected. "I guess you're not up to the challenge."

"Oh, darlin', that was a very bad idea, especially coming from a woman who just washed off most of the suntan lotion she had me put on. Are you angling for another application?"

She saw the worrisome spark of mischief in his eye right before he dove overboard. Just when she was wondering where he was going to surface, he grabbed her ankle and pulled her under. She came up sputtering.

"You rat!" she accused. "That was playing dirty."

"I wasn't aware there were any rules for this particular game," he said, bobbing just beyond her reach. "You gonna get even?"

Her teeth were starting to chatter, but she rose to the bait. "You bet," she said, diving below the surface.

She was so sure he was right in front of her, but the next thing she knew, he'd circled her waist from behind and lifted her out of the water. She shook the hair and water out of her eyes as he slowly turned her around to face him. As her body slid along his, she realized that he was totally and impressively aroused. He fit their bodies together with only the wafer-thin fabric of her swimsuit and his between them, then captured her mouth beneath his. By the time the kiss ended, Ashley was on fire.

She clung to his shoulders and looked into his eyes. "How is it possible to be this hot when the water's like ice?"

"Makes you wonder why there's not steam rising all around us, doesn't it?"

"Oh, yes," she said, not ready to move away from him. Buoyed by the water, she hooked her legs around his waist.

Josh's gaze narrowed. "What are you up to now?"

"Just holding on," she insisted innocently.

"Just tormenting me sounds more like it," he retorted.

She grinned. "Is it working?"

He shifted ever so slightly. "What do you think?"

"Definitely working."

"Are you thinking it's safe to play this kind of game out here because nothing will come of it?" he inquired curiously.

She thought about that. "Yes," she admitted.

"Then you have no intention of going back to dry land and finishing what you've started?"

Taking the question seriously, she gave it some thought. "It's not that I don't want to," she began.

"Same here," he said. "But we've agreed that the timing is all wrong."

She nodded, suddenly feeling guilty. "Sorry. I'm not playing fair, am I?"

"It's not about playing fair," he said. "It's about playing with fire. If you're counting on me being a nice guy and keeping the game under control, don't. Even I have my limits, Ashley, and you are most definitely testing them."

Ashley heard the somber note in his voice and realized she'd pushed too far. Maybe she'd meant to. Maybe she'd *needed* to, but it wasn't all about her desires. For things to go any further, they really, really needed to be on the same page at the same time.

"How about lunch?" she asked, scrambling back into the boat and pulling a shirt on over her swimsuit. She shivered, despite the warmth of the sun. "I'll buy."

Josh was a little slower getting back in the boat. Once he was seated across from her, he met her gaze, the faint beginnings of a smile tugging at his lips.

"Scary, isn't it?" he asked.

She gave him a puzzled look. "What?"

"Realizing how much you want me."

She couldn't help it. She immediately rose to the challenge. "No more than you want me," she retorted, casting a pointed look at the unmistakable evidence. "But lunch is what's on the agenda, pal."

"Then I think I'll go with a steak sandwich. Something tells me I'm going to need all the stamina I can get as long as you're around."

She shuddered at the promise behind the words. They were going to make love. Perhaps not today, or even tomorrow, but there wasn't a doubt in her mind that neither of them had the willpower to resist the inevitable forever.

By the time they got back to Rose Cottage, Josh was still shaken by the force of his need for Ashley.

When she climbed onto the dock, he stayed right where he was.

"You're not coming in?" she asked.

He shook his head. "I'm going home to change. I'll be back to get you in a half hour." After he'd spent twenty minutes of that time in a cold shower. He wasn't hopeful that it would have the desired effect, since a soaking in the icy bay hadn't done a blessed thing to cool off his ardor.

"I'll be waiting," she said, her knowing gaze filled with amusement.

Unfortunately, back at his place there were three messages from Creighton Williams, each sounding more urgent than the one before. Reluctantly, he called the office.

"You need to get back to Richmond this afternoon," his boss said without preamble.

"I'm on vacation," Josh reminded him yet again. It was typical of Creighton to forget, the minute Josh's absence became an inconvenience, that he'd signed off on the vacation request.

"Not anymore," his boss said. "I need you here."

"Why?"

"The judge is moving up the hearing on the Bartholomew acquisition."

"That's your client," Josh reminded him. "Not mine."

"I need you here," his boss insisted. "You know how much Frank Bartholomew respects you. He'll listen to you."

"That's very flattering, but I repeat, he's your client.

I'm sure he respects you even more. You've handled his legal matters for years."

Confronted with an indisputable fact, Creighton backed down. "Okay, that's not the only reason I want you back here," he admitted.

"I think you'd better explain, then."

"It'll give you a chance to get together with Stephanie face-to-face and work out this ridiculous argument before it's too late to fix things."

Josh finally saw the ploy for what it really was, a full-court press to get him back together with Stephanie. "Sir, I thought you understood. Stephanie and I didn't have some silly little argument. We're in total agreement that we're not suited to be together. There's nothing between us to fix."

"That's absurd," Creighton barked. "I've given this a lot of thought since we spoke last. This is nothing but premarital jitters. Happens to every man when he sees a wedding date approaching."

"You seem to be forgetting that we never set a wedding date," Josh said. "I'd never even proposed. We only started dating to begin with because it was what you wanted."

"But the inevitability of it was staring you in the face," Creighton said. "Same thing."

"Sir, you don't really need me in court, do you?"

His boss sighed heavily. "No."

"All right, then. I'll be in touch."

"Are you sure you won't reconsider?" Creighton asked, his disappointment evident.

"Absolutely sure, sir. If that's a condition of me coming back, then I'm afraid it's a deal-breaker."

"No, no, I already told you it wasn't," Creighton said impatiently.

"Goodbye, sir." He hung up the phone, glanced at the clock, then called Ashley.

"Where are you? I thought you'd be back by now."

"I had to deal with a crisis. It'll be a few more minutes. Would you rather meet at the café?"

"No, I'll wait. Just hurry. My stomach is rumbling."

When he finally drove up to Rose Cottage, she was already waiting out front.

"You weren't kidding about being starved, were you?" he teased.

"No. Melanie and Maggie ruined my appetite this morning, so I missed breakfast." She regarded him curiously as she slid into the passenger's seat. "Want to tell me about whatever crisis held you up?"

"Later," he said. "It wasn't that important."

"I didn't know there was such a thing as an unimportant crisis."

He laughed. "It depends on which side of the crisis you're on."

"Ah, I'll try to remember that." She glanced out the window. "There's a parking space right there," she pointed out eagerly.

Josh glanced in that direction. "And it's right behind your sister's car, if I'm not mistaken."

Ashley groaned.

"Okay, it's your call. Lunch this second with your sister or drive to someplace else?"

Even before she spoke, Josh figured the audible growling of her stomach pretty much clinched it.

"We'll stay here," she said with undisguised reluctance.

"Don't worry," he soothed. "I'll protect you."

In fact, this could work to his advantage. With Maggie and perhaps even Melanie pestering her, Ashley might forget all about that crisis in his life. He needed to know if he really was going to go back to Richmond and the fast track before he told her that he was a lawyer. He had no idea how she was going to take that news given her own ambivalence about the legal profession these days.

"Oh, look, they're at a table for two," Ashley said happily when she spotted both Maggie and Melanie inside the café. "No room for us."

Of course, no sooner had the words left her mouth than two extra chairs materialized. Apparently Maggie and Melanie had seen them coming and put in a request for the extra seating.

Ashley sighed and dutifully crossed the restaurant.

Maggie studied her with undisguised speculation. "You look amazingly bright-eyed compared to this morning. Was fishing the only thing you all did?"

Josh waited to see how Ashley would field that one. She frowned at her sister.

"That, *little sister,* is none of your business," Ashley said.

"The same way it was none of your business what we did with Mike and Rick?" Melanie inquired sweetly.

Ashley didn't miss a beat. "No. I'm the big sister. I had an obligation to keep an eye on you guys."

"Well, we might be younger, but we're old married

ladies now, so it's our obligation to look out for our un-married big sister."

"In some cultures, you two wouldn't even be married until Ashley here walked down the aisle," Josh reminded them. "You'd be wanting her to hurry up."

Melanie gave him a thoughtful look. "Are you suggesting marriage is already on the table?"

"Good grief, *no,*" Ashley said fervently.

Josh wasn't sure he appreciated the idea being dismissed so readily. "Don't be too hasty," he said, just to rattle her. "It *could* be on the table."

Eyes flashing, she stared him down. "It is *not* on the table," she repeated emphatically.

He grinned. "We'll discuss it later."

"Whose side are you on?" she demanded irritably. "You're just going to get them all stirred up. They won't give us a minute's peace. Mike and Rick will haul you out for some sort of guy talk, which will be only marginally less intimidating than having my father come down here."

Josh shrugged. "They don't scare me."

"Do the words *'What are your intentions?'* scare you?"

Not half as much as he'd expected them to. Not even a tenth as much as they had when Creighton Williams had first uttered them. Obviously, though, they terrified her.

"Settle down, darlin'," he soothed. "Nothing has to be decided till after lunch. You'll be able to think more rationally on a full stomach."

Ashley glowered at him, even as Maggie and Melanie chuckled.

"Go to hell," she muttered, then turned to beckon for the waitress. "I'd like a cheeseburger, fries and a chocolate milk shake."

Her sisters stared at her in shock.

"Oh, my gosh, she really has gone round the bend," Melanie murmured.

Maggie nodded. "Seems that way to me, too."

"I repeat, go to hell," Ashley said, then added, "all of you."

Josh chuckled. "Sounds like her old self to me." And what a pistol she was. He'd never met anyone like Ashley D'Angelo, and no matter what it took, he was pretty sure it would be a very bad idea to let her get away.

8

If she hadn't been so hungry, Ashley would have gotten up and walked all the way back to Rose Cottage just to get away from Josh and her sisters. They were having entirely too much fun at her expense. As for Josh and those crazy allusions to marriage, he'd apparently stayed underwater too long and killed off a few important brain cells. She wasn't taking him seriously, but her sisters very well might. They were eager to see her follow what they now assumed to be a family tradition and fall wildly in love while staying at Rose Cottage.

Ashley and Josh were on the way home before she called him on his ill-conceived teasing. "What on earth were you thinking?" she asked testily.

"About?"

"Oh, don't pretend you don't know exactly what I'm talking about," she retorted. "I'm referring to all that nonsense about marriage."

He gave her a look filled with feigned innocence. "Maybe it wasn't nonsense."

"If it wasn't, then you're the one who needs his head examined. I know absolutely nothing about the state of your life beyond the fact that you just broke up with some other woman, but I think we can agree that the turmoil in mine is sufficient to preclude any serious talk of the future."

"There's no harm in getting the idea out there, though, is there?"

She gave him an impatient look. "My professional life is in chaos. Don't you think I have enough to worry about without pondering marriage to a man I barely know?"

"I don't know. Thinking about getting married could be more fun than thinking about torts and trials and things over which you have no control, such as public opinion." He glanced over at her. "Don't you agree?"

The man was totally exasperating. "Marriage is not some game, dammit! You start tossing that word around with my family, and you'll be in front of a minister before you can catch your breath. Haven't you noticed that my sisters both married after whirlwind courtships? They think it's a family tradition, and they think it's all tied up with staying in Rose Cottage, as if the place had some sort of magical powers in the love department."

He grinned. "It's a unique tradition, all right. As for the cottage being enchanted, didn't you ever see that old movie?"

She sighed heavily. "Yes, I saw it. It doesn't apply. Don't you take anything seriously?"

"Sure. Actually I take marriage very seriously. That's why I broke things off with that other woman. I realized I wasn't serious enough about her for marriage. We were wasting time together in a relationship that was going nowhere. She deserved better than that."

"Then why are you joking around about the whole marriage thing with me?"

Now he sighed. "I'm not entirely sure," he admitted eventually. "The words just seemed to pop out. Since no panic alarms have gone off, I've seen no reason to take them back. Besides, it's given your sisters something to chew on besides your career status. It's pretty much gotten *your* attention off that, too."

She regarded him doubtfully. "So this has been some sort of magnanimous gesture on your part to get my sisters off my case?"

"Something like that," he said, then winked. "For now, anyway."

She studied him helplessly. "I don't know what to make of you."

"Ditto, darlin', but aren't we going to have fun figuring things out?"

That was precisely the problem, Ashley thought a little desperately. She *was* having fun, perhaps too much fun given the fact that she had an army of reporters on her trail, a career in turmoil and a guilty conscience over her part in freeing a confessed murderer.

Determined to get things back on a far safer track, she regarded Josh seriously. "What are your plans this afternoon?"

"Kicking back. Nothing much."

"Good. Then you can help me make a list."

He regarded her warily. "What kind of list?"

"Career decisions," she said with grim determination. "I could use an outside perspective."

"Bad idea," he said.

"It has to be done," she insisted. "Maybe you have

all the time in the world to relax, but I can't sit around wallowing in indecisiveness indefinitely."

He chuckled. "How many days have you been wallowing in anything here?"

"Three, four, something like that." To her amazement, she couldn't remember precisely. Maybe she was getting too good at the whole relaxation thing. That should be a warning to her. She needed to get focused—fast. A life without focus was a life that could spin out of control. Of course, hers had managed to slip off the track even with all her safeguards in place….

"And you're going to be here three weeks," Josh said. "Isn't that what you told me the night we met?"

She nodded. "What's your point?"

"You're pushing for too much, too fast. The real answers won't come to you for at least another week or so."

"Why on earth would you say a thing like that?"

"It's a proven fact that you have to spend serious time unwinding before you can get in touch with your real heart's desire."

"A proven fact?" she echoed skeptically.

He nodded. "Absolutely. Trying to force things will just set you back. You'll wind up with a decision that's based on logic, not emotion."

"You are so full of it, Madison."

"But I'm charming," he said with the engaging smile that never failed to make her heart take a tumble in her chest. "And you have to admit that the whole relaxation thing is working out exactly as I predicted."

"True," she admitted reluctantly. "But what's wrong

with logic? The world would be a better place if everyone made their decisions based on logic."

He shook his head. "No. It's critical to factor emotion into the equation. Without it, we'd all be dutiful little drones. Trust me on this. You can't be making lists this soon, or you'll just have a bunch of cut-and-dried choices."

She sighed heavily. "Then what on earth will I do with the rest of the afternoon?"

"I have a plan," he said cheerfully.

"Why doesn't that surprise me?"

"Actually, it was your sister's idea."

She regarded him suspiciously. "Which one?" She was pretty sure any ideas tossed out by Melanie would involve getting all those tulip and daffodil bulbs in the ground.

"Maggie. Why? What difference does it make?"

"Never mind. What sort of brainstorm did she share with you?"

"Trust me, it'll be fun."

She was about to protest that she wasn't going anywhere with him without details, but then she fell silent. The truth was, she *did* trust him, even though she knew precious little about him beyond his name and his ability to bait a hook. Given the way she was feeling about the whole trust thing these days, that was nothing short of a miracle.

She glanced at him and saw that he was grinning as he awaited her decision. "Okay, you win," she said.

"See, now, putting yourself into my hands wasn't so hard, was it?" he teased.

She uttered a self-mocking laugh. "Actually, you have no idea how hard it was."

But something told her it was a huge step in the right direction.

When Josh turned into the driveway at Maggie's, he saw Ashley stiffen beside him.

"We're going to my sister's? Why? So she can cross-examine us some more? That sounds like fun."

"The trust business doesn't run very deep with you, Ashley, does it?" he asked, amused.

"Frankly, no."

"Well, cool your jets, lady lawyer. We're not here to visit. In fact, as far as I know, Maggie's not even home."

"Then why are we here?"

"It's an orchard," he reminded her with exaggerated patience. "We're going to pick apples."

She stared at him blankly. "Why?"

"Because it's something you've never done before. Neither have I. We can share the experience. People bond over new experiences."

"And I suppose we'll bond even more as we share a hospital room when we both wind up with broken arms," she said cheerfully.

"You're not approaching this with the right attitude," he scolded. "We're young. We're limber. How hard can it be?"

"Unless you think you're going to shake the tree and have apples fall into our baskets, it's going to be work, Madison." Her expression brightened. "Watching you get the hang of it could be amusing, though."

Josh parked the car at the edge of the orchard. "You can forget that idea. This is a joint venture. And Maggie has promised to bake us an apple pie when we're done."

"An apple pie, huh? That can't take more than a couple of apples, right? Okay, I can do that."

Josh gave her a chiding look. "It'll take more than a couple for the pie, then we'll want some apples for our picnic tomorrow and some for snacks later on. Plus we haven't even decided which kind we want. I like Granny Smith. How about you?"

"I should have known you'd prefer something tart. I like the sweet ones. I'm not sure we have a choice, though. I think all these trees are Golden Delicious."

"Not according to Maggie."

"When did you two have this heart-to-heart about apples?"

"When I was here the other night."

"So you've been planning this outing since then?"

"No, I've been planning this since lunchtime, when I recalled the conversation she and I had after dinner. In relaxation mode, it's not acceptable to plan too far ahead."

"Which is why the whole marriage thing is so absurd," she said. "If that's not planning way ahead, I don't know what is."

"A valid point," he admitted. "We'll table that for this afternoon, though I find it interesting that you haven't forgotten it for a second." He glanced up at the trees that were laden with fruit, all out of reach. "I think getting to those apples is going to require all of our concentration."

He met her gaze. "Ever climb a tree before?"

"Do I look as if tree-climbing were a hobby of mine?"

"You could have been a tomboy. How am I supposed to know?" At least one of the D'Angelo sisters had been. He could recall their grandmother lamenting it to his mother. Neither Melanie or Maggie seemed the tree-climbing type, so maybe it had been Jo, the one he hadn't met yet.

"Trust me, not a tomboy," she said.

He gave her a very thorough once-over. "Just as well. I would hate to think of that smooth skin all scraped and scarred." Then again, he could have had himself a grand time kissing any imperfections. He decided not to share that intriguing thought.

"If that's the case, why would you insist on sending me up into a tree to pick apples now?" she inquired.

"Because we're old enough and wise enough now not to take unnecessary chances."

"Ha! I've seen glimpses of your daredevil side."

He climbed out of the car. "Come on, Ashley, stop whining. This is going to be fun." He looked around. "There should be a ladder out here somewhere, and some baskets."

"Let me know when you find them," she called out, still tucked into place in the car.

"You are not getting into the spirit of this," he accused.

"What was your first clue?"

He walked over to the car and rested his elbows on the passenger windowsill, then looked deep into her eyes. "Do you really, really hate this whole idea? We can do something else."

Suddenly a grin spread across her face. "Nope. Just seeing how far I could push you before you let me have my way. Bring on the ladder, Madison. If you want to pick your own apples for a pie, then I'm right there with you. Never let it be said that I'm not up for a challenge."

"In the tree?" he inquired, just to be sure he understood the degree of her capitulation.

"At the very tip-top," she confirmed.

He didn't like the worrisome glint in her eyes. "Don't get carried away."

"Hey, once you've gotten my enthusiasm all stirred up, it's too late to try to rein me in." She scrambled from the car. "I see the ladder. Last one in the tree turns into a toad."

Josh didn't even try to catch up with her. He had a hunch the view from the ground while she tore up that ladder was going to be something. He strolled over, steadied the ladder and took a long, leisurely survey of her trim backside and endless bare legs as she climbed agilely to the top.

"You lose," she called down, sounding triumphant.

"No way, darlin'. You may be at the top of that tree, but I am definitely the big winner here."

She scowled down from her precarious perch on a branch high above him. "How do you figure that?"

"I've got the better view."

It took a minute for her to realize what he meant. She immediately pelted him with an apple. The damn thing hit him right in the head.

"Hey, that hurt," he protested, laughing as he dodged another one.

"That was the idea. Didn't you ever play baseball? Maybe you should learn to catch. Otherwise, all we'll have is applesauce."

Josh heard the branch creak suspiciously before Ashley realized she was in danger. "Ashley, don't move," he said urgently.

Naturally she twisted around just to annoy him. The creak became a sharp crack, and suddenly she was falling. He had a split second to position himself to catch her. They both landed on the ground, but at least he'd managed to cushion her fall. The impact knocked the wind out of him.

As soon as he could speak, his gaze locked on hers. "You okay?"

"Uh-huh," she murmured, looking dazed.

"You don't sound okay. How many fingers am I holding up?"

She gave him an impatient look. "Two. I didn't hit my head, Josh. I landed on my butt, on top of you, as a matter of fact. Maybe you're the one we should be worrying about. Can you move?"

He grinned at her. "Why would I want to? I have a beautiful woman sprawled across me."

She immediately went still. "So I am. Maybe I should take advantage of that."

Now she was the one making him nervous. "How?"

She framed his face in her hands and kissed him. It was the kind of impulsive, no-holds-barred kiss that had taken them to the edge of a meltdown before. Just because they were in the middle of her sister's orchard didn't mean he had the sense to turn down what she was offering. He kissed her back. It didn't seem to matter that the ground was cold and hard or that a cloud had passed over the sun. The only things that mattered were the soft curves that fit his body like the other half of a puzzle and the intoxicating scent of her perfume.

His hands cupped her butt and held her more tightly in place. It took everything in him not to start to move, not to begin the motions that would carry them past the point of no return. He was hard and aching. She was making little purring noises deep in her throat, the kind of sounds of pure pleasure and need that could drive a man wild.

Her mouth was greedy on his, her movements restless. Another five seconds and he was going to lose the fragile grip he had on his control. Only the grim determination not to have their first time together be on the ground not two hundred yards from her sister's house kept him from granting her what she obviously wanted.

"Slow down, darlin'," he said. "You don't want this."

"Yes, I do," she insisted.

"Not here, I suspect. We're in your sister's orchard," he reminded her, then grinned as her eyes snapped open and she looked around.

"Oh, my God," she said, scrambling away from him. "What was I thinking?"

"Thinking had nothing to do with it. One of these days we need to find a nice, comfortable bed and try this again. I think we can eliminate the bay and the orchard as being bad ideas." He grinned at her. "Should we hunt one down now?"

She scrubbed a hand across her face, like a child trying to wake up from a dream. "No." She regarded him helplessly. "I was going to be so sensible about this. I was going to permit myself to have a wild, passionate fling with you."

He heard the past tense and felt his stomach clench. "And now?"

"Now it's gotten complicated." She met his gaze. "Hasn't it?"

"It's only as complicated as we let it be."

"What kind of guy response is that? It's either complicated or it isn't."

He knew better than to laugh at her obvious frustration. "Allow me to clarify. Sex is uncomplicated. Making love gets a bit trickier. Where are you coming from?"

Her gaze met his, then darted away, before finally returning. "I honestly don't know anymore. Do you?"

"Can't say that I do, but there's no rush to figure it out," he reminded her.

"Do you back-burner everything in your life until it's convenient?" she asked.

He thought of the demanding schedule he maintained at work and nearly laughed. Since he didn't want to go there, he restrained himself. "Would you believe me if I said no?"

"How could I? You seem to me to epitomize the concept of putting everything off till tomorrow."

"And you never put anything off," he commented. "Maybe I'm just trying to lead you to a middle ground.

The truth is, we tend to make our own chaos. Sure, the real world has deadlines and they're important, but we turn everything into a must-do crisis. Not everything needs to be done immediately. We can take the pressure off ourselves. We can choose not to participate in the rat race. All it takes is recognizing our own limits, prioritizing and learning to say no."

Putting that into words for her finally gave him the sense of direction he'd been craving for himself. It was just as he'd tried to tell her—answers came as soon as a person stopped trying to force them.

"If you don't grab at opportunities when they present themselves, how do you get ahead?" Ashley asked, obviously perplexed.

"Why do you have to?" he countered. "What's wrong with just loving what you do and setting a pace that allows you to live your life? Isn't that exactly what you're wrestling with while you're here? Isn't it the truth that you've allowed work to consume you to the point that the situation you find yourself in now leaves you with the sick feeling that your life as you've known it is over?"

A smile tugged at her lips. "That's exactly how I would feel if you didn't keep distracting me. As it is, the only thing I seem to be wrestling with is you."

"Is that such a bad thing?"

She held his gaze for what seemed an eternity, then finally shook her head. "No, as a matter of fact, it's not bad at all."

Josh nodded in satisfaction. It seemed both of them were finding unexpected answers this afternoon.

9

For once the thing that kept Ashley awake all night was the restless anticipation Josh stirred in her, rather than all the uncertainty about her professional future. A part of her wished they'd just gotten their first time over with, so the edginess would be a thing of the past. Instead, she was lying in bed remembering the way his body felt next to hers, the way he tasted and smelled, the way his skin heated when she touched him.

"Oh, please," she moaned when the image grew so steamy she was ready to scream in frustration. If she didn't have at least one lingering ounce of pride, she would crawl out of her bed right this instant, drive to his place and crawl into his. She doubted he would turn her away.

Still, it was a point of honor to wait for the right timing, whatever the heck that was. Josh seemed to have some vague idea that they would recognize it when it happened. She wasn't so sure. She just thought it was going to get increasingly frustrating until one or both of them exploded and they had sex on some tabletop in plain view of half the world. The idea didn't seem nearly as appalling as it should. That's how desperate Ashley was feeling.

What puzzled her was that it was a man like Josh, as laid-back as any human being she'd ever known, who stirred such passionate feelings in her. If he had even the tiniest streak of ambition in him, she'd never seen a glimpse of it. Heck, he was so low-key about work, she still didn't know exactly what he did. Whatever it was couldn't be too demanding, since he seemed to have an endless amount of time for their lazy fishing trips. She gathered he was on vacation at the moment, but he seemed so at ease, she couldn't imagine he had a high-pressure career.

Not that there was a thing in the world wrong with being content in some noncareer-track job with few demands and an obviously lax timetable, but it was totally alien to the world she'd been living in since graduating from law school. She couldn't imagine being with a man who had such low aspirations.

But, truthfully, she could imagine being with Josh. She found him to be oddly soothing, yet stimulating, which turned out to be an intriguing and unexpected combination.

She was still tossing and turning as she considered all that when the phone rang at dawn. She fumbled for the receiver. "Yes?"

"Ashley, it's Jo."

There was an unmistakably somber note in her youngest sister's voice that had Ashley sitting upright and fully alert in a heartbeat. "What's wrong?"

"I just tuned in to the morning news. They had an interview with your boss."

Ashley's heart began to thud dully. "And? Did he throw me to the wolves?"

"No. Actually he said a lot of nice things about you, but I don't think you're going to be happy about it. He's acting as if what happened in court is no big deal," Jo said indignantly. "He says all defense lawyers assume their clients are guilty. He says you were just doing your job and doing it exceedingly well, that he's proud of you."

Ashley knew she should have felt vindicated by Wyatt Blake's defense of her actions, but the unwarranted praise sickened her. It was as if he were finding a way to capitalize on what had happened in court. Obviously the PR consultant the firm kept on retainer had shown him a way to spin the story that would work to the firm's benefit. She hated that he was using the lowest moment of her career to get publicity for the firm.

"And you know the worst thing?" Jo asked. "He acted as if your feeling bad about getting Tiny off was naive. He said it in that patronizing tone of his. You know the one, Ashley. I've always found it offensive and wondered how you put up with it. Hearing it directed at *you* made me want to throw something at the TV."

Ashley had been expecting Wyatt Blake to make a public comment sooner or later, but not like this. Her respect for the man who'd once been her mentor diminished to zero. On some level she'd expected it to come to this. She really wasn't as naive as her boss had implied, but she hadn't been prepared for the awful taste it left in her mouth.

"I need to come home," Ashley said. "It's time for me to speak out. And I need to see Wyatt and let him know I don't appreciate his misguided attempt to turn this into some sort of legal triumph." If she left in the next half hour, she could be there by nightfall, in plenty of time to confront Wyatt in his office.

"No," Jo said fiercely. "You can't come home yet. You'll just make things worse."

"I'm sorry, but I don't see how they could get much worse."

"You're angry. You're liable to lash out and wind up behind bars yourself."

"I lash out with words. Not even the powerful Wyatt Blake can have me locked up for that."

"Still, he can make it very unpleasant for you if you try to contradict the spin he's putting out there," Jo said reasonably. "I didn't call to get you so riled up you'd come home. I called to warn you, so you could start thinking about whether you want to work for a firm that would twist things like this just for the chance to get some free publicity."

Ashley already knew in her heart that she could never go back there. In fact, even without a plan, she was tempted to call and quit right now, but she wouldn't. Actions taken in haste were too often regretted. Her sister was right about that.

She wouldn't go back to Boston, either. She'd stay here, think things through logically and then when she was confident that she was making a sound decision, she'd go home.

Then she'd rip the man's heart out for lumping her in with all the other criminal defense lawyers who didn't give a rip about their clients' innocence or guilt as long as the bills were paid and the headlines were big enough.

"Thanks for calling, Jo. I promise I won't do anything rash."

"You know that none of this changes anything about how the rest of us feel about you, right? We're still proud of you," Jo said. "We're behind you a thousand percent."

Tears immediately stung Ashley's eyes. "I don't deserve you."

"Of course you do," Jo said impatiently. "You're the first one there when one of us is in trouble. How could we do any less for you? Now do something fun today and forget all about that sleazeball Blake. He's not worth one second of your time."

"I'll try," she promised, though she knew it would be impossible. How could she forget that yet another man she'd trusted and respected had betrayed her? She knew he'd insist that it was all a necessary PR move for the firm, and maybe he was even right about that, but it still felt lousy being used in such a despicable way.

Even though she'd promised Jo that she wouldn't do anything hasty, even though she'd told herself it was a bad idea, she punched in Wyatt Blake's number and waited for him to pick up his private line.

"Blake here," he said, sounding distracted, probably from fielding so many media requests at the crack of dawn.

"Couldn't wait to capitalize on the furor over the Slocum acquittal, could you, Wyatt?"

"Ashley, where on earth are you?" he asked, not sounding particularly guilt-stricken to hear her voice.

"I tried to catch up with you to get you back here. We had to get a statement on the record. Ever since Slocum got off, we've been inundated with calls from the media. We had to get our position out there. We didn't have a choice. This thing's turned into a gold mine in terms of publicity. You could be in front of the cameras every night on the evening news."

Listening to him recite the line he'd obviously been given by the very powerful public relations firm they kept on retainer, she knew what she had to do. If he didn't think he had a choice, then neither did she.

"I'll give you a whole new spin, Wyatt. In your next press release, you can announce that I've quit. That ought to give the firm a few more of those headlines you so obviously covet."

"Quit? You can't do that," he said, unmistakable panic in his voice. "Come on, Ashley, think about this. You can name your own price these days."

They both knew the panic stemmed from his awareness that she pulled in the firm's highest number of billable hours each month. The media attention she drew was another plus. The partners wouldn't be happy to see all of that disappear.

"I can't work with people who obviously don't appreciate the value I put on my reputation or who deliberately diminish the fact that I have a conscience. We agreed when I came there that I wouldn't take just any case, that I wouldn't be a pawn for some rich guy who's guilty as sin, but needs a great defense."

"And we've let you do that, haven't we?"

"Yes, but in one press conference you pretty much

shattered whatever faith the public might have had that I was an honest, straight-shooting lawyer."

"Tiny Slocum did that," Wyatt said, his tone suddenly hard and unyielding. "I was just trying to make the best of it."

Ashley could see his point. She just couldn't live with it.

"Face it, Wyatt, I'm no good to you anymore," she said.

"Ashley, I'm sorry as hell you see it that way. I brought you into this company. No one's been prouder of your work than I've been."

"But you obviously never really knew or respected me. It only took you a few hours to turn me into a hero for something you know I'm ashamed about," she reminded him. "I might have made a terrible mistake when I believed in my client, but you've made an even bigger one. You thought I'd be so low, I'd let you use me and be thrilled about it. It's not going to be that way. I'll have someone come by to clear out my office."

She hung up before he could say another word. Oddly, rather than sheer gut-wrenching terror, all she felt was relief. It was the first time in days that she knew with absolute clarity that she'd done the right thing.

As for what came next, she was going to take a page out of Josh's book and wait and see. She had money in the bank, a roof over her head and people who loved her. Maybe it was time she counted her blessings, the ones that really mattered.

Josh was sound asleep when his phone rang. He rolled over and fumbled for it, then mumbled a greeting.

"Wake up, Madison. Something tells me the fish are going to be biting again today," Ashley said, sounding more cheerful than she had in days.

Josh sat up and rubbed his eyes. Funny thing how just the sound of her voice could snap him wide-awake. In an instant he was alert enough to hear the edge of hysteria behind all that cheeriness. "What's happened?"

"I'll tell you when I see you. Hurry up. I'll have the coffee on when you get here."

The promise of coffee had him rolling out of bed and reaching for his pants. Okay, maybe it wasn't just the thought of caffeine. Maybe it was Ashley's odd mood. He was curious about what could have happened since he'd left her the night before. Despite that bright tone of hers, he had a feeling it wasn't anything good.

There was a distinct chill in the air when he went outside. Fall had evidently arrived during the night. He went back for a sweater and jeans to wear over his swimsuit and T-shirt.

It was even colder on the water, but by the time he'd rowed to Rose Cottage and tied the boat up to the dock, he was warm.

Ashley was waiting for him at the back door, a cup of coffee in hand. "Thought you might need this right away. You didn't sound too alert on the phone."

"I'd decided to sleep in," he said, giving her a peck on the cheek and studying her curiously, looking for evidence of turmoil in her eyes. Her expression was perfectly bland.

"Why were you sleeping in?"

"Because I could."

She laughed. "And I picked today to call at the crack

of dawn. Sorry," she said without much real evidence of regret.

"No problem. What's up with you? You seem awfully cheerful this morning."

She lifted her cup of coffee in a mock toast. "I am, actually. I quit my job."

Josh blinked hard, sure he had to have heard wrong. A workaholic who'd just quit usually wasn't quite so chipper. At least that explained the barely concealed note of hysteria he thought he'd detected in her voice earlier.

"When did you do that?"

"About an hour ago."

"I thought you were going to take my advice and let things mull a while longer before making any decisions about the future."

She shrugged. "Things change."

"Such as?"

"My hand was forced," she said succinctly. "I did what I had to do."

"And you're okay with that?"

"I'm sure the sheer terror will set in eventually, but yes, at the moment, I am ecstatic. I am feeling strong and in control."

"I see. Mind telling me why you woke up at dawn and decided that the first thing you'd do this morning was to turn in your resignation?"

She gave him an apparently condensed version of what her sister had told her and her subsequent conversation with the senior partner in her law firm.

"How could I go on working for people like that?" she asked.

"You couldn't," Josh agreed without hesitation. He would have done the same thing. "I'm just surprised you didn't wait till you had something else lined up."

She shrugged. "So am I, but it seemed like the right thing to do at the time, so I went with the flow."

His gaze narrowed. "You aren't going to blame this on *me* later, are you?"

"How could I? You weren't even here."

"But the whole go-with-the-flow philosophy," he reminded her. "I've been its biggest proponent around here."

"And an excellent philosophy it is," she said happily. "Trust me, it won't come back to bite you in the butt, not even if I wind up destitute."

"Good to know. Have you given any thought to what happens next?"

"No. I'm on vacation."

"Actually, you're out of work. It's not exactly the same thing," he said, though he had to admire her new attitude. She seemed to be embracing it with surprising enthusiasm. Unfortunately, he wasn't buying the act for a minute.

She waved off his reminder. "Not going to worry about it today. Let's go fishing."

He nodded slowly. "Fishing it is."

"I packed a lunch. I thought we could stay out a really long time."

"Okay," he said slowly. "Why?"

"Because once my family gets wind of this, they're going to think I've lost my mind. I don't do impulsive things. I don't do much of anything except work.

I'd rather not be around when they show up with a shrink."

He laughed. "You may surprise them, but I doubt they'd go that far."

She held out an obviously heavy picnic hamper and a cooler, then said grimly, "I'm not taking any chances."

Ashley really appreciated Josh's silence. Either he was in shock or he was showing amazing restraint. Whichever it was, at least he wasn't pestering her with questions for which she had no answers.

They'd been out on the water for a couple of hours. He'd caught several fish that he declared to be too small. He'd tossed them back. Ashley hadn't even felt a faint stirring of her usual competitive spirit, which suggested she was more shaken by the morning's events than she'd realized.

"Josh?"

"Hmm?"

She nudged his foot. "Wake up."

"I am awake."

"Then look at me."

He tilted his sunglasses down and peered at her over the top. "Yes?"

"Do you think I made a terrible mistake? Be honest."

"Doesn't matter what I think. Do you?"

"No."

"Then there's your answer."

"Do you think any other firm in Boston will touch me after this?"

He appeared to give the question careful consideration. "That's hard to say," he replied eventually. "You're a good lawyer with a fantastic track record. I'd think that once the publicity dies down, any firm would be happy to take you on." He met her gaze. "Or you could start your own firm and capitalize on the notoriety."

She shuddered at that idea. How could she take advantage of all the negative publicity, when that was exactly what she'd accused Wyatt of doing? It seemed sleazy and opportunistic. "Are you serious?"

"It's just an option. I'm not making recommendations here, just tossing out ideas."

"Any others?"

"You could always open a firm here," he suggested.

His expression was casual, but she had the distinct impression that he'd given this particular option a lot of thought long before this morning's turn of events. "Here? There are probably plenty of lawyers here now."

"One or two," he said, almost sounding as if he'd looked into it. "The area's growing. You might not get rich, but you'd do okay."

Stay here in the boondocks? The idea held more appeal than it might have when she'd first arrived, intending to endure her three-week banishment from Boston, but to stay forever? Wouldn't she go nuts after a few months? A year at the outside? How challenging could the cases be? She'd be defending the occasional DUI charge or maybe a drug dealer. Those were not the kind of crimes on which she'd built her reputation. She'd handled the high-profile white-collar crime, the occasional sensational murder case. She would miss that.

Or would she? Having seen the dark side of that kind of law, was it still what she wanted? She honestly didn't know. She wasn't quite ready to turn her back on it, at least not without exploring all of her options.

"Maybe I could go to D.C.," she suggested instead. "Or even Richmond."

"You could," he agreed, though he looked oddly disappointed by her response.

She studied him intently. "Josh, is there some reason you want me to stay here? Say, for the sake of speculation, that I did, are you thinking that we'd go on being together? Is that your agenda?"

He grinned at her careful phrasing. "The thought did cross my mind. It might give us time to find that suitable bed we keep talking about."

It would also change the dynamics of everything. If she was leaving, she was free to indulge in a wildly passionate fling. If she was staying, then she'd be toying with a relationship. She didn't think she'd be any good at that.

"I don't know," she said honestly. "I can't base a decision about my entire professional future on what might or might not happen with the two of us."

"I'm not asking you to. I'm just giving you something to consider while you're weighing all those options."

"I need to make a list," she said, frustrated by the magnitude of the decisions facing her. She'd known all along that it would eventually come to this, but she'd avoided confronting it. Now she had to. No matter what

Josh said to the contrary, proper decision-making required organization, not drifting around in a rowboat.

"Not today," he chided. "The list is already dancing around in your head. It will sort itself out if you give it enough time."

"This is my life. I can't just wait around for the stars to align or something," she said impatiently. She could only do the go-with-the-flow thing for so long. As of seven o'clock this morning when she'd quit her job, it had outlived its usefulness.

He laughed. "Come here," he urged.

She studied him suspiciously. "Why?"

"Just wriggle your sexy bottom over here next to me. Otherwise, I'll just have to come over there."

Filled with suspicion, she finally maneuvered until she was next to him. He put his arm around her.

"Rest your head right here," he said, patting his shoulder.

After a moment's hesitation, she leaned against his chest, tucked her head on his shoulder and heaved a sigh.

"That's better," he said. "Now close your eyes."

"Why?"

"Because I said to."

She bristled at that. "You're not—"

"I know," he said with amusement, cutting off her protest. "I am not the boss of you."

"Right."

"Just trust me. Close your eyes."

She finally permitted her eyelids to drift shut.

"Clear your head," he instructed. "Just concentrate

on the sound of the water lapping against the boat, and on the sun on your face. Let everything else go."

Out of sheer habit and stubbornness, she fought it, but eventually his soothing tone relaxed her and her mind finally slipped away to a calmer, more tranquil place.

"This isn't so bad, is it?" he asked eventually, his voice low.

"What?" she murmured.

"Being here, with me, just existing in the moment."

She smiled. "No," she admitted, filled with wonder at just how right it felt. "It's not bad at all."

"Then why would you give it up one second before you have to?" he asked.

Good question, she thought, right before she snuggled more tightly against him. Why give up something that felt this right? She'd eventually have to think about that, worry it to death, in all probability, but not right now. In fact, it could wait till later.

She sighed happily. Much, much later.

10

To Ashley's dismay, the entire D'Angelo family was waiting at Rose Cottage when she and Josh got back late in the afternoon. She scowled at Jo. "Your doing?"

"Don't blame your sister," her mother said, stepping forward to give her a fierce hug. "Your father and I decided it was time to come down here and give you some moral support. We booked a flight right after that awful morning newscast today. Jo tried to talk us out of it, but when we insisted, she refused to be left behind."

She leaned back and searched Ashley's face. "How are you holding up?"

To Ashley's total chagrin, the sympathetic note in her mother's voice was the last straw. She burst into tears. To her shock—and probably everyone else's—it was Josh who stepped forward and tucked a finger under her chin.

"Want to go for a walk?" he asked solemnly. "Get your bearings?"

She looked into his eyes and felt the ground steady under her feet. What an amazing thing, that a man she'd known only a few days could have that effect on her.

She'd have to explore the reasons for that later, when her entire family wasn't standing around smirking. Her mother might be a bit perplexed by Josh's presence, but if they hadn't done so before, her sisters were probably now planning her wedding to the man.

Her father stepped up just then, and with a scowl in Josh's direction, took his place. "You sure you're okay, kitten?"

Hearing her childhood nickname that only her father had ever dared to call her almost brought on another round of tears, but she managed to blink them away and offer him a beaming smile.

"I'm fine," she assured him, giving his hand a squeeze. Then she announced brightly, "Since everyone's here and probably starved, let's go out for crabs." She linked an arm through her mother's, hoping to wipe the worried frown off her face. "Remember Grandma's favorite place? It was always our very first stop when we came in the summer."

Her mother dutifully fell in with the obvious distraction, and for once her sisters even cooperated. Ashley glanced back at Josh and mouthed, "Thank you."

He grinned. "Not a problem." He turned and headed toward the water.

Ashley stopped in her tracks and stared after him. "Hey, Madison, where do you think you're going?"

"Home," he said.

"I don't think so." She sent the others on ahead and went back for him. "I need you there. Please don't bail on me now."

"Why not? You've got an entire family to lean on tonight."

"Which is precisely why I want you there, to protect me from their overly zealous questions."

"Don't you think my presence during this crisis will create a few questions, as well?"

She stood on tiptoe and kissed him. "In case you missed it, they already have questions. A lot of them, if I'm not mistaken. Not to worry, though. We can handle them."

He looked doubtful. "Think so?"

"I know so."

"Did you see the way your father was looking at me? If I hadn't moved aside, I think he would have taken a punch at me."

Ashley laughed. "He looks at any male who's ever come within a mile of any of us exactly the same way. It didn't scare off Mike or Rick. And I promise you, Dad's all bluster. He's never slugged anyone as far as I know."

"All right, then," he said. "Anything those two can do, I can do."

"That's the spirit." She met his gaze. "One last thing before we join the others. Have I mentioned how grateful I am that you were here for me today?"

"My pleasure."

It was a rare man who didn't mind having a woman dump all her problems and insecurities in his lap. She studied him curiously. "One of these days we're going to have to talk about you for a change. Somehow, from the moment we met, it's all been about me."

He laughed. "Also my pleasure. You're much more fascinating than I am."

"I don't believe that. I think there are hidden depths to Josh Madison I should be exploring."

To her surprise, her teasing remark was met with an unexpected wariness.

"My life's an open book," he said, though his declaration lacked conviction.

"Then it's past time I started reading it," she said. "I've been totally self-absorbed, and you've graciously let me get away with it. I promise that's going to change." Even if it meant that her feelings for him grew even stronger and more complicated than they were now.

That flicker of wariness appeared once more in his eyes, as if he viewed her words not as a well-meant promise but as a threat.

What was it that Josh didn't want her to find out? Up until five minutes ago, Ashley would have sworn that he truly was an open book and that she knew everything important there was to know about him. She knew he had character and strength and compassion. She'd been so sure that was everything that really mattered. Now she wasn't certain of that at all.

It was time to fish or cut bait, Josh concluded as he sat with the D'Angelos at dinner. He let the conversation swirl around him, all of it lively and filled with the laughter he'd once imagined enviously from his own lonely house down the road. He could put Ashley off for a few more hours or possibly even a few more days as long as her folks stuck around, but he'd seen that glint of determination in her eyes. She wasn't going to be put off indefinitely.

How was she going to react when she discovered that he, too, was a lawyer, especially one who was about to make a decision to get out of the rat race and settle into a quiet country practice? Given the way she'd reacted when he'd floated a similar plan for her own career, he suspected she wasn't going to be impressed.

It was funny, though, that talking to her about it had just about solidified his own resolve. Whatever happened between them, he was going to settle here. He'd rediscovered the rare contentment he hadn't known since childhood, and he wanted it back on a permanent basis. Before he made the decision final, though, he needed to be absolutely sure that his contentment wasn't due entirely to Ashley's intriguing presence, that it wouldn't vanish if she did.

There would be other differences, too. He doubted he'd be able to fish all morning long, at least not if he expected to earn a living, but he imagined he could get out on the water for an hour or so most days. And this was a great place to raise a family. He'd been thinking about that more and more as he'd envisioned a future with Ashley. Her sisters had seen it. Why couldn't she? Maybe with the right sort of persuasion she would, but if she didn't, he had to make certain this was the right decision for him.

He noticed a movement beside him and realized that Mike had slipped into a chair vacated by Ashley's youngest sister.

"You look distracted, pal. Everything okay?" Mike asked. "This crowd can be a bit overwhelming the first time you meet them."

"It's not that. I was just thinking about some decisions of my own that need to be made."

"Anything you want to talk about? I'm a good listener. Rick, too."

Josh was startled to find that the prospect of confiding in a couple of male friends held a certain appeal. He'd gone through most of his life with few confidants. Most of his colleagues at the firm had been too competitive to count as friends. Stephanie had filled the role for a while, but this wasn't a decision he could bat around with her. Before he talked to anyone, though, he had to wrestle with it on his own a little longer.

"Another time, okay?"

"Sure," Mike said easily.

"I mean that. I could use another perspective."

"One night next week?"

Josh nodded. "Sounds good to me."

Mike grinned. "I'll set it up with Rick and get back to you. Maybe we can get all the women over to his place and have a guys' night at mine. When you're surrounded by these strong-willed D'Angelo women, it's nice to have backup from time to time." He glanced over at Ashley, then turned back to Josh. "The two of you okay?"

"I thought so, but it's getting complicated."

"That always happens right before the fall."

"The fall?"

"You know, when you tumble head over heels in love."

Josh laughed. "Ah, *that* fall. We're actually way past that point."

"Really?"

"I think I was half in love with her the night she creamed my car." Even as he spoke half in jest, he realized it was true. He did love her.

"When did you fall the rest of the way in love?"

"When she plowed into my boat the next day. She looked so damn vulnerable."

Mike regarded him with surprise. "Ashley? She's the family barracuda."

Josh knew the description was probably apt ninety-nine percent of the time. He'd fallen for Ashley during the one percent when it wasn't. The rest was just a challenge that promised to keep things interesting.

Much as she loved them for coming to Virginia to be supportive, Ashley wished her family would go away. She couldn't think with them underfoot. And the commotion they stirred up with Maggie and Melanie and their husbands dropping by for get-togethers at least once a day kept her from focusing on what she needed to do with the rest of her life.

She was relieved on Sunday night when her parents and Jo announced that they were heading back to Boston first thing in the morning.

"Maggie's going to drive us to the airport," Jo told her.

They sat in the backyard swing enjoying the surprisingly balmy fall night. There wouldn't be many more of them, she was sure.

"Thank you," Ashley said, giving her baby sister a hug. "I know you're responsible for convincing Mom and Dad it's time to go."

Jo chuckled. "You really do owe me. Dad wants to

stay and keep an eye on Josh. He thinks there's something fishy about him, no pun intended."

"Why would he think something like that?" Ashley asked.

"He says he can't figure out when the man works. He's sure that's not a good sign."

Ashley was not about to admit that the same thought had crossed her mind, mostly because it didn't speak well of her that she'd shown so little interest in the background of a man with whom everyone could see she was becoming involved.

"Tell Dad not to worry. If things get serious between Josh and me, I'll have him submit a complete résumé for Dad's perusal."

Jo laughed. "You think you're joking. Dad will insist on it."

"It's been good to have you here, baby sister. I've missed you."

"You've only been away for a little over a week, and we've talked almost every day. That's more contact than we have in Boston. You've hardly had time to miss any of us."

"I know," Ashley admitted. "But I like knowing you're close by."

"You'll be home soon," Jo reminded her.

"Maybe," Ashley said, admitting aloud for the first time the possibility that she might not go back to Boston.

Jo stared at her in shock. "Are you saying you might leave Boston for good?"

"Anything's possible," she said.

"Over this? That's ridiculous. You can't let the likes

of Wyatt Blake or that awful Tiny Slocum drive you away from your home and family."

"But thanks to them, my reputation's a shambles. It might be smarter to start over somewhere else."

"Such as?"

"Washington, maybe. Richmond. I don't know."

Jo's gaze narrowed. "Here?" she asked. "Because of Josh?"

Ashley refused to be drawn into that discussion again. "I don't know," she repeated emphatically. "I'll keep you posted." She gave her sister a penetrating look. "Meantime, since we have some time to ourselves for a change, why don't you explain why you've been so jumpy every time we've left the house?"

Jo turned surprisingly pale. "I have no idea what you're talking about."

"Of course you do. It's not the first time I've noticed it, either. You were the same way when we came down here to visit Melanie."

"You're imagining things," Jo insisted.

"Did I imagine that you flatly refused to go out for ice cream last night when I know for a fact that you're an ice-cream junkie?"

"I was stuffed from dinner."

Ashley wasn't buying it, but she could tell that she wasn't going to get any answers from her sister. Jo's tight-lipped expression suggested that the conversation was about to erupt into a full-fledged fight if Ashley kept pushing her.

"Okay, I'll back off," she said. "For now. But, sweetie, whatever it is, you'd better deal with it. Melanie and Maggie live here now, so coming to Rose Cottage from time to time is inevitable. I don't want you to tense up every time it happens."

"I'll deal with it," Jo said, her expression grim. She stood up abruptly. "I'm going to bed. We have to get an early start in the morning."

"Don't be mad at me for worrying about you," Ashley pleaded.

"How could I be? It's what you do," Jo said, forcing a halfhearted smile.

"Okay, then, good night," Ashley said, giving her a hug, even though Jo didn't return it. "I love you."

Jo sighed. "You, too."

Ashley stared after Jo when she headed upstairs. There was something going on here that none of them knew about. She'd always thought she knew each of her sisters inside out, but it was obvious that Jo was holding back about something. She found that more troubling than if it had been either Maggie or Melanie. They were strong. They had lots of inner resources. Jo was the quiet, sensitive one who took everything to heart. It was apparent to Ashley that something or someone in this town had hurt her baby sister. If she ever figured out what or who that was, there was going to be hell to pay.

Ashley had been so eager to see her family off that she'd barely noticed until they were gone that it was pouring rain. That put a real—and quite literal—damper on her plans to get back into the quiet rhythm of her days with Josh.

Disappointed, she made herself a cup of tea and sat down at the kitchen table. After three days of chaos, she ought to be grateful that she could finally focus on the future. Instead, she felt an inexplicable letdown. She couldn't seem to summon the energy to find one of the legal pads she'd slipped into a drawer where it would be away from her sisters' watchful gazes.

Where was her drive? Where was the sense of urgency she should be feeling? When had she changed so dramatically that all this quiet and solitude no longer made her feel as if she might jump out of her skin? She'd actually started to enjoy the peaceful mornings she spent on the bay with Josh. He didn't press her to talk. Nor did he need to fill every second with the sound of his own voice. He wasn't rushing her to figure things out. She was the one doing that, and she couldn't seem to get started. His quiet, undemanding company was a relief after getting poked and prodded by her family. She'd been looking forward to that today. In fact, she'd been counting on seeing him far more than was probably wise.

When the phone rang a few minutes later and the sound of his voice made her heart skip a bit, she was even more disconcerted.

"Where are you?" he demanded.

"At home, which you should know since you called here. Where are you?"

"In the boat about to head your way."

"Are you crazy? It's pouring outside."

"So? Do you think you're going to melt?"

No, but she would look awful. She had no illusions that soaking-wet hair would do a thing for her. "Maybe the fish need a day off," she said.

And given the little thrill of excitement she'd felt

hearing his voice, maybe she needed a day away from Josh to figure out this unexpected attraction that was developing. She couldn't spend her life with some unambitious guy who spent his life fishing to no apparent purpose. This was an interlude. It had to be. Anything else was impossible.

"Okay, then," he said in the easygoing way she found so comforting. "I'll go back in, dry off and pick you up in ten minutes. We'll go into Irvington for breakfast. I know a place that has strong coffee and homemade cinnamon rolls."

Ashley groaned. He'd found her weakness, one she almost never indulged. "Make it fifteen," she said. "I need to hop into the shower and pull myself together."

"I'll give you twenty minutes, then," he teased. "I can't possibly take you out if you're not put together properly."

By the time they reached the coffee shop in nearby Irvington, the sun was fighting its way through the thick gray clouds and the rain was tapering off.

"Want to eat first or explore the shops?" Josh asked.

She studied him with surprise. "A man who likes to shop? I didn't know such a creature existed."

"I couldn't care less about shopping. I just want to see what sort of things make your eyes light up."

Her pulse stuttered at the intensity in his gaze. She could not fall for this man, not right here on the streets of a town hundreds of miles from her home.

"We can start with the cinnamon roll," she said lightly. "After that we'll see how much more of my personality I'm willing to reveal by shopping with you."

When they sat down in the surprisingly crowded coffee shop with its spotless decor and air that was filled with the scent of freshly baked dough and cinnamon, Ashley realized that this felt more like an official date than anything they'd done before. She had coffee dates all the time back home, quick, on-the-run encounters that demanded little more than small talk and served up absolutely no expectations for the way they would end. They gave her the illusion of having a personal life without any of the complications.

Gazing across the table, though, she met Josh's eyes and knew at once that this one was different. It was going to get complicated, simply because her feelings for him had gotten deeper without her even realizing it.

When she finally glanced at Josh, he was watching her as he idly stirred sugar into his coffee. "What?" she asked.

"You seem different this morning."

"Different how?"

"More restless than usual."

"Really? I was thinking earlier about how much I've learned to relax, thanks to you."

He grinned. "You're definitely better than you were, but you seem edgy today. Did something happen with your family?"

"No, not really."

"They got off okay?"

She nodded. "Maggie called from the airport and said their flight was right on time."

"Are they pressuring you to come back to Boston?"

"To be honest, we didn't get into it that much," she admitted. "Every time they brought it up, I cut them off and explained that I have to decide what's right on my own."

"But I imagine they still expressed an opinion or two," he said.

"They're my folks. Of course they want me back home, but they also want me to be happy."

"And for you that means having a successful career," he guessed. "Wherever that might be."

She nodded. "I don't know anything besides law, so I have to go where I can practice."

"Lots of people change careers, if it comes to that," he reminded her.

To her surprise, she said emphatically, "Not me. I want to practice law."

Josh chuckled. "There you go."

"What?" she asked blankly.

"I told you the answers would come to you when you least expect it and when you stop worrying everything to death. You sounded very sure of yourself just then."

Ashley stared at him, then began to grin. "I did, didn't I?"

"Now all you have to decide is where you want to live."

"It may not be that simple," she said, trying to be realistic. "A lot of other firms probably feel the way my old one did. They'll want me but for all the wrong reasons."

"You're obviously an excellent lawyer, if you were able to win an acquittal for a man who turned out to be guilty. You may regret the outcome, but it doesn't change the fact that you did your job very, very well. That's bound to be attractive to a lot of firms."

"That's my point. I don't want a job that's tied to that."

Josh reached for her hand. "Despite the time we've spent together, I can't claim to know you well," he said. "But I think I know enough to say that you care passionately about things. You did what you thought was right at the time in that courtroom. Hindsight is always twenty-twenty, but you have to let the mistakes go or figure out how to rectify them. You can't let them destroy you. That would be a waste."

"I suppose." She wasn't quite ready to get her hopes up that offers would suddenly start rolling in the minute she let it be known that she was available. At one time that would have been true, but not now.

"Of course, I don't know why I'm trying to encourage you to go back," Josh said, his expression rueful. "It would still suit me just fine if you decided you wanted to open up a private practice right here."

Though she would never in a million years consider such a thing seriously, right here, right now, with his hand on hers and his gaze filled with desire, the idea held a certain appeal.

"Maybe we should just be grateful for the time we have," she said slowly. Yet another answer was coming to her this morning, one that had been in the making since the moment they'd met. She held his gaze. "And maybe we should make better use of it."

The heat in his eyes increased by several degrees. "Shopping's out?"

"It is unless it's the best way you can think of to spend the day."

"Oh, no. I've got all the clutter around my house I

need." He gave her a long, intense look. "Want me to show you?"

She grinned, her heart suddenly light, her pulse humming with anticipation. Whatever complications arose because of this decision, she would find a way to live with them. This was about more than having a fling to forget. It was about reaching for something it was no longer possible to resist, something too special to ignore.

"Not as clever as inviting me to look at your etchings, but yes, Josh. The answer is definitely yes."

11

As they neared his house, Josh tried frantically to recall just how many of his belongings were strewn all over the cottage. Fortunately, he was fairly tidy by nature. He was pretty sure he'd even washed the bowl he'd used for cereal that morning.

Still, he wanted Ashley's first impression of his family's home to be a good one. He'd noticed that the inside of Rose Cottage was immaculate. He imagined that it was much the way it had been before her grandmother's death. He hadn't seen one single personal item that was likely to belong to Ashley. Perhaps that was because she viewed her stay as being so temporary that she'd brought very little with her.

From the outside, Idylwild, which had been in his family for several generations, was very much like Rose Cottage, at least as Rose Cottage had been back when Cornelia Lindsey had been seeing to its upkeep. He'd noticed lately that though the inside had been painted and the gardens finally manicured after years of neglect, there were still quite a few exterior repairs needed. His own family had been much more conscientious about keeping Idylwild in excellent condition. They'd replaced the old wooden clapboards with vinyl siding, added dark green metal shutters in place of the peeling wooden ones. The only holdover had been the quaint Victorian-trim screen door, which they'd refused to exchange for a more practical storm door.

Inside was a hodgepodge of wicker furniture, oak antiques covered with several layers of paint that had changed with the whims of various occupants and modern appliances in the kitchen. The art on the walls reflected the Madison family's eclectic taste, from ridiculous paintings on driftwood to old watercolors from another era. Oddly enough, it all came together to achieve something cozy and lived-in.

Lately there were a lot more masculine touches, since it had been all but deeded over to him once his parents had moved to Arizona for the drier, warmer air.

Josh stood aside as Ashley entered, and tried to see the small, cluttered living room through her eyes. He had a feeling she preferred cleaner, more modern decor, probably something streamlined and sophisticated.

To his surprise, she immediately smiled and headed straight for a table of old photographs.

"Is there one of you here?" she asked, her curiosity evident.

"Several, more than likely," he admitted, not sure how eager he was for her to see him as the bespectacled nerd he'd been years ago. Fortunately the table had a lot of photos, many of them of his cousins, most of whom had been far more athletic and handsome than he'd been at sixteen. Given the dramatic changes he'd made physically, he suspected he'd be hard for her to spot.

"Come over here and show me," she said after several minutes of studying and discarding picture after picture.

He grinned at her evident frustration. "No way. You have to try to pick me out of the crowd. Of course, if you can't, I'm not sure whether I'll be insulted or grateful. Meantime, I'll get us some tea, or would you prefer wine?"

"Tea's good."

He left as her brow furrowed in concentration and she picked up each picture and studied it once more.

"Josh, are you sure there's one of you here?" she called out to him eventually.

"Absolutely." He poured the hot water over the tea bags and let them steep, then took the freshly brewed pot and two cups into the living room. "Any luck?"

She was holding a small wood-framed picture and studying it intently. "This one, I think. If I'm right about this one, then there are several more of you, as well."

He walked over. "Let's see." He grinned when he looked at the image of his younger cousin. "Sorry. You lose. That's my cousin Jim."

"But he has your eyes and your mouth," she said. She set the picture back, then met his gaze. "Have I mentioned how much I like your mouth?"

His heart kicked up a notch. "Not that I recall."

"You have very sensual lips." She grinned. "Or maybe I just see them that way because you're such an incredible kisser."

His ego took a satisfying lurch. "Incredible, huh?"

"Mind-boggling, in fact."

Josh leaned down and touched his lips to hers in the slightest brush. "When I kiss you like that?"

"That's nice," she said. "But then there's this other thing you do." She held on to his shirt and skimmed her tongue across his lower lip. "Something like that."

"Ah," he said, nodding. "Like this."

His mouth closed over hers. When her lips parted on a sigh, his tongue invaded. She still had a lingering hint of cinnamon and sugar on her lips, the scent of it on her breath. She was clinging to his shirt, her eyes dazed by the time the kiss ended.

"Mind-boggling," she murmured breathlessly. "Maybe we ought to find that bed before my knees give way."

He laughed. "There's no rush, darlin'. I just made tea."

Her gaze smoldered. "Forget the tea."

Josh swallowed hard. "Forgotten," he said at once, scooping her into his arms.

"How's the rest of your memory? Think you can find your way to the bedroom?"

"There are four bedrooms in this house," he said lightly. "I may not be thinking clearly, but I'm bound to stumble across one of them."

He found his own, of course, and was relieved to find that he'd tossed the covers back in place after yet another restless night. When he lowered Ashley to her feet beside the bed, he very nearly had to pinch himself to be sure this moment wasn't a dream. He wouldn't go so far as to say he'd had a crush on her forever, because it hadn't been like that. It had been impossible—at least for him—to fantasize about anything real with a girl who was so far beyond his reach.

But he'd wondered about her, wondered about all of the D'Angelo girls who were always laughing, always having spirited adventures with the most popular boys in town. The reality, as it turned out, was better than anything he'd imagined. This flesh-and-blood woman made him long for things he'd never expected to want so much…a home, a family, a future that didn't involve nonstop work to get ahead. He'd never had those thoughts as a teenager. Nor had he had them as recently as last week when he'd still been debating taking things to the next level with Stephanie.

Ashley, however, promised to provide endless fascination. As a girl, from his vantage point of distance and teenaged longing, she'd seemed strong, intelligent and invincible to him. She was all of those things as a woman, but she was also vulnerable, and that made her seem accessible in ways he'd never dared to dream about.

She touched him, then, her fingers grazing the skin of his chest, then dipping lower. The memories fled, replaced by a sea of sensations in the here and now. Need exploded inside him, but patience—years of it, or so it seemed—kept his hands steady and slow.

She didn't seem to want slow, though. She moved restlessly against him, taunting him deliberately, moving aside his careful fingers to strip away clothing in an anxious rush. She barely gave him time to appreciate her naked beauty before she was pulling him onto the bed.

Josh was no fool. As much as he wanted to linger

over every caress, to savor every touch, he caught on to her edgy, almost desperate mood and gave her what she wanted. He pinned her hands loosely above her head, then looked into her eyes, searching for her soul. It was there when he entered her with one hard thrust, all the need, all the desire, all the raw wanting that any man could ask for.

She came apart at once, shuddering beneath him, surrounding him with slick, pulsing heat. He smiled into her eyes.

"That one was for you, darlin'."

She gave him a lazy, satisfied smile of her own. "And now?"

"And now we're going to do this again," he said.

"Oh, really?"

"And this time it will be for both of us."

He waited for her body to grow still, waited for the longing to rise once more in her eyes and then he began to move, slowly at first, letting the sweet tension build, until she was pleading with him for yet another release.

"In time," he murmured. "In good time."

Given her penchant for control, he wasn't surprised when her body tried to take the decisions away from him, but he was more determined. He held her in place, his rock-hard arousal sheathed in her, not moving a muscle until she calmed, her gaze alert and filled with interest in what he had planned.

Satisfied that he had her full and captivated attention, he began to move again, this time responding to her little cries of pleasure with deeper, harder thrusts until the rhythm was no longer his—or hers—to control.

They were both caught up in the passion, in the frantic need. He was pretty sure they were going to go up in flames, if something didn't happen to lessen the mounting heat, the sweet, powerful friction that was driving them wild.

Josh had no idea what it would take to send them flying, but he hadn't expected it to be a smile. Ashley's lips curved ever so slightly into a Mona Lisa smile of purest satisfaction and he came undone. The smile spread as she came with him.

As they slowly fell back to earth, Josh cradled her against his chest and fell into the deepest, most contented sleep of his life, only barely resisting the urge to whisper that he'd fallen in love with her. Only the shock of that, the wonder, kept him silent. That and the fear that even after what they'd just shared, she wouldn't feel the same way.

"Do you have any idea how intimidated I was by you?" Josh asked Ashley as they lay side by side in his bed after making love for yet a third time during the long, lazy afternoon. The rain had started once again and was beating a staccato rhythm on the old tin roof.

Taken aback, Ashley stared at him. Of all the things he'd said and done since they met, this was the one that most astonished her. "Intimidated? Why?"

"Because you're one of the totally unattainable D'Angelo sisters, the most beautiful, most intelligent one. When I was sixteen, I never in a million years would have dreamed we'd be together like this."

She was even more astounded by that. "You knew me when you were sixteen?"

He laughed. "Hardly. I knew *of* you. Every boy in three counties knew who you were. You and your sisters breezed in here every summer and left behind a trail of broken hearts each fall. Your poor grandmother was constantly apologizing to all the mothers." He regarded her intently. "Is that what you're going to do to me? Will I wind up being your autumn fling?"

His tone was light, but Ashley heard the note of real concern behind it. "You know I can't make any guarantees right now, Josh. This is what it is, for as long as it lasts. We have to agree to that, or it's pointless to even start."

He gave her a wry look and ran a hand over her hip. "I'd say we've already started."

Indeed, they had. Ashley hadn't felt this way in a long time. Her body was still quaking inside from the power of what they'd just shared. And based on the shiver that Josh's light touch had just sent over her, she was eager to try it again. Before she could indulge herself, though, she wanted him to explain how they'd never met.

"Why didn't we know each other back then?" she asked him, tracing the outline of his wickedly clever mouth. "It's not as if we were living miles and miles apart."

"You and your sisters were way out of my league," he said with a self-deprecating smile. "It was sort of like the difference between standard-issue white bread and one of those crusty loaves of olive bread that come from a gourmet bakery. No comparison."

Her gaze narrowed. "Are you saying we were snobs?" The possibility rankled, most likely because she feared there might be some truth to it. Look at the judgments she'd been making about men her entire adult life. Look at how stunned she'd been that Josh had slipped past the careful screening system that tended to weed out anyone she deemed unsuitable by some ridiculous standard that combined ambition and success to the exclusion of character.

He shook his head. "Not at all. I just wasn't on your radar. That's obvious, since you couldn't pick out my picture from those photos in the living room. I was the one with glasses and a pained smile."

She immediately remembered a picture that had charmed her. The boy, barely a teenager, had looked miserably self-conscious as he gazed at the camera. "I know exactly which picture it is," she said. "Wait."

She scrambled from the bed and ran to get it. "This is you," she said, holding it out to him when she'd returned.

He winced as he looked at it, then nodded. "That's me, all right."

"You were a cutie," she said.

"Please. If you believe that, then you have a very broad definition of the word."

"You were a cutie," she repeated. "I can't believe I never spotted you."

"That was as much my fault as yours. I was shy and got along better with the characters in books than I did with real-life girls my own age."

"That's amazing," she said.

"What? That I turned into this sexy stud muffin?"

Ashley couldn't contain the laugh that bubbled up. "No, that I missed knowing you back then. I've always had a thing for shy bookworms."

Josh scoffed at her. "Kenny Foster was about as far from a shy bookworm as this region ever produced."

She blinked at the mention of a name long forgotten. "Kenny Foster," she repeated. "My gosh, whatever happened to him?"

"You didn't keep up with him?"

"Obviously not."

Josh grinned. "Just as well. You'd have had to defend him on an embezzling charge. His fingers got a little sticky down at the bank."

"You're kidding! My dad always said he had shifty eyes."

"Your dad's obviously a very wise man."

She met his gaze. "Want to know what he says about you?"

His expression sobered. "I don't know. Do I?"

"He thinks there's something fishy about a man who never goes to work."

To her surprise Josh didn't seem to take offense.

"If only he knew," he said dryly.

"Knew what?"

"That this is the first time off I've taken in five years."

She studied him with surprise. "Really?"

"No lie."

"Me, too," she said, holding up her hand to give him a high five. "I don't suppose you're having the same kind of career crisis I'm having, though."

"I wouldn't call it a crisis," he said. "Just thinking about a few things."

She sat up beside him. Now was her chance to return

the favor and listen to him, just as he'd allowed her to go on and on. "Talk to me."

He shook his head. "I have the woman of my dreams in my bed and you want to do career counseling? I don't think so."

"What did you want to do?"

"This," he said, reaching for her.

When his mouth closed over hers, all thoughts of jobs and just about everything else flew out the window. He was right. Why waste time on anything else, when there were so many sensations they had yet to share?

"Where exactly were you all day yesterday?" Maggie asked when Ashley finally returned her call the next morning after she got home from Josh's. "I called three times after I got back from dropping everyone off at the airport."

"I know. I got the messages."

"And I dropped by the house."

"Doesn't surprise me a bit," Ashley said.

"Well?"

"Well, what?"

"Oh, stop it, were you with Josh or not?"

"None of your business."

"Which means you were," Maggie concluded. "Just how serious are things getting between the two of you?"

Ashley didn't have a good answer to that. The sex was definitely serious. In fact, it was magnificent. She couldn't say the same about the relationship. There were some huge gaps that needed to be filled in before she could honestly say they had one.

"I can't answer that."

"Can't or won't?"

"Does it matter?" she asked irritably.

"Yes, it matters. I'm coming over. We obviously need to talk."

"We do not need to talk. And I don't want you and Melanie to get the idea that you need to start planning the wedding."

"I should hope not," Maggie said so emphatically that it caught Ashley off guard.

"I thought you liked Josh."

"I do. We all do. In fact, all the guys are going over to Melanie's tonight to bond over beer and burgers, which is why I was calling you. Melanie and I want you to join us here."

"Why? Are you serving beer and burgers, too?"

"Please. I'm the sister who cooks, remember? I'm serving roasted pork with apricot sauce, mashed potatoes and an asparagus salad. Melanie's bringing a decadent chocolate cake."

"Do the men know about this meal? It might make them rethink the whole beer-and-burgers thing."

"I think it's more about the bonding than the menu," Maggie told her. "And I've instructed Rick not to come home without a few answers about the mysterious Josh Madison."

"Meaning?"

"We all like him, but what do we really know about him?"

"About as much as you knew about Rick before you climbed into bed with him," Ashley reminded her tartly.

"Ha-ha," Maggie retorted. "But I learned a whole lot more before I agreed to marry him."

"I haven't agreed to marry Josh."

"Then the subject has come up?" Maggie said, seizing on Ashley's inadvertent slip of the tongue.

"In passing," she admitted. "But do you honestly think I'd consider spending my life with a guy I hardly know?"

"Not without running his Dun and Bradstreet rating," Maggie said. "Have you done that?"

"No, I have not done that," Ashley said, wounded yet again by the suggestion that her standards for men were suspect. "In fact, that's insulting. I'm not a snob."

"Not a snob, just very certain of the kind of man you want in your life. Are you telling me you no longer care about the designer apparel and the Rolex watch?"

"It's never been about the damn clothes," she snapped, even though Josh's wardrobe had been one of the first things she'd noticed. It hadn't impressed her. Lately, though, she'd hardly noticed what he wore. It simply hadn't mattered.

"No, it's been about the man having enough ambition to be able to afford them," Maggie agreed. "Maybe I've missed something. What does Josh actually do for a living? Do you know something about his career that the rest of us don't?"

"No, I'm not entirely sure, either. I do know that he's thinking of making a change, same as me."

"Great, two of you in career crisis. That ought to provide a nice solid foundation for marriage."

"Go to hell," Ashley said, losing patience with the whole conversation, mostly because she didn't have any of the answers about Josh she probably should have, given the increasing intensity of her feelings for him. She didn't do anything impulsively, yet she'd managed to get involved with a virtual stranger in barely more than a week. And, like it or not, she was involved with him.

"We'll discuss this some more tonight. I'll see you at seven," Maggie said sweetly.

"I never said I was coming."

"But you will."

"Oh? Why is that?"

"Because you know if you don't, Melanie and I will be on your doorstep by seven ten."

"Fine. Whatever."

"I mean it, big sister. You need a plan of action. You need to find out who Josh is before you get any more deeply involved with him."

"Now who's being a snob? Isn't it enough that he's been amazingly supportive and kind? Isn't it enough that he's smart and fun, to say nothing of sexy?"

Maggie chuckled. "Nice defense for a woman who's only casually interested in the guy. We'll talk some more about that, too."

"I can't tell you how I'm looking forward to it," Ashley said sarcastically and hung up.

If she had half a brain, she'd stay as far away from her sister's tonight as she possibly could. Unfortunately, unless she hid out in another state, Maggie and Melanie wouldn't hesitate to track her down. No, it was better to go and save all of them the trouble. She'd just perfect her technique for saying *no comment* to anything she didn't care to answer.

12

Josh studied the uneasy expressions on Mike's and Rick's faces and concluded that he was about to be served up along with the burgers. "Okay, guys, what's the deal?"

They were surprisingly reticent. Mike flipped the hamburgers on the grill and avoided looking at him directly. Rick sighed.

"I'm waiting," he prodded.

"We're on a mission," Rick finally admitted. "From our wives," he added, as if there were any question about who'd put them up to it.

Josh bit back a chuckle at the idea of these two men, both of whom obviously had a very strong sense of who they were, being manipulated by the women in their lives. It was a testament to how deeply they loved their wives. "Interesting. And you felt obligated to accept this mission?"

"Oh, yeah," Mike confirmed. "If I were you, I'd run right now. The list of very intrusive questions we were given is endless." He reached in his pocket and pulled out a wrinkled piece of paper. "Melanie made notes. She didn't trust my memory."

Rick held out a similar sheet of paper. "Neither did Maggie." He frowned at Mike. "I think we were supposed to be more subtle about it."

Josh laughed. "You definitely missed the boat on that. Doesn't matter, though. I'm afraid I can't hide from a few questions," he said with some regret. "It would send the wrong message, don't you think?"

"That's what I said," Rick commented. "Once those two scent blood, they'll be all over you like a couple of hound dogs. You can forget about pursuing Ashley. Maggie and Melanie will take up all your time, pestering you with the same questions, making your life a living hell. We're your best bet. At least with us, you'll have sympathetic male ears."

"Yeah, I can see that," Josh said wryly. "I don't suppose there's any chance at all that you can just tell them I'm a great guy and let it go at that?"

"Fat chance," Mike said. "It's details they're after. They think you're keeping a lot of deep, dark secrets from Ashley."

"Nothing important," he assured them. "But I suppose my word on that isn't enough."

"Afraid not," Rick said apologetically.

Josh took a long swallow of his beer, then sat down in one of the Adirondack chairs on the deck. "Okay, go for it. Ask whatever you want to."

"Maybe we should at least wait till after you've eaten," Mike suggested, obviously not at all anxious to get started. "These are going to be outstanding burgers.

I'd hate to ruin your appetite. And a couple of beers from now, the inquisition won't be quite so painful."

Josh shrugged. He was in no hurry to get into this discussion. "Works for me. And make it two burgers. I'd like to put this off as long as possible, too." He turned to Rick. "Did you really have this much trouble with the sisters when you were courting Maggie?"

"To tell you the truth, the sisters were great," Rick confided. "Maggie was the tough sell. She thought it was all about the sex. She figured the fire would burn itself out eventually and we'd have nothing."

Josh lifted a brow. "But it wasn't about the sex?"

"Well, sure it was, at first," Rick admitted. "I'd played a very gorgeous field for a very long time. Done it damn well, too. I couldn't imagine myself settling down."

"What changed?" Josh asked.

"Maggie ran. Naturally, since no woman had ever done that to me before, I came after her. She still didn't trust me or what we had. I fought. She resisted. It didn't take long for me to weigh settling down against a future without Maggie. I realized very quickly that it was no contest. Once I got to that point, marriage was the obvious answer."

"And that took how long?" Josh asked.

"A few weeks."

"Same with me," Mike said. "My first marriage had pretty much been a disaster. I wasn't looking for a wife, especially with Jessie wildly out of control. I'll be grateful till the end of my days that Melanie looked beyond the mess we were in and took us on. She's made everything since then seem easy."

Mike handed each of them a burger, then sat down with his own. After he'd taken a couple of bites, he glanced slyly at Josh. "Why are you so interested? Are you thinking about marrying Ashley?"

"It's crossed my mind a time or two," Josh admitted. "Like I told you before, though, there are a lot of issues that need to be resolved before either one of us could take the idea seriously. Ashley's career means a lot to her and it's pretty messed up. She needs to work that out. She's not entirely sure who she is or what she wants right now. Me, I think it's clear what she ought to do, but it's not my opinion that counts."

"You could steer her in the right direction," Mike reminded him. "Make the idea of relocating her practice here irresistible."

"I've planted the idea in her head, but so far she's been fairly resistant."

The two men exchanged a look that Josh couldn't interpret. "What?" he asked.

"Maybe you should offer to go into practice with her," Rick suggested casually.

Josh choked on his beer. "Excuse me?"

Mike grinned. "Hard to keep a secret like that in a town this small. Ever since you showed up, I've been running into people who've been only too happy to tell me how lucky I am to have such a successful lawyer for a neighbor. Seems a lot of these folks read the Richmond papers. Lucky for you, Melanie hasn't gotten wind of it yet."

"Neither has Maggie," Rick added. "What I can't figure out is why you'd want to keep it quiet from Ashley. You haven't told her, have you?"

Josh shook his head. "I know it doesn't make a lot of sense, but the night we met she made some crack about me obviously not being a lawyer since I wasn't ready to sue her for damages after that accident. Since I'd been wrestling with whether to change careers or at least leave my firm in Richmond, I sort of went along with her. I figured I could use a break from the whole big-time lawyer image. It was only later, when I realized just how deep her own issues with the law ran, that I saw how stupid it had been not to tell her in the first place. Now I'm not sure how she's going to take it." He regarded them hopefully. "She could be thrilled to discover we have that in common, couldn't she?"

Rick chuckled. "She could be, but my guess is she's going to be mad as a hornet."

"I agree," Mike added. "I'm no expert, but I have figured out that women don't like being lied to."

"It wasn't a lie," Josh said. "It was an omission."

"Well, pardon us all to hell," Rick said, obviously amused. "An omission." He nodded sagely. "Yes, indeed. Explain it just that way. I'm sure that'll make all the difference."

Josh sighed at the grim reality check. "Okay, okay, she's going to be furious."

"Add in the fact that her client lied to her, her boss at the law firm betrayed her and, according to Melanie, her last relationship ended because of a lie, I think furious is putting it mildly," Mike added.

Josh looked from one man to the other and decided it was definitely time to cast pride aside and plead for help. "What the hell do I do now?"

"Grovel," Rick suggested cheerfully.

"Get the truth out there and *then* grovel," Mike corrected.

"I'm not sure I know how," Josh said. He'd never had to grovel before in his life. But to save what he had with Ashley, he was willing to give it a try. "Do I start with flowers?"

Rick laughed. "You are so pathetic. I seem to recall being exactly like you, right, Mike?"

"You were pitiful," Mike concurred.

"Not helping, guys," Josh said. "Clue me in on the groveling thing. I've never had to do it before."

"Send flowers and candy," Mike suggested. "Take over wine and candles and dinner."

"No, no, no," Rick protested. "You have to remember who she is."

Josh stared at him blankly. "I thought all women loved the whole flowers and candy business."

"They do, but keep in mind what's important to Ashley. Buy her a briefcase or the latest handheld computer gadget. Buy her a shingle for a law office."

"Hey, I like that one," Josh said.

"Just don't make it Madison and D'Angelo on the sign," Mike recommended. "D'Angelo and Madison is better. Aside from getting top billing, she'll think she has the upper hand."

Josh laughed. "She does have the upper hand. She has since the day we met."

He didn't see that changing in this lifetime, not as long as he continued to be completely dazzled by her. He pretty much expected that would last forever.

"How could you, of all people, get so deeply involved with a man you barely know?" Maggie asked, regarding

Ashley incredulously. "You pride yourself on digging beneath the surface, scrambling all over for every bit of evidence in a case that could exonerate a client. Didn't you stop for one single second and ask yourself what you really knew about Josh before you climbed into bed with him?"

Trying not to feel foolish, Ashley shook her head. "He was just sort of there. It's not as if we were really dating. We literally drifted into spending time together. It was fun and uncomplicated, at least at the beginning. I didn't want a lot of information. I didn't figure I needed it, since I was going to go back to Boston in three weeks and probably never see him again. Besides, he wasn't my type."

"As if tall, dark and gorgeous isn't everyone's type," Melanie scoffed.

"That barely registered," Ashley admitted.

"Because you didn't think he was polished enough or ambitious enough," Maggie guessed.

Ashley sighed at how that made her look, but it was true. Dammit, she was a snob, after all. "Okay, yes," she admitted. "He seemed to lack some of the essentials that have always been important to me."

"And now?" Melanie asked, regarding her sympathetically.

"And now it's gotten complicated," Ashley said. "Those things don't seem to matter quite so much."

"How so?" Melanie asked.

"She's fallen for him," Maggie replied before Ashley could say a word. "She's slept with him, the sex was fantastic and now she has stars in her eyes that enable her to overlook his possible lack of a bank account or decent wardrobe of designer suits and Italian shoes."

Ashley frowned at her. "You're one to talk about falling in lust, then falling in love. Wasn't that precisely how it was with you and Rick? Isn't that exactly why you hightailed it out of Boston—because you were falling for him because the sex was good?"

"Great," Maggie corrected. "The sex was incredible." She grinned. "Still is, in case you were wondering."

Ashley groaned. "Too much information."

Melanie chuckled. "Besides, she wants us to stay focused on her."

"Trust me, not so much," Ashley retorted. "We could drop this entire subject and it wouldn't bother me a bit. I can deal with my personal life on my own."

"Obviously," Maggie said. "That's why you know so much about the man you're sleeping with."

"You don't have to be sarcastic," Ashley told her.

"I think I do," Maggie said. "This isn't like you at all, big sister. It's a recipe for disaster. You need to start asking some questions. What if you find out he just got out of jail?"

"Don't be ridiculous," Ashley said, then realized she truly didn't know enough to dispute the possibility. And her judgment hadn't been sharp enough to recognize a murderer when he'd been sitting right next to her for weeks. Who knew what secrets Josh might be keeping? He seemed so down-to-earth and sincere, she couldn't imagine that there was a dark side lurking somewhere inside him, but she couldn't swear it didn't exist. That was worrisome.

"Okay, I promise I'll sit down and have a heart-to-heart with him before this goes any further."

Maggie studied her with a narrowed gaze. "How much further is it going to go? All of this could be moot, if you're going back to Boston soon."

Ashley sighed. "I don't know if I am or not," she told them. "And I really, really don't want to discuss that tonight. I've made a promise to myself that first thing tomorrow I'm going to sit down and start making a list of my options."

"Is staying here one of them?" Melanie asked.

"It'll be on the list," Ashley conceded. "But not near the top. It'll be there because I can't afford to dismiss anything out of hand."

"Will it be on there at all because you like the idea at least a little or because of Josh?" Maggie asked.

"What difference does it make?" Ashley replied.

Her sisters exchanged a knowing glance. It was Melanie who answered. "A big one, I would think," she told Ashley. "Whatever you decide, it has to be what's best for you. Josh shouldn't even enter into it. Not unless you're more serious about him than you're letting on."

"It's complicated," Ashley said again. She was crazy about him, but she didn't want to be, didn't think she should be. In fact, if she had an excuse, any excuse at all, she'd disentangle herself from the relationship and flee back to Boston. As bad and as unpredictable as her professional life there was, it was a whole lot easier to understand than the current roller-coaster ride of her emotions.

She stood up. "I'm going home," she announced. She didn't bother explaining that the home she intended to run to was in Boston. She needed to get her emotional feet back under her.

"We haven't even had dessert," Melanie protested. "You have to stay for chocolate cake."

"Not tonight," Ashley said. She gave each of her sisters a fierce hug. "Thanks for helping me to get a clearer picture of all this."

Maggie looked surprised. "We actually helped?"

"Yes, brat. You helped. You, too, Melanie. I think I know exactly what I need to do next."

But she had to make one important stop before she left town. She had to see Josh and try to explain why she was bailing on him and everything that had been building between them.

Ashley had forgotten about the whole guy-bonding session. When she got to Josh's, the house was dark. She could leave him a note, try to explain her decision without having to bear the disappointment that was bound to be in his eyes, but when she really thought about it, she knew she couldn't take the coward's way out. If nothing else, she owed him for being there for her during the worst days of her life.

Since it was a mild enough night, she left the car and went to wait for him on the porch. She was idly rocking when his car finally turned off the road and pulled to a stop.

"Hey," he said, his tone cautious as he approached. "I wasn't expecting you to be here."

"Is it okay?"

"Of course." He dropped a light kiss on her forehead,

then leaned against the porch railing. "How was your evening with your sisters?"

"About as much fun as walking barefoot through glass. How about yours with the guys?"

"Interesting," he said in a way that made her instantly alert.

"What did they say?"

"I'll tell you in a minute," he promised, lifting her out of the rocker, then settling in it himself with her on his lap. "Much better."

Ashley linked her arms around his neck and rested her forehead against his. "I missed you tonight," she admitted, surprising herself. It wasn't what she'd intended to say at all. She'd planned to keep the conversation cool and impersonal, explain that she had to leave town, had to figure things out without him to distract her. Now she couldn't seem to summon the words.

"That's a good thing, isn't it?" Josh asked, studying her worriedly.

"In a way, I suppose."

"Then why do you look so sad? Were your sisters that hard on you?"

"They worry about me, that's all. They're not convinced I'm thinking clearly these days." She shrugged. "They could be right. At the very least, they gave me some things to think about."

"Such as?"

"I don't want to get into it," she said. Talk wasn't what she needed now. She wanted to feel the way only this man had ever made her feel...cherished. "Make love to me, Josh, please."

He searched her face. "You sure we don't need to

have a long talk first? I know your sisters were probably plaguing you with questions about me, since that's what their husbands were doing to me. I figure they'll spend the rest of the night comparing notes. Don't you feel a need to be as up to speed as your sisters will be?"

"Eventually," she said. "But right now I want to be in your arms."

"Happy to oblige," he said. "But then I think we'd better talk about this evening."

"Yours or mine?"

"Both," he said, sounding serious.

"Okay," she agreed reluctantly, then brightened. "Maybe if we go inside and make intense, passionate love, we'll forget what we wanted to talk about."

He grinned. "You do have the ability to make me forget my own name from time to time."

She met his gaze, for some reason needing more. She wanted to know that she made him half as crazy as he made her. "Only from time to time?" she taunted.

"Okay, most of the time," he responded, a glint of knowing amusement in his eyes. "Is it vital that you know how much power you have over me?"

It had been, but now it scared her, especially since she knew what she had to do. She touched his cheek. "I'm not sure I want to have power over you."

"Why?"

"Because that means I could hurt you."

"You won't hurt me, Ashley." He sighed, looking sad. "If anything, it will be the other way around."

She was shocked by his assessment. "You've been wonderful to me," she protested.

"I've tried to be. I've wanted to be," he said. "But I'm not perfect."

She wanted to put a smile back in his eyes, so she said, "Next best thing to perfect, then. Besides, perfection is highly overrated."

"I hope you go on thinking that forever," he said in a way that told her he was sure it would be otherwise.

Ashley swallowed hard. Hadn't she warned herself just a short time ago that this was going to get increasingly complicated? She was beginning to think she might have underestimated just how complicated it could be. Maybe it needed to be reduced to the basics, at least one last time. Maybe that would help her to clarify her feelings before she went back to the relative safety of Boston to think things through. Instead of providing a safe haven, Rose Cottage had only placed her in the middle of a deeper quagmire.

"We're talking too much," she told him.

He hesitated, then nodded. "Entirely too much."

He stood up with her cradled against his chest and went inside, then kicked the door closed behind them.

This time they never made it to the bedroom. There was something almost desperate pulling them together, making each caress as wickedly hot as a flame, making their coming together as explosive as dynamite.

Kisses stole breath. Touches tormented. Clothes flew in every direction as they tumbled onto the sofa in a mad frenzy, arms and legs tangled, bodies uniting.

Ashley shuddered as wave after wave of pleasure crashed over her, taking her under to a dark, dangerous place where only Josh mattered. She lost herself in him and then, when a climax ripped through her, found herself again in his eyes.

It was the first time in her life she'd fully understood the meaning of magic and why women craved it.

13

Josh woke up to find the other side of his bed empty. He should have been accustomed to the feeling, but it felt lonely somehow after having Ashley in his arms for most of the night. He shivered in the chilly air, then dragged on a pair of sweatpants and a T-shirt and went hunting for the woman who'd spent the entire night making his heart pound and his blood race. He doubted he would ever get enough of her.

But today could change everything, he warned himself. Once he told her the truth about his career, about all of the issues that had brought him to Idylwild and that he had kept from her, she might walk out of his life. The prospect made his heart ache. He simply couldn't allow it to happen. He would fight with everything in him to see that she understood his reticence and forgave him.

First, though, he had to find the words and the courage to utter them.

"Hey, beautiful, where are you?" he called out, heading for the kitchen and the aroma of freshly brewed coffee.

When she didn't respond, his heart began to thud. Despite her silence, he sensed that she was still in the house, which meant something was very wrong.

"Ashley!"

Again, nothing.

He found her standing by his dining room table, where he'd been doing some work the day before. It had become his makeshift office, which meant there were papers there that could have given him away. He knew in an instant that that was exactly what had happened.

She was staring out the window. Though the sun was glistening on the bay just outside, he had a sick feeling that it wasn't the beauty of the view that had made her so still. He knew in his gut that the revelation he'd intended to make was now out of his hands. She knew.

"Ashley?"

She turned slowly, an expression of hurt and betrayal written all over her face. Whatever slim hope he'd held out that there was still time for him to tell her everything himself vanished.

"What is it?" he asked, praying that he'd gotten it wrong. "What's happened?"

"I was looking for some paper to make a list," she whispered. "I found this instead." She held up a piece of stationery—letterhead from his firm—in a hand that trembled visibly. "You're a lawyer," she said as if it were some sort of crime. "You're with a very prestigious firm, in fact."

"Yes," he admitted, knowing the wounded expression in her eyes would haunt him forever. "I'm an attorney."

She shook her head as if she still couldn't quite believe it. "I don't understand, Josh. Why didn't you tell me? That first night, when I made that crack about you definitely not being a lawyer, why didn't you say right then that I had it all wrong? All this time, when you were so sympathetic to me, you could have told me that you understood because you know firsthand what it's like, but you never once said that. Why not? Why keep it a secret?"

"Because at that moment, I didn't want to be a lawyer anymore. I liked that you thought I was something else."

"That doesn't make any sense," she said impatiently. "Are you ashamed of it for some reason? Are you one of those lawyers who bends the rules, does whatever it takes to win, the kind you described with such disdain? Is that why you didn't think there was anything wrong with the way I handled Tiny Slocum's case?"

"It wasn't about you, Ashley. And, yes, sometimes I am ashamed of being a lawyer," he admitted. "And like you, I've spent a lot of time lately wondering about the path I'm on. Not for the same reasons, of course, but it's still an identity crisis and, frankly, I was no more ready to talk about it than you were to talk about your situation. I came here to think, to make some tough choices. You know my philosophy on all that. I mull things over, push them to the back of my mind until the answer finally makes its way through the chaos. I'm not like you. I don't worry it to death, make lists, debate the pros and cons."

"Not even with me? I thought I mattered to you."

"You did," he said. "You do. It wasn't about you. It was about me."

"But you had to know I had issues about people lying to me. There were a dozen different times when you could have told me and you didn't," she protested. "Why hide it, especially after I'd told you what was going on with me? All you had to do was say, 'Hey, Ashley, I'm a lawyer, so I get what you're going through.' Period. That's it. If you didn't want to talk about your issues, fine. I could have understood that."

"I see that now," he said honestly. "I see that keeping it from you was wrong, that I turned it into a big deal when it shouldn't have mattered at all. And I can tell you that I regret staying silent. It was foolish and unfair. Rick and Mike made me see that last night."

"They know?" she asked incredulously. "You told them before you told me?"

"No. I didn't have to tell them. Apparently several people in town had mentioned it to them. They confronted me about it last night, told me that I was being an idiot for not telling you, that I was putting your trust at risk. That's why I wanted to talk when I got back here and found you waiting. I knew I'd kept silent too long, that you had to know before you found out some other way."

"Too little too late," she said disdainfully. "You made a fool of me," she whispered. "Just like before, and once again I never saw it coming. What is wrong with me? How did I turn into such a lousy judge of character?"

"Ashley, it's not as if I've committed a crime or kept another woman from you. Law is a job, and at the time I wasn't very happy with it."

"But it's who you are. Now I have to question whether I ever really knew you."

"You do," he argued. "You know everything important."

He reached for her, but she pulled away. Fighting the panic clawing at him when he realized he really could lose her over this, he tried to explain. "It just didn't matter, Ashley, especially when being a lawyer was something I was questioning anyway. Why does what I do for a living matter so much to you, anyway?"

"That's not the point," she said defensively. "You lied. That's what I care about."

He studied her curiously. He had a feeling she wasn't being entirely honest herself. His career did matter to her in some way he had yet to discern. "What did you think I did for a living?"

She hesitated then, her turmoil evident. "I wasn't sure. Fished maybe."

Josh laughed at the absurdity of that. "You must have thought I was damned bad at it. The biggest catch we brought in was three rockfish, and *you* caught those."

Her defensiveness came back. "I figured since you were on vacation, that you weren't really trying."

He regarded her skeptically and waited.

She sighed, then admitted, "Okay, it felt safe that you were nothing more than some halfway idle guy."

His heart sank as he realized what she was really saying. "Because you could never fall for a man like that, right? A man with no ambition?"

She nodded, looking miserable. "I'm sorry. I know that sounds insulting."

"It *is* insulting, especially considering what went on here last night and on at least one other occasion. If you think what I did was so awful, think about how it makes me feel to know that essentially you were using me to scratch some itch, that you figured a mere fisherman couldn't be hurt by whatever game you were playing."

She looked as if he'd slapped her. "It wasn't like that, Josh."

"Really? Then how was it? Please explain it, because right this second I'm pretty sure I feel like an even bigger fool than you do."

"I was falling for you," she insisted.

"Despite me being some unsuccessful fisherman," he said sarcastically, letting his fury reach a boil. Everything was falling apart and anger was just about the only thing that was going to get him through the pain of it. "How gracious of you to look beyond my lowly lifestyle. How did I miss the fact that you are such a snob?"

"I'm sorry." She scraped a hand through her thick hair, leaving it more tousled than ever.

Josh had to tear his gaze away. That was the way he liked her best, looking sexily rumpled and accessible. He couldn't let himself think of her that way now. He had to hang on to his outrage.

"I guess we're both lucky," he said.

"Lucky?" she repeated incredulously. "How do you figure that?"

"We've just avoided making a horrible mistake. I thought I was in love with a brilliant, generous-hearted woman. You thought you were falling for a guy who was good in bed and nothing more. Turns out we were both wrong." He met her gaze. "I guess the reality isn't nearly as appealing as the fantasy."

She winced at that. "I should go," she said, then

waited, almost as if she were hoping that he'd try to stop her.

He didn't say a word. He couldn't. He could only think about the irony of this whole mess. He'd been falling in love with her and she'd been using him for easy, uncomplicated scx. That was definitely a turnabout in his life. One of these days when it stopped hurting so damn much, he might even laugh about it.

Ashley drove back to Rose Cottage in a daze. How had everything spun so wildly out of control in little more than a heartbeat? She wished she'd never found the stupid letter, never discovered that Josh was a lawyer.

Maybe in another hour, he would have told her himself. It would have shaken her, but at least the news would have come from him. Maybe that alone would have been enough to redeem him, so they could go on together.

"Don't be ridiculous," she told herself as she went inside and made herself a cup of tea. She would have been just as angry, felt just as betrayed, if the announcement had tripped off his lips. His being a lawyer was a big deal. His hiding it from her was an even bigger one. She simply couldn't stomach being with another person who couldn't tell her the truth. How could anyone be expected to build a relationship on lies and half-truths?

She sat at the kitchen table, sipping her tea and trying to work up the energy to pack for the return to Boston. It didn't seem half as urgent to run back home now. The decision about what to do about Josh and her feelings for him had been made. It was a nonissue. They were over.

Even if she weren't furious at him for the lie, he would probably never forgive her for the judgments she'd made about him.

As for the whole question of her professional future, she could just as easily decide that sitting right here at the kitchen table.

Determined to get on with it, she pushed aside her emotions and retrieved a yellow legal pad and a handful of pens. Just spreading them on the table in front of her immediately made her feel better, more in control. Making lists was something she excelled at doing. She liked being organized and practical. It was about time she remembered that. Idle mulling might work for Josh, but it simply wasn't her way. It was ridiculous. Decisions that were made like that couldn't be trusted. They were little more than impulse. She liked her decisions to be based on sound logic and clear thinking.

Okay, then, she thought, she had four basic choices.

First, she could go back to Boston and begin applying at other law firms. Under that she jotted down a couple of quick notes on the positive side; that she would be near her family and that she had a reputation in Boston. She sighed and put that reputation down as a negative, too. It was hard to tell which way that one would go, to her advantage or her disadvantage.

Next, she listed the option of looking for jobs in other cities, such as Richmond or Washington. More negatives than positives immediately popped into mind. It would mean relocating to cities where she knew no one, taking the bar exam again, being separated from her family. Those were all huge, though not insurmountable, drawbacks. On the plus side, such a decision would offer a new challenge, a fresh start. There was a lot to be said for that.

Or, she wrote down, she could change careers entirely. She was a bright woman with many interests she had yet to fully explore. She could certainly find some way to utilize those skills and talents to find a whole new direction for her life. She sighed. If only that didn't seem like such a waste, she thought, not just of her degree, but of her passion for justice. No, she was simply meant to be a lawyer. She just had to rethink the way she practiced, which cases she accepted.

Satisfied that the third option wasn't really an option at all, she crossed it off the list.

That left one last possibility, at least for now. She could stay right here, open her own practice and be near her sisters. It would combine several advantages. She could have her fresh start, stay in law and still be close to family. The only negative was the prospect of running into Josh from time to time, but maybe he'd go back to his fancy Richmond law office any day now and never set foot in this region again.

If it turned out that he did pop up occasionally, she could live with that, she concluded thoughtfully. They were both adults. What was the big deal? They'd had an affair and it hadn't worked out. Happened all the time and people got over it and moved on. It didn't have to make her heart ache forever that he'd betrayed her and she'd apparently hurt him just as badly. She'd just have to chalk it up to bad timing, bad karma, something like that. She'd get over it. He would, too.

Tears pricked the back of her eyes, and she knew it

was a lie. She wasn't going to get over it. Certainly not anytime soon. That meant she had to deal with it.

She ripped off the sheets of paper on which she'd listed her career options and wrote down another heading: *What to Do about Josh?*

The answers weren't half as clear-cut as she would have liked. Much as she hated to admit it, she needed another perspective. The prospect of going to Maggie and Melanie and telling them what a mess things had become held no appeal at all. Sooner or later, she would be forced to do it, but not this afternoon.

What she needed this afternoon was a distraction. She needed to mull things over, let her mind drift until the answers rose to the surface.

There was only one good way that she could think of to do that, since fishing with Josh was not a possibility. She hauled out the kayak and the new paddle she'd purchased. With any luck, a couple of hours of hard exercise would drive the whole Josh dilemma from her mind.

But the instant she put the kayak in the water, the memory of the first day she'd taken it out came flooding back to her. She pulled the paddle out of the water and let the tears she'd held back earlier come flooding out. They were hot and endless, proving that it wasn't going to be half as easy to put Josh behind her as she'd hoped.

Her tears eventually slowed to a sad trickle, and she was drifting when he pulled alongside her in his rowboat.

"Ashley?" There was an unmistakable note of worry in his voice.

She wanted to disappear. She didn't want him to know that he'd caused her one second of anguish. "Go away."

"Not with you floating around fifty feet from shore crying your eyes out. I could hear you from a hundred yards away."

Embarrassment turned her cheeks red. She'd had no idea she was sobbing so noisily. "I'm not crying over you," she said, feeling it vital not to let him think she was.

"Never thought you were," he said, though his lips quirked just a little.

"And I don't need you to rescue me."

"Of course not," he agreed. "I'll just stick close by, in case the waterworks get out of hand again and the kayak starts filling with water. Doesn't take much to swamp a little thing like that."

She finally lifted her gaze to meet his and wiped away the traces of tears on her cheeks. "Not going to happen," she said fiercely. "See, dry-eyed. You can go now."

He looked as if he wanted to say something more, but eventually he merely nodded. "Okay, then. I'll see you around."

She held on to the paddle until her knuckles turned white as she waited for him to disappear from view.

Oh, yeah, it was obvious she could handle bumping into him, she thought with self-derision. She'd all but come unglued just at the sound of his voice. A part of her had wanted to dive over into that rowboat so she could fling herself into his arms. Given that he was just as furious with her as she was with him, that could only have come to a bad end. It was entirely possible he'd have tossed her straight overboard. Just because he'd been worried finding her drifting along on the water didn't mean he was any more ready to forgive her than she was to forgive him. He would have done the same for anyone, because that's who he was…a nice guy.

Well, she didn't need his concern. Or his sympathy. Or his pity. In fact, the last would be unbearable.

Which meant she had to get over him. Right now. A nearly hysterical sob rose up. Sure, like she could snap her fingers and make that happen.

Much as she hated to admit it, she was probably way too much like her sisters. Once she gave away her heart, which she'd apparently done without giving it a conscious thought, it was all but impossible to take it back.

Josh hadn't wanted to feel a damn thing when he'd spotted Ashley out in that ridiculous kayak that she didn't know how to handle. He'd wanted to turn around and row away before she even knew he was around, but the instant he'd heard her sobs, his heart had flipped over. He hadn't been able to make himself leave, not without assuring himself that she would be okay. He figured his appearance alone would snap her out of it, and it had up to a point.

Making her mad had accomplished the rest well enough. He knew she'd hate his pity, so he'd done his best to act solicitous and sympathetic, knowing that she would place the worst possible spin on that and assume it was based on pity. What he'd wanted to do was to haul her into his boat and into his arms. That wasn't a good idea for either of them right now.

He figured he'd eventually get over his own hurt feelings, but first he had to understand how he'd allowed her opinion to matter so much. He had a feeling it went back to those days when he'd known she was out of reach and he'd felt inadequate.

This afternoon, for the first time since they'd met as adults, she'd made him feel inadequate all over again. To have that happen after being so close to her had ripped all of his hard-earned self-confidence apart. It was like discovering indescribable joy only to have it snatched away because he didn't measure up in some way that couldn't be changed.

He arrived back at Idylwild in time to hear the phone ringing. He managed to grab it before it stopped.

"Hello," he said breathlessly.

"Josh, I thought you were in better shape," Stephanie teased. "Or have I called at a bad time?"

"Very funny. What's up?"

"You're making my father very unhappy," she said. "And the worst of it is, he's blaming me."

"You? Why?"

"Because I won't bend to his will and come chasing after you," she said dryly. "He's sure we can work out all the pesky things bothering us and eventually find our way to the altar, after all."

"That just shows how stubborn he is," Josh said. "He's obviously not listening to either one of us. At least I assume you've told him the same thing I have, that we're not right for each other."

"I've tried," she said, "but you know my father. He ignores anything that doesn't agree with his view of the world."

"Then what do you suggest?"

"Come back to Richmond. We see him together and present a united front, so he can't dismiss this as some silly misunderstanding. Maybe then he'll get it and get off my case. Otherwise I'm afraid any other man I bring around will be doomed. Dad will only compare them to you and find them lacking."

Josh laughed. "Is there a compliment in there somewhere?"

"You are a tough act to follow, Josh. There's no question about it." She hesitated. "Did you need reminding of that for some reason?"

"As a matter of fact, I did," he said. "If it'll help you out, I'll come back to go with you to see your father." In that instant he made up his mind about something else that had been weighing on him. "But I have to warn you, Steph, I intend to quit while I'm there."

"Oh, jeez," she said with an exaggerated moan. "Can you at least wait till I get out of town?"

"Afraid not."

"Out of the room?"

"I can do that," he promised, smiling.

"What are your plans?" she asked him.

"I'm going to move down here and open up a practice," he said decisively. "It's what I should have done from the beginning. I'm not cut out for the barracuda pool."

"No, you're not," she agreed. "You have the talent, but not the bloodlust. That's one of the things I like most about you."

"I think that could be the nicest thing you've ever said to me," Josh told her.

"Oh, I'm sure I said a few more flattering things from time to time," she teased, then turned serious. "Are we okay, Josh? Can we go on being friends? I'd miss that a lot."

"Absolutely. You're the best one I have."

"Can I ask you something?"

"Anything."

"Is she worth it?"

His heart lurched. "Is who worth it?"

"Whoever you're moving down there to be with. There has to be a woman involved."

Josh sighed. He saw no point in denying it. "I thought she was."

"Has she done something to change your mind? Has she hurt you?" Stephanie demanded indignantly.

"Whoa, girl! You don't need to swoop down here to protect me."

"I will, you know."

"I know and I'm grateful."

"So are you sure this a good time for you to get away? I don't want to mess up whatever you have going on."

"Actually, your timing couldn't be better," he told her honestly. A day or two away might allow the dust to settle.

"Then when will you come down here to see my father?"

"Is tomorrow okay? We might as well get this over with."

"I'll set up lunch at the club," Stephanie told him. "He'll be much more mellow after a Scotch, a steak and a cigar."

"Mellow or dead," Josh said wryly. "He needs to quit all of those things."

"Which I've told him repeatedly, but since he hasn't, I intend to use them to my advantage," she said, sounding decidedly chipper. "See you tomorrow at noon."

Josh hung up, then went to stare out the same window where he'd found Ashley earlier. Had it only been that morning? He felt as if an eternity had gone by. He waited to see if he would catch a glimpse of her on the water, but she didn't appear.

He wondered how she would take the news that he was relocating, or if it would even matter to her. Probably not. He couldn't let her reaction matter to him, either. This was the right thing to do. He'd known it the minute he'd uttered the words to Stephanie. For the first time in months, he honestly felt as if his future were on the right track.

Now if only he had the right woman by his side.

14

When Josh stopped for coffee on his way out of town, he ran into Mike and Rick. He hesitated at the café door, but they spotted him before he could turn right around and leave. Reluctantly, he went to join them. He had a hunch they were going to want to get into things he had no intention of discussing.

"Going somewhere important?" Mike asked, noting the unaccustomed suit Josh was wearing.

"I have a meeting in Richmond," Josh admitted, figuring that was safe enough ground.

"Big case?" Rick asked.

"Nope, my boss and his daughter, the woman he expected me to marry."

Both men regarded him with amazement. "And you're walking into that willingly?"

"Eagerly, in fact," he told them. "Stephanie and I intend to convince her father that we would have made each other miserable, then I intend to quit my job. It's not going to be a great morning for Creighton Williams. He doesn't like being thwarted when he has things all planned out."

"Isn't he the lawyer who cuts the opposition into itty-bitty pieces at trial?" Mike asked worriedly.

"The very one."

"You're a braver man than I," Mike said.

"It has to be done," Josh told them. "Then I'll be free to come back here and open a practice."

"Does anyone else know about this?" Rick asked.

"If by anyone you mean Ashley, the answer is no. We're not exactly on speaking terms these days. This has nothing to do with her. It's a decision I should have made years ago, but I was blinded by dollar signs."

"Mind if I ask why you think this doesn't affect Ashley?" Mike inquired.

Josh regarded him with surprise. "You don't know?"

"Not me," Mike said. He turned to Rick. "You?"

"Haven't heard a word," Rick confirmed.

Josh wasn't sure what to make of that. He'd been sure Ashley would run to her sisters with the tale of how he'd betrayed her. Maybe she'd been too embarrassed that she'd missed something so obvious about the man she was sleeping with.

"Bottom line, she found out I was a lawyer before I could tell her." He gave them a rueful smile. "You underestimated her fury. Then I discovered that she'd assumed I did some sort of menial, undemanding labor and that it suited her just fine, because that made me safe, since she couldn't possibly fall in love with someone with so little ambition."

"Safe and unambitious?" Mike said, his expression puzzled. He glanced at Rick, then back toward Josh. "Is that as demeaning as it sounds?"

"I certainly thought it was," Josh said. "Things pretty much went downhill from there."

"Yet you're coming back here to go into practice," Rick said. "Why?"

"Because it will give me the chance to practice the kind of law I always wanted to practice, helping regular folks with the things that matter to them, instead of big corporations that only want to get bigger."

"And you honestly don't see Ashley anywhere in this picture?" Mike asked.

Josh hesitated. He didn't want to admit just how badly he wanted her to be a part of it, not after what had happened between them. What would it say about him that he was willing to grovel to make it happen? Bottom line, though, she had to discover on her own exactly how well-suited they were and that they could be professional as well as emotional partners.

"You can admit it, pal," Rick teased eventually. "We won't think any less of you. We've both been there. The D'Angelo women are worth whatever it takes to keep them."

Josh was surprised by Rick's understanding. "You don't think I'm an idiot for wanting her, even after she proved how little respect she had for me?"

"Personally, I think you're looking at it all wrong," Mike said. "I think it's a testament to how much she respected you that she overlooked what she was sure were your shortcomings and fell in love with you anyway."

It was an interesting spin, but that's all it was. Even so, Josh desperately wanted to believe him. "You think so?"

Rick grinned. "If that's the interpretation that gets you through this impasse, then hang on to it for dear life. Pride's a mighty cold bedfellow."

Josh nodded slowly. "I'll keep that in mind. Now I'd better hit the road, so I can get this over with. I can't have much of a future, if I don't deal with the past once and for all."

"Good luck," they both told him as he scooted out of the booth.

"Thanks." He wasn't going to need it, though. It was an image of the prize at the end of it all—the albeit slim possibility of a future with Ashley—that was going to get him through today.

"Are you seeing the big picture here?" Maggie asked when Ashley told her the whole story about discovering that Josh was an attorney with a firm in Richmond that was so influential she'd heard about it all the way in Boston.

"He lied to me," Ashley said flatly. She didn't want to hear her sister's spin on that. The lying was the only thing that mattered. "How can trust flourish when one person lies about something so basic? And without trust, what kind of relationship can we possibly have?"

"Maybe it was a lie. Maybe not," Maggie said anyway. "Josh said he was here to think about what he wants, the same as you have been. Haven't you wrestled with that on your own without asking for his input?"

"I suppose, but that hasn't stopped him from giving it to me," Ashley grumbled.

"But my point is," Maggie continued as if Ashley

hadn't said a word, "this just gives you something more in common besides the great sex."

"Who said the sex was great?" Ashley retorted irritably.

"You did. Besides, if it wasn't, you wouldn't be so rattled by all of this," her sister said confidently. "You'd write him off, finish making up your mind about what you want to do for the rest of your life and then get on with it. Have you thought about that, by the way? Or has the issue that brought you running down here taken a backseat to your feelings for Josh? If so, what does that say about your priorities these days?"

The truth was she hadn't thought about anything except Josh for days now. Since everyone around her knew it, she might as well admit it. "No," she responded testily. "My priorities have gotten a little confused. That's all the more reason to forget about Josh and get back to what's important."

"There is nothing more important than love," Maggie said. "A very wise older sister once told me that."

"Must have been someone else," Ashley insisted sourly.

"Come on, Ashley, admit it," Maggie chided. "Doesn't it tell you something that your priorities have changed since you came here? You've actually found someone who's more important to you than work."

"He's not," Ashley said fiercely. "I won't let him be."

Maggie laughed. "Too late, sweetie. You don't get to control everything, you know. Some things just are. Love is one of them."

"I will not be in love with Josh." She said it with more

wistfulness than conviction. Naturally her sister picked right up on that.

"Good luck with that one," Maggie replied. "Keep me posted."

Ashley scowled at her. "I can still go back to Boston. In fact, that was exactly what I intended to do as soon as I talked to Josh night before last. Then one thing sort of led to another, I wound up spending the night there and then yesterday morning I stumbled across this little bombshell."

"Why did you come here today?" Maggie asked. "Why didn't you just leave for Boston? What's keeping you here?"

"I wish to hell I knew." She gave Maggie a bemused look. "God, I hate this uncertainty. I used to know how to make quick, clean decisions and live with the consequences."

Maggie laughed. "Tell me something I don't know about you." She gave Ashley a penetrating look. "Why are you confused? Seems to me if you're really through with Josh, if you really think he's a pig, then there's no reason to stick around."

"Logically, you're right," Ashley admitted.

"But logic has nothing to do with it, sweetie. Josh suddenly seems more suitable, now that you know he's a lawyer, doesn't he?"

"Yes," she admitted. "That's part of it."

"Do you realize just how shallow that sounds?"

"Yes," she said miserably. "Believe me, he called me on it, too."

"You still haven't answered my question. Do you want to go back to Boston as much right now as you did when you first found out? Or do you want to stay and fight for what you could have with a good, decent guy who happens to love you?"

"I like it here," she admitted, still a little stunned by that fact. Even in the throes of discovering that Josh had lied to her, she'd realized how much she would miss him and Rose Cottage. That realization had changed everything. In fact, it had left her torn. It had ruined the cold logic she usually used when analyzing her lists.

"Then stay," Maggie said as if the decision were easy.

"It's not that simple. I like being here with Josh, and maybe we could get past this monumental lie or omission or whatever, but Josh doesn't live here, or have you forgotten that?"

"I haven't forgotten anything," Maggie said calmly. "Not even the fact that D'Angelo women fight the hardest when they're about to go down for the count."

Rick wandered in just then and overheard them. "Guess you haven't heard," he said, picking up an apple and biting into it.

"Heard what?" Maggie prodded.

"Josh is gone."

Ashley felt her heart tumble straight to her toes. "He's gone? Where? Back to Richmond?"

"Uh-huh. I spoke to him this morning right before he took off."

"I see," Ashley said, her voice flat. It really was over then. He hadn't stuck around to fight for her. That hurt a hell of a lot more than she'd expected it to.

"Not sure you do," Rick said, a surprising twinkle in his eyes.

Maggie gave him an impatient look. "If you have something to say, spit it out. This is not the time for games."

He looked unrepentant. "I thought maybe it was. Seems to me that your sister's reaction was very telling." He turned to Ashley. "You felt as if the wind had been knocked out of you, didn't you?"

She stared at him with a narrowed gaze. "Your point?"

"That you're in love with the man."

"Well, of course, she is," Maggie said.

"I am not," Ashley said, but without much conviction. "Okay, of course I am. Admitting that does me a fat lot of good when he's gone back to Richmond."

"You could go after him," Rick suggested, then added slyly, "Or you could wait till he gets back tomorrow."

The sudden pounding of Ashley's heart told her everything she needed to know. "He's coming back?" she asked, trying to keep the hope out of her voice. It was humiliating how badly she wanted to have another chance.

Rick nodded. "He went down there to quit his job. He's decided this is where he wants to live."

Maggie scowled at him. "And why did he confide all this to you, rather than Ashley?"

"Because we were there," Rick said simply. "Besides, the way I hear it, they aren't speaking."

"Where?" Ashley asked, ignoring the comment about the lack of communication between her and Josh at the moment.

"At the café. He had breakfast this morning with Mike and me."

"And he thought you should be the first to know about this important, life-altering decision? Guess that shows where I fit in," Ashley said.

"Hey," Rick protested. "I thought you women were all in favor of us bonding with him and pumping him for information."

"You're supposed to share it," Maggie reminded him impatiently.

He stared at her. "I just did. Was I supposed to call on my cell phone from the café? You know the damn thing never works."

"Okay, you two," Ashley scolded. "Play nice. I won't have you fighting because of me and my problems."

"Sounds to me like you don't have any problems," Maggie said, suddenly more cheerful. "Josh is coming back. You can make things right with him, if that's what you want. Is it?"

"He's furious with me, too," she reminded her sister. "He might not want to make things right." She glanced at Rick, to see if he'd admit to any insights on this point, but he was suddenly silent.

"Oh, no," Maggie scoffed. "He's just giving up his thriving law practice with a prestigious Richmond firm so he can be near the water."

"Actually, that's exactly it," Rick said.

Maggie frowned at him. "You're not helping."

Ashley turned to Rick. "It has nothing at all to do with me?"

"How could it? He doesn't know what you intend to do."

Her spirits sank. "I see."

Maggie gave her a hard hug. "Stop it. You look as if

it's over. It's not. You have a second chance. You just have to grab it the minute he gets back to town."

Ashley nodded slowly. Her pride was screaming that Josh ought to make the first move. She'd try to tell her pride to shut up and be reasonable, but the reality was that she usually let it rule her decisions. Wasn't it pride that had made her scurry out of Boston just when she should have stayed there with her head held high? Her uncharacteristic retreat had probably only fueled the media frenzy she'd left in her wake.

She made a decision of her own then. "I have something I need to do," she told Maggie and Rick, gathering up her purse and the jacket she'd worn over.

"What?" Maggie asked.

"I'm going home."

"Home?"

She nodded. "To Boston. There are some things I need to take care of."

Her sister's gaze narrowed. "But you'll be back?"

"In a few days."

Rick looked completely confused. "What should I tell Josh if he asks?"

Ashley and Maggie both turned to him at once. "Stay out of it!" they said in a chorus.

He frowned at both of them. "Is it any wonder men don't understand women? You keep changing the blasted rules on us."

Ashley gave her brother-in-law a kiss on the cheek. "Stick around, pal. You'll get the hang of it eventually. I can see your potential. Obviously Maggie can, too, or she wouldn't have married you."

"Small consolation," he grumbled, but he pulled

Maggie into his arms and kissed her so thoroughly it made Ashley's mouth go dry.

"I'm out of here," she said hurriedly.

She was pretty sure neither one of them heard her or even gave a damn.

The meeting with Creighton went off with surprisingly few hitches, Josh concluded after the lunch ended. Oh, the man had grumbled and carried on about Josh being ungrateful and shortsighted, but in the end it was obvious that he wanted his daughter to be happy and he respected Josh enough to accept the decision he had made, as well. They had parted on good terms, with the door at the firm always open if Josh woke up one morning and realized he'd made a tragic mistake, which Creighton direly predicted Josh would most certainly do.

Josh was so eager to get back and find Ashley that he decided against staying over in Richmond for the night to put his condo on the market, and drove straight back down to Idylwild instead. Rick and Mike had been right. He couldn't allow this misunderstanding to fester until it turned into something insurmountable. He had to be the one to hold out an olive branch.

But when he arrived around dinnertime, he couldn't find Ashley at Rose Cottage or anywhere else in town. Finally, as a last resort, he drove out to Maggie's. When she answered the door, she gave him a hard look.

"Yes?" she said in a tone that would have made him quake if he hadn't seen the twinkle in her eyes.

"I'm looking for Ashley."

"You're too late."

His heart fell. "Too late?"

"She went back to Boston."

Josh felt as if someone had punched him in the stomach. "I see."

Maggie shook her head and regarded him with pity. "You'd better come in. I can't have you passing out on my doorstep. Ashley would never forgive me."

"I'm not going to pass out," he said with more spirit.

"Come in, anyway. Based on your unmistakable reaction to the news, we probably need to talk."

He frowned at the determined note in her voice. He didn't trust that tone one bit. "Again?"

She laughed. "Oh, don't whine, Josh. I'll make it relatively painless."

"You might as well do it," Rick called out. "Otherwise she'll just have to hunt you down. Believe me, persistence is one of her best traits. Sticking around now will save time in the long run."

Josh focused on Rick as he stepped inside. "Thank goodness," he muttered. "A friendly face."

"Don't rely on my husband to save you," Maggie warned. "I want to know what your intentions are toward my sister and I want to know now. And just to give you a fair heads-up, they'd better be honorable."

Josh gave her an amused look. "Isn't that a little old-fashioned?"

"What can I say?" she said, not backing down. "I'm an old-fashioned girl. And in the absence of my father, it's my duty to get a few things straight with you." She gave him another of those hard looks. "Or, if you prefer, I can call him and drag him down here first thing in the morning. He's chewed up and spit out men like you every day since we hit sixteen."

Josh glanced at Rick, who was clearly getting entirely too much enjoyment out of the whole scene. "You could help, you know."

Rick shook his head. "Sorry, pal. You're on your own with this one. Maggie's a reasonable woman."

She beamed at him. "Thank you."

"Just being honest," Rick assured her. He grinned at Josh. "Tell the truth and you have nothing to fear."

Josh shot a sour look in his direction, then turned it on Maggie. "I repeat, isn't this a conversation I should be having with Ashley?"

Maggie returned his look with a perfectly bland expression. "That depends," she said sweetly. "She's not here at the moment. I am. And, trust me, you won't ever get close enough to talk to her unless I like what I hear."

Josh shook his head. "Then I'd say we're at an impasse, because I don't intend to discuss this with you. Suffice it to say that it is not my intention to hurt your sister."

"You already have," she reminded him.

"Not deliberately," he replied. "And she didn't exactly make me feel all fluttery and special. She thought I was a fisherman."

"There's nothing wrong with fishing for a living," Maggie said. "It's a perfectly respectable profession, especially around here."

"I agree, but it was plain that your sister didn't see it in such a positive light. She acted as if she'd been doing me a damn favor by condescending to sleep with me when I had nothing at all to offer her." The bitterness welled up again as he spoke. He hated that their relationship had begun with lies, evasions and misunderstandings, but it was too late to change that. They had to deal with who they really were and the undeniable attraction that couldn't be dismissed just because of hurt feelings.

Maggie regarded him with surprising compassion. "I'm sorry. You have no idea how terrible she feels about that. Ashley isn't a snob. If anything, she was just trying to protect herself from emotions that were too huge for her to accept."

"Small comfort," Josh said. Ironically, even as he spoke with such sarcasm, he realized it was true. It was some comfort to know that she'd been in deeper than she'd expected to be and had latched onto any excuse for an escape.

"She loves you," Maggie said more gently. "She really does."

He met her sympathetic gaze and finally found the courage to admit what he hadn't said to anyone else, including himself. "I love her, too."

A grin filled with unmistakable relief spread across Maggie's face. "There now," she said, patting his arm. "That wasn't so difficult, was it?"

He couldn't help grinning at her obvious sense of triumph. "No worse than a tooth extraction," he retorted. "Now may I please go?"

"Where? Boston?"

"Absolutely not," he said at once. "If this is going to work, it has to work here. She has to come back on her own." He studied Maggie intently. "Think she will?"

"Not a doubt in my mind."

Josh nodded. He was counting on the fact that no one knew the D'Angelo sisters any better than they knew each other.

15

Ashley stood in front of a bank of television and radio microphones and drew in a deep breath. This was it. This was what she should have had the courage to do weeks ago. She was going to face the people of Boston and the family of Letitia Baldwin and admit that she had lost sight of the promise she had made to herself when she first went into law…to focus on justice, not winning. Perhaps it simply wasn't practical to believe that every client she defended would be innocent, but she had intended to do her very best not to fall prey to the cynicism that afflicted too many criminal defense attorneys.

"Good morning, ladies and gentlemen," she said at last, proud that neither her gaze, nor her voice faltered, not even when she spotted her parents and Jo in the back of the room. Her sister gave her a broad smile and a thumbs-up gesture.

"Thank you for coming. I have a brief prepared statement and then I'll take a few of the questions I'm certain you've stored up in my absence."

The last drew a laugh from some of the veteran

reporters at the front of the pack. They all knew that she'd never before been reticent with the media. In fact, she'd always enjoyed a lively give-and-take with most of them. Her silence since that awful day in the courtroom had spoken volumes. It had conveyed her sense of shame and guilt, emotions she had to put behind her if she was ever to function effectively in a courtroom again.

She glanced at the cameramen to be sure they were set up. "Shall we get started?" At their nods, she looked directly into the closest camera. "Although I have done so privately, I would like to publicly apologize to Letitia Baldwin's family, as well as to the people of this city for the part I played in the miscarriage of justice that occurred in Tiny Slocum's trial. I could tell you that I was just doing my job and that would be true, but it's a sad truth when a guilty man goes free because of it. I could tell you that I believed in Tiny Slocum's innocence and that would be true as well, but it doesn't say much about my judgment, and for that I am deeply sorry."

Her chin rose a notch. "I know that I can't change any of that, but I can promise you and, just as importantly, myself, that I will never again go into a case without evaluating the impact of my defense more thoroughly and being absolutely certain in my heart that what I'm doing serves the cause of justice. I owe that much to the honor of this profession."

She swallowed hard and fought to hold her gaze steady. "Now I'll take those questions."

"Ms. D'Angelo, will you continue to practice law?" Lynda Stone, daytime anchor for a network affiliate, asked. "And why haven't you been around to answer questions?"

They'd never gotten along and it seemed to Ashley as if the woman was eager to gloat over Ashley's current professional predicament. Ashley met her gaze evenly. "Let me answer the last question first. I needed some time to think about what had happened and my role in it. As for your other question, absolutely, I will continue to practice law, though I'll admit to having had a lot of self-doubts in recent weeks. In the end, I realized that I still believe passionately in our legal system. Nothing is perfect, but it's the best one on the face of the earth. And I think I can still make a valuable contribution."

"Really?" Ms. Stone asked, her voice laced with skepticism. "You honestly think you can be effective after this? Will any jury trust you?"

"One case, one mistake, doesn't negate a track record like mine," Ashley said succinctly. "And cases should be won or lost based on the evidence, not the attorneys involved. In the end, that's what happened in this one. Sadly, the prosecutor didn't come into the case fully prepared with indisputable evidence. I'll leave it to others to decide if the fault was his or the police department's. Unfortunately as it turned out, I was able to take advantage of that in defense of my client."

"Would you conduct the defense the same way if you had to do it over?" the anchorwoman asked.

"If you're asking if I'd defend Mr. Slocum in the same way knowing he was guilty, the answer is no. I would have done everything in my power to persuade him to accept a plea bargain."

"And if he had refused?" Ms. Stone asked.

"I would have stepped down as his counsel," she said.

"Even though he's entitled to the best defense available?" Ms. Stone persisted.

Ashley nodded. "Yes. I have to live with my conscience. Besides, Boston has plenty of qualified criminal defense attorneys who could have handled his case, including others at my own firm."

"Very noble, now that you have the advantage of hindsight," the anchorwoman said bitingly. "Will you stay with that firm?"

Ashley was certain from the malicious glint in the woman's eyes that she already knew the answer. "I believe some of you already know that I've quit."

"Why is that?" The question came from an unfamiliar reporter in the back of the room.

"I no longer felt we were a good fit. I'm sure the partners agreed," she said wryly. "But, of course, I wouldn't dream of speaking for them."

"Even though they had no problem speaking for you?" Frank Lyman asked. "In fact, they seemed quite eager to jump into the spotlight."

Ashley had always found Frank's biting wit a breath of fresh air. It was so again this morning. "Some people abhor a vacuum," she commented. "And if there was one in this instance, I created it by running away. I'm sure they felt they had to fill the void."

"You're being very gracious," someone commented. "Don't you feel as if they were capitalizing on a tragedy?"

"I'll leave it to you to interpret their motives."

Lynda Stone gave her another smirking look. "Any other firms in town made an offer to you?"

Ashley refused to lose her cool. "None knew until this moment that I might be available, but thank you for giving me an opportunity to put the word out." She smiled. "Unfortunately, though, my plan is to go into private practice elsewhere."

"Where?" the woman prodded. "New York? Washington?"

Ashley saw what she was trying to do. Unless Ashley came up with some dream offer, anything else Ashley said would sound like a demotion of sorts, a step down. She gave her reply careful thought. She refused to let anyone think she was running away because she thought she couldn't cut it in the big leagues anymore.

"I've had a few weeks to sort out my priorities," she began slowly. "I've found that not everything begins and ends in Boston. There are plenty of places in need of a lawyer with my skills and much satisfaction to be had in making sure that everyone has an equal shot at justice. I've also realized that there's more to life than the law and I hope to have an announcement on that front in the very near future."

Determined to end the press conference on her own terms, she beamed directly at Lynda Stone. "Thanks so much for giving me this opportunity to speak out. I'm sure we'll cross paths again."

She turned and walked away, this time with her shoulders back and her head held high. For the first time in weeks she felt as if she'd reclaimed her self-respect. As her parents and Jo came up to flank her, she realized it felt damn good.

Now it was time to get back to Virginia and fight for the man she loved.

* * *

Damn, but she was magnificent! Josh caught a snippet of Ashley's press conference on the national news. The miscarriage of justice in the Tiny Slocum case had made the network newscast a few weeks back. Because the attorney involved had been all but invisible, he hadn't realized at the time that it was Ashley. In fact, he hadn't put it all together until she'd told him about the dilemma that had brought her to Rose Cottage. Now he had to give the network credit for following up with Ashley's side of the story, albeit they gave her time for little more than a footnote compared to the length of the original segment.

He had a hunch offers would pour in once the other major law firms in Boston caught wind of the fact that a high-profile, talented lawyer was without a job. Any sensible firm would want such a class act with her incredible legal mind on staff. What would she do once they started dangling money and power in front of her? He wished he were convinced that she would choose Virginia, would choose *him*.

He couldn't sit around Idylwild waiting for her to come back, though. He'd go stir-crazy. He had decisions of his own to make, office space to lease, letterhead to be designed and printed. He had to go back to Richmond and put his condo on the market, pack up the few things that really mattered to him and sell the rest. None of that was contingent on Ashley's return.

But for some reason, he couldn't make himself get started. He wanted to know if they were going to be a team. More than that, he needed to know if she'd forgiven him, if she was even remotely interested in marrying a man who had a hefty bank account and a professional job.

He was still staring listlessly at the now-dark television screen when Mike appeared in the doorway. He'd gotten in the habit of strolling over whenever he was at loose ends. This visit had to mean that Melanie had taken Jessie somewhere for the day and left Mike to his own devices. It was almost pathetic how lost the man was without his wife and daughter. Josh was beginning to understand how he felt. He felt a little lost and vulnerable himself these days.

"You look like hell," Mike observed cheerfully.

"It's a good thing you're not hoping to pursue a career as a motivational speaker," Josh retorted.

"Want to go out for a beer?"

"No."

"Want to order a pizza?"

"No."

"I'm sensing a pattern here," Mike commented. "Are you up for company?"

"Not really." He regarded Mike speculatively. "I don't suppose you know if or when Ashley's coming back?"

"Sorry. I'm not in the loop on that one. Melanie's been walking around all grim-faced ever since that press conference on TV. She saw maybe ten seconds and concluded that the world is out to destroy her sister. I pity Lynda Stone if they ever cross paths. I'm not sure I realized my wife had such a vicious streak in her."

Josh stared at him in surprise. "Did Melanie see the same clip I saw? I thought Ashley was amazing."

Mike grinned. "You'd think she was amazing if she drew little stick figures and called it art."

"Possibly," he admitted.

"I assume, though, that seeing her on TV is what put you in this odd mood," Mike said.

He nodded.

"Why?" Mike asked.

"What if she decides she has to stay up there and fight for her reputation?"

Mike gave him a bland look. "What if she does?"

"How the hell will we work things out then?"

"Creatively," Mike said. "Planes fly. The phones around here work. You'll manage, at least if you want to badly enough." He gave him a sly look. "Or you could move to Boston."

Josh shuddered. "Not likely."

"You would if you loved her enough and it was where she had to be."

Would he do that in the name of love? Josh tried to imagine it and couldn't. Unfortunately, he couldn't en-vision his life anywhere without Ashley in it. He sup-posed if that meant moving to Boston, he'd find a way to handle it. He'd played in a shark-infested pool before. He could do it again, especially with Ashley added to the stakes.

In the meantime, though, maybe he'd take a leap of faith and put a deposit down on office space right here in town. With luck, he'd find a place with room enough for two lawyers just in case she decided to come back and they worked things out.

He got to his feet, grabbed a jacket and headed for the door.

Mike stared after him without budging. "Where are you going?"

"To put a down payment on my future," he said at once. "Want to come?"

Mike grinned. "Can I call Melanie first?"

"Absolutely not."

Mike seemed to weigh that for a minute, then shrugged. "Oh, well. How much hell can she put me through? Count me in."

Ashley had been back in town for twenty-four hours and she still hadn't seen Josh. She'd debated simply calling him, but each time she'd reached for the phone, she'd stopped herself. She'd done a lot of thinking in Boston and she knew what she wanted. At least she thought she did.

She did know that they needed to have this conversation in person. She wanted to look into his eyes when she told him she was staying. She needed to see if that mattered to him at all.

Half a dozen times she was tempted to take her kayak out on the water and paddle along until she ran into him, hopefully not literally again. But she had too much pride to do it. Besides, it was cold as hell out and he was the one who owed her an apology, at least almost as much as she owed him one. She had to give him time to reach that conclusion on his own. If he didn't, well, she could still take matters into her own hands. She wouldn't let this absurd impasse go on forever.

Maybe the delay was a good thing. Maybe she could manage to think clearly about what she really wanted without getting her hormones all tangled up in the decision. In Boston, she'd all but made up her mind to open a practice right here, but was it what she really wanted? Or had it been a knee-jerk reaction after she'd accepted that there was nothing left for her back home?

And how much of her thinking had been based on having a future with Josh? Could she stay here in this quiet place, maybe go into private practice, if Josh were never to be a part of her life?

She sat beside her kitchen window looking out at the brilliant blue sky, the calm water reflecting the trees that had already turned, their leaves now bright splashes of autumn colors. She felt the once-familiar calm steal through her. How long had it been since she'd known such a blissful lack of stress? Years, if she were being totally honest about it. She'd thought she needed the stress to survive, but she didn't. She'd discovered that other things made her feel alive.

Yes, she could stay. In fact, she was eager to stay. She'd tapped into a serenity here that she'd never expected to want or enjoy. Now she knew she needed it to be a whole woman and not just a workaholic lawyer.

And she had family here. Maggie and Melanie were building their lives here. Boston would always be home, but with her parents and Jo still there, she could visit as often as she wanted to. Maybe this place was even in her soul, just as it was in her mother's. Maybe there was something to this whole roots business that made her feel as if she'd *come* home, rather than run away from it.

She glanced around Rose Cottage and considered the whimsical notion that it was magical. Maybe it was.

Two of her sisters had fallen in love here. There was no denying that. Now she was on the same path.

"I want to stay," she said aloud, testing the words, testing the sentiment. The instant she'd said it, the last of the second thoughts faded and she felt an even deeper kind of peace steal through her.

An hour later she was standing in front of a building with office space for rent in Irvington. Real estate wasn't exactly easy to come by now that the area had been discovered by other professionals looking for a more leisurely way of life.

"Sorry I'm late, but my other appointment took longer than I expected. I have to tell you that someone else is interested in this space, too," the real estate agent said when she finally arrived looking harried. "He looked at it an hour ago."

Ashley seized on what the woman hadn't said. "But he didn't put down a deposit?"

"No. He had to go home for his checkbook. I probably shouldn't even be showing it to you, since he said he'd be back any minute now, but I've had enough be-back customers in my day to know to hedge my bets. I want to be honest with you, though. If he does show up, he has first crack at it."

Ashley slipped into full-lawyer mode. Even without going inside, she could tell this space would be perfect. It was on a main street in a Victorian house that had been converted to offices. The available space was on the first floor with windows facing the street and the giant oak tree that shaded the porch. The building had history, substance and charm. She was ready to fight for it. "Did he sign any papers? Did you make a verbal agreement to hold it?"

The woman looked at her curiously. "Let me guess. You're a lawyer."

Ashley gave her a rueful nod. "I guess it shows."

"Funny. It showed on him, too." Her eyes lit speculatively. "It's a big space. If you hit if off, maybe you could hook up, go into practice together."

"I don't think so," Ashley said, but the words trailed off when she spotted Josh pulling into a parking space right beside them.

"Is that the other prospective tenant?" she asked the woman.

"Oh, my," she said worriedly. "It is. I hope he's not furious about this."

"Let me handle it," Ashley said, then snatched a dollar out of her pocket. "There's my deposit. You'll get the rest in ten minutes."

"But you haven't even seen it."

"Doesn't matter," Ashley said. "It will do. Now I have another negotiation to complete. Meet me inside in ten minutes."

The agent glanced from Josh to her and back again. "If you say so."

He looked so good. Better than he had a right to. He should have looked as miserable as she had felt every minute since they'd fought. He stood where he was, regarding her suspiciously.

"What are you doing here?" he asked.

"Same thing you are, apparently. Trying to rent office space."

An unmistakable spark of hope lit in his eyes. "Really?"

She nodded, her gaze locked on his face. "I'm staying, Josh. You'll just have to get used to it."

"So am I," he said easily. "Think you can get used to that?" There was an undeniable challenge in his voice.

She nodded confidently. "I know I can. In fact, I was counting on it."

Silence fell. It lasted for what seemed like an eternity before he finally spoke again.

"Think we can get past the mistakes we both made?" he asked. "You were awfully furious with me."

"Are you reminding me of how angry I was just so I'll give up and let you have this office?"

"I'm reminding you because I need to know that's in the past. I'm reminding you because I love you and I hate being separated from you. I want you to be sure, because it would kill me if you walked away again."

She barely contained a sigh of relief. "I have an idea," she said, kicking pride out of the window to reach for what she wanted, what she needed. "Want to rent part of that space from me? I'll negotiate a fair deal."

He grinned. "Nice try, but that space is mine. I might consider letting you share it."

She gave him a wicked grin of her own. "I'm the one who put a deposit down, smart guy."

"But I had a verbal agreement with the agent. I can sue to make sure she honors it."

"You could," Ashley admitted.

"Then, again, I think I might have a better idea."

"Oh?"

"We could get married and share a life that just happens to include this office space."

Why quibble over terms, when it was the deal she'd been praying for? She held out her hand. "Deal."

"Just like that?" he asked, looking vaguely surprised.

"I'm going to trust my judgment on this one. I don't think it's letting me down, after all."

"I won't let you down, that's for sure. Not if I can help it."

Instead of taking her hand, he pulled her into his arms and kissed her thoroughly. "Now we have a deal," he said firmly. "We'll seal it in a church with all the appropriate bells and whistles, but it's binding now."

"Spoken like a true lawyer," she said, oddly pleased. It was something she would have said herself, if he'd given her the chance.

"You're not still furious that I don't fish for a living?"

She shook her head. "Not as long as you take me with you from time to time when we play hooky from the office."

"That's a promise."

"And you'll bait my hook," she said, going for broke as long as he was in such an amenable mood.

He laughed. "You can bait your own hook, sweetheart. In fact, I should probably have you bait mine. You've reeled in more fish lately than I have."

She wound her arms around his neck. "Reeled myself in a big one just this afternoon, in fact."

Ashley glanced up just then and saw the real estate agent staring down at them with a stunned expression.

"We'll take it," she called up.

A grin spread over the woman's face.

"What made you say yes so quickly?" Ashley asked Josh. "I know I'd hurt you."

He shrugged. "Maybe I saw you slip her that dollar and this was the only way I could think of to make sure my law practice didn't wind up homeless."

"You'd marry me just to have a decent law office?" she inquired with a hint of indignation.

"No, I'd marry you under any condition. The office is just a nice bonus," he assured her.

"How will I ever know that for sure?"

"To prove how much I love and respect you, I'll let you put your name first on the door. How about that?"

"D'Angelo and Madison? Sounds good to me."

He shook his head. "Madison and Madison sounds even better."

Ashley laughed. "You really are a clever lawyer, aren't you?"

"Takes one to know one, darlin'."

Epilogue

"**I** am getting very tired of my daughters getting married in such a hurry that there's no time to plan a proper wedding," Colleen D'Angelo said wearily as the entire family relaxed in the parlor of the family home in Boston after Ashley and Josh's wedding ceremony.

The guests had gone, but Ashley and Josh were still there. He'd insisted on going over the marriage license one last time to make sure every *t* had been crossed and every *i* had been dotted. Ashley could have told him they had been because she'd gone over it herself, several times, in fact.

She slipped her arms around his waist. "You know that piece of paper isn't what really matters," she told him.

"Then why'd we go through all this fuss that obviously wore your mother out just to get it?"

"Because living in sin wasn't in the cards. In this family, we do things the old-fashioned way."

He turned and pressed a kiss to her lips. "You don't strike me as an old-fashioned woman, Mrs. Madison. Are you going to stay home with the kids and bake cookies?"

"Nope," she said complacently. "I'm going to bring them with me to the office and pick up cookies from the bakery on the way. I think they'll get over the trauma of it."

He laughed. "I imagine they will." He studied her intently. "We never talked about kids. Maybe we should have. How many do you want?"

"Two, three. How about you?"

"I'm rather partial to four. I like the way you and your sisters stick together. I want our kids to have that."

"That doesn't have anything to do with the fact that there are four of us. It has to do with the way we were raised. Loyalty was ingrained in us."

"I know." He glanced over at Jo. "What will happen to Jo now that the rest of you are going to be in Virginia? Won't she be a little lost?"

Ashley had worried about the very same thing. She'd even tried discussing it with Jo, but her baby sister had insisted she was going to be just fine in Boston. Unspoken was the fact that Jo had always kept herself a little apart from the rest of them.

"She says she's content here," Ashley said.

"I suppose she can always come and visit," Josh suggested.

"I said the same thing, but she had the oddest reaction. She brushed me off. She said she wasn't like the rest of us, that she had no intention of running away to Rose Cottage, not ever, no matter what happened in her life."

Josh looked as perplexed by that as Ashley had been. "I suppose there's no law that she has to like it down there, just because you, Melanie and Maggie do," he said.

"But that's just it," Ashley protested. "She always loved it as much as we did when we were kids. In fact, she could hardly wait to get back there each summer."

"Things change," Josh said. "She's an adult now."

"I still think it's weird. A couple of times when she drove down with us, she acted almost as if she didn't want to go out in public, as if she was afraid of something."

Josh's gaze turned speculative. "Or someone."

Ashley stared at him, her indignation immediately rising. "Do you think someone there hurt her?"

Josh grinned. "Slow down, tiger. I'm merely speculating. And to tell you the truth, I think there are a lot more interesting things we could be doing on our wedding night than worrying about your baby sister and manufacturing problems where there might not be any at all."

Ashley immediately responded to the heat in his eyes. "Think so?"

"Know so," he said. "I know this cozy little gathering is all for us, but I say it's time to head for our hotel room. We can get a head start on our honeymoon."

She laughed. "I think we've been getting a head start on that for weeks now. Where are we going, by the way? You still haven't told me."

"Because it's a surprise."

"I hate surprises."

He grinned. "I know, my darling control freak, but you'll love this one. Trust me."

She sighed and pressed her forehead to his, surrendering. "I do," she said softly. Despite everything that had happened to her, despite the betrayals she'd suffered, she did trust this man with her heart.

That didn't mean she didn't want to know where they were going first thing in the morning, though. "How am I supposed to pack?" she groused.

"Maggie packed for you," he assured her, his eyes glinting with amusement. "Besides, it's a honeymoon. How much clothing could you possibly need?"

"A lot more than you're obviously anticipating," she said, "especially if you keep playing games with me."

"I've got it covered," he insisted. "I promise."

"Is it warm? Cold?"

"There will be heat," he said cheerfully.

"Indoors or out?"

"Wherever we are," he assured her.

"You're really not going to tell me, are you?"

"No."

"Why?"

"Because it's a man's job to plan the honeymoon."

"Who says?"

"I read it somewhere."

She laughed at that. "You have not been reading books on wedding etiquette."

"I needed something to put me to sleep during all those lonely nights you were up here planning the wedding."

"I was gone for a week."

"Too long," he insisted. "One night is too long."

She smiled. "Then isn't it lucky that we're going to be together for the rest of our lives?"

"Damn straight," he said, waving the marriage license under her nose. "I made sure of it."

"No loopholes?" she teased.

"Not a one. This thing is airtight. Not even a lawyer as clever as you could find a loophole."

"Good," she said, pleased. "Because I intend to hold you to it."

Josh laughed. "Never doubted it for a minute."

* * * * *

For the Love of Pete

Prologue

"**P**ack your bags and come to Virginia," Ashley commanded the morning after Jo's life had been turned upside down by her lying, cheating ex-fiancé.

Jo sighed. She'd planned to spend the whole day in bed, licking her wounds in private, maybe eating the entire pint of Ben & Jerry's ice cream she had stashed in the freezer. Her funk had been interrupted before it could even get going by this call from all three of her sisters. She knew they were all on the line, even though Ashley was the only one who'd spoken so far. She could hear them breathing, while they left the coaxing to their big sister.

"How did you find out?" She thought she'd made it absolutely clear to their folks that her broken engagement was something she'd wanted to announce to her sisters herself…maybe next June, when the shock had worn off.

Unfortunately Max and Colleen D'Angelo weren't great at keeping quiet. They thought families should stick together in times of crisis. Her sisters had learned the lesson well. Until now, Jo had always found that comforting.

"Nothing stays secret in this family for long," Ashley responded, stating the obvious. "What I don't understand is why you didn't say something yourself. You should have called us the minute you caught James cheating."

"Why?" Jo grumbled. "So you could come up here and personally rip his heart out?" The image gave her a certain amount of bloodthirsty satisfaction, which she found deeply troubling. She liked to think of herself as kindhearted.

"That or some other part of his anatomy," Ashley said.

"That's precisely the reason I didn't call," Jo explained, shaking off the chill that had run down her spine at her sister's words. Ashley was perfectly capable of making good on such a threat. She had the protective-big-sister thing down pat. "I handled it in my own way. Besides, I didn't want all this sympathy, and I definitely don't want to run away. The humiliation of discovering James in bed with another woman was bad enough. I won't let him chase me off. My life is here in Boston. I'm not budging because of that scumbag."

In fact, this whole mess had reminded her of just how determined she was to make a life for herself in Boston. It had brought back way too many memories of another man she'd loved, another man who had cheated on her and forever ruined the love she'd once felt for Rose Cottage, her grandmother's home in Virginia. Even now, fresh as this was, she was having a hard time deciding which betrayal had been more devastating.

Worse, even though they'd never known about that earlier disaster, Jo had anticipated exactly how her sisters would react to this one. Though she sometimes thought of herself as the odd man out—the only one whose name wasn't somehow tied to *Gone With the Wind,* her Southern mother's favorite book—she'd known they would rally around her and insist that she come to Virginia, where they could fuss over her. The scene of that heartbreaking first betrayal was the last place on earth she wanted to be—not that her sisters had any way of knowing that. She'd kept her own counsel back then and dealt with the anguish in private. Only her beloved grandmother had known the details, and she'd honored Jo's wishes never to discuss what had happened.

"You may as well give in and do this gracefully," Maggie chimed in on another extension, dismissing Jo's protests.

"Yes," Melanie added. "Don't make us come up to Boston to get you."

Jo's chuckle turned into a sob. It was too late to regret her part in insisting that each of her sisters go to Rose Cottage after their lives had fallen apart. How could she explain that it was different for her without divulging the secret she'd kept from them all these years? Then the fussing would really begin in earnest.

"I can't," she whispered. It was one thing for Ashley, Maggie and Melanie to make new lives for themselves in Virginia, but Rose Cottage was where Jo's heart had been broken the first time. How could she go there to heal now, when there were so many ghosts from the past to be faced in that place? Visiting for a day or two had been difficult enough. Staying any longer, risking a chance encounter with the man she'd once loved so deeply, would be torment.

"I'd like to know why not," Ashley demanded. "If you can't take the time off work, quit."

"Work's not the issue," Jo said miserably, though it didn't surprise her that it was the first thing her big sister had thought of. Even now, with her workaholic tendencies held in check by her new husband, Ashley was still driven.

"Then what is?" Ashley asked.

"I'm better off here," Jo said, knowing it was a weak response but unwilling to admit the truth. None of them knew how crazy in love she'd been during that last summer she'd spent at Rose Cottage. They'd all been busy with summer jobs back in Boston that year. She'd spent the entire summer alone with her grandmother...and with Pete.

She'd been so sure Pete Catlett was *the* one. She'd believed him when he said he loved her, believed it enough to make love with him, believed it well enough when he'd promised to be waiting when she returned the following year.

But even before the last of the autumn leaves had fallen, her grandmother had casually mentioned that Pete had gotten married. A few months later, there had been mention of a baby, too. A boy.

She and her grandmother had both maintained the pretense that Cornelia Lindsey was doing little more than passing along local gossip about an acquaintance, but Jo had heard the compassion underlying the words, the awareness that what she was telling Jo would devastate her.

Jo had felt utterly betrayed, especially because the young man she'd loved and trusted hadn't even had the courage to tell her himself. Not that that would have made the pain any easier to bear, but it would have reassured her that she hadn't misjudged him entirely, that she had mattered to him, at least for a time.

It had taken her years to find the courage to risk her heart again, and just look what had happened, the same damn thing...or something that felt a whole lot like it.

No, Virginia was definitely not the place for her. She needed to stay right here in Boston and bury herself in work. She liked her job as a landscape designer. She had her friends, even if none of them were as close as the sisters who were insisting she come to Rose Cottage so they could hover over her.

"I can't come to Virginia," she said again, her tone flat and, she hoped, unequivocal.

Melanie heaved an exaggerated sigh. "I guess that means we leave in the morning, right, Ash and Maggie?"

"I can be ready by 5:00 a.m.," Ashley said. "How about the rest of you?"

"Absolutely," Melanie responded.

"Guys!" Jo protested with what she knew was wasted breath. They weren't going to be satisfied until they'd seen her for themselves, babied her for a few days or weeks. It was the curse of being the youngest that they thought she needed extra care at a time like this.

"You can stop us," Ashley reminded her. "All you have to do is agree to come quietly. Settle in for the winter, Jo. It'll be peaceful and quiet. We won't bug you unless you want us to."

"That's a joke. You're already bugging me," Jo pointed out.

"Yes, but with the best intentions," Melanie said cheerfully.

"Let me see what I can work out," Jo said finally. "Maybe I'll come for the weekend so you can see that I'm not a complete basket case. James isn't worth falling apart over."

She figured she could hide the truth about her aversion to Rose Cottage for a couple of days, then scamper straight back to Boston. In fact, two days seemed safe enough, however she looked at it. After all, she hadn't run into Pete on any of her previous brief visits. She'd been very careful not to spend too much time in public.

Though her reluctance to go places had clearly aroused her sisters' suspicions, they'd never called her on it with more than the most cursory questions. Any hesitation she showed now, they would blame on her broken heart. They'd never guess it had anything at all to do with a long-ago relationship that had ended badly and a panicky fear that she would encounter Pete Catlett again.

Not that her self-imposed isolation had worked all that well when it came to her own feelings. She'd been aware of Pete every second of every visit. Just driving to Rose Cottage, she'd seen his name on construction jobs all over in the small waterfront towns of White Stone and Irvington. Knowing that he had built a reputation for himself doing what he loved had only stirred mixed emotions. She wished she were a big enough person to be happy for him, but a part of her had seen that success as further evidence of betrayal. She was the one who'd encouraged him to fight for his dream, despite his mother's insistence that he attend college instead. Now he'd achieved that dream with some other woman by his side.

"A weekend won't cut it," Melanie said firmly. "We made Ashley come for three weeks. If Ms. Workaholic could do that, you ought to be able to commit for at least a month, minimum."

"Right," Ashley agreed. "Besides, you work for a landscape company. How much work do you do in winter, anyway? And if you get the itch to design something, I'll bet Mike can put you to work. He has more landscaping jobs than he can handle these days."

"You worked all of this out before you called, didn't you?" Jo said, increasingly resigned to her fate. "You even have Mike in on it. Does he know you're now hiring employees for him, Ashley?"

"Of course," Ashley said. "I never go into a courtroom or into an argument with you unprepared. Besides, this was Mike's idea, right, Melanie?"

"Absolutely," Melanie said, speaking for her husband. "He really is swamped, Jo. You'd be doing him—and me—a favor. I'd like to see a whole lot more of my husband than I do. Come on, Jo, say yes."

Jo sighed.

"Call us when you're a couple of hours away," Maggie said, obviously convinced that they'd won. "We'll get a fire going and some dinner on the table. Rose Cottage is a wonderful place for you to be. It certainly did the trick for the rest of us. I can't think of anything cozier than sitting in front of a fire and letting all your cares drift away while the snow falls outside."

"It snows in Boston," she reminded them, making one last halfhearted attempt to put them off. "I hate snow."

"You do not," Melanie protested. "Besides, it's common there. It's so rare here that it's magical. Just wait. Maybe you'll follow tradition and meet the man of your dreams here, too."

"Whatever," Jo said, seeing little sense in trying to shake their faith in the cottage's magical properties when it came to romance.

In her current mood, however, she couldn't imagine that there was enough magic on earth, much less at Rose Cottage, to make her feel one bit better, not about snow, and definitely not about love.

The irony, of course, was that she was the first of the D'Angelo sisters to find the right man at Rose Cottage. She wondered what they'd think of the tradition if they knew how badly that had ended.

1

As if to prove her sisters' point, snow had started falling an hour after Jo's arrival at Rose Cottage. She stared out the window as the big, wet flakes landed on the ground. With some effort, she bit back an hysterical sob.

"What?" Ashley asked, coming up to slide a comforting arm around her shoulders.

Jo turned to her big sister, her eyes stinging with tears. "Do you guys have to be right about everything?" she asked in frustration.

Ashley grinned. "Pretty much. Why?"

"The snow's started right on cue. Surely you don't actually control the weather."

Hearing that, Melanie and Maggie rushed over to join them.

"It's going to be beautiful," Melanie promised, stepping up beside her and circling an arm around Jo's waist. "You'll see. By morning it will be like a winter wonderland out there."

"And I'll be trapped in here all by myself," Jo grumbled, awash in an unbecoming and uncommon sea of self-pity. "I'll have nothing to do but think." She shuddered at the prospect. Her thoughts were not all that happy these days. She didn't want to be alone with them.

"We'll rescue you," Ashley promised.

"I'll bring Jessie by and the two of you can go sledding," Melanie suggested, referring to her energetic stepdaughter. "That'll put some color in your cheeks."

"It's cold out there."

"Please," Melanie commented. "Compared to Boston, this is practically tropical. Besides, you used to love sledding."

"When I was eight," Jo muttered.

"Okay, if that doesn't appeal to you, we can all sit here in front of the fire and drink hot chocolate and eat s'mores," Ashley said, her tone soothing, as if she sensed that Jo was about to come unglued on them. "Or Maggie can bake. The whole house will fill up with all these wonderful scents, just the way it did at home when Mom made us cookies on snowy days."

Jo knew they would all be on her doorstep first thing in the morning tomorrow and every day after, unless she put a stop to it right this second. If she ate as many cookies as Maggie was likely to bake, she'd be a blimp by spring.

"Okay, enough," she said firmly. "Don't listen to all my grumbling. You can't turn your lives upside down for me. I appreciate your concern, but I'll be fine. If my thoughts start getting too dark and dreary, I can always go for a walk."

"Of course you can. And there are a few things around this place that need to be taken care of," Ashley said briskly. "Since I was the last one here, I'll make a list of the stuff I never got to do. In fact, I'll make a couple of calls first thing tomorrow and try to line up the right people to come by. You'll just have to be here when they show up."

"I can't afford to spend a fortune on repairs," Jo reminded her. "Until Mike needs me for something, I'm on an unpaid leave of absence. My boss was generous in agreeing to keep the job open for me."

"Generous, my ass," Ashley retorted. "You're the most talented person he has."

Jo grinned at her. "Thanks, big sister, but you're not only biased, you don't know a thing about landscape design."

"But Mike does," Melanie chimed in. "And he says you're good. Don't worry about money, Jo. You'll have all the work you want while you're here. You just have to speak up whenever you're ready."

"And in the meantime, don't worry about the repair bills," Ashley said. "We've pooled money to get this place fixed up. Melanie got the rooms painted and worked on the garden, Maggie made improvements in the kitchen." She shrugged. "I didn't do much, since Josh was teaching me to relax, so I've chipped in for the work that still needs to be done. All the bills will come to me. You'll just need to supervise."

Jo regarded them with bemusement. "Why waste any more money on this place? You all have your own homes now, and Mom hasn't been here since Grandmother died except to see you. Why spend a fortune to fix up Rose Cottage?"

"It's not a fortune. We've all agreed Rose Cottage

needs to stay in the family, which means it's sensible to keep it in good repair," Ashley said. "And it's yours for as long as you want it."

"Thanks," Jo said, her voice choked. Until she'd actually gotten here, she hadn't realized how much she missed her big sisters. Right this second, it didn't even matter that they were gathered around her in Rose Cottage, the site of her first painful love affair. "You guys are the best." She sniffed and brushed away a traitorous tear.

"Don't start bawling now," Maggie scolded, handing her a tissue. "Or we'll have to stick around till you're finished and we'll wind up being snowed in. Much as you love us right this second, I doubt you're up for a slumber party."

Jo forced a misty-eyed smile. "True." The last thing she wanted was to give her sisters too much time to cross-examine her. "Go, while you can. And call me when you get home, so I won't worry that you've skidded off the road and landed in a ditch."

Relieved by their acquiescence, she stood in the doorway watching until they were out of sight, then sighed heavily. The ground was almost covered with snow already, and there was no sign that it was stopping. It was a little like a winter wonderland, she admitted as she stared toward the Chesapeake Bay.

Once, when she'd been starry-eyed and in love, she had thought this would be the place she'd spend the rest of her life. Now it felt more like a beautiful prison.

At least she could leave it when it got to be too much, she reminded herself. If she managed to plaster a cheery smile on her face each time she saw her sisters, eventually they'd relent and let her go home. Until then, she'd lay low and pretend that she'd never even heard of Pete Catlett, much less loved him enough to let him break her heart.

Pete's answering service relayed the message that there were some loose and rotting boards on the porch at Rose Cottage, along with a plea that he get to them first thing in the morning if at all possible. The service hadn't said who'd called, though his guess was Ashley.

Damn, he thought, his mind immediately going back seven years to the summer when Rose Cottage had been like a second home to him. Maybe even more like the first real home he'd known. Mrs. Lindsey had had a soothing temperament, especially compared to his mother's quick flashes of irritation.

And, of course, there had been Jo with her huge blue eyes, scattering of freckles dusted across a pert nose and a mouth that had tempted him from the first time he'd seen those lush lips curve into a shy smile.

They had shared so many hopes and dreams that summer. He'd been so sure that in a few years they'd find a way to be together forever. He'd made a lot of promises that he'd had every intention of keeping.

Then he'd made one stupid, idiotic mistake in the first weeks after Jo had gone back to Boston, and his life had been sent in another direction entirely.

He'd wanted to blame Kelsey Prescott for getting pregnant, but the one thing he'd vowed to do the moment his father abandoned him and his mom was to be responsible. He'd sworn he would never walk out on a child of his, not even if he wasn't in love with the child's mother. He'd find some way to make it work. In his head, if not his heart, he'd accepted that he was every bit as responsible for that baby's creation as Kelsey was.

And he'd tried doing the right thing. Lord knows, he'd tried. But Kelsey had felt trapped and angry from the very beginning. She couldn't seem to let go of her bitterness the way Pete had tried valiantly to do. Nothing Pete had done could make up for the fact that she'd had to give up her dream of moving away to someplace more exciting than the rural area where they'd both grown up.

For five years, he'd fought a losing battle to keep her and his son, but now she and Davey were living in Richmond and Pete hardly ever saw his boy, except for the occasional weekend or holiday visits or a few bittersweet weeks each summer. In the end, things had turned out exactly the way he'd sworn they wouldn't, with him separated from his son. Had he been able to see into the future, maybe he would have done things differently. Maybe he and Jo could have found some way to work past the stupid mistake he'd made and the two of them could have been there for his son, giving him the kind of stable family he certainly didn't have now.

As it was, Pete had never had the courage to face Jo. He'd known she would never understand how he could claim to love her, then have sex with someone else a few weeks after she'd gone. Hell, he didn't entirely understand it himself, except that he'd been young and stupid and living in the moment. At twenty, he'd been more attuned to his hormones than his brain. He'd actually tried explaining that to Jo's grandmother, but even though Cornelia Lindsey hadn't said a single harsh or accusing word, the disappointment in her eyes had only compounded his sense of shame. He couldn't bear the prospect of seeing that same disappointment in Jo's eyes, so he'd stayed silent and let others break her heart with the news.

Over the past year, he'd seen people coming and going at Rose Cottage. He knew that, one by one, Jo's sisters had come there, fallen in love and married. All were now living in the area, but he hadn't caught the first glimpse of Jo.

Feeling awkward and ill at ease the whole time, he'd even done some work for Ashley and her new husband, Josh Madison, but the subject of Jo had never even come up, eventually convincing him that Ashley didn't know about the betrayal. As clannish as they were, he'd supposed they all hated him on Jo's behalf. It had been a relief, in a way, to know that she'd kept silent, though it worried him some that she apparently hadn't even turned to those closest to her back then. Still, his guilt ran deep.

Even after that reassuring encounter with Ashley several weeks back, he dismissed the message he'd received this morning. He told himself it was because he was swamped with work. Now, though, he had no more excuses. On his way home, he ignored the churning in his gut and drove to Rose Cottage to take a look at what needed to be done.

Snow still clung to the trees and lay several inches deep on the front steps. Even though the snow was undisturbed by footprints, there was smoke curling from the chimney. A light was burning in the living room, and another shone brightly in the kitchen.

Pete sat in his car and debated whether he ought to drive right on. He wasn't sure he was ready to face any of the D'Angelo women, not at Rose Cottage. He'd only been able to work for Ashley because the job had been at Josh's home. He knew that stepping through this door would strip away the scab on an old wound.

"Don't be an idiot," he finally muttered. It was a job. No big deal. They'd probably rented the place to some stranger. There was nothing here to be afraid of. Chiding himself for his cowardice, he strode to the front door and knocked.

When the door swung open, he wasn't sure who was more stunned, him or the pale woman who stared at him with sad, haunted eyes.

"What are you doing here?" he and Jo said in a chorus.

He tried for a smile. "Sorry. I had a call to come by about some needed repairs. I had no idea you were here. Frankly, I can't believe you called me."

She regarded him with bewilderment. "I didn't. What repairs? Ashley said something about making a few calls, but I had no idea she'd done it. We never even went over her list of what needs to be done."

"Whoever called said something about some loose and rotting boards on the porch."

"It was dark when I got here. I didn't notice."

"You just arrived, then?"

She shook her head. "Last night, actually."

"And you haven't been out all day," he said.

She regarded him with suspicion. "How do you know

that?" she asked, a surprisingly defensive note in her voice.

"Settle down, darlin'. Nobody's been tattling on you, at least not to me." He gestured toward the steps. "The only footprints out here are mine."

Her temper deflated at once. "Sorry," she said stiffly.

He hesitated, then forced himself to ask, "Would you prefer I send someone else over to check out the porch? I could have someone come by in the morning. Your sister obviously didn't know that calling me would be a problem."

Indecision was written all over her face. She looked so lost, so thoroughly miserable, that Pete wanted to haul her into his arms and comfort her, but he no longer had that right. Once she would have slapped him silly if he'd tried, but something told him that whatever had sent her fleeing to Rose Cottage had wiped away that feistiness and strength.

"No," she said at last. "You're here. I don't want to try to explain to Ashley why I sent you away. I'll flip on the light so you can take a closer look."

Pete nodded. "Thanks."

A moment later, the light came on, and then the door shut firmly. He tried not to feel hurt at being so plainly dismissed and locked out, but he couldn't help it. Once he'd been warmly welcomed in this home. Once he'd been joyously welcomed by this woman. Having that door close quietly in his face was as effective as any slap. The message was just as clear: Jo would tolerate his presence as long as there was a job to do, but she wanted no further contact with him. Her reaction was only what he deserved, yet it rankled.

He spent a few minutes surveying the porch, determined that it needed to be totally replaced since half measures would only delay the inevitable. He made a few rough calculations on the notepad he always kept in his pocket, then knocked on the door again.

It took a long time for Jo to answer, and when she did, it was obvious she'd been crying. Her pale skin was streaked with tears. Pete's heart turned over at the sight.

"What?" she asked impatiently.

Forgetting all about the porch for the moment, he asked, "Jo, are you okay?"

"Nothing a little time won't cure," she said. "Or so they say. Personally, I think that's a crock."

He heard the unmistakable bitterness in her voice and concluded she was referring to something recent, though it could just as easily have had something to do with his betrayal all those years ago and a wound he'd caused that had yet to heal.

He shoved his hands in his pockets and risked another rejection. "Want to talk about it?"

"No, and certainly not with you," she said flatly. "What I want is to be left alone."

He knew he should take her at her word, but how could he? She looked as if she were on the verge of collapse. What were her sisters thinking, leaving her alone like this? Ignoring her words, he brushed right past her and walked inside the cottage, determined not to go until there was more color in her cheeks, even if anger at his presumption was what put it there.

It was like coming home. The paint was fresh and there were a few unfamiliar touches, but essentially it had hardly changed from the way he remembered it. It was warm and cozy with the fire blazing, the chairs covered with a cheery chintz fabric, the walls decorated with delicate watercolors of the Chesapeake Bay and one or two of the garden right here at Rose Cottage. Jo's grandmother had painted them. What they lacked in expertise, they made up for in sentiment.

"Have you eaten?" he asked briskly, heading for the kitchen as if he had a perfect right to do so. "I haven't and I'm starved."

Jo hurried to catch up with him, then faced him with a stubborn jut to her chin. "What is *wrong* with you?" she demanded. "You can't barge in here and take over, Pete."

"I just did, sweetheart. How about some soup?" he asked cheerfully, opening a cupboard to find it fully stocked with everything from chicken noodle to tomato soup. "Seems like the right kind of night for it. It's cold and raw outside."

The suggestion was greeted with silence. He took that as a good sign.

"Tomato soup and grilled cheese sandwiches," he decided, after checking out the contents of the fridge. "Your grandmother used to fix that for us all the time. Is it still your favorite?"

"I'm not hungry, and you need to go," Jo insisted, trying to reach around him to shut the cabinet door without actually touching him.

"I have time," he said, deliberately misinterpreting her objection and making it impossible for her to succeed in thwarting his actions. "Sit down. I'll have it ready in no time."

He began assembling the ingredients for their make-shift dinner with quick, efficient movements, finding pans where they'd always been, bowls and plates in the same cupboard. He was pretty sure the flower-trimmed plates had the same chips he remembered.

"Ah, you've already boiled water," he said, noting that the teakettle on the stove was still hot to the touch. "Tea bags in the same place?"

He didn't wait for a response, just kept on making the meal, flipping the sandwiches as the bread turned a golden brown, stirring the soup. This was Davey's favorite meal, too, so Pete had become something of an expert.

He took heart from the fact that Jo hadn't blown up and insisted that he go. At the same time, it was telling that she apparently didn't have the strength to fight his obviously unwanted presence. Eventually, she simply sighed and sat down.

"So, what brings you to Rose Cottage?" he asked as he set the soup and sandwich in front of her.

She stared at the food, then scowled at him. "I don't want this and I don't want to make small talk, especially not with you," she said with a bit more spirit.

"I get that," he said. "But the food's hot and I'm here, so why not make the best of it?"

She frowned. "Were you always this annoying?"

"Probably," he admitted. "You tended to see the good in people. You probably overlooked it."

"Must have," she muttered, but she picked up her spoon and tasted the soup.

Pete felt a small sense of triumph when she swallowed the first spoonful, then went back for more. When she picked up her sandwich, he did a little mental tap dance. The food—or her annoyance with him—was putting a little color back into her cheeks. She didn't look nearly as sad and defeated as she had when he'd first arrived. He would have put up with a lot worse than what she'd dished out to see that change in her.

When she finally glanced his way, she asked suspiciously, "Who really called you to come by here? Are you sure you didn't make the whole thing up?"

He shrugged. "I can't say for certain who called. The answering service took the message. You said Ashley had told you she was going to call someone, so I assume it was her."

"But you?" she asked skeptically.

He grinned. "My number's in the book, so why not me? Besides, I did some work for her and Josh a while back. They were happy with it. Unless you filled her head with a list of all my shortcomings since then, it makes perfect sense."

"I've never even mentioned your name to her."

"Then what's the big deal?"

"I think you know the answer to that."

"It's a coincidence, Jo, not some big, diabolical conspiracy I worked out with your sister. Trust me, I have more than enough work to keep me busy—I don't need to drop in on unsuspecting people and beg for little nuisance jobs like this. I got a call. I came by to check things out. That's it. Till I saw the lights and the smoke coming from the chimney, I had no clue anyone was staying here."

"Okay, so you're just following up on a call," she finally conceded. "You've done your duty. Leave your estimate. I'll get another one. You'll lose."

"I don't think so," he said. What he'd said was true—this was a nothing little job for him, but he intended to do it. In fact, he was going to stick to Jo like glue till he found out why she'd looked like death warmed over when he'd turned up. "Whoever called was right. The porch is a disaster. Better to rip it off and start from scratch before someone gets hurt."

"Fine, but I'm sure someone else can do it cheaper," she said flatly. "Heck, I could probably do the work myself if I put my mind to it."

He grinned at that. "Really? You think so?"

"How hard could it be to nail a few boards together?" she said brashly. "And I wouldn't be charging Ashley some exorbitant price for labor."

"You haven't seen my estimate yet," he reminded her, not even trying to hide his amusement at her obvious ploy to get rid of him. "You just don't want me hanging around."

She met his gaze, then looked away, the color in her cheeks deepening. "No," she said softly, then immediately apologized. "Sorry."

"No offense taken," he said easily. "I could have someone else come by, but whoever called asked specifically for me. When loyal customers do that, I do the work. It's a point of honor."

She frowned at him. "As if," she said bitterly.

Her comment was like a slap. It stung. "I suppose I deserved that," he admitted.

"And more," she retorted. "Look, Pete, you can forget

that whole trumped-up honor thing. I'll deal with my sisters. Besides, I thought you were building all these huge homes around here. Why would you want to waste time fixing up a porch?"

"Keeps me humble," he said lightly, though what he wanted to say was that it would give him a chance to be around her again, to maybe make amends for what he'd done to her seven years ago. Now that he'd actually seen Jo again, he knew that all those feelings he'd tamped down so that he could stay married to Kelsey were as strong as ever.

"It's a bad idea," she said, half to herself.

"Why?" he asked, though he knew perfectly well precisely why she would see it that way. Seeing her had shot his defenses to hell, too.

She skewered him with a disbelieving look.

"Okay, scratch that. You're still furious with me. Can't say I blame you. What I did to you was inexcusable."

"You're wrong," she said fiercely. "I don't feel anything at all where you're concerned. Seven years is a long time, Pete. What we had is so over."

It was a blatant lie. Pete could see that in her stormy eyes, which was why he decided there was no way in hell he was backing off on doing this job, no matter how hard she fought him.

"Then having me underfoot won't bother you at all," he said pleasantly.

"Why are you doing this?" she asked plaintively.

He ignored the question. He figured she already knew the answer. She just wasn't ready to acknowledge it yet.

"I'll be by around eight," he said decisively. "Hope you weren't planning to sleep late. I'm going to be noisy, and I could use a cup of coffee when I get here. Mine's lousy, but I seem to recall you brewed the strong stuff."

He decided he'd done what he could for tonight, declared his intentions as plainly as he could, gotten her blood to pumping in the only way he knew how short of kissing her. He got to his feet.

"'Night, darlin'. Good to see you." He dropped a kiss on her already overheated cheek and tried not to notice that she was sputtering with indignation as he left.

In fact, as he crossed the lawn, she uttered a few words he'd never even realized she knew. They weren't complimentary.

Even with those words echoing in his head as he climbed into his car, he caught himself whistling happily. Whatever was going on with Jo that had brought her scurrying to the safe haven of Rose Cottage, he intended to see that he was there to help her through it. Last time she'd been hurt, he'd been the cause. This time, he would be the solution.

And when all was said and done, when fences were finally mended, who knew what might happen next?

2

Of all the arrogant, annoying, impossible men on the face of the planet, how had Ashley somehow managed to come up with the one guaranteed to drive Jo insane? For a normally calm, placid individual, she'd used more curse words at top volume in the ten minutes following Pete's visit than she had in her entire lifetime. He'd apparently heard a few of them cross her lips, too, and they'd only made him laugh. The sound had reached her and, if anything, had only made her more furious. The man was absolutely insufferable. She definitely hadn't recalled that about him. It might have made things easier for her.

How dare he barge into Rose Cottage as if he had every right to be there? How dare he take over as if she were some basket case he didn't dare leave alone? Okay, so maybe she had looked a little pitiful when he'd first arrived, but that definitely wouldn't happen again. In the morning, she'd be ready for him. Too bad her grandmother had never kept a shotgun on the premises. Maybe waving one of those in his direction would convince him to leave her the hell alone.

She sighed as her flash of temper died. If that was what she really wanted.

The truth was her stupid heart had raced when she'd first glimpsed Pete on the porch. She could deny it till the cows came home, but on some level she'd been glad to see him. In fact, she'd shut the front door so securely to keep him from seeing any telltale reaction on her face. Or maybe just to prevent herself from flying straight into his powerful arms. On some primal level, that was exactly what she'd wanted to do. How idiotic was that? One glimpse of the man, and in five seconds her self-control and her good sense had been wrecked.

And that was before he'd ignored all her protests and barged in. After that, she hadn't had to fake her indignation. It took a lot of nerve for a man who'd all but destroyed her to walk inside her home and act as if nothing had happened, as if he belonged there. If he thought that half-assed acknowledgment that he'd mistreated her seven years ago was an acceptable apology, he was seriously mistaken. It was going to take more than a few pitiful words to win her forgiveness. She was going to make him work for it.

Now, unfortunately, it seemed that he was going to have plenty of time to come up with all the pretty words she needed to hear. He was going to be underfoot for who knew how long, and there wasn't a blessed thing she could do about it except stay as far away from Rose Cottage during the day as she possibly could.

As he'd probably guessed, firing him was not an option. It would only stir up more questions than she was prepared to answer. And perverse as he was, he'd probably see it as an admission that she was still attracted to him.

Which she was, dammit!

Her plan of action, such as it was, decided, Jo went to bed and tried to forget about how good Pete had looked in his snug, faded jeans and dark green sweater. Seven years had only made him more handsome. His face looked stronger and sexier with a day's stubble of beard shadowing his cheeks, and there was even more mischief in his dark eyes. Hell, the man radiated sex from every pore, which was something she had no business thinking about a married man, especially not a married man who'd broken her heart.

Come to think of it, for a married man he'd been awfully carefree about hanging out with her for a couple of hours when he should have been home with his wife and son. Obviously, his morals hadn't improved since the days when he'd slept with another woman shortly after professing his undying love for her. That alone should be warning enough for her to give him a very wide berth.

Because of that, she set the alarm for six. She'd be showered, dressed and on her way somewhere by seven, long before Pete showed up in the morning. It was one thing to agree to let him do the job Ashley had hired him to do. It was another thing entirely to stick around and watch and be tormented—and tempted—in the process.

Pete knew exactly how Jo's mind worked, which was one reason he was pulling up in front of Rose Cottage shortly after six-thirty in the morning. The fact that every light in the house was blazing told him he'd been right to guess that she would be preparing to be long gone before he turned up.

He sat in his truck with the heater pumped up on high and waited. Sure enough, at seven o'clock the lights began to switch off. Immediately after the last one went out, the front door opened. She was so busy concentrating on getting her key into the lock, she apparently didn't even notice when he cut the truck's engine, swung down from the front seat and stepped into her path. She turned around and ran smack into him. He steadied her and looked straight into eyes blazing with anger and dismay.

"Going somewhere?" he inquired, regarding her with amusement. "I don't recall you being such an early bird."

She frowned at him. "Why are you here?" she asked, guilt written all over her face.

"I told you I'd be here first thing this morning."

"You said eight o'clock."

"I did," he agreed. "And then I got to thinking."

Her gaze narrowed. "About what?"

"How likely it was that you'd bolt before I got here, if you had the chance."

"Maybe I was just going out to grab breakfast," she said defensively. "Maybe I'd planned to be back by eight."

"Did you?"

She avoided his gaze, apparently unwilling to utter a blatant lie. "Why does it even matter where I was going? You don't need me here. I'm sure you're perfectly capable of handling this very difficult job all by yourself."

"True, but I was counting on that coffee," he said cheerfully.

"I didn't make any coffee."

"Not a problem," he said, circling an arm around her shoulders and turning her in the direction of his truck. "Since I got such an early start, there's plenty of time for us to go into town and have breakfast together. I'll even treat."

"I am not going into town with you," she said, sounding horrified by the suggestion.

"Why not?"

"Because I'm not. It's a terrible idea. What on earth is wrong with you?"

Pete couldn't imagine why she found the idea so abhorrent. He concluded, though, that asking wasn't likely to get him a straight answer. "Then I'd say we're at an impasse," he said with a shrug. "Everyone knows it's vitally important to have coffee for the men on a job site. It's like an unwritten rule."

Her scowl deepened, but she whirled around and headed for the house. "Fine. I'll make your damn coffee, but then I'm leaving."

He beamed at her. "Works for me," he said.

Inside, though, he opened the refrigerator and took out eggs, bacon and butter. "Might as well have breakfast while we're at it."

Her color was definitely better this morning, but she still had that sad, haunted look in her eyes, and she was too damned thin. Whatever was bothering her had evidently ruined her appetite. He was no gourmet chef, as he'd heard her sister Maggie was, but he could handle breakfast.

"What makes you think I wasn't planning on meeting my sisters for breakfast in town?" she inquired testily.

"For one thing, you didn't mention it," he said reasonably. He leveled a look straight into her eyes. "Were you?"

Her gaze wavered before she finally sighed. "No."

"Then have a seat. I'll whip something up in no time. We can catch up."

"Pete, I don't want to catch up with you," she said with evident frustration. "I don't want to talk to you. I don't want to see you."

He shook his head. "Is that anything to say to an old friend?"

"You are not my friend."

He met her gaze. "I was. I could be again."

"I don't think so." Her anxious gaze settled on the coffeemaker as if she could will it to brew the coffee faster. "As soon as this is ready, I'm out of here. In fact, since it pretty much does the work all on its own, I'll go now. Help yourself when it's ready. Enjoy your breakfast."

When she reached for her coat, Pete put his hand on hers. She jerked away.

"Stop it," she ordered fiercely. "I don't want you touching me."

He winced at the evidence of her aversion. Okay, so he understood it, but that didn't mean it didn't cut right through him.

"Jo, come on," he pleaded. "We obviously need to talk. We need to settle a few things."

She glowered at him. "We needed to talk seven years ago, but I didn't see you beating down the door to do it."

Another direct hit, he thought wearily. She was getting good at it. "I was twenty years old and stupid. I should have talked to you, but you'd already left town."

"And what? The phones didn't work?"

"I was embarrassed and ashamed."

She gave him a disbelieving look.

"Okay, I was a coward," he admitted. "I came by and talked to your grandmother. That was hard enough. I didn't have the guts to face you. I figured she'd tell you everything. I convinced myself it would be easier for you to hear it from her."

"Of course you did," Jo accused bitterly. "And believe me, it was so much easier having my grandmother be the one to share the news that was going to break my heart," she added in a voice rich with sarcasm. "She tried hard to be nonchalant. So did I, but we were both lousy at it."

Pete winced at the image she'd painted. "I'm sorry," he said. "It was a rotten thing to do to you and to her."

"Yes, it was," she said, not giving an inch. "Now if we've rehashed the past sufficiently, do you mind if I take off?"

He made one last try to keep her there. "Sure you don't want to stay? I make a terrific omelet."

"So do a lot of people. It's not that hard." She gave him a withering look. "I trust I won't find you here when I get back."

His own appetite ruined, Pete put the food back in

the refrigerator, then turned to face her. "I suppose that depends on how long you intend to hide out."

"As long as it takes."

She would do it, too. Pete could see in her eyes that she would find some way to avoid him until the job was done. Maybe he should let her, but he couldn't imagine himself giving up so easily. If she wanted him to pay penance for what he'd done to her, that was only fair. If she wanted to rail at him, curse him, keep him at arm's length, that was okay, too. He deserved whatever she wanted to dish out.

But he would keep coming back, not because he was stubborn. Not because he wanted to be a thorn in her side. He'd keep coming back because the moment he'd laid eyes on her again, he'd known he had no choice.

He was still in love with her, or at least with the sweet, vulnerable girl she'd once been. It remained to be seen if the woman was as captivating. Based on the way his hormones were raging, he was pretty sure she was.

Jo knew she wasn't thinking straight when she drove straight out to Maggie's farm, her temper still boiling. What was it going to take to make Pete see that she wanted absolutely nothing to do with him? She didn't want him as a friend. She certainly didn't want him as anything more. What did it say about him—or her— that he even thought she might? The man was married, for goodness sake, though he apparently didn't seem to care much about that little detail.

If she'd spent one more second with him at Rose

Cottage, she might have slapped him silly for his presumption.

Or she might have kissed him. That had been a definite possibility, too. She was willing to admit that. She was such an idiot! Maybe she'd sunk so low that her morals were no better than his.

Before getting on the road, she'd spent a long time in the driveway thinking about that, shocked that she would even consider such a thing for a single second.

When he'd walked out of the house while she was still sitting there, her gaze had fallen on him with seven years of pent-up longing. She knew he was aware of her, knew he was counting on her staring when he hefted that heavy ax over his head and started his demolition of the porch.

Her hand was shaking so badly, she almost hadn't been able to turn the key in the ignition. She'd actually stalled out twice before she finally got away from Rose Cottage and Pete's barely muffled laughter. He hadn't even tried to hide his gloating.

All the way to Maggie's she kept telling herself to calm down. If her sister saw her like this, she would know something was up. It didn't take a genius to see that Pete had rattled her. Since she was never, ever rattled, it was going to be a dead giveaway.

When she pulled up outside of Maggie's, she spotted Ashley's and Melanie's cars. She cursed another blue streak at the sight and almost turned right around and headed back to town, but with all this adrenaline pumping, she was hungry. She cut the engine, drew in a deep calming breath and went inside.

She'd barely stepped into Maggie's gourmet, professional kitchen before her temper stirred again. All three women were seated at the table, the last crumbs of a pecan coffee cake on their plates, mugs filled with fragrant coffee. They looked so blasted innocent, but one of them was a traitor, albeit an unwitting one. Her money was definitely on Ashley. Jo figured she'd ask anyway, just in case she and Pete both had gotten it all wrong.

"Okay, which one of you did it?" she asked before she'd even removed her coat.

"Did what?" Maggie asked, then went right on as if the question and the answer were of no consequence. "There's more coffee cake if you want it. It's in the oven to keep it warm. And I just brewed a fresh pot of coffee. Help yourself. If we'd known you were coming, we'd have waited."

Jo tried to tamp down her irritation and act just as cool. She took off her coat, tossed it over a chair, retrieved the coffee cake, then poured herself some coffee before sitting down at the table. She cut herself a huge slice of the coffee cake as she inquired, "Who called Pete Catlett and sent him to my doorstep last night?"

Three perfectly bland expressions greeted her.

"Then he did come by?" Ashley said, confirming her role in getting him there. "Good."

"You seem upset," Melanie noted, looking more curious than repentant.

"I'm not upset," she said, struggling to keep her tone neutral. She thought she was doing an admirable job of it. "Just surprised."

"Everyone, including Ashley, says Pete does the best work of anyone in the area. Do you have a problem with letting him fix the porch?" Maggie asked.

"Yes, I have a problem with it," she blurted without thinking. Damn, damn, damn. So much for neutrality. She should have taken some other approach. Now she'd all but admitted that it was personal.

"Which is?" Maggie persisted.

Jo tried to backtrack and come up with an explanation that wouldn't stir up more questions. "You didn't consult me," she said finally. "It's got nothing to do with Pete. I'm sure he's very qualified, but I'm the one who's going to have to deal with having him underfoot day in and day out. He's there right now, brandishing some sort of weapon that smashes boards. I'll be lucky if the place is standing when I get back."

"Come on, Jo. Don't exaggerate. He knows what he's doing," Ashley soothed, then grinned. "And he's easy on the eye, don't you think? He did a lot of the work for us, when Josh and I were fixing up our place. If I'd been single, I'd have definitely given him a second look."

Jo rolled her eyes. She was beginning to get a much clearer picture. Pete's presence was a gift from her big sister, a male distraction, eye candy. Geez-oh-flip, she was distraught over a broken engagement and Ashley was serving up more testosterone. If only she and the others understood the irony of this particular gesture.

Jo glanced up and realized Melanie was studying her with obviously increased curiosity.

"Is there some particular reason you don't want Pete underfoot? I mean Pete specifically," Melanie inquired. "I wasn't even aware that you knew him, yet you seem to have taken an almost instant dislike to the man."

Jo sighed. That was not a road she intended to travel down, even with her sisters. Her life was pathetic enough in their eyes at the moment without rehashing ancient history. She'd already stirred up more suspicion than she'd intended to.

"I don't dislike him," she lied. "I just wish you'd let me find my own contractor. I have a broken heart, not a broken brain. I need to find things to do, if I'm going to stay here for a while. I can't just mope around the house all day. And despite what you think, looking at some hunk you've found for me is not the answer."

"It's an interesting start, though, don't you agree?" Ashley asked. "I'd think you'd be more appreciative."

Jo tried to muster up the expected gratitude, but all she could think of was just how badly their good intentions had gone awry.

"Have you spoken to him?" she asked Ashley instead. "Has he told you how long this job will take or how much it will cost? The man builds huge houses. I've seen the signs for them everywhere. He's bound to charge a fortune for a minor little repair like this. I'm sure someone else, a handyman for instance, could do the work for a lot less."

"Too late now, if Pete's already started. Besides, I told you not to worry about the cost," her big sister said. "And I trust Pete to do what needs to be done and to give me a reasonable price."

"Really?" she said skeptically. "You trust him?"

Ashley's antennae went on full alert. "Is there some reason you think I shouldn't? I thought you said you didn't know him."

Jo saw that she wasn't going to maneuver her sister into firing Pete, not without giving her something specific to go on. Since she wasn't about to admit the one thing that might have done it, she merely shrugged.

"It's your money," she told Ashley. "I suppose I can put up with him for however long this takes. I don't know how much thinking I'll get done with all that clatter going on, though."

"Just as well," Melanie said. "You're probably thinking too much. Forget about what happened in Boston. Forget about everything and relax."

Jo bit back a laugh. As if she could relax when she was brushing up against the past every time she turned around! "Sure. I'll try."

"Maybe I should stop by and tell Pete he needs to clear everything with you," Ashley suggested, her expression thoughtful. "That way you can decide when it's most convenient for him to be there. He's an accommodating guy."

"No," Jo said hurriedly. The last thing she wanted was to have her very perceptive big sister watching the interaction between her and Pete. "I'm sure we can devise some sort of schedule that works for both of us. I have no idea why I'm making such a big thing out of this. It's silly, really."

"Are you sure? The last thing I want to do is add more stress to your life," Ashley told her.

Too late for that, Jo thought. She plastered a smile on her face. "Not to worry," she assured Ashley. "I'm sorry I got you all worked up over this. It's not a big deal. Really." She stood up. "Now I've got to run."

"Run where?" Maggie asked. "You haven't even touched your coffee cake."

Somewhere, anywhere, Jo thought desperately.

She grabbed up the slab of cake and wrapped it in a napkin. "Errands," she said succinctly. "I'll take this with me."

"I'll come with you," Melanie offered, pushing back her chair and standing. "I have some errands of my own."

Jo frowned at her. "I don't need a babysitter."

Melanie immediately sat back down. "Sorry."

Relenting, Jo crossed the room and gave her a hug. "I need to do things for myself, okay? It's not that I don't appreciate the offer."

"I know," Melanie said, regarding her with sympathetic understanding. "We're hovering."

"You're hovering," Jo confirmed.

"Okay, then, go off on your own, baby sister," Ashley said. "If you need us, all you have to do is call."

Jo grinned. "I have all your numbers on speed dial on my cell phone."

She hurried away before they remembered that down here in the boonies, her cell phone was virtually useless.

Pleased with herself, she noted that it was her second fast escape of the morning. At this rate, she was going to wind up being the family expert at quick getaways. Of course, unless she turned to bank robbery, it probably was a wasted talent.

3

As he worked, Pete thought about how skittish Jo was around him. He couldn't honestly blame her, but it was more distressing than he cared to admit. Once they'd been as close as any two people could be. They'd sat out in the backyard swing right here at Rose Cottage with the moon overhead and the Chesapeake Bay lapping at the shore and talked for hours on end. A fierce attraction had burned between them, but more than that, they'd been comfortable together, in tune with each other. They'd shared their hopes and dreams.

Jo had been the first person he'd told about his desire to build homes right here in Virginia's Northern Neck region. His uncle—his mother's brother—had taught him the construction trade, taught him all about being a craftsman who took pride in his materials and his work.

For as long as he could remember, Pete had wanted to follow in his Uncle Jeb's footsteps. Maybe that was only because Jeb was the only male role model in his life, but he didn't think so. If he'd had to explain it, he would have said it was because his uncle had shared with Pete his lifelong passion for crafting something strong and solid.

"I think it's because you want to build homes that will endure," Jo had said to him one night, picking up on an emotion Pete hadn't been able to express. "To make up for not having had one yourself. I'll bet you can see families living in the homes you build. I imagine you can hear the laughter and feel the love that you think you missed."

She'd understood him so well. Even at eighteen, she'd been able to put things into words that at twenty he'd barely recognized in himself—the hurts, the heartaches, the longings.

"We'll have a home like that," he'd promised her one night. "It will withstand the salt air, the winds, the storms. We'll fill it with kids and laughter. The only thing more solid will be our marriage."

Her eyes had been luminous in the moonlight. "I want that, Pete. More than you can imagine. Let's not wait too long."

"Just till you finish college and I'm established," he'd said, thinking they had all the time in the world.

She'd gone back to Boston a few days later to begin her freshman year at Boston University, and he'd buried himself in work. His uncle was a demanding taskmaster, but the long, hard days had been worth every backbreaking minute because he had a goal, making a life for himself that he would one day share with Jo. He'd been so sure that the first house he built entirely with his own hands would be for the two of them.

But then Kelsey, whom he'd known most of his life, had started hanging around. She'd never gone to college, either, but unlike Pete, she was in a dead-end job she hated at the local grocery store. Whenever she had the time, she was looking for uncomplicated, undemanding fun.

Pete saw no harm in going out with her for a few beers. They both knew the score. She even knew he was in love with Jo and claimed not to care. "I'll just keep your bed warm for her," she promised when they'd tumbled into it. He'd had too many beers to think with anything other than his hormones. It was stupid. It was irresponsible and reckless. He regretted it even before he realized that he hadn't used a condom. Then he'd known it was the worst mistake he'd ever made.

He hadn't been surprised when Kelsey had told him she was pregnant. He'd been waiting with dread for just that news. It meant the end of his relationship with Jo, the end of his dreams.

But he'd accepted responsibility with no argument. He'd offered marriage and was determined to make the best of it. There had even been a few months at the beginning when he'd thought it might work, mostly because he and Kelsey were so in love with the baby they'd created.

Then there had been the endless months when he'd been forced to accept that it wasn't working at all, would never work.

Even now, two years later, thinking about the misery of that time, about his son's tears when Kelsey had dragged Davey off to Richmond and away from his dad, tore Pete apart. Distracted by his dark thoughts, he carelessly smashed his thumb with a hammer, then cursed.

"You'll ruin your reputation if people catch you doing stuff like that on the job," Josh Madison commented, startling Pete so badly that he almost whacked his thumb again.

Grateful to have an excuse for a break, Pete stepped away from the remains of the porch. "What brings you by?"

"Ashley mentioned you were going to do some work over here. Thought I'd stop by and say hi, see how things are going."

Pete's gaze narrowed at the hint that Josh was somehow here to supervise. Did they not entirely trust him, after all? "That deck I built for you guys okay?" he asked Josh.

Josh chuckled. "Couldn't be better. I'm not here to hassle you. I'm just killing time."

"Good to know." He gave Josh a curious look. "Things slow at your law practice?"

"Just right, actually. I have a lot of time for Ashley and for fishing. For the first time in my life, everything's in perfect balance."

"Sounds like every man's dream," Pete said enviously. Since he suspected there was something more on Josh's mind, he waited to see if Josh would get around to it without prodding.

"You getting along okay with Jo?" Josh asked eventually.

So that was it. Pete gave him a sharp look. "Why wouldn't I be?"

"Just wondering," Josh said innocently. "She's a little uptight these days. Just thought I'd warn you."

Pete nodded. "I'd noticed."

"Cut her some slack, okay? Ashley and the others are worried about her."

Pete was glad to hear that they shared his concern. He also realized this was his chance to dig a little deeper into the circumstances that had brought Jo to town. "Any idea what the problem is?"

"Broken engagement," Josh said. "Turns out the guy was a real jerk. She caught him cheating on her."

Pete's stomach fell. No wonder Jo was looking at him with even deeper disdain and distrust than he'd anticipated. She'd been twice burned by betrayal. He'd been the first, and now he was right here rubbing her nose in it when she was trying to recover from this latest heartbreak. His presence was probably going a long way toward reinforcing her impression that all men were worthless bastards.

"That's tough," he said, trying to keep any trace of emotion from his voice.

"I met the guy once," Josh said. "She brought him to the wedding when Ashley and I got married. To tell you the truth, I think she's better off, but that's not something she wants to hear right now, I'm sure."

Curiosity got the best of Pete. He wanted to know about the man Jo had chosen to marry, even if just thinking about her with someone else twisted his gut into knots. "You didn't like the guy?"

Josh shook his head.

"Any particular reason?"

"Let's just say he spent the wedding chatting up every other woman in the room. Since most of them were members of Jo's family and married themselves, it seemed to me the handwriting was on the wall. He even put a couple of less-than-subtle moves on my wife. If I hadn't walked up when I did, I think Ashley would have decked him."

"Why the hell didn't she warn her sister?"

"I think she tried, but Jo didn't want to hear it. She was convinced Ashley had misread the man's intentions. She was sure he was just being friendly, hoping to get the family to warm up to him. The D'Angelos are a tight-knit clan."

Pete regarded him intently. "Any chance Jo was right, that it was innocent?"

Josh laughed. "You know my wife. Does she strike you as someone who'd misread that kind of situation? No, she got it exactly right, and remember, I heard most of it, too." He shrugged. "But you know how people are when they're in love. They have to figure out their mistakes for themselves. And there's not a more loyal, trusting woman around than Jo. She didn't want to believe the worst."

"I suppose," Pete said, his guilt stirring all over again. Jo had trusted him once, and look what he'd done. She was probably convinced now that her judgment about men sucked. That meant it was going to be a whole lot harder for him to convince her otherwise.

Josh regarded him curiously. "You seem awfully interested."

"You know me. I'm a sucker for a woman in distress."

"I doubt she'd want your pity."

Pete laughed. "No kidding. I do have a few functioning brain cells. There hasn't been a woman born who wants a man coming around out of pity." He studied

Josh curiously. "Why'd you tell me all this? Just so I'd keep an eye out for her?"

Josh rolled his eyes. "Come on, Catlett, get serious. Everyone in town knows your reputation. Since your divorce, you date a lot, but you don't get serious. Let's just consider this conversation fair warning. Jo's vulnerable. A lot of people will be upset if you hurt her."

Little did he know, Pete thought wryly.

"Yeah, I'll keep that in mind," Pete promised. "I'll try not to jump her bones first chance I get."

Josh scowled at him, clearly taking the comment at face value. "I'm trusting you to keep that promise."

He was gone before Pete could reply. Of course, the truth was that he hadn't needed Josh's warning to know to take things slowly with Jo. She had warning signs posted around her that all but shouted her vulnerability.

And even if she hadn't, she'd made it abundantly clear that she was strictly off-limits to Pete in particular.

Of course, he admitted to himself, that only made things interesting. There was nothing on earth that Pete liked better than a challenge. That it happened to be provided by a woman he'd once loved just made it that much more fascinating.

Jo managed to hide out till dusk, certain that once the light died Pete would be forced to quit for the day.

Now she stood in the front yard and gaped at what had once been the porch. It was a yawning, empty space that stretched out between where she was and the door. Four-by-four posts propped up the porch roof.

Thanks to the dimming light and shadows, getting inside suddenly seemed treacherous. The only alternative was to go around back, but she wasn't even sure if her key worked in that lock, which raised something of a quandary. How the devil was she supposed to get inside without crawling over the threshold in some awkward spectacle?

She was still pondering her choices when the front door opened, startling her so badly, she dropped the bags she was carrying. Thankfully, nothing she'd bought on her shopping spree was breakable.

"There you are," Pete called out from inside. "I was wondering when you'd be back. I didn't want to leave till you turned up."

Jo frowned. His presence was precisely why she'd stayed away so long. She'd hoped to outwait him. She should have guessed he'd stay put just to be perverse.

"Where's your truck? Did you deliberately hide it?"

He grinned. "Took it home and walked back," he admitted. "I figured you'd turn right around and leave if you saw it parked out here."

"Damn straight," she muttered.

His grin broadened. "Still stubborn as a mule, I see. Come on, Jo. What's the big deal? I thought you might have some trouble getting inside, so I stuck around. End of story. I didn't stay just to annoy you."

He glanced at the bags now scattered at her feet. "Did you buy out the stores?"

"Only a few of them," she said, regarding him warily. "Since you're here, make yourself useful and open the back door."

"Why haul all that stuff around back when you can come in this way?"

"How do you suggest I step up and into the house?"

"You always have me to help," he suggested. "That's why I'm here, after all."

Jo couldn't see his eyes at this distance and in this light, but she suspected there was a wicked glint in them. "You?" she asked skeptically.

He leapt down, then came toward her. When he was closer, she could spot the amusement glittering in his eyes. She backed up a step, bent over and grabbed haphazardly for the bags, holding them in front of her as if they would somehow ward him off.

He just kept coming. "Hope none of that stuff you're carrying weighs too much," he joked as he scooped her up, then shifted her till she was snuggled securely against his chest. "Nope. Light as a feather."

"Pete, put me down this instant," Jo grumbled, even though the faint scent of his aftershave and the masculine scent that was as familiar to her as salt air made her feel vaguely weak with a sudden, unwanted longing.

He stopped in his tracks and gazed into her eyes. "Now, the way I see it, you have two choices. You can let me give you a little boost inside or you can face the indignity of trying to scramble up there on your own while I stand here and watch." He grinned. "I imagine it'll be quite a show. You always did have the cutest little butt around."

"You're a pig!"

"You're not the first to suggest that," he noted calmly. "So, what's it going to be?"

"Just get me into the damn house and then go away," she said.

"You'd send me away even after I got dinner all ready for the two of us?"

"I would send you away if you'd spent your last dime on it," she said firmly.

"Heartless," he said mildly. "I'd never have guessed it."

"Some traits develop over time," she commented wryly as he stepped onto a precarious arrangement of cinder blocks she hadn't even noticed, then stepped inside the house as easily as if there were actual steps.

"Why didn't you just tell me you'd rigged up some temporary steps? I could have gotten in here on my own," she noted, punching him in the chest.

"True," he agreed, his grin unrepentant. "But this was more fun."

"Not for me," she said, scrambling out of his arms and snatching away her packages. "Go away."

"Not till you eat."

"I told you you weren't invited to stay for dinner," she said, even as she sniffed the air and noticed the appealing aroma of baking chicken.

"That's fine, but I don't intend to leave until I see you put a few forkfuls of food into your mouth."

"Do I look as if I need coaxing to eat?"

"Yes," he said readily. "You're too skinny. It was the first thing I noticed when I saw you last night."

"Now you're just being insulting."

"That's me, known far and wide for my complete lack of charm. Dinner's in five minutes, if you want to put this stuff away and wash up."

Jo sighed and accepted the fact that she wasn't getting rid of him. She didn't pretend to understand why he was insinuating himself into her life like this. Maybe Ashley had hired him to do more than fix the porch and look good while he was at it. Maybe he was an undercover babysitter. Whatever was keeping him around, he seemed to be serious about it. She knew from bitter experience that he wouldn't be shaken off till he was good and ready. That's why it had hurt so much when he'd simply vanished without a word seven years ago. It had told her he was ready, if not eager, to be rid of her and move on to his new life.

"If you're staying, you may as well eat," she finally said grudgingly.

"Thank you," he said solemnly.

To her surprise, the table was set. He'd even lit a couple of candles and plunked a bouquet of flowers in a water glass in the center of the table. It had all the trappings of romance to it, and a tiny little shiver of anticipation danced along her spine.

"What's all this?" she asked suspiciously, as if it weren't plain as day.

"Ambience," he said, looking vaguely uncomfortable. "I hear women are fond of it."

"Maybe when they're being courted, but the circumstances are a bit different with us."

"Are they?" he asked in a tone clearly intended to have her blood humming.

She regarded him with frustration. "Pete, you can't say stuff like that."

"Why not?"

"It's not appropriate."

"Because we parted a long time ago?"

"No, idiot. Because you're married and have at least one child. What is wrong with you? You can't start hitting on me. I am not going to have a fling with a married man just for old time's sake."

Something dark and painful flashed in his eyes. "Thanks for the vote of confidence about my morals," he said tightly. "Just to set the record straight, I have a son who lives in Richmond with his mother. I'm no longer married."

Jo had picked up a glass of water, but her hand shook so badly she had to set it down again. His news was the last thing she'd expected. It changed everything. It made her nervous in ways she hadn't been before. His marriage had been like a safety net, the only thing keeping her from forgetting about all the anguish he'd caused her.

"You're divorced, not separated?" she asked, just to be sure she'd gotten it right.

"Two years now. I can bring the divorce papers by for you, if you don't believe me," he said, his expression bleak.

"What happened?" she asked instinctively.

He gave her a shuttered look. "I don't want to talk about it."

"But—"

Now he was the one on the defensive. "Look, I fixed you a little dinner and stuck around to make sure you ate it. No big deal. It doesn't give you the right to start poking around in my personal life."

"You tried to poke around in mine," she reminded him.

"And you told me to butt out. Now I see your point. Let's stick to safe, neutral topics."

Jo nodded, but somewhere deep inside, where Pete's announcement had lit a ridiculous spark of hope, she realized that things would never be entirely safe or neutral between her and this man.

She swallowed a whole litany of questions and searched frantically for something they could talk about.

"The chicken looks good," she said eventually. "When did you learn to cook?"

"After the divorce," he said, his gaze avoiding hers.

So, not even dinner was a safe topic, apparently. Jo regarded him with frustration. "You could help me out here. Say something."

An unwilling smile tugged at the corners of his mouth. It was obvious he was fighting it. "There never was much that was safe or simple between us, was there?"

"Not much," she admitted.

"There's always the weather," he said. "I hear it might snow again."

She went along with him. "Really? When?"

He did grin then. "Sometime this winter."

Jo laughed and the tension was broken. "You made that up, didn't you?"

"Hey, it's as accurate a forecast as any we're likely to get on the news," he protested.

"I suppose so." She grinned back at him. "Think it will rain this spring?"

"Pretty certain," he said.

"If we work at this, we could carve out whole new careers for ourselves."

"Personally I like the one I have," Pete said. "You can go for it if you want to."

She shook her head. "Not me. I like landscape design."

Pete's eyes lit up. "That's what you do?"

"Yes," she said, surprised by his apparent enthusiasm. "Why?"

"I don't suppose you're looking for any work while you're here, are you?"

"Mike said he might have some jobs for me," she admitted. "We haven't discussed the specifics, though."

He nodded slowly. "You could work through him," he said. "Or work directly for me. I've been on his waiting list for weeks for a couple of houses I just built. He told me the other day he might have help soon. I imagine that's you."

Jo swallowed hard. So there really was more work around than Mike could handle, but working for Pete? Could she do it? Wasn't that just asking for disaster? She needed more information on just how closely she'd have to work with him. It might be smarter to keep Mike as a buffer.

"Are you making the decisions?" she asked. "Or are the new owners of the houses?"

"I'm making the decisions for now. I've built these places on spec. I want the grounds in good shape by spring when the real estate market kicks into high gear around here." He studied her intently. "Is that a problem?"

She put her fork down and met his gaze. "I don't know. Is it, Pete?"

"What are you asking me?"

"It's been a long time. I was a girl when you knew me. Now, not only am I a woman, but I'm a professional. Can you treat me with the respect I deserve and trust my judgment? Or will our personal history constantly be getting in the way?"

"I could ask you the same thing," he reminded her.

Her lips curved. "But I asked first."

His gaze never wavered. "I always trusted you. I'm the one who blew it, Jo, not you. I may not have shown you the respect you deserved at the end, but the whole mess was caused by my stupidity. It had nothing to do with the way I felt about you. I know that doesn't make a lot of sense, since you were the one who got hurt."

"No, it doesn't," she said.

"I guess the real question is whether you trust me enough to give me another chance, at least enough for us to work together on a few projects. We can take it one day at a time. Anytime you say it's not working for you, that's it. No hard feelings."

"I don't walk out on jobs," she said. "I'll finish whatever I start. You can count on that."

"And you can count on me not to hurt you again, Jo. I mean that."

Sincerity radiated from him. Jo wanted desperately to believe what he was saying. He clearly was talking about a whole lot more than a couple of landscaping jobs, but the work was all she could think about for now. It was a start, and it would keep her from going stir-crazy here.

She finally held out her hand. "Deal. I'm going to want to clear this with Mike, but if he doesn't have a problem with it, I'll do it."

"Sounds fair to me." Pete took her hand in his, but instead of shaking it, he raised it to his lips and kissed her knuckles. "You won't regret it, darlin'."

She kept her gaze on his steady and cautious. "I hope you're right," she said softly. For both their sakes.

4

First thing the next morning, Jo opened the back door to Mike and, to her dismay, Melanie. She frowned at her sister.

"I didn't know you were coming," she said.

"Mike said you'd asked him to stop by, so I figured I'd tag along." Melanie returned her gaze curiously. "Is that a problem?"

Jo bit back a sigh. She'd really hoped to have this conversation with Mike in private. She was afraid her sister would read too much into it. Too late for that now. She could hardly kick her out. Melanie really would read too much into that.

Jo forced a smile. "Of course not," she said with exaggerated cheer that was as phony as her smile. Hopefully it was too early in the day for Melanie to pick up on that. "Come on in. The coffee's ready. Have you two eaten? I can scramble some eggs, or make you some toast at least. I'm afraid if you want baked goods, you're at the wrong place. That's Maggie's province."

"I'll pass," Melanie said, still regarding her with a puzzled look.

"Me, too," Mike replied. "I have to be on a job site in twenty minutes. I'd have been here sooner, but I had to wait for my wife to get ready. It's actually astounding how fast she can move when she's highly motivated."

"Oh?" Jo asked.

"She was dying of curiosity about why you wanted to see me," Mike said, giving his wife an affectionate look.

"Then I'll get right to the reason I called," Jo told him. "Pete Catlett has asked if I'd be willing to do the landscape design for a couple of houses he built. He said you were too busy to get to them right away. I said I'd do it, but only if you didn't have a problem with it. I don't want to poach on one of your clients."

"Hell, no, I don't have a problem with it." Mike grinned. "That would be great, in fact. Pete's been very patient. The minute Melanie told me you were coming, I started hoping you'd agree to take on those jobs, but I didn't want to rush you."

Although he sounded very convincing, Jo pressed him. "You're sure? We can work it out so you bill him and then you can pay me whatever you figure the going rate is around here."

"Absolutely not," Mike said. "Why make extra paperwork? Make your deal directly with Pete. I don't need to be involved." He gave her a sly look. "Although, if you decide you want to work around here on a more permanent basis, I'd like you to consider teaming up with me. There's more than enough work for a partnership."

Melanie's eyes lit up. "What a fabulous idea!"

Jo frowned at her. "As if you weren't the one who planted it in his head."

"I most certainly did not," Melanie retorted. "This was Mike's idea."

Jo glanced at him. He nodded in confirmation.

"In that case, thanks. I appreciate the offer. I'll think about it. Let's see how these two jobs go first. You might hate my ideas."

"Don't wait. Say yes now, Jo," her sister pleaded. "It would be so great to have you living here."

"She's right," Mike agreed. "It would sure help me out."

Jo held up her hands. "Hey, slow down, you two. I've agreed to take on a couple of jobs. Even if I agreed to do a few more, I'm not making some long-term commitment. I still intend to go back to Boston at some point."

"But why?" Melanie asked. "This is perfect for you. You'd be your own boss, instead of working for someone who doesn't really appreciate you. And who knows? If you settled here, maybe Mom and Dad would retire down here. Wouldn't that be fantastic?"

Things were moving way too quickly for Jo. "Don't get ahead of yourself. Mom and Dad are nowhere near ready to retire and, despite what you think of my boss, I did tell him I'd be back. It was very generous of him to give me a leave of absence."

"An *unpaid* leave," Melanie retorted. "Where's the generosity in that?"

"He could have hired someone else for that position," Jo argued.

"In winter?" Melanie asked skeptically, then gave a gesture of surrender. "Okay, okay, I won't push."

Jo hooted at that. None of her sisters were the shy, retiring type. They'd push like crazy, especially if they sensed she was weakening. "Yeah, right."

"I promise," Melanie said, sketching a little X across her heart. "The decision's all yours, even if your staying would mean that Mike and I would have more time to work on our baby project."

Jo stared at her sister. "Baby project?"

"We think it's time Jessie had a little sister or brother," Melanie said. "But Mike's so busy, we barely even see each other, much less have time to, well, you know."

Mike nudged her in the ribs. "We will always find time for that, sweetheart." He winked at Jo. "On that note, I think I'll get out of here. I meant what I said, Jo. The door's always open if you do decide to stay, even if it's just through spring. That's my busiest season and it's worse than ever with all the construction going on."

She stood up and impulsively gave him a hug. "You're the best."

"So my wife tells me," he said lightly, dropping a kiss on Melanie's lips before taking off.

As soon as the door was closed behind him, Melanie regarded her intently. "Now we can get to the good stuff."

Jo stared at her blankly. "What good stuff?"

"You and Pete. You seem to have formed a bond awfully quickly."

Jo frowned. This was exactly what she'd been afraid would happen the minute any of her sisters heard about this job. "It's not a bond. I mentioned that I do landscape design. He said he needed help. That's it."

Melanie obviously wasn't satisfied. "And when did you share this information?"

Jo saw the trap. "Yesterday," she said cautiously.

"Oh? I thought you intended to stay away as long as he was working."

"That was the plan," Jo agreed. "It didn't work out. Turned out he was still here when I got home."

"What time was that?"

"Melanie, is there some point you're trying to make?"

"No," she said cheerfully. "I'm just fishing for information I can share with Maggie and Ashley. It's so rare that I know anything before they do."

"And what is it you think you know?"

"That something's clicking between you and Pete."

"Indeed there is," Jo said. "He's thrilled about my job experience. I'm excited about his offer to pay me for my expertise. If that's clicking, then we are definitely on the same wavelength."

"Joke if you want, but I think there's more going on," Melanie insisted.

"Such as?"

"Chemistry."

"More like botany," Jo said dryly. "We have plants in common."

"Ha-ha," Melanie responded with a roll of her eyes.

"I thought it was amusing."

"Where is he, by the way?"

"Working, I imagine."

"But not here?" Melanie said, looking disappointed that she wasn't going to get to put him through the wringer on this visit.

"Not till later," Jo said.

Melanie brightened at once. "After hours? How much work can he actually get done once it's dark?"

Jo groaned at her sister's determination to make something of the situation. She would have expected it from Ashley or Maggie, but Melanie usually had better sense. "I think maybe this whole baby project of yours has put your mind on a single track," she told her.

Melanie beamed. "Could be. Mike and I certainly don't think about much else." She gave Jo a pointed look. "At least when we get five minutes alone together."

"Oh, no, you don't, big sister," Jo chided. "You are not going to guilt me into staying here, just so you and your husband can have more sex."

"It's not about the sex. It's about a baby," Melanie said. "A little niece or nephew for you. Wouldn't that be wonderful?"

"Wonderful," Jo agreed readily. "But making it happen isn't my responsibility."

Melanie laughed. "Oh, well, it was worth a shot. Now I have to be going. I have things to do and places to go."

"I imagine Maggie's will be your first stop," Jo said.

Her sister didn't even try to pretend otherwise. "Of course," she said at once. "Want to come?"

Something told Jo it was the only way to protect her own interests. Otherwise Maggie and Ashley would only hear Melanie's spin on the news that she was going to do a little work for Pete. That would only fuel their eagerness to turn it into a budding romance. And once inspired, who knew what lengths they'd go to in order to make sure that love bloomed by spring, right along with the forsythia?

She gave Melanie a cheerful smile. "I'll be right behind you."

She knew she'd made the right decision when Melanie didn't even try to hide her disappointment.

When Pete finally caught up with him, Mike had a sketchbook in hand and was apparently trying to rough in a landscape design for a piece of waterfront property on which a Cape Cod–style house was under construction. Unfortunately, it was so damn cold out that he was forced to wear gloves and he kept dropping his pencil.

Pete retrieved it from the ground and handed it to him. "Ever think of doing this inside your truck with the motor running and the heater blasting? The wind off the bay cuts right through you this morning."

Mike gave him a sour look. "I noticed. Unfortunately, the builder piled all his construction debris beside the house. There's no way around it except on foot. That means I get to stand out here and freeze my butt off and hope my hand's not shaking so badly that I won't recognize what I've sketched in."

"If you were working with me, you wouldn't have that problem," Pete told him.

Mike gave him a hard look. "But I hear you've found yourself a backup landscape designer."

Pete regarded him with surprise. "You know?"

"Jo called last night. I stopped by to see her on my way over here. She told me. She wanted to be sure I had no objections."

"Do you?"

"Not a one. She'll do a good job for you. I've seen some of the places she landscaped up in Boston. She's good at it."

"Boston's not here. You sure she'll understand what plants work in this climate?"

"Hold it," Mike said. "Let's have this conversation in your truck. Something tells me it's going to require my full attention. Your heater will probably warm up faster than mine, since you just got here."

"And there's coffee," Pete said. "I picked up an extra cup in case you were in this precise predicament. Some builders aren't nearly as thoughtful as I am." He winked. "Just one reason you ought to make my jobs your first priority."

When they were finally settled in the cab of Pete's truck with the heater blasting, Mike gave him a hard look. "Okay, what's up? What's with the crack about me making you my first priority? I thought you were content with having Jo do the work. Are you having second thoughts about that?"

Pete weighed his response. He didn't want to get into all the complicated reasons why it might be a bad idea. Those had only started churning in his head after he'd left Rose Cottage the night before. By morning, he'd concluded he ought to try to find some way out of their agreement. Her qualifications were the only legitimate excuse he could come up with.

"You have to admit this area requires a different approach than some house in suburban Boston," he said defensively.

"Her credentials are impeccable," Mike said. "She'll do her homework, Pete. You don't need to worry about that. And she'll show you site plans and sketches, same as I would. You have any questions, you can bring 'em to me."

Pete knew how that would go over if Jo found out he was taking her work to Mike behind her back. "You know I can't do that. It's insulting."

Mike grinned. "Glad you have sense enough to see that. Now tell me what's really going on here. It's not about Jo's experience, is it?"

Pete tried a different tack. "She's got a lot going on in her life right now. Josh told me about the broken engagement and I've seen for myself that she's an emotional wreck. Maybe she shouldn't be taking on work."

Mike studied him intently, then began to chuckle. "You're scared of her, aren't you?"

Pete glowered at him. "Why on earth would I be scared of a little bitty thing like Jo D'Angelo?"

"Maybe because you're attracted to her," Mike suggested. His expression sobered. "I know about the two of you, pal. I know you had a thing once."

Pete slapped his hand on the steering wheel in frustration. "Dammit, where'd you hear about that?" he demanded, knowing even as he asked that he was giving himself away. "I know you weren't around back then."

"Then it's true?"

Pete nodded. "What exactly did you hear?"

"That the two of you had a summer fling, maybe more than that."

"It was more than that," Pete admitted. "And I broke her heart. Do her sisters know about that?"

"I don't think so," Mike said. "You'd never have set foot inside Rose Cottage if they knew. In fact, Ashley would most likely have taken a shotgun to you when you showed up to do that work for her and Josh."

"That's what I figured." He gave Mike a worried look. "Are you going to tell them?"

"Not unless it seems like you're going to hurt her again. You and I are friends, Pete, but Jo's family now. I have to look out for her."

"I respect that," Pete said. "I certainly don't want to hurt her again, but I'm wondering if we should start spending quite so much time together when there's all this past history that needs to be resolved."

Mike's expression turned thoughtful. "Okay now, it's a given that I'm no expert on women, not even my wife, but it seems to me if Jo agreed to do this, then she's ready to spend more time with you. Maybe this is your chance to make things right with her. A couple of jobs will give you plenty of uncomplicated time together."

"It gets complicated when we're in the same room," Pete said dryly.

Mike laughed. "A whole lot of pheromones bouncing around?"

"You have no idea."

"Okay, this is definitely a guy approach, but maybe you should just take her to bed and get all that out of the way," Mike suggested.

Pete gave him a horrified look. "Her engagement just

broke up. She's an emotional mess. And you want me to take her to bed?"

"Just a thought," Mike said.

Pete shook his head. "How the hell did you ever land a classy woman like Melanie?"

"I didn't. She landed me."

"I hope you count your blessings every night," Pete told him.

"Believe me, I do. Every night and every morning," Mike said fervently. "So, are you okay with this work arrangement? You're going to let Jo do the design work?"

"Yes," Pete said. And he'd suffer the torment of the damned every single minute he was around her.

It was nearly dark when Pete finally pulled up at Rose Cottage with a load of lumber. Jo heard the truck rumble into the yard, grabbed a jacket and went outside and around to the front of the house to meet him.

"I was expecting you earlier," she said as he jumped down from the cab of the truck.

"Sorry. I got held up. I ran into problems on every job this morning."

"Anything major?"

He shook his head. "Nope. Just time-consuming. I figured I'd drop this lumber off tonight, then come by first thing in the morning to get in an hour or two of work here before I head over to the house I'm building in White Stone. I thought maybe you'd like to go with me, since that's one of the ones I'd like you to land-scape."

"Sure." She studied him curiously. He hadn't once

looked directly at her. "Pete, is everything okay? You seem a little distracted."

"Just one of those days, I guess." He began pulling the boards off the back of his truck and stacking them neatly.

Without being asked, Jo went to help him, but as she reached for a board, he scowled at her. "What do you think you're doing?"

"Helping."

"You don't need to do that."

"But I can, so why shouldn't I?" she asked, meeting his gaze. There was something dark and dangerous in his eyes, a look she couldn't quite interpret.

"I'm getting paid to do the job," he said, trying to nudge her aside.

"And I imagine you're being paid by the hour, so if I help, it will cost Ashley less," she said, grabbing for another board.

"Jo!"

She bit back a grin at the frustration in his voice. "Yes, Pete?"

His fierce look finally vanished and he sighed. "What am I supposed to do with you?"

"Let me help," she suggested lightly.

"I don't think that's the answer," he said, and took a step toward her.

"Pete?"

"Yes, Jo," he said, a smile tugging at his lips.

"What are you doing?"

"Give it a minute and I'm sure you'll figure it out," he said softly, just before he lowered his lips to hers.

She should have protested. She should have pushed

him away. But his kisses had lived in her memory for so long, how could she resist a chance to see if she'd gotten it right?

His taste was as familiar to her as her morning coffee. The texture of his lips was soft. His tongue was wickedly clever. A tiny spark turned into a full-fledged conflagration in a matter of seconds, just as it always had.

It wasn't supposed to be like this. She was supposed to be over him, not putty in his hands. She wanted to mold herself to his body, wanted his hands to work their inevitable magic, but he seemed to be satisfied with the kiss. In fact, he seemed dedicated to perfecting it.

Her head was spinning, her knees were weak and her body was on fire when he finally dragged his mouth away with obvious reluctance. *No, no, no,* she wanted to protest, but she couldn't summon up the strength to utter a word.

Calling herself every kind of idiot under the sun, Jo stepped away from him and grabbed onto the truck for support. At least, Pete looked a little dazed, she decided, taking some satisfaction in that. It would be hell knowing that he'd emerged from that kiss unscathed, while her whole world had been rocked.

"Why did you do that?" she asked shakily.

"Because I had to," he said. "I couldn't survive one more second without it."

Her lips quirked. "Really?"

He laughed. "Don't be smug, darlin'. It's not becoming."

"I thought maybe you kissed me because I was annoying you," she retorted.

"And if that had been the reason, would you be on your best behavior from here on out?"

Jo considered the question, then shook her head. "No. Actually I think I'd go right on annoying you."

"And damn the consequences?"

"Pretty much."

He gave her a curious look. "You've changed."

"We all do."

"But this goes deeper than changing hairstyles or getting a college education."

"Oh?"

"You're obviously willing to play with fire."

Jo thought about that with a sense of shock. Was she? Ten minutes ago she would have sworn that the opposite was true, that she never wanted to take another emotional risk in her life. That kiss had changed everything.

"Maybe I am," she said slowly, then regarded him with an innocent expression. "Is that a problem?"

Pete stared at her for a very long time before a grin spread across his face. "Not for me."

"Okay, then, let's get the rest of this lumber off the truck and after that I'll fix dinner." She met his gaze. "If you're free."

He hesitated then. "This is just about dinner, right?"

She wanted to throw caution completely to the wind and say no, that it was about seduction, but some lingering shred of common sense crept in. This was the man who'd almost destroyed her, after all.

"It's just about dinner," she confirmed.

Pete nodded. "Good to know."

Because he looked so sweet trying to hide his disappointment, she couldn't resist adding, "I'll let you know about dessert later."

That ought to keep his hormones twisted in a knot all through dinner, she thought with satisfaction. Maybe she had a wicked streak, after all.

If so, nobody deserved to see it in action more than this man, who'd left her questioning everything about herself seven years ago. Maybe they'd met again just so he could help her restore her self-esteem and move on with her life.

5

Pete was pretty sure if Jo so much as brushed up against him, he was going to go up in flames. That kiss had reminded him of the way they were together, and he knew he wasn't going to shake the memory anytime soon. Hell, five years of marriage—some of it actually good—hadn't dimmed the memory of the way she'd once come apart in his arms.

Face it, he told himself, Jo was seared into his heart and his soul.

Worse, though, than the stirring of old memories was that deliberate little taunt she'd uttered about dessert. They both knew she wasn't talking about apple pie. Sweet heaven, the woman had turned into a temptress. He wasn't sure how he felt about that. He'd liked her just fine when she'd been a shy, inexperienced young girl. He had a feeling the woman might just turn out to be too much for him.

He thought of Mike's advice to take her to bed and get the whole sexual attraction thing out of the way, but he now knew better than ever that it wouldn't be like that. Once they slept together again, there would be no turning back, at least not for him.

That would be all well and good if they were on the same page, but how could they be? His life was chaotic. His son was his first priority, which shouldn't be half as complicated as Kelsey tended to make it. How could he drag Jo into that, especially when it was the very situation that had hurt her so deeply years ago? Add in Josh's warning that Pete not hurt her, and any involvement was bound to be risky business.

And her life was no less complicated. Some other man had broken her heart, quite recently if Pete understood what she and others had told him. Much as he might like to believe that the man meant nothing to her, he doubted that was true. If Jo had given her heart to him, then she hadn't walked away from his betrayal unscathed. The shadows in her eyes had been proof enough of that.

Thankfully, it appeared he wasn't going to have to resolve the whole dilemma tonight. By the time they were inside, Jo seemed to have lost that feisty edge that had scared him to death. Obviously she was beset by second thoughts, too. In fact, she was suddenly giving him such a wide berth, it was almost insulting, as if she feared he was the one who'd put moves on her she wasn't ready to handle.

After putting up with her undisguised skittishness for several minutes, Pete knew they had to settle things between them. He stepped in front of her and grasped her shoulders. Alarm immediately flared in her eyes.

"What?" she asked, her voice shaky with obvious nerves.

"Listen to me, Jo," he said quietly. "Nothing is going to happen between us tonight." He was pleased by the faint flicker of disappointment that registered on her face, but he stuck to his guns. "I'm going to stay for dinner. Then I'm going to give you a chaste peck on the cheek and go home to my own bed."

The declaration put some color back into her cheeks. "Oh, really? What makes you think you get to decide that's how the evening is going to go?"

Pete laughed at the show of feistiness. "Did you have another ending in mind?"

As he'd expected, she faltered at that. "No," she finally admitted.

"Okay, then, let's just agree to the ground rules, so you can stop looking like a deer I've caught in my headlights."

"I just wanted to prove how sophisticated I've become," she grumbled, stepping past him and chopping an onion with a ferocity that gave him chills.

He finally worked up the courage to ask her what the devil she meant by that.

She gave him a helpless shrug. "I honestly don't know. I suppose so you wouldn't think I'm some basket case who'd jump into bed with you on the rebound."

He hid a smile at that. "So if you had jumped into bed with me tonight, that would have been the only reason—the rebound thing?"

She nodded.

"Oh, darlin', don't make me prove you wrong about that," he said seriously.

"You can't prove me wrong, because it's the truth," she declared, her eyes flashing with defiance.

Pete couldn't resist calling her on it. "I've got five

bucks and a kiss that says otherwise," he said, slapping a bill on the counter.

Her eyes widened with shock. "Are you crazy?"

"More than likely."

She forced the money back into his pocket, then immediately stepped gingerly away as if she'd belatedly realized her mistake. "I am not going to kiss you and I'm certainly not going to make a bet that says you can't seduce me."

"Because you know I'm right," he said, satisfied with the admission.

She frowned at him, and for a minute it seemed as if she might continue the debate until Pete was forced to kiss her to prove his point. Unfortunately, though, she finally drew in a deep breath and leveled a cool look into his eyes. "Would you prefer green beans or peas with dinner?"

Pete knew better than to laugh at the quick retreat to neutral turf. She might have felt compelled to take him up on his impulsive bet and, truthfully, he wasn't the least bit sure if he would have been able to resist.

The kitchen was filled with the scent of onions and garlic and tomato as Jo's spaghetti sauce simmered on the stove, but it was the pheromones swirling in the air that were getting to Jo. Somehow in the last few hours, she'd completely lost her mind. What she'd been doing ever since Pete had arrived rivaled the stupidity of waving a red cape at a bull. Did she want the man to seduce her?

Okay, yes, of course, she did. At least she wanted to know that he wanted to take her to bed. And it *was* about the rebound thing, no matter what he said to the contrary. She wanted to prove to herself that she was still a desirable woman, and who better to prove that than a man who'd once walked away from her? If she could attract Pete now, wouldn't that prove…something?

She tried to figure out what exactly it would prove and couldn't. Maybe it would only prove that she really was an idiot.

"How about some wine with dinner?" Pete asked. "I found a bottle of merlot in the wine rack."

Not a chance in hell, Jo thought. She needed all her wits about her if she was going to negotiate the minefield she'd set up for herself tonight.

"No, thanks, but you have some if you'd like."

He shrugged. "I'm okay with a beer. Are there any in the fridge?"

"There should be," she said, opening the door. There were half a dozen bottles of beer inside. She took one out, twisted off the top and handed it to him. "Want a glass?"

"Nope. The bottle will do." He kept his gaze locked with hers. "Anything I can do to help with dinner?"

"The sauce is almost ready. You can drain the pasta, if you want to."

He put his bottle on the table and picked up the heavy pot, held it over the colander and dumped in the boiling water and pasta. More of the angel hair slithered down the drain than into the colander.

Jo chuckled as he tried to grab a handful. "Let it go," she said. "I made more than enough. We won't starve if some of it gets away."

He gave her a frustrated look. "You didn't warn me how slippery it would be."

"Haven't you ever cooked pasta before?"

"Sure," he said. "From a can."

Jo rolled her eyes. "Please don't ever let Maggie hear you say that. You'll absolutely destroy her respect for you. She thinks it's disgusting enough that I don't own a pasta machine so I can make my own."

"If Davey wants spaghetti, we go out," Pete said defensively. "I like the stuff in the can."

"See if you can still say that after we've eaten tonight," Jo said. "Of course, Maggie is right about one thing. This would be even better if we'd made the noodles from scratch."

He regarded her with surprise. "You can do that?"

"If you're asking if it's possible for a person to make pasta in his own kitchen, the answer is yes. If you want to know if I personally can do it, then, no. I'm hopeless at anything complicated—piecrusts and pasta are beyond me. The prepared stuff suits me just fine."

He grinned. "Nice to know there are some principles you're willing to compromise."

"Not the important ones."

She watched as he expertly wound some of the angel hair onto his fork, then took his first bite of the homemade sauce that was one of her Italian father's specialties. He'd insisted all his daughters learn the recipe. "It's a family tradition," Max D'Angelo had told them. "I won't have it dying out with me, so no matter what else you learn to cook, you'll learn this sauce."

Maggie was the only one who'd inherited his love of cooking, but the rest of them at least had this one dish they could use to impress guests. Pete was no exception. He regarded her with an expression bordering on awe.

"I think I love you," he said after his first bite.

Jo's pulse jumped, but she ignored it. "That's the sauce talking," she assured him…and herself. "I'll send some home with you. You can freeze it and try it out on your son next time he visits."

"If you think I'm sharing this with a kid who eats peanut butter and mayo sandwiches, you're nuts. It would be wasted on him."

"I'm sharing it with a man who likes spaghetti from a can," she reminded him.

"Not anymore," he said fervently. "I'll be here once a week for spaghetti. I'm writing that clause into whatever terms we set up for working together."

They ate for a while in silence, but Jo finally worked up the courage to bring up the one topic they'd avoided from the moment Pete had turned up on her doorstep. She figured he'd opened the door by mentioning his son's love of spaghetti.

She swallowed hard, then asked hesitantly, "Tell me about your son."

Pete's eyes lit up at once. "He's something. Sometimes I look at him and marvel that I had anything to do with creating such a great kid."

She swallowed the envy crawling up the back of her throat. "Does he look like you?"

"He looks a lot like I did when I was his age, the same dark hair, dark eyes and the exact same stubborn chin."

Jo smiled, thinking about the handful of pictures

she'd once seen of Pete as a kid. He'd had a snaggle-toothed smile and a dimple that wouldn't quit. She hoped there was no trace of the sadness she was feeling in her eyes when she asked, "Do you have a picture of him?"

"Sure." He pulled his wallet out of his pocket and flipped it open, then handed it to her. "That's his school picture. He's in first grade. Believe me, he's not normally that neat. I'm sure five seconds after they took it, his shirt was tugged out of his pants and probably torn. He reminds me of that kid in the *Peanuts* comic strip, the one who's always going around in a cloud of dust. That's Davey. Five minutes out of the tub and he looks like he's gone ten rounds in the mud."

"He sounds wonderful," Jo said wistfully.

So many times over the past seven years she'd wondered about Pete's child. A part of her had respected his refusal to turn his back on the boy's mother, even though it had hurt like hell. So many times her heart had ached at knowing that they would never have the children they'd talked about together.

Now, looking into that gaping, six-year-old smile, she couldn't seem to stop the tide of emotions that washed over her—sorrow, envy and even an undeniable trace of anger that she'd been deprived all of this.

"Jo?"

Pete's voice cut through the anguish.

She forced a smile. "I'm sorry," she said, handing him back his wallet.

"No, I'm the one who's sorry," he said, his expression filled with regret. "I shouldn't have gotten into this with you."

"I asked," she reminded him.

"Still, I am sorry. It should never have been this way."

"No," she said softly, "it shouldn't have been." A lingering trace of anger crept into her voice. "Why *was* it, Pete? Why did it happen?"

He regarded her with a gaze filled with misery. "I wish I could tell you that it was all Kelsey's fault, that she set out to seduce me and trap me into marriage, but I have to be honest. It wasn't like that."

Jo almost wished she hadn't asked, but she needed to know. "Did you love her?"

"No," he said fiercely. "You were the one I loved. I promise you that. But you had gone home. Kelsey and I thought there was no harm to hanging out together, having a few beers. It wasn't about attraction or sex or even friendship, though I guess we were friends. We'd known each other since we were kids."

"Had you dated before?"

He shook his head. "No. It was all about being lonely, Jo. I missed you. And I was too damn young and stupid to realize that sleeping with some other woman wouldn't make that loneliness go away. It only happened once, because I knew right away that sex with anyone who wasn't you wasn't the answer."

"But once was enough," Jo said.

"Yeah, once was enough. It's an old story," Pete said. "When I found out Kelsey was pregnant, there was only one thing to do. I wasn't going to let my child grow up without a dad."

"The way you'd grown up," Jo said, understanding at last. The marriage had been about far more than some moral obligation to Kelsey. It had always been about his son.

And knowing who Pete was and all the things that had shaped him into the man he'd become, she accepted that it couldn't have turned out any other way.

With that understanding came relief. She felt a weight lift from her heart. Forgiveness, which had always been an elusive concept to her, flooded in, and for the first time in seven years, she felt at peace.

"I should have told you all this back then," he said apologetically.

"I'm not sure it would have meant anything then," she admitted. "I was too hurt and too angry." She met his gaze. "I'm sorry the marriage didn't work out."

It seemed such a waste to her that it hadn't, that he'd sacrificed so much only to lose his son in the end, after all.

"So am I," he said.

It hurt to hear him say that. A part of her wished that he was glad to be rid of Kelsey, but it was a small, petty reaction. Again, he wouldn't be the man she'd loved if he'd been relieved that the marriage was over.

"I know it's none of my business, but what happened?" she asked him.

"I wasn't what she wanted," he said simply. "I never was."

The woman must be an idiot, Jo thought, but kept her reaction to herself. If Pete didn't cast aspersions on his ex-wife, she certainly wouldn't.

"You said they live in Richmond. That's not exactly around the corner. Do you get to spend much time with Davey?"

His eyes were filled with heartache when he replied, "Not nearly enough. We've worked out a schedule, and Kelsey usually sticks to it."

"Usually?"

"When she doesn't forget or make other plans—deliberately, more than likely."

"Does that happen often?"

"Often enough."

"That must be awful for you and your son."

He gave her a grim look. "I try not to let it be. I don't ever want Davey to be some pawn between his mother and me. That's why I didn't fight her for custody. He needs both of us. And as long as she's doing right by him, he'll never hear a harsh word about her from me."

"But if she's not living up to the agreement—" Jo began.

"I deal with her," Pete said. "We don't need the court involved."

Jo's respect for him grew. "You're an honorable man. I hope she knows what a treasure she threw away."

He laughed, but there was little humor in the sound. "I think she'd dispute that." He met her gaze. "Enough about me. Tell me about the man who didn't have the good sense to hang on to *you*."

She gave him a wry look. "You mean besides you."

He winced. "Ouch. I deserved that."

"You did," she agreed. "But I promise it'll be the last time I take potshots about the past. There's no point in living there."

"Amen to that," he replied. "Now stop avoiding the subject."

"The short version is that I came home and found him in bed with someone else," she said without emotion.

She had thought the image would be burned into her head forever, but ironically she couldn't picture it anymore. In fact, it hardly seemed to matter. Seeing Pete again had done that for her. Feeling the stir of those old emotions, knowing that the depth of what they'd once shared was so much more than anything she'd ever felt for her ex-fiancé, had put her heartache to rest. Since her love for Pete hadn't died nearly as quickly, she could only wonder if she'd ever loved James at all. Maybe that relationship had been on the rebound, despite the years it had taken for her to let another man into her heart.

Pete's gaze was steady and serious. "Want me to go beat him up for you?"

She returned his gaze with a solemn expression. "That's a lovely thought, but Ashley already offered. I turned her down."

"I'm meaner."

"You obviously don't know my big sister all that well."

"I saw her use a hammer," he said, then added with a grin, "She's a sissy."

Jo burst out laughing. "Please tell her that," she begged. "I want to be there."

"Think she'll pummel me to a bloody pulp?"

"I certainly think she'll try."

"It's good to hear you laugh, Jo," he said, his expression suddenly serious again.

"It's good to have something to laugh about," she

admitted. "I was beginning to think I'd lost my sense of humor along with my fiancé."

"That would have been the real tragedy," Pete told her.

She lifted her gaze to his and felt the familiar stir of old desires. "It would have been, wouldn't it? I think I'm just beginning to see that."

"I could always make you laugh," he reminded her.

Because it hadn't always been that way, she reminded him. "You made me cry, too."

"And it's something I'll regret till my dying day," he told her.

Jo shook off the desire to weep one last time for all they'd lost. Instead, she met his gaze and lifted her glass of water in a solemn toast. "Here's to concentrating on the laughter from now on."

Pete lifted his bottle of beer and tapped it against the glass. "To laughter."

But even as they made the pact, Jo knew that there were no guarantees. The one thing certain about the future was its unpredictability. In fact, she would never in a million years have predicted that she would be sitting here in the kitchen at Rose Cottage sharing a meal with Pete again. Moreover, they'd found a way to laugh together again. That wasn't just totally unpredictable, it was a miracle.

But looking into Pete's eyes, feeling her heart begin to heal at long last, she realized that miracles truly could happen.

6

Pete cursed himself six ways to Sunday all the way home from Jo's for having gotten drawn into even the briefest mention of his marriage. Up until tonight, he'd had a hard and fast rule: He didn't talk about it, not with anybody. What was the point, anyway? It was over and done with. Nobody needed to know the gory details. He'd always told himself he was keeping silent for his son's sake, but it was more than that. He didn't want anybody to know just how badly he'd screwed up.

Tonight he'd broken his own vow, and now he was regretting it. It would have been bad enough no matter whom he'd opened up to, but he sure as hell shouldn't have gotten into it with the woman who'd suffered because he hadn't known at twenty how to keep his pants zipped.

Then, again, maybe he had owed Jo that conversation. Maybe it was long overdue and damn the consequences to his pride. Possibly it would give her some satisfaction to know that he'd suffered too for the mistake he'd made. Maybe the humiliation of reliving it all would turn out to be worth it, if she'd been able to take some comfort in finally hearing the truth about his hasty, ill-advised marriage. Surely she couldn't think any worse of him than she did already. If she did, so be it. He could live with that, knowing that he'd finally been honest with her.

If they were ever going to have a second chance, Jo had to know the whole story. The fact that such a chance was even possible was a miracle, Pete realized. Mike had opened his eyes to that and made him see that it was a gift that shouldn't be tossed aside lightly. Since his attraction to Jo clearly hadn't died, he should be grateful for every second that gave him time to make amends and explore whether there was a chance for the two of them to recapture what they'd once had and build it into the dream they'd once shared.

Jo had been so damn innocent back then, so trusting. She'd believed in him—and in them—enough to give him not just her body, but her heart. He'd been way too careless with that gift. Because of that, he wasn't sure if he deserved a second chance, but obviously fate had other ideas since it had tossed them together now.

So far Jo had said nothing about how long she intended to stay, but he planned to use every minute to see if there was anything left of the feelings they'd once shared. One look at her had stirred something inside him, something he'd convinced himself was dead and buried. If he'd had to put a label on it, it wouldn't have been love exactly. No, it was more like hope.

When she'd been in his arms for those few brief moments, he thought he'd seen a fleeting spark of desire, a hint of longing in her eyes. He knew she'd responded to that kiss they'd shared. In fact, she'd looked as shaken by it as he had been. That could be the building block to something more. He just couldn't rush it. He had to keep in mind that she was in emotional pain herself. Her break-up was far fresher than his own. Taking advantage of that was out of the question.

No, he was older and, hopefully, wiser now. He was in it this time for the long haul. No mistakes. No blunders that would leave him racked with guilt and pain.

And with her entire family watching him like a hawk, he wasn't about to do anything that would give them cause to question his motives. Nope, he was going to be the perfect gentleman…even if it killed him.

Satisfied that he'd worked everything out—at least as much as he could control—he walked into his house with a lighter step. Immediately, he heard the phone ringing. By the time he snatched it up, the person had hung up, but the Richmond number on the caller ID told him it had been either Kelsey or his son. Though he had no particular desire to speak to his ex-wife, he couldn't take a chance that it had been Davey or that Kelsey was calling about his son. He dialed back immediately.

It was Davey who answered on the first ring. "Hello," he said, his voice quavering in an obviously frightened whisper.

All lingering thoughts of his unexpected evening with Jo fled. Trying not to overreact, Pete kept his own tone light. "Hey, buddy, it's Dad. How's it shakin'?"

"How'd you know it was me who called?" his son asked, his voice filled with surprise and unmistakable relief.

"Caller ID. How come you didn't leave a message?"

"I dunno."

"You know it's always okay to call me, right?"

"I guess."

Something wasn't right. Davey loved to call, but he usually had a reason and was usually bubbling over with enthusiasm. Tonight, he was being surprisingly vague. Pete pressed gently for answers. "What's up, buddy? You okay?"

"I guess."

"Is everything going okay at school?"

"I guess."

"Is your mom around?"

Davey hesitated so long, Pete knew he'd finally hit on the problem. "Where's your mom?" he asked.

"She's on a date with that guy, the one I told you about," Davey said.

"Harrison something."

"Yeah."

"Is someone there with you?"

"I don't need a babysitter," Davey said bravely. "I'm almost seven."

Pete bit back a curse. Almost seven! Typical kid. He'd barely turned six, and he was already anxious to be a year older. Six was entirely too young for a kid to be on his own at night, especially in the city. So was seven, for that matter.

Down here was something else, but even here Pete would think long and hard before leaving his son rattling around in the house by himself. Kids needed supervision, whether they wanted it or not. His skin crawled when he thought of the mischief and danger the boy could have gotten into.

"How long has your mom been gone?" he asked, careful not to let Davey know just how furious he was.

"Not that long. A couple of hours, I guess."

"Did she leave you a number?"

"I've got her cell phone number," Davey said. "She promised to leave it on."

Pete's temper hit a boil. Despite everything he'd said to Jo earlier about trying to keep his relationship with Kelsey civil for Davey's sake, he'd just about had it with her irresponsibility. He obviously needed to have another talk with her about her neglectful approach to parenting. Until now, he'd tried just talking things out with her, but he was beginning to wonder if it wasn't time for him to press the issue in court. He hadn't fought her before, because he'd believed she was seriously trying to be a good mom. Lately, though, he didn't like some of the decisions she was making. Too often she was choosing her social life over their son's well-being.

"Dad, please don't be mad at Mom," Davey said, obviously sensing that he'd revealed too much. "I'm okay, really. I just thought maybe we could talk for a while."

"Of course we can talk," Pete said, trying to calm his fears. As long as Davey was on the phone with him, he'd know he was safe. He shrugged out of his jacket and settled into a chair. "Why don't you tell me what's happening at school these days?"

First grade apparently was more exciting than Pete remembered. He kept his son on the phone for an hour, listening to the increasingly carefree chatter about an awesome science project he'd seen.

"I could have done a really cool one that was better,"

Davey said. "But our teacher said we're too little. Isn't that dumb? What difference does it make how big we are?"

"None I can see," Pete agreed.

"Did I tell you I have a spelling test tomorrow? I'm going to ace it. I spelled all the words for Mom and she said I was perfect," Davey boasted.

"That's great," Pete told him. "Want to spell them for me?"

Davey giggled. "Dad, you're a lousy speller. You won't even know if I'm right."

"Hey, kid, mind your manners. I'm not that bad," he retorted.

"Mom says you are. She told me if I needed help with spelling, I'd better get it from her."

"Okay, maybe she has a point," Pete admitted. "But I'd like to hear the words anyway."

Davey spelled a couple, then yawned.

"You tired, buddy?"

"I guess."

"Then crawl into bed and get some sleep. Take the portable phone in with you. If you wake up and want to call me, it'll be right there, okay?"

"Okay."

"And don't answer the door, you hear me?"

"Dad, I know that," Davey said. "You've told me."

"Yeah, I guess I have," Pete said, grinning at his son's evident exasperation. "How about I come down this weekend and we can see about doing that science project you want to do? Nothing says you can't do it, even if it's not for school. We'll grab some lunch, too."

"Really?" Davey asked, then immediately tempered

his excitement. "It's not a regular visit. I already looked on the calendar to see when you'd be coming again."

"I'll work it out with your mom. Now get some shut-eye, kid. Tomorrow's a school day."

"Bye, Dad. Love you."

"Love you more," Pete said, his heart aching.

He didn't waste so much as a split second on self-pity, though. He immediately punched in Kelsey's cell phone number. It took several rings before she picked up, and when she did, her voice was slurred. Even in that condition, he'd rather have her home with Davey than having the boy in the house all alone. Hell, maybe he should have called the cops instead and let the chips fall wherever they would, but he could only imagine the mess it would create with Davey caught smack in the middle. He'd probably end up in foster care before Pete could get it all straightened out. That wasn't an option, not even for a night.

"Get home right now," Pete said without ceremony. "And don't leave Davey there alone again or I'll haul you into court and take him away from you."

"What?" she asked, clearly fighting to grasp his words.

"I said to go home. I'll be calling there in fifteen minutes, and you'd better be there. If you're not, my next call will be to the police."

"You can't tell me what to do anymore," she protested.

"I think I just did," he responded. "When it comes to our son, I do have some say. If you don't believe it, try me."

"This is because you hate that I have someone new in my life and you don't," she said.

Pete clung to his patience by a thread. "I don't care who you date or what you do, unless and until it affects our son. Go home, Kelsey. You're down to twelve minutes to get there."

He slammed the phone down, waited the promised number of minutes with his eyes on the clock the whole time, then dialed the house. Kelsey picked up at once.

"Don't ever do that to me again," she said tightly. "You embarrassed me with a friend."

"That's nothing to what I'm likely to do if I find out you've ever left that boy in the house alone again. I don't care if it's day or night—he's too young to be there by himself. I've warned you before, and I'm beginning to think it fell on deaf ears."

"Okay, okay, I hear you, but I think you're getting worked up over nothing. Davey's a very responsible kid."

"He's six, dammit. What's he going to do if there's an emergency?"

"He knows how to call 911."

"Fat lot of good that will do him if the house is on fire and he can't get to a phone."

"Dammit, Pete, you're acting crazy," she said in a tone that was all bluster. "Davey is perfectly fine. How'd you find out he was here alone anyway?"

"He called me," he said. "And don't even think about taking this out on him. He called because he was scared. He did exactly the right thing."

"He's sound asleep," she protested, sounding a bit more uncertain. "How scared could he have been?"

"Scared enough to call me and spend an hour on the phone just to have a little company."

She didn't seem to have an answer to that.

"Okay, here's the deal. I'm coming down on Saturday," Pete informed her without leaving any room for argument. "I promised him we'd go out for the day."

"But—"

"Don't even think about trying to stop me, Kelsey."

"Fine. Whatever."

"Think of it this way. You can finish up your hot date, while I've got our son covered."

He slammed the phone down, satisfied that Davey was safe enough at least for tonight.

Then he grabbed a beer from the fridge, but before he'd taken the first sip, he dumped it down the drain. Getting stinking drunk wasn't the solution. It hadn't worked when his marriage was crumbling. It wouldn't work now.

The only thing that might marginally improve his mood would be seeing Jo, but he couldn't go barging in over there again tonight. And this definitely wasn't a problem he could dump on her shoulders. She didn't deserve getting dragged into this quagmire. It would just be rubbing salt in an old wound.

It was only a few hours till morning, though. He could make it till then. He'd pick up some of those blueberry doughnuts she used to love and be on her doorstep right after dawn. Maybe then this ache in the region of his heart would go away. And those doughnuts might earn him enough goodwill that he could sneak in another of those mind-blowing kisses.

He grinned for the first time since he'd called Davey. Now *that,* he thought, was something to look forward to.

Jo was still half-asleep when she heard Pete outside. She squinted at the clock and saw that it was barely six-thirty. She fell back against the pillows with a moan. It wasn't even daylight yet, but he was already hammering the heck out of something. She was surprised he could even see.

That didn't seem to be stopping him, though. Since the racket showed no sign of lessening, she dragged herself up and into the bathroom. She took a quick shower, pulled on jeans and a heavy knit sweater, ran a comb through her damp hair and walked downstairs in search of her shoes and socks. The minute she switched on the downstairs lights, Pete knocked on the door, then stuck his head in.

"You awake?"

Jo laughed at the ridiculous question. "As if anyone could sleep with all that racket you were making. What on earth were you doing?"

"Starting on the porch."

"In the dark?"

"I could see well enough." He surveyed her, then grinned. "You're not much of a morning person, are you?"

"I am when I have to be."

He dangled a bag in front of her. "Will this help?"

She sniffed and immediately smelled the heavenly

aroma of sugar and blueberries. "Oh, my God," she said, snatching the bag away from him and burying her face inside. "I can't believe the bakery is still making these."

"Yes, and they're fresh from the oven. I stopped by on my way over here and wheedled a few out of Helen. She remembered how you loved them."

"You're a saint."

"Hardly, but am I at least forgiven for dragging you out of bed?"

"That depends." She peered inside the bag again and counted. "A half dozen," she said with a blissful sigh. "You're definitely forgiven." She grinned at him. "For waking me, anyway."

"You gonna share?"

"Do I have to?"

Pete chuckled. "No, but it's a darn good thing I bought a couple for myself."

She took out the first one, slowly savored the aroma of sugar and blueberries, then bit into it. The sugar rush went straight to her brain. She'd never tasted anything quite like these and she'd been looking for years.

"Oh, my," she murmured after the first bite. "These are heaven."

"Does your sister the gourmet chef know that the only food you really crave in life is a blueberry doughnut?"

Jo nodded. "It pains her greatly. She even tried to learn to make them, but good as she is, hers never measured up. How did Helen remember that I love these? It's been years since I've been in there."

"Hey," he protested. "Don't I get some of the credit?"

She chuckled. "Yes. I thought I'd already praised

you. How did *you* remember that this was my favorite breakfast in the whole world?"

"You'd be surprised at the things I remember," he said in a way that made her heart skitter crazily.

It was way too early in the morning to go there. "Pete, don't say things like that," she pleaded, as if that would stop the sizzle in the air between them.

"Why not? It's true. I remember everything about that summer." He stepped closer and gazed into her eyes. "I remember the way you looked first thing in the morning, all dewy-eyed and fresh. You were no better at crawling out of bed early back then, either." He touched a finger to her lips. "And I remember how your lips tasted of blueberries and sugar. I was addicted to that taste for years. Couldn't get it out of my head, but just eating doughnuts wasn't enough. I kept telling Helen she was leaving something out, till I realized that what I needed was you. You were the missing ingredient."

He touched his mouth to hers and skimmed his tongue along the seam. Jo felt the earth shift beneath her feet.

"Pete," she protested, but without much energy.

"What, Jo?"

"We can't go back," she whispered, even though she couldn't seem to tear her gaze away. "Too much has happened. And if we dredge it all up, it'll make it impossible for me to work with you."

"So we should pretend it never happened?" he asked incredulously.

She drew in a deep breath and said firmly, "I think that's best."

"I think it's impossible."

So did she, if she were being honest. She'd just

planned to push down the old feelings in the vague hope that all the new ones would vanish, as well. Her reaction to this morning's treat proved that old and new were bound to be all tangled together.

"How about a compromise? I won't talk about the past if you won't," she said. "We don't have to pretend it didn't happen. We just won't talk it to death. We pretty well covered it last night anyway."

He didn't look convinced. "Then there's nothing more you think we need to say?" he asked.

"Nothing," she said staunchly.

He looked as if he wanted to debate the point, but he finally nodded. "Okay, I can ignore it, if you can." He turned away from her, hands shoved in his pockets. "I'm going to spend another hour working on the porch and then we can go over to the house I was telling you about. Will you be ready?"

She hated the sudden distance in his voice, as if they were little more than colleagues…or strangers. But she was the one who'd insisted it be this way, so how could she complain?

"I'll be ready," she told him. "I just need to hunt down my shoes and socks."

He left the kitchen, taking the life from the room when he went. She sagged into a chair and absentmindedly picked up another doughnut. After one bite, though, she realized that she wasn't really tasting it and put it aside. Why waste something so delicious?

She sipped her coffee, but it left a bitter aftertaste in her mouth. Acknowledging that her conversation with Pete had pretty much ruined a morning that had started out brightly, she scowled in the direction of the porch where he was hammering away again.

She didn't want it to be like this. Last night, things had felt natural, comfortable. Today, the air was filled with tension, and it was all her fault. What had she been thinking with her stupid ground rules? She was smart enough to know that as soon as a topic or a person was declared off-limits, it became huge, far more important than it otherwise might have been. Now the past and their old feelings for each other loomed between them.

She noticed that Pete had left his cup of coffee on the table and made a decision. She freshened it up, then carried it outside and handed it to him silently.

He watched her warily. "Thanks."

"You're welcome." She swallowed hard. "I'm sorry."

"For?"

"Being a first-class idiot."

He grinned and the tension vanished. "You? Never. You were always the smartest girl I knew."

"Maybe I grew into being dumb," she said, not entirely in jest. "I know we can't pretend that the past never happened. Last night we promised to concentrate on laughing again. Can we still do that?"

"Fine with me." He studied her over the rim of the cup, waiting. Finally, he said, "So, know any good jokes?"

She grinned. "Not a one."

"Me, either—at least none I can tell to a lady."

She shrugged. "Just as well. I'm freezing. I'll go back inside. I just wanted to, you know, settle things, make them okay again."

He tucked a finger under her chin. "Things are fine."

She felt the smile build from somewhere deep inside. "Good to know."

"Skedaddle, woman. You're distracting me."

She gave him one last look before she went back inside. He winked at her, and her heart did a predictable somersault.

Inside, she asked herself why it was so important to her that she and Pete be friends again. It was only opening the door to more potential heartache. She knew it wasn't because he'd offered her work. She could have managed for a bit without those two jobs he'd discussed with her. Nor was it because she didn't like being on the outs with anyone.

No, this was very personal. It was about her relationship with Pete—the one they'd had and the one she had a terrifying hunch that she wanted again.

7

Pete was still feeling completely off-kilter when he stopped work on the porch and told Jo it was time to drive over to the job site. He'd come damn close to dragging her into his arms after that kiss earlier, but he'd known he wouldn't be content with a few more kisses. Better to keep some distance between them. Jo needed to get used to the idea of being around him again, and rattling her was no way to accomplish that.

Of course, it was fairly difficult to get too much distance between them in the cab of a pickup. He could smell that familiar, old-fashioned scent she'd always worn, something light and flowery. It had always reminded him of her grandmother's garden. For a long time he hadn't been able to smell a rose without being transported to Rose Cottage. When Kelsey had wanted to put rosebushes all around their house, he'd vehemently protested. To Pete's relief, she'd grudgingly substituted a hodgepodge of lilacs, hydrangeas and azaleas, which she'd then neglected.

He'd eventually come to hate that little house with its haphazard, struggling garden. No more than an aging beach cottage, it was cramped and filled with reminders of all the mistakes he'd ever made. He'd kept the roof solid and the exterior painted, but he'd been so busy building his business, he hadn't had the time or money to invest in any of the extras that would have made it more livable. If the people whose homes he'd built in recent years had ever seen where he lived, he wasn't sure they would be trusting him with their dream homes.

He was about to change that, though. One of the places he wanted Jo to landscape was going to be his. He hadn't told her that. He wasn't sure why, except that he hadn't decided which house to keep just yet. He was half hoping that her reaction would help him decide. Maybe he even feared she'd back out of the job if she thought he was the client she was ultimately going to have to please. After all, he'd pretty much agreed to give her carte blanche to landscape the places for some anonymous buyers who'd hopefully come along in the spring.

They rode the few miles to the first house in silence. That was another thing he'd always loved about Jo. She'd never felt the need to fill every minute with chatter. It was yet another way in which Kelsey had fallen short by comparison. Kelsey couldn't keep quiet for ten minutes if her life depended on it. It had driven him nuts. A million other traits had driven him just as crazy, but the one positive—his son—had made him struggle to ignore the rest.

When he turned onto the dirt road that led to the first Cape Cod–style house with its soft gray shingles and white trim, he slanted a look at Jo. She was sitting on the edge of the seat, her eyes filled with anticipation. When the house finally came into view, she gasped.

"Oh, Pete, it's absolutely beautiful." She turned to him with shining eyes. "Can I see the inside?"

He grinned. "You planning to landscape in there, too?"

"Very funny." She gave him a pleading look. "Please?"

He laughed, taking pleasure in her delight. "Of course you can see the inside. It's still a work in progress. A lot of the finishing touches won't be done until March or so. The real estate market around here kicks into high gear in April, so I'm not rushing to complete it too much ahead of that."

"That's okay, I can use my imagination."

The minute he pulled to a stop, she leapt eagerly from the truck without waiting for his assistance. She was halfway to the front door by the time he caught up with her.

"You're awfully eager," he teased. "Or are you just cold?"

"Eager," she said without hesitation as she crossed the sweeping porch and waited for him. "Come on, slowpoke. Open up."

Pete unlocked the front door, then stepped aside and waited, his heart admittedly in his throat.

"Oh, my," Jo murmured as she stepped into the foyer with its shining hardwood floors and a skylight that sent sunlight cascading over everything, turning the oak to a golden hue. "It's beautiful."

She walked through the downstairs rooms almost reverently, expressing delight with the windows, the fireplace, the crown molding, the French doors in the dining room that led to a soft pink brick patio, the bright kitchen with its view of the Chesapeake Bay from the window that would eventually be over the sink as well as from the bay windows around the built-in breakfast nook that had been framed in, but not completed.

"It's charming," she said over and over. "Absolutely perfect." She grinned at him. "You have incredible taste. What kind of cabinets will you have in here?"

"White with glass doors. I want to use the old-fashioned glass that has a few bubbles and ripples in it, so the place will look as though it has some age to it. What do you think?"

"I think that's exactly right," she said. "Every detail is just what I would have chosen."

Pete had to bite back the desire to tell her that she was the one who'd inspired him. He couldn't remind her that they'd built this same dream house on a dozen different occasions over that incredible summer. It hurt in some way he couldn't name that she didn't seem to share that memory, that she wasn't recognizing the details he'd worked to get just right.

"How many bedrooms upstairs?" she asked.

"Five, including the master suite. Most of the work that's left is up there and here in the kitchen."

"I still want to go up. May I?"

"Of course."

This time he let her go alone. He stood at the kitchen window and stared out at the view, remembering how careful he'd been to be sure it was at exactly the right angle to capture the sunlight on the bay in the morning. He heard Jo's footsteps going from room to room, even heard the occasional exclamation and tried to guess what she was seeing. Her delight filled his heart with satisfaction and, maybe just a little, with regret.

This house could have been theirs. They could have finalized every detail together, but instead it had all been up to him. It wasn't enough that he knew her so well that he'd pleased her anyway. The real joy would have come in the sharing, in the excursions to look at everything from faucets to ceiling fans and flooring.

Still, he couldn't deny that it felt good knowing that he'd built something she liked. He could hardly wait to see how she reacted to the second house. It was ironic given how long they'd been apart, but he'd actually felt as if she were with him as he'd designed and built it.

"Hey, it's cold in here," he finally hollered. "Are you ever going to get down here and do the job I hired you for?"

She danced down the steps, her cheeks glowing. "That's some tub you installed in the master suite," she teased him.

"Big enough for two," he confirmed.

"Lucky couple."

He grinned. "Indeed. Ready to look around outside?"

"I'll need to get my notepad from the truck so I can make a few sketches and jot down my ideas."

Pete nodded. "I'll meet you out by the oak tree in back. Wait till you see it in the spring and next fall. It's spectacular."

Some of the light in her eyes died. "I'll have to take your word for it," she said. "I'll probably be back in Boston by then, but I'm glad you saved it. Too many builders just slash down everything in sight these days."

"There was no way I'd cut this down. I kept imagining a swing hanging from its branches or a tree house built way up high. Besides, it adds to the feeling that this place is substantial. Even makes it feel as if it's been around for a while."

To his astonishment, she stood on tiptoe and planted an impulsive kiss on his cheek. "Nice to see you getting all sentimental about a tree."

She was gone before he could react. He wandered around back and leaned against the massive trunk of the saved oak that had earned him an unexpected kiss. He nudged it with an elbow. "Thanks," he murmured, then felt like an idiot.

Even with the sun shining brightly, the air off the water was frigid. Pete shivered as he waited for Jo to join him. When she didn't appear after several minutes, he went looking for her. He found her by his truck, her pad resting on the hood as she made some sketches, her pencil flying over the page. He went up to peer over her shoulder.

There, in front of his eyes, was a climbing rosebush creeping up to the porch railing. A pond was taking shape off to one side, surrounded by some sort of flowering bushes. She blinked and looked up at him.

"Where'd you come from?"

"Around back, where I was waiting for you."

"Sorry," she said, but with little real repentance. "Inspiration struck and I wanted to get it down on paper. I'm thinking a wildflower garden over here with a birdbath. It will draw butterflies and birds, so people sitting on the porch will be able to watch them. What do you think?"

"People actually sit around and watch birds?"

She laughed. "We used to."

He thought back and recalled how they'd been endlessly entertained by the turf wars over her grandmother's birdbath and the hummingbird feeder. "I'd forgotten," he admitted. "Where's the hummingbird feeder going?"

"With the plants I have in mind, you won't need one. They'll be drawn to the flowers."

"You know, if you're going to go into this much detail all around the yard, we'd better come back another day. I don't want you to freeze to death out here. How about grabbing some lunch while we warm up a bit, then taking a quick look at the other place?"

She waved off the question, her attention back on the page. She was sketching something else, some sort of arbor.

"What's that?" he asked.

"Wisteria. This place cries out for a white picket fence and an arbor. It'll give it a nice, old-fashioned touch."

"If you say so. Now, how about lunch?" he prodded again.

"Since I think my fingers are turning into blocks of ice, lunch sounds good."

Pete impulsively clasped her hands in his and rubbed them, then kissed the tips of her fingers. She gave him a startled look, but then a slow smile crept across her face.

"Is this one of those perks that comes with the job?" she asked.

"I'll even put it in the contract, if you want me to."

She nodded slowly. "Just be sure you make it an exclusive."

Pete chuckled. "Believe me, you're the only person who works for me whose hands aren't scarred up and calloused. This treatment is definitely reserved for you."

As if the whole exchange had suddenly made her nervous, she withdrew her hands and tucked them in her pockets. She headed around to the passenger door of the truck, then shot one last grin over her shoulder. "I'll want that in writing."

Pete laughed. "Done, darlin'."

She was playing with fire, Jo warned herself as she sipped the hot seafood chowder she'd ordered for lunch. Something daring had crept over her back at the job site and she hadn't been able to help herself, but she could not keep tossing out innuendoes and letting Pete steal kisses. Not only was it unprofessional, it was dangerous. For hours now her blood had been humming through her veins the way it had that long-ago summer. She felt every bit as giddy and impulsive as the schoolgirl she'd been back then, too.

And look what had happened, she reminded herself sternly.

She glanced across the table and realized Pete's gaze was resting on her. "What?" she asked.

"You look as if you're giving yourself a very stern lecture," he teased.

"I am," she admitted.

"About?"

"You."

"Oh?"

"Just reminding myself that you're a client."

Something flickered in his eyes, something she couldn't really interpret. Hurt, maybe.

"I thought we were more than that, Jo," he said quietly. "I thought we were friends."

"We *were* friends," she agreed. "In fact, we *were* even more than that. You changed everything. I can't let myself forget that."

"Yeah, I suppose you're right. Trust doesn't come easily once it's been destroyed. I guess I need to remember that, too." He glanced at her bowl. "You finished? We should probably get going."

Sorry that she'd spoiled the easygoing mood between them yet again, Jo merely nodded. It was just as well. They'd been getting too comfortable together…again.

Pete threw a couple of ones on the table, then paid the check. "Are you up for seeing the other house?"

"Of course," she said, not even trying to hide her eagerness. If it was anything at all like the first one, she was going to love it.

A few minutes later, Pete turned off the main road and cut through a densely wooded lot. When they finally emerged into a clearing, Jo felt her heart begin to pound. She recognized this house as if she'd seen it a thousand times before. In a way she had, because she and Pete had talked about it so often.

She'd had a similar reaction to the first house, but not like this. This morning, certain touches had seemed vaguely familiar, like a distant memory stirring but not quite gelling. Her reaction to this house, though, was intense and instantaneous. There was no mistaking that this was their dream house.

Unlike the first one, this was all on one floor, sprawling over the waterfront land to take advantage of every view, every breeze. Even from where they sat, she could see through one set of French doors straight through the house to another set that faced the Chesapeake. She already knew there would be ceiling fans in every room, that the porch facing the water would have Victorian trim and railings meant to hold flower boxes spilling over with color.

Despite its obvious size, it somehow captured the feeling of a seaside cottage, something cozy and filled with light and the scent of salt air. She was willing to bet that the master suite would be at one end with rooms for kids and guests at the other, giving the owners privacy even when the house was overrun with family or company.

Despite all her earlier admonitions, she turned to Pete with her heart in her throat. "You built our house," she said softly. "Just the way we talked about."

Hands stuffed in his pockets, he nodded. "I tried."

"But why? And how can you turn around and sell it?"

He looked vaguely embarrassed, which in itself was a shock.

Pete never looked anything other than confident.

"In a weird way, it started out as punishment, sort of a torment," he admitted, "but in the end it made me feel close to you again. I brought in plumbers and electricians, but all the rest I did myself. I started it right after my divorce became final."

"Then I'll ask again—how can you sell it?"

"I'm not going to," he said, as if he'd just reached a decision. "I'm going to live here."

"But you told me before you intended to sell both of these houses."

"I think I might have, if you hadn't reacted the way you did just now. The minute I saw your face, I knew I couldn't part with this one, after all." His gaze lingered on hers. "Want to see the inside?"

"Yes," she said at once, then, "No."

He regarded her with amusement. "Which is it?"

"I'm not sure. I think I'm afraid to see the inside."

"Afraid I've gotten it wrong?" he asked.

"No. I'm terrified you've gotten it exactly right," she confessed.

"Would that be so awful?"

Yes, Jo thought to herself. Because Pete would live here without her.

Aloud, she forced herself to say, "No, I suppose not."

He hopped out of the truck and went around to open her door. When he held out his hand, she took it, then reluctantly stepped down.

At the front door, she hesitated again. She lifted her gaze to meet his. "You know if I walk through this door and fall in love, there's going to be a problem, don't you?"

He looked perplexed. "What sort of problem?"

"You're going to have to fight me to keep this place."

Pete laughed, then sobered when he apparently realized she was at least halfway serious.

He shrugged. "There's an easy solution to that, you know. You can just move in here with me."

Even though his tone was light, Jo's heart tumbled straight to her toes. The suggestion was too damn tempting. "You know that's not possible," she said at once, a reminder meant as much for her as for him.

"Of course, it is," he said just as readily, then winked at her. "But I've got another few weeks' worth of work to do. You have time to decide."

But when the door swung open and Jo stepped through, she knew it wouldn't take nearly that long. She felt as if she'd just come home.

"He's gotten every single detail exactly right," Jo complained to her sisters when they stopped by later that evening.

"And that's a bad thing?" Melanie asked cautiously, clearly not quite certain what to make of Jo's mood.

"Yes, dammit. I am not supposed to fall in love with a house here, but I have to tell you, I want that house."

Ashley and Maggie exchanged a grin. "Maybe he'll sell it to you," Ashley suggested. "Building and selling houses is what he does, after all."

"And what will I use to buy it? I don't have any savings, at least not enough to put a down payment on that house."

"What was he going to ask for it?"

"I have no idea, but with real estate booming here and that incredible water view, it's got to be at least half a million. Maybe more. That's way out of my league," Jo said with regret.

"But you do want it?" Ashley persisted. "It's more than sentiment talking?"

"Absolutely," she insisted, knowing it was impulsive and irrational and completely out of character, especially since until a couple of hours ago she'd had every intention of going back to Boston. "The minute I stepped inside, I knew that house was mine."

"Unfortunately, Pete seems to be thinking of it as his," Melanie reminded her.

Jo frowned. "Don't you think I know that? He was grinning like a fool when he saw me drooling over the place. Now he knows he has leverage. He has something I want, and he knows I'll do just about anything to get it."

For the first time since they'd started talking about the house, Ashley looked alarmed. "What do you mean by anything?"

Jo scowled at her. "I'm not going to murder the man in his sleep, if that's what you're worried about. I'll probably be doing free landscaping design for him till my dying day trying to persuade him to sell me the house."

"Actually I wasn't worried so much about murder. I could defend you against that," Ashley said with a dismissive wave of her hand. "I'm more concerned that you're going to get mixed up with a man you barely know just because he happened to build your dream house."

Jo stared at her blankly, then realized that none of her sisters had a clue that Pete had actually built the house because of her. If they knew her history with Pete, Ashley's mild worry would turn into utter panic. Jo should have kept her mouth shut about this whole stupid mess. It wasn't as if she could have the house, after all. It was just that they'd arrived while her desire for the place was still fresh. She hadn't been able to stop talking about the house from the moment they'd arrived.

"Me getting mixed up with Pete is not an issue," she assured her sister. "Let's forget about the house. I can't have it, and that's that. I shouldn't have brought it up."

"But you did, and you obviously feel passionately about it," Ashley said. "Let's get practical. Maybe Pete will build you another house just like it, maybe something on a smaller scale and more affordable."

"It wouldn't be the same," Jo said wistfully.

"Come on, Jo. That's a great idea," Melanie enthused. "If you go into partnership with Mike, you'll have the money for a down payment in no time. Heck, maybe you can even barter a few jobs with Pete to get the rest."

Jo knew it was ridiculous, but she didn't want an exact replica. She wanted this one, at least in part because she knew she'd been on Pete's mind when he'd designed and built it.

But it was out of the question, and that was the end of it.

"Come on, guys, I never should have gotten into this. You just caught me in a weak moment. Let's talk about something else."

"Such as?" Maggie asked.

Though she tried desperately, Jo couldn't think of an alternative topic. Images of the house kept flashing in her mind. She'd been mentally decorating the place ever since she'd seen it. There would be lots of blue-striped cushions and chintz, and old-fashioned wicker furniture for the porch.

"There you go," Ashley said, when it was clear Jo was stumped for another subject. "This is the only thing that really matters to you. Let's come up with a plan."

Jo studied her with a narrowed gaze. "What kind of plan?"

"To get that house away from Pete, of course."

"Feminine wiles," Melanie said at once, only to draw scowls from the rest of them. "Hey, it works. Isn't that all that matters?"

"No, it is not," Jo said firmly. She couldn't see herself seducing the house away from Pete. That would just complicate an already tricky situation. In fact, he'd probably be delighted to have her try. He had invited her to move in, after all. Even if the offer had been made in jest, she knew he'd be thrilled if she took him up on it. Only she knew how impossible that was. She was not putting her heart at risk, even for the home she'd always wanted.

"Money talks," Ashley said, shooting a daunting look at Melanie. "Let's see what kind of down payment we can scrape together and make the man an offer he can't refuse."

"It's not about the money," Jo assured her. "Pete loves this house as much as I do."

"Men don't fall in love with houses. They want a roof over their heads," Ashley scoffed.

"Excuse me," Jo protested. "But don't you think it might be different with Pete? He builds houses for a living. They have to mean something to him for him to be so good at it."

Melanie regarded her curiously. "You're certainly quick to jump to his defense. And you seem to understand what makes him tick. How well have you gotten to know him?"

"Oh, for pity's sake," Jo muttered. "You all are impossible. It's about the house, not Pete. How did we get off track?"

"I thought it was because the two were so intertwined," Ashley said, a smug expression on her face.

Jo saw she was not going to win an argument with this crowd, not without divulging a whole lot more than she wanted to about her history with Pete.

"How about some ice cream?" she asked cheerfully. "I have hot fudge sauce."

"It's thirty degrees outside and you want ice cream?" Ashley asked.

"With *hot* fudge sauce," Jo said. "That makes all the difference."

"Count me in," Melanie said at once.

"Me, too," Maggie agreed,

Ashley clearly wasn't going to be so easily distracted, but when she opened her mouth, Maggie frowned at her, and she clamped her lips together.

"Ashley will have ice cream, too," Maggie said with a grin.

"Yes, I will," Ashley said primly. "And then we'll get back to Pete."

Jo sighed, but she dished out the ice cream and prayed she could get them all out of the house before her big sister made good on her promise.

8

It was Friday before Pete came around to Rose Cottage again. Despite her desire to keep her emotions in check where he was concerned, Jo realized she'd missed him. She was too honest not to admit that, at least to herself. She told herself it was merely because she was anxious to look for some chink in his determination to keep that house. She also told herself that her long-held hurt and anger over his betrayal were as strong as they'd ever been. They had to be.

Maybe so, she admitted ruefully, but she couldn't seem to stay away from him. He was on the porch, hammering away, when she took him a mug of steaming coffee.

"How's it going?" she asked as she handed it to him.

He paused, took a cautious sip of the coffee, then surveyed what he'd accomplished. The new tongue-and-groove flooring was about halfway finished. "It would move a lot faster if I weren't tied up on so many other jobs right now."

"There's no rush," Jo assured him. "Have you had

time to do any work on your two spec houses since we went by there the other day?" She'd deliberately chosen to refer to them as "spec houses" in order to minimize the attachment they both clearly felt, at least to the one.

He grinned, as if he understood her ploy. "I haven't had much time. I usually work over there on the weekends, but that's out this weekend."

"Oh?"

"I need to go down to Richmond Saturday morning to see Davey," he said, then studied her as if to see if the reference to his son was upsetting.

Jo worked to keep her expression neutral so he'd continue. Eventually, he shrugged.

"Something came up the other night," he said. "I promised him I'd get down there to spend some time with him."

Envy streaked through Jo, though she didn't pause to define the cause. "The two of you have big plans then?" she asked.

"Any time I get to spend with my son is a big deal," he said at once, a surprising edge in his voice.

"Well, of course, I just meant—"

He cut her off. "I know what you meant. I'm sorry. Look, I won't bore you with the details, but things got a little tense between Kelsey and me the other night. I need to straighten some things out with her. I'm not looking forward to it, and I really don't want to talk about it, especially not with you. I won't drag you into the middle of this. It's not fair."

"You don't get to decide what's fair," she retorted. "Maybe I could offer a woman's perspective."

"No," he said flatly.

There was a finality in his voice that told Jo he wouldn't appreciate her prying any more deeply into what had happened. She bit her tongue and deliberately changed the subject.

"Since you won't be around, do you mind if I go over to the houses tomorrow and do some more sketches?" she asked.

"Of course not. That's what I hired you for."

She grinned at him. "You haven't actually hired me yet. Maybe we ought to talk about the exorbitant rates I charge for my expertise before we go any further."

"Whatever your going rate is, I'll pay it," he said without hesitation. "I want the landscaping done right. Mike says you can handle it, and that's good enough for me. Besides, I saw those preliminary sketches you did in just a few minutes the other day. I know you've got a feel for these houses."

"I'm glad you're pleased, but I still think we ought to talk about my fee," she said. "I don't want there to be any problems when I turn in the bill. This is a professional thing, Pete. It doesn't have anything to do with, well, us. You'd write up a contract with Mike, wouldn't you?"

"Okay, you're right. Why don't you put something down on paper, and I'll come inside in a half hour or so and sign it?"

Jo nodded. "Perfect."

He regarded her with amusement. "And just so you know, I'm going to read the fine print, darlin'. I didn't miss the gleam in your eyes when we left that second house the other day. I don't want you sneaking in some deal to get that house away from me."

Jo laughed. "Never crossed my mind."

"Yeah, right," he said skeptically. "I know how your mind works, but just so you know, there's only one way you're ever moving into that house and it's with me."

She frowned at him. "Be careful. You saw how much I love that place. I might take you up on that, and then where would you be?"

"In heaven," he retorted lightly. "Or the closest thing to it."

The expression in his eyes was just serious enough to make her tremble. "Pete," she whispered in what sounded more like a plea than a protest.

A wicked grin spread across his face. "Don't panic, Jo. I'm not going to push you into anything you don't want to do."

But, of course, that was precisely the problem. Despite all the stern lectures, despite her best intentions, this was something she was starting to *want,* desperately in fact. Not just that house, but Pete. He wasn't just a rebound romance, despite what she'd told him. She realized now that he was the only man she'd ever truly loved. It should have scared her to death, but with every day that passed she was growing more at peace with that knowledge.

Pete finished up as much work on the porch as he could before dusk fell, then went inside Rose Cottage. Jo was sitting at the kitchen table, still looking rattled by their earlier exchange. He could relate to the feeling. He'd been in a state of perpetual turmoil ever since she'd opened the front door the first night he'd come by about fixing up the porch. The unexpected wonder of seeing her then was still with him.

"Penny for your thoughts," he said when she looked up at him with a startled expression as if she hadn't been expecting him.

"My going rate's a lot higher than that," she said, dragging her attention back from wherever it had wandered.

He picked up the piece of paper on the table. "I assume our deal is all spelled out on here."

She nodded. "I gave you a break from what I'd charge in Boston."

Without even looking at the paper, Pete frowned at her. "I don't want a break."

Her chin came up. "Well, I gave you one anyway."

He tossed the paper on the table. "Take it back."

"I most certainly will not. Stop being so blasted stubborn. You haven't even looked at it." She handed it right back to him. "See? It's not like I'm going to go broke."

It was a nice round number, but it wasn't enough. "Fair is fair, Jo. This isn't even half as high as what Mike would charge me."

She faltered at that. "Really?"

"Really," he assured her. "If you won't make the change, I will." He picked up the contract, filled in a new set of numbers, then scrawled his signature across the bottom.

"This is more like it," he said as he handed it back to her.

She frowned as she read it. "You can't be serious."

"Oh, but I am. Ask Mike. He tells me all the time that he's being conservative, too."

There was a spark in her eyes he couldn't quite interpret,

"That lowdown scumbag," she muttered under her breath, her gaze still on the paper.

Puzzled by her reaction, he stared at her. "Who's a scumbag? Mike?"

"No, of course not," she said. "My boss in Boston. Everyone told me he was a tightwad, but I'm just beginning to see how much he was probably making, thanks to me."

"Seems to me that's a good reason not to go back there," Pete said, then added casually, "Assuming you need one."

"I might go back to Boston, but I sure as hell won't be working for him again," she said fiercely.

Pete laughed at her infuriated tone. "Maybe I ought to call Mike right now and tell him this might be a good time to sign you up for a partnership."

She gave him a sly look. "It might be, if I had the perfect place to live."

He chuckled. "Very clever, but you have Rose Cottage. There's nothing wrong with this place that a little loving attention won't fix right up. Your sisters have already done a lot to whip it back into shape. The foundation and roof are solid. The porch is the last big investment you'll be making."

"But there's an even more perfect place a few miles from here," she told him.

He regarded her innocently. "But the price is way

too high for you, isn't that what you've been telling me? And it's awfully big for one person living all alone."

"Give me a price in dollars and cents, and there might be bargaining room," she countered.

"There's lots more to life than money," he reminded her.

"That's not what you used to say," Jo replied. "When I knew you, all you could think about was getting your business started and making a name for yourself. You were very ambitious."

"But now that I've done that, I see the flaw in my thinking," Pete confessed. "None of it matters a damn, if there's no one around to share it."

Jo met his gaze and released a sigh. "I can't argue with that," she said. She got to her feet and opened the refrigerator door. "Can you stay for dinner?"

Pete walked over behind her and pushed the door closed. "Jo?"

When she turned to face him, tears were glistening on her cheeks.

"What is it?" he asked, rubbing the pad of his thumb across the damp, silky skin. He had to fight the desire to swoop in and claim her lips.

"Nothing," she insisted, trying to duck under his arm.

Pete dropped a hand on her shoulder and kept her in place. "Talk to me," he pleaded. "What did I say to upset you?"

"It wasn't you," she insisted. "I'm just an idiot."

"Never."

"I am. I'm always wanting something I can't have or something that's wrong for me."

"Such as?"

Her gaze met his, then darted away.

"There's nothing you can't say to me," he told her. "Nothing. What is it you can't have that you want?"

A spark of anger flickered in her eyes as she faced him. "I wanted you once," she said with such quiet regret that it made Pete's heart twist. "And I wanted James, at least till I figured out what a dope he was."

"Anything else?"

Her lips curved slightly. "I want that house."

Pete cupped her chin in his hands and looked into her eyes. "It was made for you," he said quietly.

Surprise lit her eyes. "You'll sell it to me?"

Maybe he should. It was obvious the place meant something to her, perhaps even more than it meant to him, though he didn't see how that was possible. But that house was the one thing that might keep the door open for him to get back into her life. He couldn't relinquish it too easily.

"Sorry," he said. "I can't sell it to you."

The excitement in her eyes died. "Can't or won't?"

"Doesn't matter. The house is mine."

"I could hate you for the ten seconds when you let me get my hopes up," she muttered.

"Just add it to the list," he advised. "You have bigger reasons to hate me."

"But I've been working on forgiving you for those," she said.

He grinned. "How's that going?"

"Not half as well as it was about five minutes ago," she replied.

"I figured as much," he said, then dropped that kiss

on her lips after all. "I think I'll skip dinner tonight. We both have a lot of thinking to do. I'll see you when I get back."

"Maybe you will, maybe you won't," she said airily.

Pete picked the contract off the table and waved it under her nose. "This says I will. I know you'd never go back on your word."

"Why shouldn't I?" she asked. "You did."

"But you're a better person than I ever was, darlin'. Everybody around here knows that."

In fact, he was exercising astounding restraint to keep from capitalizing on that kiss and seducing her right here and now. He knew the attraction was there on her part. He felt it every time he crushed her mouth beneath his. It was in her eyes when she looked at him. She wouldn't fight him. In fact, she would come to him as eagerly as she had at eighteen, when she'd been way too young and he'd been way too stupid to see what a gift she was giving him.

With the taste of her still on his lips, he made a hasty exit before he was tempted to stay and prove just how low-down and sneaky he could be.

Jo sank down on a kitchen chair after Pete had gone and touched a finger to her still-burning lips. She could deny it from now till the cows came home, but she wanted him. It didn't seem to matter whether it was sensible or insane. It didn't seem to matter that he'd broken her heart once. All that mattered was the heat and need that simmered every time he was around. Even tinged with hurt and regret and anger, that need was a powerful force. In fact, its overwhelming power scared her to death. She liked being in control, but she wasn't with this. The need controlled her.

"You ought to be upstairs packing your bags right this second," she muttered aloud.

"Oh, my God," Maggie said, scaring Jo half to death. "She's in here talking to herself."

"Do you ever knock?" Jo groused as the door slammed shut behind all three sisters.

"Why would we?" Ashley asked reasonably. "We all have keys."

"Maybe you should turn them in to me. I'd like to know I can count on some privacy around here," Jo retorted.

"To do what?" Melanie asked, regarding her with amusement. "You having a fling you want to keep secret?"

There was no smart answer to that question, so Jo ignored it. A yes would definitely intrigue them. An honest answer—that she needed a break from them—would offend them.

"Why are you here?" she asked instead. "Just to make me nuts?"

"It's our sisterly duty to check on you," Ashley said.

"But daily? Is that really necessary?" she asked wryly.

"At a minimum," Ashley said. "Maybe more if we don't like what we find. Fortunately, it's a small town. It's not inconvenient for us to drop by."

Now *there* was a barely veiled threat, Jo concluded. She regarded her sisters with dismay. "Don't you all have husbands now?" she grumbled. "Shouldn't they be the focus of your attention?"

"You wish," Maggie said with a grin. "We know what they're up to. They're at my house grilling steaks. We give them an occasional men-only night, so they appreciate us more."

Jo laughed. "How's that working?"

"Amazingly well," Melanie complained. "We're beginning to think they get together just to talk about us and plot against us. It's worrisome."

"Really? Yet you still do it," Jo said with an exaggerated shake of her head. "Very sad. I thought you all were smarter than that. You were my role models. Now I'm not so sure I should pay a bit of attention to you *or* your unsolicited advice. What exactly do you think they're plotting?"

"Not so much plotting as exchanging information," Maggie said. "For instance, Rick came home the other night and insisted on fixing me dinner. He knows I'm the cook in the family. I take pride in it. But one of them must have told him it would be a treat for me to have a night off. He would never have thought of that on his own."

Jo stared at her. "Okay," she said slowly. "You say that as if it's a bad thing. What am I missing?"

Melanie nudged Maggie in the ribs. "Come on. Confess. You got all bent out of shape because you thought he was telling you he didn't like your cooking."

"Well, it did cross my mind," Maggie said, looking vaguely flustered by having to admit to an uncharacteristic dip in her normally healthy self-esteem in the kitchen. "But after my second glass of wine and my first taste of the pesto sauce he made from scratch, I decided maybe I should just go with the flow. The man seems to know his way around the kitchen. Who'd have guessed it?"

"And that's it?" Jo asked. "That's the kind of devious plotting they're up to over there tonight?"

"Pretty much," Ashley said.

"Well, thank God they haven't thought to include Pete yet," she said with exaggerated relief.

"Pete?" All three women seized on her comment at once.

"Should they be including Pete?" Ashley inquired, her gaze narrowed. "What's happened? Do our men need to check him out more thoroughly? Should I run a check into his background? I can do that, no problem."

"Oh, stop it," Jo ordered. "Nothing's happened. I just meant that he *is* underfoot around here, so some people might leap to the conclusion that he should be dragged into this family mix thing. I was trying to make the point that I'm grateful he hasn't been lured into such a web of male intrigue."

"But these people who'd leap to that conclusion, they'd be wrong?" Ashley persisted. "You haven't done something crazy, have you?"

"Crazy like what?" Jo asked, struggling to contain her impatience.

"Well, you do want that stupid house," her big sister reminded her.

"We've been over this," Jo said irritably. "There are limits to what I'll do to get it."

"Glad to hear it," Ashley said. "I drove by it, by the way."

"Me, too," Melanie and Maggie chimed in.

"I can see why you adore it," Ashley said. "It's charming. It reminds me of Cape Cod."

Jo bit back a grin. "Maybe that's why they call that architecture the Cape Cod style."

Ashley frowned at her. "You're such a pain when you're being smug."

"If I'm so annoying, why didn't you all go to a movie tonight, instead of coming over here?"

"I think we've established that it's our duty to be here," Maggie said. "Whether you want us here or not. Let's play Scrabble. I'm feeling particularly brilliant tonight."

"Give her a glass of wine," Ashley ordered. "That ought to dull her brain. Nobody in this family is allowed to beat me at Scrabble."

"Is that so?" Jo asked, exchanging a look with her sisters. It was evident they were as eager as she to rise to the challenge. "What do you say, ladies? Do we make her regret those words?"

"I'm in," Melanie said at once.

"Oh, yes. I am so in," Maggie agreed.

Jo laughed. "Then, Maggie, you get the wine and I'll get the game. Just make sure you fill big sister's glass to the very brim. I'll have water, by the way."

"Me, too," Melanie said, winking at her.

Maggie nodded as she retrieved the glasses. "That'll be two waters and a brimming glass of wine for the smart-alecky big sister."

Ashley frowned at Maggie. "What about you? What are you drinking?"

Maggie plunked the wine bottle down at her own

place at the table. "I'm going with the rest of the bottle."

"Oh, no," Melanie whispered, laughing. "That leaves me to drive them home and try to explain to Josh and Rick why they're drunk as skunks."

"I say we just pour them both into bed upstairs and let their husbands come and fetch them in the morning," Jo said. "Then we can watch while these two try to explain what happened. It'll be fun."

To her surprise, it was Ashley who regarded her with evident approval. "You have a very diabolical mind, little sister." She lifted her wineglass in a toast. "I salute you."

"Which should tell you something," Jo said.

"What?" Ashley asked, looking perplexed.

"That the rest of you can stop worrying about me. I'm not the nitwit you take me for. I can handle Pete Catlett and anything else that comes my way."

Her sisters exchanged a look, then grinned at her.

"You're our baby sister. We'll never stop worrying," Ashley said, patting her hand. "Get used to it."

Jo sighed. Right there in a nutshell was the primary reason she shouldn't even consider getting mixed up with Pete—or trying to buy that house that would keep her close to her overprotective sisters.

Somehow, though, as daunting as the prospect was, it wasn't nearly enough to stop the yearning for either one.

9

Fearing the confrontation that was bound to happen the minute he laid eyes on his ex-wife, Pete approached the ranch-style brick home he'd bought for Kelsey and his son with more than his usual trepidation. Kelsey's moods could be unpredictable at best. This morning, she might be humble and conciliatory, given the fact that she was clearly in the wrong, but more than likely she'd be defensive and spiteful.

This should have been such a tranquil place for Davey to grow up, Pete thought with another surge of anger. The house was in a quiet residential neighborhood with good schools nearby. It had cost more than he could afford at the time, but he'd wanted his son to have nothing but the best, and he'd been determined to be fair to Kelsey, too. Whatever else he thought of her, she would always be the mother of his son, and for that alone, he wanted to show her the respect she deserved.

Sometimes, though, she made it damn hard.

As he tried to settle his temper, he noticed that despite the money he sent her each month in alimony, none of it was apparently being spent on upkeep. The shutters needed painting and the garage door looked to be stuck halfway up.

He parked behind his ex-wife's brand-new SUV—a car which told him exactly where her money was going—and crossed the lawn to the front door. Davey came charging out before he got there and launched himself straight at Pete with a wild whoop of excitement.

"Hey, buddy," Pete said, laughing as he scooped the boy up and noted that his clothes were surprisingly neat for nine in the morning. Usually by now, Davey would have managed to make a mess of whatever he'd put on. "You look good." He buried his nose in the kid's stomach till Davey started giggling, then added, "Smell good, too."

"Mom let me take my bath this morning instead of last night, so I'd look good when you got here. Can I go next door and play now? Mom says you guys have gotta talk or something. Grown-up stuff, huh?"

"Yeah, it's grown-up stuff," Pete agreed. "I can't believe you want to play and spoil these nice, clean clothes." He paused, leaned closer, then asked with an expression of mock horror, "What if you have to take another bath?"

Davey giggled. "I'll be careful," he promised.

Pete rolled his eyes at the likelihood of that. "A half hour, pal. Then you and I are going to look for supplies for whatever it is you want to make as a science project."

"And we're having lunch out, too, right?"

"Absolutely. Whatever you want."

"Hamburgers and pizza," Davey said at once.

"That might be overdoing it," Pete said. "Think about

it and pick one or the other. Now let me go in and say hello to your mom."

Davey was about to bound off down the street to his friend's house, but he suddenly turned and came back, his expression worried. "You and mom aren't gonna yell, are you?"

Pete tugged his son's baseball cap down over his eyes. "Nope."

"Promise?"

"I promise." It was a promise he had every intention of keeping, unless Kelsey failed to listen to reason.

Apparently satisfied, Davey took off running toward the neighbor's house. Pete watched till he went inside, then turned toward Kelsey's. When he walked in, he could hear the noise of cartoons coming from the family room and concluded that Davey had left the set on as usual. He listened some more and finally heard the faint sounds of water running in the kitchen. He headed in that direction.

Kelsey was at the kitchen sink, her hands in soapy dishwater. She stiffened when she heard him enter.

"Hey," Pete said, shrugging out of his jacket.

She turned slowly and he noted her unusually pale complexion and the worried expression on her face.

"I'm not going to jump down your throat again," he assured her.

She relaxed some at that. "Look, I'm sorry about what happened," she told him. "I honestly don't know what I was thinking. You were right. I was wrong."

He met her troubled gaze and reminded her, "You've said that before."

"I know, but we're living here in the land of families,

and this place gets so damn lonely sometimes. I just wanted to go out with an adult for a change, instead of a carload of six-year-olds."

"Nothing wrong with that," Pete agreed, "but Davey can't be here by himself. Work out a deal with another mom to keep him, or find a reliable babysitter. I don't care what you do, but I meant what I said, Kelsey. If I find out he's here alone—and I don't care if you've just gone to the store for milk—I will go to court. I don't want to do that to him or to you, but I will. His safety is the priority here."

She looked thoroughly rattled by his quietly spoken declaration, more disconcerted than she might have been if he'd been shouting. "You really mean that, don't you?"

He nodded. "Yes."

She sucked in a deep breath and nodded. "Okay, then," she said. "I won't do anything to make you resort to that."

Pete prayed she'd keep that promise, but he knew from past history that the commitment could be just as fleeting as all her other promises. For now, though, he'd done all he could to warn her and to protect his son.

"So, how are you?" he asked. "Everything else okay?"

Her hands trembled slightly, but she nodded. "Great. What about you? Is everything good back home?"

"It's been busy," he told her. "I got several houses started and under roof this fall, so my crew's been working on the interiors now that the weather's a little rough out there."

"Anybody ask about me?" she inquired.

She sounded so wistful, Pete wished he honestly could say yes, but the truth was that most people in the town who knew both of them had taken his side in the divorce. They asked about Davey regularly, but any mention of Kelsey was likely to draw scowls, if not disdainful comments. Fortunately, they all knew better than to react that way when his son was around. He saw no point in telling her that, though.

"Sure," he said, choosing his words carefully. "You grew up there. Your name's bound to come up. People want to know how you're doing."

"What do you tell them?"

"That you're happy living in Richmond." He studied her intently. "You are happy, aren't you? This is what you wanted, after all."

Her cheeks flushed a bit at the reminder and for an instant he thought she might tell him the truth, for once, but then her pride apparently kicked in and she forced an obviously phoney smile. "I love it. Even here in 'Familyville,' it's better than that hick town any day."

"That's how I thought you felt," he said. "Though if you were ever to change your mind and decide you want to come home, we could get you a place down there. You know what it would mean to me to have Davey close by."

"Forget it," she said fiercely, either out of pride or some stubborn determination to keep him separated from his son. "You couldn't pay me enough to get me back there."

"Whatever," Pete said with a sigh. "Look, I'd better go next door and get Davey. Any particular time you want me to bring him back here?"

"Suit yourself," she said with unmistakable bitterness. "You're the one who insisted on coming today."

Pete told himself not to rise to the bait. "Then I guess I'll see you later. I'll have him back around five. I might stick around for an hour or so to help him with this science thing he's dreamed up."

His announcement was greeted with silence as Kelsey turned her back on him and went back to washing dishes. He stared at her with regret, then walked away.

Just once, he thought as he left the house, he wished that they could attain a level of civility and maintain it throughout his visit. It never failed, though, that something would set her off and the contact would turn, if not into an argument, then at least into a cold war of sorts.

It struck him then that his ex-wife was simply one of those people who would never be truly happy. She'd gotten exactly what she wanted with the divorce, custody of their son and this house in Richmond, but she still wasn't satisfied. It seemed likely she never would be, and that struck him as unbearably sad.

"So, can we, Dad?" Davey pleaded as Pete turned into the empty driveway at the house just before five o'clock.

Trying not to overreact to the obvious evidence that Kelsey had taken off, Pete forced his attention to his son. "Can we do what?"

"Weren't you listening?" Davey asked, his exasperation plain.

"Obviously not as well as I should have been," Pete

told him, reaching over to muss up his hair. He'd lost his baseball cap somewhere along the way and his gloves. He probably would have left his jacket behind, too, but Pete had seen that on the floor under their table at the hamburger joint where they'd had lunch a few hours earlier. Pete had grabbed it before they left.

"I was asking if we could play a video game before you go home," Davey repeated.

"Sure, but what about that whole science thing you were so anxious to get into? We bought a whole bag full of stuff for that."

"Next time," Davey pleaded. "This game is so awesome. I want to show you."

"Okay, pal, a video game it is. Now grab that stuff from the backseat and I'll get the pizza." He'd bought a large one for dinner, thinking they would be sharing it with Kelsey.

They hadn't agreed to that, he reminded himself as he went inside. He couldn't get all worked up over her not being here. She was bound to be back soon. She knew he was bringing Davey back at five, because he'd told her.

But by the time he and Davey had eaten and played the video game for over an hour, there was still no sign of Kelsey. He sent his son off to take a bath and get ready for bed, then dialed Kelsey's cell phone number. She didn't pick up.

When Davey finally came padding downstairs, his hair standing up in damp spikes, his feet bare and his pajamas inside out, Pete had to bite back a grin. At least the kid had tried.

"Where's Mom?"

"I have no idea, buddy. She didn't leave a note."

Worry immediately creased his son's brow. "You're not going to go, are you?"

"No way. Come on. Let's go upstairs and I'll tuck you in. You can read me a bedtime story."

Davey giggled. "You're supposed to read it to me. I don't know enough words yet."

"Oh, that's right," Pete said. "I'd forgotten how it worked. You're so smart I figured you'd know a bunch of words by now. Maybe you could show me the ones you do know."

Davey nodded eagerly. "I could do that."

Upstairs, he picked a book from the stack beside his bed, then crawled in and scooted over to make room for Pete.

With his kid snuggled up next to him, Pete almost forgot about his exasperation with Kelsey. He'd missed nights like this. They were far too rare.

Together they read the story, but by the last page Davey's eyes were drifting shut. Pete closed the book, slipped off the bed, then pressed a kiss to Davey's forehead. "'Night, son."

Davey's blue eyes blinked open. "'Night, Dad. I love you."

"Back at you, kid."

After Davey drifted off again, Pete stood looking down at him, his heart filled with such aching joy he could hardly stand it. This boy was a part of him. He deserved nothing but the best, but he wasn't getting it, not from either of his parents. And there didn't seem to be a damn thing Pete could do to change that.

He went downstairs, poured himself a glass of milk,

then settled into a chair in front of the TV to wait for his ex-wife.

His eyes repeatedly drifted closed, then snapped open at some unexpected sound, but it was well after midnight when he finally heard Kelsey at the front door.

Pete flipped off the TV and stood up. When she rounded the corner into the family room, he stepped into her path. "Where the hell have you been?" he demanded, unable to keep his temper in check.

Defiance flashed in her eyes. "Out."

"Not good enough," he said coldly. "You knew I was bringing Davey back at five."

"You said you were going to stick around, so I figured there was no reason for me to be here, too," she said.

"An hour, Kelsey. I told you I'd be here an hour or so, not till after midnight. Dammit, didn't you hear anything I said to you earlier? Didn't your promise mean a damn thing?"

"Davey wasn't alone," she reminded him. "That was the deal."

He sighed at her twisted logic. "Is this the way it's going to be? Do you really want things to get complicated?"

She scowled at him. "Do whatever you need to do to feel like a big man, Pete. Frankly, I don't care."

He knew he'd pushed his luck by insisting on coming down here today, but he intended to push it even harder. It was past time he exerted a few more of his own parental rights, rather than bending over backward to keep things calm between them. Maybe she'd eventually get the message that he was losing patience with her games and that he was going to stick to the letter of the court's ruling, which guaranteed him a lot more time with Davey than he'd taken advantage of up till now for the sake of peace.

"Okay, then, this is what I need to do," he told her flatly. "I'll be back next Friday to pick Davey up from school. I'm taking him home with me for the long President's Day weekend."

Fear flashed in her eyes at that. "Oh, no, you're not. That's not one of his weekends to be with you. I didn't fight you this time, but I will fight you on that."

He regarded her with bemusement. "Why? It's obvious you'd rather be doing something besides taking care of our son. Consider this a bonus break for you. Besides, the court granted me four extended holiday visits a year. I intend to take this one."

"No."

"Why not?"

"Because you'll find some way to use it against me. I love that kid. You're not going to take him away from me. And I won't let you spend time turning him against me."

"You know I'd never do that, Kelsey," he responded patiently. "What's the real problem here?"

"I want him with me next weekend."

He knew better, but he asked anyway, "Did you already have something special planned?"

"No, but—"

Pete didn't know why he felt the need to push so hard for this, but he couldn't seem to let it go. He cut her off. "You need a break, Kelsey. Let me give it to you. I promise I won't hold it against you for saying yes to this. Have you ever known me to break my word?"

She looked as if she wanted to argue, but he knew she'd also started to consider what she could do with all that free time. "Okay, but just this once, right? You're not going to start making it a habit?"

"No. We'll stick to the schedule," he promised. To the letter, he added mentally.

"Okay, then. I'll let the school know you're coming on Friday."

They both knew it was a halfhearted attempt to prove she was in control. Both of their names were on the school list. Pete could have picked up his son without her permission, but he let her have her momentary feeling of power.

"Thanks. I'll call during the week to find out when you want him back on Monday, so there's no confusion."

She nodded, suddenly looking oddly defeated. "Look, it's late. Why don't you just stay till morning? You could see Davey again before you go."

Pete was tempted, but he'd learned a long time ago it was best not to accept Kelsey's hospitality. The last time he had, she'd tried to crawl into bed with him. Getting her out had been awkward and unpleasant.

"I'll be fine. I had a nap while I was waiting for you." He pulled on his jacket and headed from the room. When he turned back, she still looked so dejected that he came back and pressed a kiss to her forehead. "Take care of yourself."

"Yeah, sure," she murmured.

As he drove away, he realized she was standing in the shadows at the front window, staring after him. That, too, struck him as unbearably sad. It was the second time that day he'd felt a surge of pity for his ex-wife.

Pete was in an odd mood from the second he turned up on Monday morning. Once upon a time, Jo had been able to read him easily, but not this morning.

He'd arrived with another bag of those warm blueberry doughnuts, two extra large coffees and the usual lighthearted quips, but there was definitely something on his mind. There were unmistakable shadows in his eyes. To her dismay, she wanted to know what had put them there. She knew that asking would only draw her more deeply into his life, but she couldn't seem to stop herself from wondering.

Even as he was outside pounding nails into wood with more force than necessary, she watched him, startled by the anger and tension that seethed just beneath the surface. He hadn't said why he wasn't going on to another job site, and she hadn't asked about that, either. Maybe he was suddenly anxious to get this one finished so he could steer clear of her. She wasn't sure she wanted to know, if that was the case.

But by lunchtime, she'd had enough. Two could play at the game of poking and prodding.

"Lunch is ready," she announced cheerfully, enjoying the look of surprise in his eyes. He clearly hadn't been expecting the invitation. In fact, he didn't even look as if he'd realized what time it was.

Jo had made thick sandwiches with the leftover chicken, then made a pot of homemade vegetable soup with noodles, the way her grandmother used to make it. Pete eyed it suspiciously.

"You went to a lot of trouble."

"Hardly. It's soup and a sandwich, the same sort of thing you fixed me when you were worried about me."

"Does that mean you're worried about me?"

"Worried about all that lumber Ashley paid for, actually. The way you're pounding on it, I expect it to split."

"I know what I'm doing."

"I imagine you do," she agreed. "Usually, anyway. Otherwise I wouldn't see your name in front of half the houses under construction around here. Today must be some sort of off day."

"I don't want to talk about it," he said at once.

She studied him intently and concluded that the exact opposite was true. He was bursting to talk about whatever had him so upset.

"Is it that you don't want to get into it at all or that you don't think you should get into it with *me?*"

His expression turned sad. "There was a time we could talk about anything," he said, a wistful note in his voice.

She nodded. "We still can, even if it has something to do with your marriage or your son. Is that it? Didn't things go well when you went to see him?"

He gave her a hard, searching look. "Are you sure you won't mind if I get into this?"

"I won't know until you start, will I?"

He told her about his call from his son and then his argument with his ex-wife. Before he could go on, Jo was already seething with indignation. "She actually left a six-year-old boy by himself at night?" she demanded

incredulously. "How could she do something so irresponsible?"

"Then I'm not crazy?" he said, looking oddly relieved by her immediate and forceful reaction. "That
is a really lousy idea?"

"Well, of course, it is. What was she thinking?"

"She wasn't thinking. She was on a date and she
was drinking. It happens more than it should. In fact, it
might have happened again night before last, but I was
there. I stuck around till she finally wandered in after
midnight."

"Then you have to do something," Jo said flatly.
"Protecting your son is the only thing that matters."

Oddly, talking about Pete's son didn't hurt half as
much as she'd expected it to. In fact, she found herself
longing for a glimpse of him. She already knew from
his picture that he looked just like his dad, but what
about his personality? Was he full of mischief? Was
he smart as a whip, the way Pete had been?

"I wish I could meet Davey," she said, then faltered.
"But that's probably a bad idea."

"Why would it be?" he asked. "At least from my
perspective. What about you, though? Are you sure you
really want to see him? I would certainly understand if
you never wanted to set eyes on him."

"How can you say that? What happened wasn't his
fault. And he's a part of you. Of course I'd love to meet
him."

"Then you can have your chance to do that next
weekend," he announced, catching her by surprise. "I'm
picking Davey up on Friday. He'll be here till Monday.

If you're sure about this, we could get together on Saturday and do something."

A part of her wanted to agree, wanted to say, "Of course, bring him by." But somewhere deep inside, she was terrified of what might happen next. What if she fell in love with Pete's little boy? He would never be hers. In fact, he was likely to be snatched away from her. Could she bear that? And how would his mother feel about Pete introducing another woman into Davey's life—especially *her?* Would it only cause more problems between Pete and his ex?

In the end, though, it was the prospect of yet more heartache for herself that led her to a decision.

"I'm sorry," she whispered eventually, "I think maybe it's a bad idea, after all."

She would have run from the room so Pete couldn't see the tears gathering in her eyes, but he stopped her before she could take the first desperate step.

"I'm the one who's sorry," he said, gathering her close. "For everything. I shouldn't have asked."

She managed a watery smile. "It was my idea," she reminded him. "Then I got scared."

"Of what?"

"Falling for a six-year-old and then losing him the way I did his dad."

Pete closed his eyes and pulled her close again. She could feel the steady beat of his heart under her cheek. It was reassuring and familiar.

"Just think about it," he said at last. "I swear I won't push you, but he's such a great kid. I'd like you to know him. And I'd like him to meet you."

"How will you explain who I am? Or has he met a lot of women in your life?"

"There haven't been a lot of women in my life since his mom and I split up, but Davey hasn't met any of them. You'd be the first."

Her heart flipped over at that. "Then why me?" she asked.

His gaze locked with hers. "Don't you know?"

She was afraid to guess. "No."

"Because you matter, Jo. You always have."

10

Jo's head was spinning. She'd never expected Pete to tell her that she mattered to him, not like that, not so soon. She'd almost come unglued and burst into tears right there in his arms. Wouldn't that have been a pretty picture?

She couldn't let those impulsively spoken words turn her world topsy-turvy, she told herself a thousand times in the following days. It wasn't as if he'd declared his undying love, after all. *You matter to me,* that's what he'd said. Not *I love you.* Heck, the accountant who kept his company books probably *mattered* to him. So did the guys on his crew.

But even though she tried hard to put those four simple words in perspective, Jo kept hearing the underlying meaning in his voice. It was as close to an admission of love as he could give her right now, probably as close as he thought she could accept.

But was it enough to give her the strength it would take to meet his little boy? That child, through no fault of his own, had changed her life forever. How would she react when she saw him? She knew instinctively that she would open her heart to him, and that terrified her most of all.

But as terrified as she was of being hurt again, Jo knew she had no real choice. She wanted to see that child, to get to know him, to see how much of Pete she would find in his eyes. If anguish and regrets over dreams lost came with that, so be it. That was a small enough price to pay for sharing something—someone— so important to Pete.

Even though her decision was essentially made, she kept it to herself. She didn't want to have to take her words back later if she chickened out. She could tell, though, that her silence on the subject was driving Pete just a little bit crazy. He'd promised not to push her, so he wouldn't, but every time they were together during the week, he watched her, his gaze questioning, asking all the questions he'd promised not to verbalize.

Finally, on Thursday, Jo couldn't stand the wary, surreptitious glances another second.

"Okay, yes," she said as they drank coffee and ate doughnuts at the kitchen table in what was turning into their morning ritual. It felt so damn comfortable and right, that the routine scared her, too.

Pete blinked and stared at her. "Yes?"

"Let's all do something together on Saturday. You, me and Davey."

His eyes lit up and a smile spread across his face. It was as if she'd granted his wish or something. Perhaps if she'd realized how much it meant to him, she would have told him sooner.

"Really?" he asked. "You're sure?"

She held up a cautioning hand. "Let's not make a big commotion out of it, though, okay?"

His gaze narrowed. "Meaning?"

"We could just hook up at one of the sites, make it look accidental. You know, like it's no big deal."

He looked as if he might argue, but evidently he, too, saw the wisdom in that. "You're probably right," he said at last. "That would be best."

"Then, if you wanted, we could grab some lunch or something. Maybe a burger. Does he like hamburgers?"

"Next to pizza, they're his favorite."

"Would it be better to go for pizza, then?" she asked worriedly, wanting this meeting to go right. She knew she was placing way too much importance on it, but she couldn't seem to help herself. No matter how they played it, for her it would be a very big deal.

Pete reached across the table and put his hand on hers. "Hey, stop fussing. We're not going to place too much importance on this, remember?"

"I know, I know. I don't want to make a big production out of it for your son's sake, but for me it's different." She drew in a deep breath and steadied her resolve. "That doesn't mean it needs to be a big deal for him, though. I just want him to have a good time, do things he enjoys doing, you know?"

"You want him to like you," Pete concluded, cutting straight through to the bottom line.

"Okay, yes," she admitted, chagrined.

Pete grinned at her. "With any luck, all of this plotting every minute will be wasted, anyway."

"Why?" she asked in alarm, fearing that her already

out-of-control hopes were about to be dashed. "Do you think he might not come?"

"Oh, he's coming," Pete said, his expression filled with grim determination. "But there's snow in the forecast for Friday night. Quite possibly, we'll be able to spend Saturday sledding and building snowmen." He winked at her. "Then I can send the kid to bed and you and I can get all cozy in front of a fire."

The prospect sounded so inviting, she forced herself to put up at least a token protest. "I don't think so."

"Why not?"

"With your son in the house?" she asked, her tone chiding.

He gave her a piercing look, as if he'd read something into the comment she hadn't intended. "What about after he goes home?" he asked. "Can we get cozy then?"

She met his gaze and made a decision that had been a long time coming, even though it had been inevitable. "I'd have to say that's a definite maybe."

"Not as much conviction as I'd like to hear, but I'll take it as a positive sign," he said. "Now I can hardly wait to take the kid home. What kind of father does that make me?"

"A human one," she said. "And maybe it's something you need to remember when your ex-wife doesn't stop to think. She's only human, too."

"The difference is that I would never leave Davey on his own, no matter how desperate I was to be with someone else."

Jo slid out of her chair and walked around to the other side of the table. Impulsively, she slipped onto

Pete's lap and cupped his face in her hands. "I know. That's what makes you amazing."

Heat immediately blazed in his eyes. "And I thought all along it was my hard muscles you liked."

"Nope. Your tender heart," she told him, tapping on his chest.

"You know," he said quietly, "Davey's not here now."

She met his gaze, her heart in her throat. "I know, but there's no snow on the ground, either."

"Do you think that's entirely necessary?"

Her heart tumbled to her toes as an old and wonderfully familiar desire nearly overwhelmed her. "Now that you mention it, I don't think it's necessary at all."

In the back of his mind, Pete had been imagining this moment for days now, maybe even weeks. Maybe forever. Now that it was here, he could hardly believe it was real. He stroked a finger along Jo's cheek just to reassure himself it wasn't a dream.

"Nope," he murmured. "Definitely real."

"Make love to me," she said, her hand on his cheek. "That ought to convince you I'm very real."

He knew he should keep his questions to himself and accept this precious gift, but he couldn't seem to stop himself from asking, "Why now?"

Her lips curved. "Why not now? Are you going to talk this to death? I thought men were the impulsive, spontaneous ones when it came to sex."

Pete knew he had to be candid with her. As desperately as he wanted this, he didn't want to make a mistake they'd both regret. "It's been a very long time, Jo.

A lot's happened between us. If I take you upstairs now, if I make love to you, it's not going to be the start of some casual fling. It's going to mean something."

She swallowed hard. "Please don't say that," she said, her gaze pleading.

"I have to say it. You need to understand where my head is. I'm not saying you have to be in the same place, but you need to know how I feel." He looked into her eyes. "I guess, in a way, I'm giving you the power to hurt me, because I'm telling you that my heart's on the line. You'll be able to get even with me for what I did," he said. "Or you can love me back."

To his dismay, a tear spilled down her cheek. "Dammit, Pete. Don't you know how I feel? I *do* love you. I don't want to, but I do."

He chuckled despite her obvious distress. "Now there's a declaration guaranteed to make a man's heart sing."

She nudged him in the stomach with her elbow. "Don't joke about this."

"I know, darlin'. It's not a laughing matter."

"No, it's not."

He looked into her eyes. "Does that mean we're not messing around?"

Her lips twitched, then broke into a wide smile, the kind of smile that had once twisted his heart into knots.

"Think you can beat me up those stairs?" she taunted, already out of his lap and heading for the doorway.

Laughing, Pete caught up with her in two strides and scooped her into his arms. "How about we get there together?" he said as he took the stairs two at a time.

"I think I'm beginning to admire those muscles more than I did before," she said as he carried her without hesitation into the right bedroom. "How'd you know which room I'd be in?"

"I stood outside under your window often enough when I was a lovesick twenty-year-old. I know which room is yours." He glanced around. "I've just never had a chance to see it from the inside before."

It was a girly room with lots of pale pink and soft green in the flowery materials of the comforter on the old iron bed. The bed was piled with lace-trimmed pillows. There was a dark burgundy stripe in the cream wallpaper that somehow tied it all together and made it just right for the sexy woman she'd become.

He sat down on the edge of the bed and pulled her into the V between his thighs. Holding her loosely, he gave the mattress a test bounce, then grinned. "Good. No squeaks."

"Even if there were, there's no one in the house to hear them," she said. "Do you realize we've never actually made love in a bed before?"

Pete frowned at that. It was true. They'd had to steal their moments to be together and be inventive about their privacy. He pulled her closer. "Then I think it's way past time to change that, don't you?"

"I don't know," she said. "I thought there was something awfully exciting and special about trying not to get caught."

"Ah, so it was the thrill that got to you back then," he teased. "It had nothing to do with me. In that case, let me run downstairs, unlock the front door and make a call to your sisters. Knowing they could turn up at any second could add a little spice to the afternoon."

"Heaven forbid," Jo said fervently. "They can't know about this."

Pete's heart thumped unsteadily at the implication. "Why not?"

"For your protection," she said at once.

"My protection?" he echoed, stunned. "Why on earth do you need to protect me?"

She grinned at him. "Let's think about this. We're talking about three overly protective big sisters, who've just recently gone from whirlwind courtships into marriage. Can you connect the dots yet?"

Pete saw her point, but he wasn't nearly as terrified by the outcome as she apparently was. "Think they'll try to push us into walking down the aisle?"

"I know they will," she confirmed.

"Maybe that's not such a bad thing. It's what should have happened seven years ago," he said.

"No," she said fiercely. "That was clearly the wrong time for us. Either you would never have had your son or he would have been born without a father. Can you honestly say either of those would have been for the best?"

"No," he admitted. As much as he regretted the way things had turned out for him and Jo, he could never regret having Davey. He tunneled his fingers into her hair and looked deep into her eyes. "Do you have any idea how amazingly generous you are?"

"Me?"

"Yes, you. You're thoughtful and smart and sexy, too."

"All those things?" she said, clearly pleased. "I *am* amazing. Maybe I'm too good for the likes of you."

"You are," he said at once. "Which makes me the luckiest man on the face of the earth since you're here with me now."

Jo lowered her face until her lips were almost on his. "Then let's take advantage of your luck," she whispered right before her mouth settled against his.

Pete felt his pulse jolt, then scramble. His blood shot straight from his brain to another part of his anatomy. He still had just enough sense left to remind himself to go slow, to savor this moment, to savor *her*.

He took that soft, sweet kiss and turned it into something greedy and primal. Jo turned restless, her body seeking his, rubbing against hardness and heat and need in a way that almost had him bolting off the bed.

"Slow down, darlin'," he whispered against her fantastically seductive mouth.

In response, she took his hand and slid it up under her sweater until it met flesh and lace. She was so hot, so soft, Pete wanted to bury his face between her breasts, wanted to stroke his tongue over the hard, sensitive peaks until she was moaning with pleasure.

But not just yet, he told himself. He wouldn't rush her or himself. He'd waited seven years for this. He could wait a little longer, make sure that she knew what a treasure she was, what pleasure she was capable of giving and receiving. He'd been too impatient at twenty. He'd loved her then, but not well—not with a man's patience and desire.

He did, however, strip away that soft sweater so he could gaze at her full breasts and the surprising black lace bra that was such a contrast to the innocence of the plain white garment she'd worn all those years ago. Sexy as this was, he almost regretted the change, or maybe what he really regretted was the loss of innocence. It was something he'd taken and could never give back.

He skimmed a finger across the lace, smiled as she trembled. "Fancy," he said, grinning.

"When I turned twenty-one, my sisters thought it was time to upgrade my lingerie wardrobe." She winked at him. "Wait till you see the pitiful excuse for panties I'm wearing."

Pete moaned. "Don't tell me that. I'm trying to cling to some control here."

"Why?"

"Because you deserve to be properly seduced."

"And you can't do that if I start talking about my skimpy little lace thong?"

He covered his ears. "No, I cannot."

"It's black, too."

Pete groaned.

She grinned. "Good to know just how to rattle you," she said, reaching for the zipper on her jeans and slowly sliding it down.

Pete tried not to look, because he knew he'd be lost. Slow and sweet would be out of the question if those panties were half as sexy as she'd implied.

One glimpse of black lace and he nearly swallowed his tongue. There was barely enough there to cover... well, anything. He finally tore his gaze away and met her eyes.

"I warned you," he whispered, scooping her up and settling her on the bed. He reached for her jeans and yanked them down and off with one smooth motion, then turned all his attention to that skimpy little bit of fabric.

He cupped her, rubbing fabric against the sensitive bud that was already hard, then slipped two fingers over flesh and deep into moist heat. She convulsed around him, her hips lifting off the bed. A ragged moan tore from her throat.

That was all it took to strip away his last shred of control. He kicked off his own jeans and Jockey shorts, then ripped those dangerously wicked little pants right off of her before plunging into her with a thrust that had her bucking against him.

He stayed perfectly still, counting to ten, thinking about the weather, doing anything he could not to give in to the desire to claim her for his own once and for all time. She whimpered against his throat and her hips moved with a will of their own, seeking, pleading, demanding.

Pete looked into her eyes and saw the yearning, the hunger that he knew was reflected in his own and then he began to move, faster and then faster still until the heat and tension exploded, sending shudders rocking through both of them.

It was a long, long time before his brain cleared enough to think, before he could shift his weight off of her to roll over, carrying her with him. He caught a finger through the ruined scrap of lace and dangled it in the air. "I'll buy you a dozen more just like this," he promised.

"Oh, sweet heaven," she murmured, her breath still

ragged. "Forget the panties. What have you done to me? I'm limp."

Pete grinned and shifted beneath her. "I'm not."

She gave him a startled look and then a smile spread across her face. "No, indeed. You're definitely not. I suppose it's up to me to do something about that."

He laughed. "Only if you feel so inclined," he said, putting his hands behind his head and waiting.

She rose up and settled herself astride him. He watched her face as she rode him, laughed at her exultant expression, but then his body went on a wild ride of its own. His vision blurred, his breath snagged in his chest and for just a minute, he was pretty sure he could reach out and touch heaven.

Jo woke to the sound of a door closing downstairs. She rolled over, expecting to find nothing but empty mattress, but there was Pete, still beside her, still looking magnificent and very, very naked.

Which meant that door downstairs had been opened and closed by one of her sisters...or all three of them. She bolted out of bed as if someone had lit a fire under her. She peeked out the window, praying that she would see them driving away, probably confused by not finding her inside, but none the wiser about how she'd spent her day.

But, no, there was Maggie's car—right behind Pete's pickup—and not a sign of Maggie herself, which meant Jo's goose was cooked. Probably well done, in fact.

She frantically pulled on clothes without stopping to consider the effect, then shook Pete. He blinked sleepily and reached for her.

"Not now," she whispered, pushing his hands away. "Sister alert. I'm going downstairs. Whatever you do, do not follow me. Understand?"

He gave her a vague smile and rolled over, burying his face in the pillow. She rolled her eyes and headed for the door, then thought about it and took the time to run a brush through her tangled hair. There wasn't much she could do about her swollen lips, except to touch them up with fresh lipstick.

Five minutes later, she walked into the kitchen, yawning mightily. Three expectant faces turned to her.

"Hey, you guys. I didn't know you were here. Why didn't you wake me?"

"We just got here," Melanie said, then tried ineffectively to swallow a chuckle.

Ashley didn't seem nearly as amused. "I hope, just in the nick of time," she said.

"Oh, please," Maggie chimed in, not even attempting to hide her own amusement. "Nick of time? Not unless Jo's wardrobe has taken a serious dive into flannel."

Jo glanced down and realized for the first time that the shirt she'd grabbed was Pete's. It hung down to her knees and was buttoned so haphazardly, there was no mistaking the haste with which she'd put it on.

"Oh, no," she whispered and sank onto a chair. "I wanted so much to pull this off."

"What?" Ashley inquired. "A deception? You wanted to lie to us?"

Jo's chin rose a notch. "Yes, as a matter of fact."

Her oldest sister looked stunned. "But why?"

"Because you're going to get all protective and nosy and pushy. I know you, remember?"

"We love you. We're concerned," Ashley said. "You should appreciate that."

"And I do, in a general, nonspecific sort of way. But right here and now, with you three in my face, I could live without it."

"I just have one question for you," Ashley said. "What kind of man would let you come down here alone to face us?"

"A man who was instructed to stay put," Jo said.

"In your bed, I presume," Ashley said.

"Yes, in my bed. I'm a grown woman. I get to decide who's in my bed."

"And you want Pete Catlett there?" her sister persisted.

"Yes," Jo said emphatically.

"And it has nothing to do with that house you want?" Ashley pressed.

Jo scowled at her. "Do you have any idea how insulting it is that you would even ask me that?"

"It is," Melanie and Maggie agreed.

Ashley didn't look fazed by their reaction. "It's a fair question. Why is that man in your bed?"

"Because I love him, dammit!" she all but shouted. "There, are you satisfied?"

Filled with heat and dismay and anger, she grabbed her jacket off a hook by the door and slammed out of the house. At first, the frigid blast of air felt good against her overheated flesh, but within seconds she knew it was too darn cold to be going for a walk just to get away from her sisters. Worse, she hadn't brought her keys, so she couldn't even go and sit in the car with the heater on. Then she thought of Pete's truck out front and the keys he usually left in the ignition.

"Thank you," she muttered gratefully with a glance toward her bedroom window. She climbed into the pickup and started the engine. In no time, the heater kicked in and the windows steamed up.

When the passenger door opened, she didn't even turn. "Go away. I'm not talking to you."

It was Pete who responded. "Not even to me?" he asked quietly.

Jo sighed. "I probably shouldn't be talking to you, either, but no, you're not the problem. Well, you are, but not the one that has me ticked off at the moment."

He studied her for what seemed like an eternity, then chuckled. "I like the way that flannel looks on you. I'll never be able to wear that shirt again without getting turned on."

"Don't even mention this blasted shirt to me," she grumbled. "I might have pulled this off if I hadn't grabbed it by mistake."

"Maybe it wasn't a mistake," he said. "Maybe you wanted them to know."

She frowned at him. "Believe me, I did not want them to know about us."

"Are you so sure? Maybe you were hoping they'd kick up such a fuss it would give you an excuse to call things off before they get any more complicated."

"No," she said with certainty. "I wanted time, Pete."

"Time for what?"

"To figure out if we can get it right this time."

"Oh, darlin'," he whispered, pulling her into his arms. "We've got all the time in the world for that."

"Did you see those three?"

"Actually, no. I did the cowardly thing and snuck out the front door after I saw you crawl into my truck. When I heard the engine turn over, I was afraid you might just head for Montana to get away from all those prying eyes."

"Definitely not a bad idea. They're sitting in there waiting to pounce all over this. It's Ashley mostly, but even Maggie and Melanie will get in on the act sooner or later."

"Then tell them to butt out."

"I did," she said.

"And then you ran out here to hide in my truck. You let them chase you out of your own house."

She regarded him with dismay. "I did, didn't I? I gave them all the power. How stupid was that?" She cut the engine and wrenched open the door, but before she could climb out of the truck, Pete pulled her back.

"Hold on," he said.

"I need to go back in there and tell them to butt out."

He grinned. "In a minute."

She stared at him blankly. "Why wait?"

"For this," he said, and kissed her till her head went spinning. He grinned, obviously satisfied. "Now, then, warrior princess, let's go get 'em."

"You don't need to get involved," she protested. "You could leave."

"I am involved." His grin spread. "Besides, I can't very well leave without my shirt, and I doubt you want to strip it off and give it to me before you go back inside. Neither one of us would hear the end of that."

Jo laughed at the image of her sisters' reaction to that. "Might be worth it," she said. "Then again, it might be smarter to go in there with backup."

He winked at her. "Always said you were smart."

Jo suddenly felt stronger, as if she really could conquer the world. Then, again, she'd settle for keeping her sisters' noses out of her business.

11

Pete had to admire the way Jo stood up to her sisters, all but daring them to make a comment when they came in from the truck with him wearing his undershirt and jacket and Jo still in his flannel shirt. She stared them down when all three women gave him smiles that made his blood run cold. The tactic was only partially successful. They pretty much ignored her and kept their focus on him.

"Hello, Pete," Ashley said, her voice frosty.

"Hey, Ashley. Good to see you."

"Do you know Maggie and Melanie?"

He nodded at them, feigning total composure. "Nice to meet you," he said, even as he thought that only an idiot wouldn't recognize this polite charade for what it was—the prelude to an inquisition.

"We've heard a lot about you," Melanie said, barely containing a grin.

"But apparently not nearly as much as we should have," Ashley said, casting a pointed look in Jo's direction.

There went the gloves, Pete thought, and waited to

see how Jo reacted. Adding to his deep respect for her, Jo beamed at Ashley.

"I thought you knew all you needed to," she informed her older sister. "You're the one who hired Pete, right? And he had worked for you before. I figured you'd checked him out six ways from Sunday before you called him the first time."

Ashley frowned at the retort. "Actually, Josh was the one who found him to do the work for us. I trusted my husband's judgment."

"Well, there you go," Jo said triumphantly. "And Pete must have done good work, or you'd never have called him to do another job for you, correct?"

"I called him to fix the porch," Ashley said impatiently. "Not to sleep with you. You have to admit the qualifications are somewhat different."

"Then I guess it's just a lucky bonus for me that's he more than qualified to do both," Jo said gaily, while Pete choked back a laugh. "Now if you all don't mind, Pete and I have things to do this afternoon."

Ashley looked absolutely stunned. "You're kicking us out?"

"Pretty much," Jo said without hesitation.

Pete regarded her with admiration. He gave her a thumbs-up signal that put a smile back on her lips.

"Next time you might want to call first," she told her sisters. "Make sure I'm not going to be busy before you drop in. Perhaps we'll be able to avoid another of these awkward situations."

"You've changed," Ashley told her. "I'm not sure I like it." She frowned at Pete. "Is this your doing?"

"You mean Jo standing up for herself?"

"Is that what you call it?" Ashley asked.

"Sounds that way to me. And no, it's not my doing. I think she's always had it in her."

Ashley's gaze instantly narrowed, and Pete realized he'd gone too far.

"Now how would you know that?" Ashley asked him.

Pete read the panic in Jo's eyes and knew he had to extricate himself from the inadvertent slip. "Don't you think most people are born with a certain amount of strength? They just have to learn how to tap into it."

Relief shone in Jo's eyes.

Ashley still looked skeptical, but she didn't force his hand. Instead, she turned to her sisters. "Are you guys ready to go? We're obviously in the way here."

"Personally I think it's a lot more fascinating here," Maggie said, but she got to her feet. Melanie followed.

After a flurry of goodbyes, they were gone. Jo sagged onto the chair next to Pete.

"Oh, my God," she murmured.

"You were great!"

She whirled on him. "Great? Are you crazy? Thanks to that expression of insolence and ingratitude, I have just launched a full-scale investigation into our private lives that won't end till we've walked down the aisle of some church. They left quietly enough, but only so they can go someplace and plan some scheme that will hit us when we least expect it. Just wait till they get their husbands in on it. Our lives won't be worth living. We'll never have another second's peace."

"But we're onto them," Pete reminded her, unfazed

by her panic. "They won't catch us off guard. Besides, what can they do, really?"

"Make our lives a living hell?" she suggested, her tone deadly serious.

"Come on. It won't be that bad."

"Ha!"

"Want to go back upstairs so I can show you why it's all going to be worthwhile?"

She shot him a withering look. "That's what got us into this mess."

He shook his head. "No, what got us into this was the fact that we couldn't keep our hands to ourselves. We never could. Personally, I think that speaks volumes."

"No, that should have been a lesson to us seven years ago," she retorted. "You'd think we'd be smarter now."

"We are," he insisted. "We're smart enough to go after what we want and fight for it. I want you. What do you want?"

"The truth?"

"Of course."

"The only thing I know with absolute certainty that I want is that house."

Pete's heart sank. He knew this afternoon hadn't been about the house, but he never in his life would have guessed he could be jealous of a pile of shingles and some hardwood floors.

He forced himself to respond with a careless shrug. "Maybe one of these days you'll decide to take the package deal."

In fact, he was counting on it.

* * *

Jo's thoughts were such a jumble, she didn't know which problem to grapple with first. She was going to have to deal with her sisters sooner or later. She wasn't naive enough to believe that kicking them out of Rose Cottage had been anything more than a temporary reprieve. She was going to have to figure out what to do about her feelings for Pete, which were getting more powerful and more complicated by the day. And she was going to have to spend time with his son without letting her heart get broken.

So many problems and not a solution in sight, she thought wearily.

Fortunately, for one day at least, she could simply avoid the whole lot of them. She was up and out of the house before daybreak on Friday. She merely got in her car and set out on an aimless drive. At least that was how it started.

She realized once she'd stopped for breakfast and caffeine that what she was really on was a research mission. She wanted to study the landscaping around the region, see what plants were thriving, which ones didn't seem to do well, and which created the old-fashioned country cottage or beach house ambience she wanted at both of Pete's houses. It would be better to do this sort of tour in spring or summer, but midwinter was the only time she had to do it. She'd just have to use her expertise and imagination to fill in the gaping blanks.

Since she'd been in the habit of doing this sort of thing whenever she went for a drive back in Boston, she had a pad and pencil handy in the car so she could jot down notes every time she stopped by the side of the road. By the time she got back to Rose Cottage at dusk, the pad was filled with scribbled notes and sketches. At least one thing in her life was under control, she thought happily right before she spotted Ashley's car in the driveway. If only the rest were, she added with a sigh.

She emerged from her own car reluctantly and went inside. She found her sister sitting in the kitchen with a cup of tea and a troubled expression.

"Where have you been?" Ashley asked. "With Pete, I assume, since he's nowhere to be found, either."

"Actually I've been working," Jo said, tossing the pad of paper on the table. "Doing some research. And I was alone, not that it's any of your business."

The sketches and notes distracted Ashley for a time. She turned the pages slowly, grinning from time to time.

"These are good. Really good," she told Jo.

"Thanks, but I'm sure you didn't come by to tell me I'm good at my job."

"No, to be honest, I came by to tell you to watch yourself with Pete."

"You're the one who sent him over here," Jo reminded her again. "If you meant him to be nothing more than eye candy, you should have said as much at the beginning. Maybe plastered a look-but-don't-touch sign on his very attractive behind."

Ashley didn't seem to appreciate the humor. "I know. I did think he'd provide a good distraction, get your mind off the broken engagement." She regarded Jo worriedly. "I might have made a mistake."

"Hold the presses!" Jo exclaimed. "You're admitting to a mistake?"

"It's not a joke," Ashley said. "I'm trying to tell you something here. Pete's life is a mess. I didn't realize that. He has an ex-wife and a son."

"I know."

Ashley looked surprised. "He told you, then? That's something, I suppose."

"Did you really think he'd try to hide it? It's a small town. I was bound to find out." She wasn't about to admit that she'd known about the marriage and the son for years.

"I wasn't sure. I don't know him that well. I gather the divorce wasn't pretty. There's probably a lot of baggage there. You've already been through a lot, Jo. Why go looking for more trouble?"

"I appreciate your concern. I really do. But you don't need to worry. I'm on full alert where Pete's concerned." If only Ashley knew just how alert, she might take some comfort in it. Then, again, it might only make her worry more.

Ashley studied her somberly, then finally gave her a satisfied nod. "Okay, then. I'll butt out."

Jo grinned. "As if you could."

"I'll *try* to butt out," Ashley amended.

Jo crossed the room and hugged her fiercely. "Thanks. Now go home to your husband."

"What are you going to do tonight? Want to come to dinner?"

"No, I think I'll stay here. I have a lot going on right now."

"Pete coming by?" Ashley inquired with feigned nonchalance.

"Less than a minute and she's butting back in again,"

Jo teased. "No, Pete is not coming by. He's in Richmond picking up his son. Davey's coming for the weekend."

"Oh, I see." Ashley studied her intently. "How do you feel about that?"

"Ask me after tomorrow."

"Why then?"

"I'm going to spend the day with them. I'll be able to give you a better answer."

Ashley gave her shoulder a squeeze. "I almost wish you hadn't told me that. Now I'll be worried sick all day. Do you think it's a good idea for you to spend time with his son? Not just for your sake, but for the boy's?"

"See what happens when you go poking around for information?" Jo teased. "Sometimes you find out things you'd rather not know. And believe me, Pete and I have discussed all the pitfalls. We're going to make sure it doesn't turn into a big deal."

Once more, her sister frowned at her joking. "Promise me one thing."

"Anything."

"Don't get your heart broken."

Jo nodded. "That one's easy. I'm certainly going to try like hell not to."

She was just terrified it might be easier said than done.

Pete was jostled awake at dawn on Saturday when Davey started bouncing on his bed, his face alight with excitement.

"Guess what, Dad?" He nudged Pete. "Are you awake?"

"How could I not be awake? Somebody's using my bed for a trampoline," Pete mumbled sleepily. "What's up, buddy? Couldn't you sleep?"

Davey gave him a disgusted look. "I slept, but then morning came, and I got up," he explained with exaggerated patience. "Come on, Dad. You still haven't guessed."

Pete was pretty sure he knew based on the way his son's eyes were shining, but he pretended to give the question serious thought. "I know," he said at last. "The tooth fairy came and left a million dollars under your pillow."

Davey giggled. "No." He opened his mouth wide. "See. All my teeth are still there." He wiggled one in front. "This one's getting ready to go, though. Will I get a million dollars?"

"Not likely, kid. So, if it's not that, what could it be?"

"It snowed!" Davey said, obviously thrilled. "And not just a little bit, either. Lots and lots! Can we go outside?"

Pete glanced at the clock. It was barely six-thirty. "How about breakfast first? Maybe by the time we're done, it will at least be daylight."

"But I want to build a snow fort."

"And you don't think you'll have time to do that if we start at, say, seven-thirty?"

"But that's a whole hour from now," Davey protested.

"Trust me, the time will fly by. It takes a long time to make pancakes and eat them."

The mention of pancakes immediately wiped the

beginnings of a pout off of his son's face. "Big ones or little ones?"

"Does it matter?"

"I like the little ones," Davey announced.

"Any particular reason?"

"Sure. 'Cause then I can eat about a hundred of them."

Pete rolled his eyes. "In that case, you'd better go in the kitchen and check to see if we've got enough pancake mix. You can get it out of the cabinet and find a big bowl, but do not, I repeat, do not, get started till I get in there."

"But I can pour the flour into the bowl," Davey said.

And onto the table and the floor, Pete imagined. "Wait for me," he repeated firmly. "Ten minutes, okay?"

"Okay," Davey agreed and ran out of the room at full throttle.

Pete grinned. Oh, to have that much energy again. He rolled over, picked up the phone and called Jo. She answered groggily.

"Did you know it snowed last night?" he asked.

"Is this one of those nuisance calls?" she grumbled. "I'm hanging up."

"You'll be sorry," he said. "And no, it's not a nuisance call. It's a news alert. Snow means the plans have changed."

"Changed how?"

"We need to get started a whole lot earlier, because little boys can hardly wait to get outside."

She laughed. "How about big boys?"

"Personally, I could have used another hour of sleep, but I'm not the one who counts over here. Get moving, darlin'. We'll meet you at your favorite house at eight-thirty, unless you want to switch gears and come over here for pancakes."

She was silent so long, Pete knew she was wrestling with the choice, but eventually she sighed.

"Let's stick to the plan," she said with an unmistakable hint of regret in her voice. "I'll see you at eight-thirty. Arc we building a snowman or sledding?"

"We're building a snow fort. And just so you know, forts take time when they're crafted by Catlett Construction. Wear something warm."

"You're talking to a woman from Boston. We know how to dress for snow. See you soon."

Pete was smiling as he hung up, but a glance at the clock showed him he needed to hurry. Davey wouldn't wait forever for those pancakes. He'd either turn the kitchen into a disaster area trying to fix them himself or he'd slip outside to play in the snow until Pete finally ventured into the kitchen to make them for him. The kid was good and usually listened to a direct order, unless it happened to bump up against his own exuberance.

Sure enough, when Pete got to the kitchen, Davey was on a chair, the box of mix upside down over a bowl. He'd poured in enough to feed an army battalion.

"Whoa, kid! Let's not get carried away," Pete said, extracting the box from his hands and putting it back in the cabinet. "How about setting the table? You remember how to do it?"

"Yeah, but how come it has to be all fancy when it's just us?"

"It's not fancy to put silverware and a napkin where they belong. Knowing where things like that go will impress a girl someday."

Davey stared at him blankly. "How come?"

"It's just one of those rules of life, pal. Girls like things done a certain way. When guys understand that, life goes a whole lot more smoothly."

Davey shook his head, his expression still perplexed. "Dad, you're weird."

"Maybe, but you love me, right?" Pete asked, scooping him up and holding him upside down till he squealed.

"I love you. I love you," Davey said, squirming till Pete set him back on his feet.

"Then set the table."

Davey did as he was told, but even after Pete put the first batch of pancakes in front of him, he was bouncing in his chair, clearly eager to be finished and outside.

"How deep do you think it is?" he asked Pete.

"Maybe if it were light enough to see outside, I could tell you."

"It's almost light," Davey argued.

"How can you tell?"

"Way over there, where you told me to look, you can see a tiny little bit of light right at the bottom. And pretty soon, it will turn all red and streaky and stuff and then, bam, the sun will come up."

Pete grinned at him. "I guess you've got this sunrise stuff nailed, after all."

"That's 'cause you taught me." Davey's expression suddenly turned solemn. "You always teach me really cool stuff. Mom teaches me spelling and words and things, but the things you tell me about are way better."

Pete knew it was Davey's way of broaching a subject that had come up in the past. He wanted to spend more time with Pete and didn't get why he couldn't. Pete refused to get drawn into a debate of the merits of Kelsey's lessons versus his own. Nor did he want to explain yet again that their time together had been spelled out by the court.

Instead, he met his son's gaze. "Spelling and words are important, pal. Don't ever forget that."

"So is how to hammer a nail and where the sun comes up," Davey retorted.

"And how to set a table," Pete added. "Let's not forget that."

Davey rolled his eyes and climbed out of his chair. "Can we go outside yet?"

"I've barely taken the first bite of my pancakes, much less had my first cup of coffee," Pete protested, then relented. "Bundle up and go on out, but stay right by the house. I'll be out in a little while and we can go build that fort."

"How come we can't build it here?"

"Because I know a better place."

"But we don't have to wait long to go there, right?"

"No," Pete assured him. "We don't have to wait long."

Just until he got sufficient caffeine in his system to guarantee he could keep up with his son.

12

Not that she was eager or anything, but Jo was over at Pete's house by the bay twenty minutes ahead of the agreed-upon time. As she sat in her car with the heater blasting, she studied the snow-covered landscape and knew, once again, that she simply had to live here. It was like a fairyland now that the sun had come up and the ground and trees were sparkling as if they'd been dusted with diamonds overnight.

Seeing it like this gave her some new ideas about what ought to be planted—holly trees with their dark green leaves and bright red berries certainly, and perhaps a grove of pine trees and blue spruce that would look like something on a Christmas card on mornings like this. Most properties around here couldn't afford the space for an entire grove of trees, but Pete had bought up at least two acres. He'd only cleared a small portion of that facing the water.

Jo was lost in a sketch of the proposed grove, when she was startled by a tap on the window of her car. She turned to find Pete grinning at her and beside him a pint-size replica bundled into a bright red jacket with blue mittens on his hands and a knitted blue cap pulled low over his ears. He was frowning at her.

"You're trespassing," he announced when she rolled down her window. "This is my dad's house."

Pete started to say something, but Jo stopped him.

"You must be Davey," she said, fighting the sting of tears as she looked into that precious face with its startling blue eyes and freckled nose.

His frown only deepened. "How come you know that? I don't know you."

"Because your dad told me how handsome and smart his son was, so that has to be you." She slid out of the car and held out her hand. "I'm Jo. I'm doing some work for your dad."

Davey stared at her hand, clearly torn between suspicion and every lesson he'd ever been taught about being polite to grown-ups. He finally gave her hand a reluctant shake, though the scowl still hadn't left his face.

"What kind of work?" he asked, his voice laced with skepticism. "Girls don't build things."

"Uh-oh," Pete muttered, clearly amused at the sexist controversy his son had just unwittingly opened up.

Jo grinned at Davey. Six definitely wasn't too early to start teaching a kid about equality. "Is that so? Who told you that? Not your father, I'll bet."

"Definitely not me," Pete acknowledged hurriedly.

"Your mom, then?" Jo asked Davey.

He suddenly looked a little less sure of himself. "Nah. She always says girls can do anything boys can do."

"She's absolutely right," Jo said, surprised to find

herself siding with Kelsey Catlett about anything. "Then who gave you the ridiculous notion that girls can't build anything?"

The smart kid promptly turned the tables on her. "Have you ever built anything?"

"In a way."

"Like what?"

"I design gardens and then I put them together for people. That's why I'm here. I'm designing some things for this house. Want to see?"

Clearly intrigued, he nodded and inched closer when she pulled her pad out of the car. She flipped it open to the page she'd just completed. Davey's eyes widened.

"Wow!" he said. "It's like Christmas!"

Jo beamed at him. "That was exactly my idea."

"Where's it gonna go?"

"If your dad agrees, I thought right about there," she said gesturing toward an open spot on this side of the house that wouldn't block any of the water views. Instead, it would offer a completely contrasting view to anyone sitting in the dining room having breakfast on a morning like this one. Turning one way, they'd see the bay. Facing the other, they'd look into a small forest of evergreens. Either view would provide a tranquil backdrop for their morning coffee.

"Are you gonna do it, Dad?" Davey asked excitedly. "It would be so cool to have Christmas trees growing right outside. We could even put lights on 'em at Christmas. We'd look outside and it would be like a fairyland."

Pete grinned at him indulgently, then faced Jo. "I

guess that's a yes on the trees. Anything else in that notebook of yours?"

She handed it to him. "It's more like notes right now. I drove around yesterday to get some ideas. I haven't worked them into any sort of plan yet."

With Davey tugging on his arm begging to see, Pete knelt down so his son could look over his shoulder at the drawings. They lingered intently over each one. Jo watched Davey almost as intently as she did Pete and was pleased by the reactions she detected on their faces.

"Cool," Davey pronounced when they'd looked at every page. "Can you teach me to draw like that?"

"I'd love to," Jo said, thrilled by his eagerness and his apparent acceptance. She knew it could have been a whole lot harder to win him over. And maybe this was just détente.

"Now?" he asked.

"Hey, buddy, I thought you wanted to build a snow fort?"

"Oh, yeah," Davey said, readily distracted. He grinned up at Jo. "You want to help? Dad and me can show you how."

"I would love to help," she said. "Where are you going to build it?"

"By the water," Davey said at once. "That way when the bad guys come up by boat, we can nail 'em."

Jo laughed. "Good plan."

"The kid is definitely full of ideas," Pete said, tagging along behind them as Davey led the way to his chosen location.

Jo turned and met his gaze, hoping he could see the

gratitude in her eyes for this chance. "Thank you," she mouthed silently.

When they finally reached the site for the fort, she turned to Davey. "Okay, Captain Catlett, what do we do first?"

Davey giggled. "First we make really big snowballs, right, Dad? Big as me."

Jo nodded thoughtfully. "Then who gets to lift them? Your dad?"

"He's really, really strong," Davey said with evident pride. "He could probably even lift you."

Jo chuckled. "I am definitely bigger than a giant snowball," she agreed, loving the way the boy's mind worked, to say nothing of his enthusiasm for whatever he set out to do. What an absolute joy he must be!

Oddly, she was feeling none of the anguish she'd expected to hit her when she first set eyes on him. She was simply gathering up every precious moment and storing it away to think about when he wasn't around. She wondered if that's how Pete survived the separations, by making so many memories that his son was never far from mind.

It took them two hours to build the fort to Davey's very precise specifications. Once it was done, Jo was the first to get behind the wall and lob a snowball straight at Pete. It hit him squarely in the chest, catching him completely by surprise. Jo ducked down behind the wall when he started to reach for his own fistful of snow. While he was distracted, Davey hurled another one that he barely managed to duck.

"Okay, you two, this is war," Pete declared, pelting

them with snowballs of his own, then chasing down Davey and rubbing snow on his neck.

Next he came after Jo, a diabolical expression in his eyes, but she was quick. She whirled away and ran, laughing as she danced out of his path.

The laughter died, when he snagged her ankle, somehow managing to land beneath her, so that he took the brunt of the fall. She grinned down at him. "You are such dead meat," she said, picking up a handful of snow to rub in his face.

But before she could do that, a fistful of snow was shoved down the back of her jacket by his sneaky little boy, whom she'd mistakenly assumed to be on her side. She should have known better.

"Way to go, Davey!" Pete enthused, giving his son a high five. "We guys have to stick together."

Laughing, Jo got up to shake the snow out of her jacket. "I'll remember this," she warned Pete. "Just wait."

His gaze locked on hers. "You gonna get even, tough girl?"

"You bet," she said at once. "And you won't even see it coming."

"Uh-oh," Davey said, grinning at his dad. "You're in big trouble, huh?"

Pete winked at him. "Nothing I can't handle."

Jo laughed at the pair of them. "Okay, macho guys, let's go have lunch before we all catch pneumonia. Soup and burgers? How about it?"

"With fries?" Davey asked at once.

"If your dad agrees," she told him.

"He will," Davey said triumphantly. "Dad loves fries better than anything."

He always had, Jo thought, and barely managed to keep herself from saying it aloud.

"Not better than anything," Pete replied quietly, his intense gaze fastened on Jo. "Some things are even more incredible."

Jo lost herself in the heat in his eyes for a moment, but then the moment was lost when Davey demanded to know what could possibly be any better than French fries.

Pete tugged his blue cap a little lower to cover his eyes. "Kissing girls," he said at once, then stole one from Jo before Davey could rip away the impromptu blindfold.

His son regarded him with blatant skepticism. "Gross," he declared.

"Tell me that when you're sixteen," Pete said. "Hop into the truck, buddy. I'll be there in a minute as soon as I open the car door for Jo."

"Can't she open it herself?" Even as the words left his mouth, Davey's expression brightened with sudden understanding. "It's another one of those things to keep girls happy, huh?"

Pete winked at him. "Exactly."

Davey ran on to the truck, while Pete went with Jo and opened the door.

"See you in ten minutes in town," he said.

"Do you think it's going okay?" she asked worriedly.

"Are you kidding? The kid's fallen in love with you," he said. "Same as me."

He winked and left, leaving her with her heart thundering in her chest and a million and one dreams coming alive again.

Lunch was an unqualified success. Pete watched his son with the woman who should have been the mother of Pete's children and knew that they could become the perfect family. Jo was a natural with the boy and Davey was responding to her effortless teasing with increasing affection. He told himself he wasn't leaving Kelsey out of the equation, just adding Jo into it, but it was hard to imagine Kelsey fitting in to the idyllic image in his head.

"Hey, Dad, I have an idea," Davey said, when they were all stuffed with hamburgers, fries and slices of pie. "You said we could rent a movie tonight. Maybe Jo could come, too. It would be like a party. You could make popcorn and hot chocolate and stuff."

Pete grinned at him. "Maybe Jo doesn't like popcorn and hot chocolate and silly kid movies."

"Bet she does," Davey said confidently. "Right, Jo? You think all that stuff is cool, don't you?"

"Nothing better," she agreed at once. "*Finding Nemo* was one of my all-time favorite movies."

"See," Davey said. "So, can we ask her?"

Pete laughed. "I think you just did."

Davey gave him a baffled look, then grinned. "Oh, yeah. So, will you come, Jo?"

She cast a look at Pete, clearly seeking his permission. "What do you say, Dad?"

"Fine with me," he said at once. He glanced at his

son. "Maybe we should let her pick the movie. What do you think?"

Davey looked doubtful. "You aren't gonna pick some mushy thing, are you?"

"Nah," she said at once. "How about I show you my choices and you can help me decide?"

Davey nodded eagerly, then glanced worriedly at Pete. "That sounds fair, right, Dad?"

"More than fair," he said with amusement.

He wasn't sure who was manipulating whom anymore. It was just plain as day that these two knew how to work each other. It couldn't have made him happier, but it was worrisome, too. The instantaneous bonding was going to cause problems down the road. Kelsey would hear all about this, and there would be hell to pay. But Pete had accepted that going in. Sooner or later, his ex-wife would have to come to terms with the fact that he really had moved on. He knew it would dash the hopes he suspected she had that one day he would come to his senses and chase after her.

"Okay, let's head for the video store and pick out a couple of movies, one for tonight and one for tomorrow. Then Davey and I can run by the store for supplies."

"Sounds good," Jo said.

"You want to come by around six-thirty and have dinner with us? We're going with the canned spaghetti thing," he told her with a grin.

"I think I'll pass, unless you can be persuaded to sacrifice the canned stuff in favor of homemade. I still have sauce in the freezer."

"Awesome," Davey said at once.

Jo slapped his hand in a high five. "There's the man," she said approvingly.

"Okay, then, I guess dinner's under control," Pete said.

"I'd better come at six, though, to boil the pasta and heat up the sauce."

Pete nodded. "We have a plan, then."

It was the kind of plan he'd always imagined making on a snowy Saturday with his family, but Kelsey had always insisted that Saturday was a date night, not a family night. She didn't care where they went, as long as it was out and they were alone. He looked into Jo's shining eyes and saw no hint of hesitation or dismay. If anything, she looked as eager as his son.

How had he ever for a single second forgotten that she was the perfect match for him? Okay, if he was being totally honest, he hadn't forgotten. He'd just buried the knowledge in order to live the life he'd been forced to choose.

And now, at long last, he had a second chance. He vowed here and now that he wouldn't waste it.

It was nearly midnight when Jo finally got home from their outing. She was on such an emotional high, she didn't think it was possible that she'd ever come back to earth. The spaghetti had been a big success with Davey, as had her special hot chocolate with just a hint of peppermint in it. They'd eaten a huge bowl of buttered popcorn and watched both movies, though Davey had fallen asleep fifteen minutes into the second one. Pete had carried him to bed, then returned to snuggle with her in front of the TV.

Neither of them had paid much attention to the plot of the movie, which was probably just as well, since she assumed Pete was destined to see it again on Sunday night when Davey realized he'd slept through most of it.

Tonight had been bittersweet. It had given her a taste of all she'd lost…and maybe all she could have, if she was brave enough to take another chance on loving Pete.

Was she that brave? She was beginning to believe she was, but now and then a vague feeling of panic would roll over her. At its core was always the faceless woman who'd stolen Pete from her the first time. Kelsey still had a powerful claim on him. Something told Jo that she wouldn't give it up lightly. Worse, Davey was bound to be caught in the middle. Pete didn't seem to be half as worried about that as she was, but she knew she could never do anything that might turn that wonderful child into some sort of pawn between his parents.

Too wound up to sleep, she made herself a cup of chamomile tea, then sat at the kitchen table, wishing for once that her sisters were here to listen to her jumbled thoughts and help her make sense of them. Unfortunately, if she told them everything now, she had a feeling not one of them would see Pete for the incredible man he was. They would focus exclusively on the fact that he'd broken her tender young heart.

When the phone rang, she almost laughed. It was bound to be Ashley, checking up on her, putting her mind at rest that Jo had survived her day with Pete and his son without any emotional scars.

"Hello, worrywart," she said, when she picked up.

"How'd you know it would be me?" Pete asked.

"Actually I was sure it was going to be Ashley. I thought you'd be sound asleep by now."

"I couldn't sleep till I knew you were home safe and in bed. Are you in bed?" he asked hopefully.

"Nope, fully dressed and in the kitchen. Sorry to spoil your fantasy."

"Ah, well, I have a pretty vivid imagination anyway. I'll make do."

"Today was fun," she told him quietly. "Thank you."

"It was fun for me, too, and Davey was over the moon. Of course, he'll never be satisfied to eat spaghetti from a can again."

"An educated palate is never a bad thing," she told him.

"I'll add that to the list of lessons I can take credit for," he said lightly. "'Night, darlin'."

"Good night, Pete."

It was fully a minute before Jo finally hung up the phone and cut the connection. She sighed when it rang again.

Smiling, she picked it up. "I thought we'd said good night, Pete."

"So that's who you were on the phone with," Ashley said. "Didn't you just leave him?"

"You're up late," Jo commented, ignoring her sister's testy tone.

"I wasn't waiting up for you to get home, if that's what you're thinking. Josh and I had to go to some big dinner-dance thing with his old law partners in Richmond tonight. We just got back. Thought I'd check on you before going to bed, but your line was busy."

"How was the event you went to?"

"Boring," Ashley said. "I'd almost forgotten how dull a roomful of lawyers can be."

"Oh, my God," Jo said with exaggerated alarm. "Let me check outside to see if the sky is falling."

"Very funny. How was your date with Pete and his son?"

"Amazing," Jo admitted. "And scary."

"Scary? Why?"

"I love that kid," she admitted. "Now the stakes have really gotten high, Ashley. I want them both in my life. I'm not sure if I'll be able to handle it if I lose them."

"Why would you lose them?"

"It could happen," Jo insisted. It was something she knew only too well.

"Do you want me to have the guys take Pete out and have the honorable intentions talk?"

The very idea filled Jo with horror. "Absolutely not."

"It's one way to get answers," Ashley reminded her.

"I think I'll use my own technique, thank you very much."

"You have a technique?"

"Well, no," she admitted. "Unless you count leaving it up to fate."

"Normally I'd be the first to tell you to forget that and take charge of your own future," Ashley said.

"But?"

"I'd have to say destiny's done all right by the rest of us, wouldn't you?"

Jo chuckled. "You have a point. Maybe I will just trust in fate."

"You might want to toss in some mind-boggling sex to seal the deal," Ashley suggested tartly. "Worked for me."

"I'm sure Pete would appreciate that technique," Jo agreed. "I'll give it some thought."

"Just be happy," Ashley said. "If you think that man can make you happy, then fight like heck to keep him."

Ashley's words continued to ring in Jo's head long after she'd hung up. That was the big difference between seven years ago and now. Back then, she hadn't known how to fight for her man, hadn't even known until too late that she needed to. Now, though, she was all grown-up and stronger than she'd realized. This time she would fight with everything in her to hold on to the happiness she'd found once again with Pete.

And heaven help anyone who got in her way.

13

It was barely seven in the morning when Jo's phone rang. Sure that it would be Pete, she already had a smile on her face as she answered. When she heard Davey's voice, her smile spread even wider.

"Well, good morning," she said, instantly cheerful despite the early hour. "How are you?"

"I'm great," he said, his voice brimming with exuberance. "I wanted to call you before, but Dad said it was too early and that we had to wait till at least seven, so we wouldn't wake you. I know it's not quite seven, but I couldn't wait anymore. So, did we? Wake you up, I mean?"

Jo laughed. "No. I was awake."

"See, Dad? I told you it wouldn't be too early," Davey called out triumphantly to his father.

Jo couldn't hear Pete's mumbled response, but grinned as she imagined his side of the exchange. She could practically see the tolerant amusement on his face.

"Dad says to ask you if you want to go have waffles with us," Davey said. "He can't make waffles, 'cause you need some kind of iron thing, which is dumb, if you ask me, 'cause waffles aren't smooth."

Jo laughed. "It is dumb, now that you mention it. Are waffles a favorite of yours?"

"They're the best," Davey confirmed. "Even better than pancakes, 'cause there are all those little places for the syrup to go. So, will you come? Dad says we can come get you."

"How soon?"

He relayed her question at his father, then said, "He says twenty minutes. Can you be ready then?"

"I'll be ready," Jo promised.

"With your coat on and everything?" Davey asked worriedly. "I'm starving."

"I'll even be waiting outside," she assured him. "We definitely can't have you starving."

"Okay. Bye," he said, then put the phone down with a clatter.

Jo stared at the receiver, a smile on her lips, then finally hung up and raced to put on a little makeup and do something with her hair before her allotted time was up.

She was outside in the driveway when Pete turned in. He frowned at her as she got into the truck.

"Why are you standing outside?" he scolded. "It's freezing. You should have waited till we pulled in before coming out."

She winked at Davey. "I promised not to hold things up."

Pete turned to the backseat and frowned at his son. "You don't make girls stand around in the cold for your convenience," he chided.

"Are we gonna waste time while you tell me another one of those things about keeping girls happy?" Davey asked plaintively. "It's going to be years and years before I need to know that stuff."

Pete regarded him with resignation. "Have you gotten the message?"

"Yes," Davey said at once. "Can we please go now?"

"Yes, please," Jo added. "I'm starving, too."

Pete laughed. "Something tells me this breakfast is going to cost me a fortune. Hope I have enough cash."

"I have my allowance," Davey said. "I can pay for my own."

"How about mine?" Pete retorted. "Can you pay for mine, too?"

Davey immediately reached in his pocket and brought out a fistful of dollars and some change. He shoved it in Jo's direction. "Is this enough?"

She solemnly counted out his four dollars and sixty-seven cents, then shook her head. "Not quite," she told him. "But don't worry. I've got it covered."

"Girls don't pay," he responded at once. "Right, Dad?"

"That's right," Pete confirmed.

"It's okay for girls to pay for things some of the time," Jo corrected. "But it's always nice when the guys offer."

Davey regarded her with confusion. "How am I supposed to know when it's okay?"

Jo laughed at his perplexed expression. "Sweetie, it is not something you need to worry about for at least ten years or so."

"I don't think I'm ever gonna need it," Davey said. "It's probably easier just to stay away from girls."

"Easier, maybe," his dad said, clearly amused. "But not nearly as much fun. You'll see."

"I doubt it," Davey said with blatant skepticism as Pete pulled into a parking spot in front of the café in town.

When the three of them walked through the door, a half-dozen curious glances were directed their way. People spoke to Pete and grinned at Davey, but faltered a bit when they came to Jo. She was relieved when they were finally seated in a booth toward the back. She hadn't stopped to think about how awkward this might turn out to be. Naturally, most people here had known Kelsey. Many of them might have a vague recollection of Jo, but after seven years they obviously didn't recognize her as the young girl who'd spent an entire summer coming in here with Pete.

At least none picked up on the connection until the waitress came to take their order. She'd worked here for years and took one look at Jo and beamed. "Jo D'Angelo, if you aren't a sight for sore eyes. It's been a long time, girl. I see your sisters in here all the time these days, but you've been keeping yourself scarce. Heard you were with them once, but I missed you. Glad you're finally back, though I can't see that your taste in men has improved much over the years." She grinned at Pete when she said it.

Jo laughed. "Hello, Gloria. I just came down recently to stay at Rose Cottage for a bit."

The waitress immediately looked disappointed. "You're not moving here?"

"I haven't decided yet," Jo said, ignoring Pete's stunned expression.

After the woman had gone to place their order, Pete looked at Jo. "What did that mean? I thought you'd pretty much decided to stick around."

She used his obvious dismay to sneak in another play for his house. "Maybe if I had the perfect house..." she said and let her voice trail off.

He shook his head. "Don't you pull that on me," he scolded. "Don't make me responsible for your going or staying."

Jo simply stared at him, letting the words sink in. Even though they'd been spoken lightly, she doubted he realized how telling they were. It was a warning, in fact, one she would do well not to ignore. If she stayed here, it had to be all about her and what she wanted, not about what might or might not happen with Pete. She'd very nearly forgotten that in the warm glow of being with him—and with Davey—these past couple of days. Her spirits, so high when she'd left Rose Cottage, took a nosedive.

When the waffles came, they might just as well have been sawdust. Even though Pete was watching her with a worried look, she barely managed to choke down more than a few bites. Even Davey seemed to notice that something was wrong. He fell silent and concentrated on his breakfast, finishing his own waffle in record time.

"Can I go outside?" he begged his father.

Before Pete could reply, Jo said, "If your dad's not finished, I'll come with you."

"He can go by himself," Pete countered. "I think we should talk."

"Not here and not now," she said just as firmly, already scooting out of the booth and pulling on her jacket.

"But you didn't eat. You said you love waffles and that you were as hungry as me," Davey said. "Did you get sick?"

"No," she assured him. At least not the way he meant. She held out her hand. "Maybe we can walk to the park and build a snowman. What do you say, Davey?"

His concern for her mood vanished at once. "Cool. Is it okay, Dad?"

Pete looked as if he wanted to argue, but he finally relented. "I'll meet you there in a few minutes," he said, his voice tight.

On the way to the park, Jo was grateful for Davey's nonstop chatter. And once they were there, she forced herself to concentrate on helping him build a snowman. Since the temperature had risen slightly once the sun came out, the snow was melting fast now. The poor snowman wasn't nearly as plump as he should have been. He looked about as defeated and sad as she felt. Not even the curved stick Davey found to use as a mouth could perk him up. The makeshift smile looked forced.

How had things turned upside down in less than twenty-four hours? Jo wondered. This time yesterday, she'd been filled with joy and hope. Now it was as if she'd run headlong into reality, all because of a few careless words that Pete had spoken, probably half in jest.

While Davey scrambled through the park looking for more sticks to create arms and something to use for eyes and a nose, Jo sat on a nearby bench and watched. She released a sigh when Pete sat down next to her, his expression troubled.

"Mind telling me what happened back there?" he asked quietly. "One minute everything was fine and you had a smile on your face, the next you looked as if you'd caught me kicking your dog."

She could have lied and pretended that nothing had happened, but he would never buy it, not after she'd all but walked out on him. She might as well admit to the truth.

"You said something that reminded me that all this is just temporary."

He stared at her blankly. "You were the one who said you were only here for a while, not me. What did I say?"

"That you couldn't be responsible for my decision to stay or go." She met his shocked gaze. "And you were right. It has to be about me. All of this…" She waved a hand to encompass him and Davey. "It's not mine."

"I was just teasing you about the house," Pete said, clearly contrite. "I thought you knew that."

"I know that's what you intended," she agreed. "But there was an underlying truth that I can't ignore."

"Underlying truth," he repeated as if it were a foreign concept. "I only say what I mean, Jo. There was no underlying truth or undercurrent or hidden meaning. That's a female thing."

She shot a sharp look at him. "You really don't want to go there."

"I just meant that you can count on whatever I say. I don't have hidden agendas."

She gave him a sad look. "I used to believe that. Now I know that I have to listen to what you don't say as much as what you do."

"And you got all this from some stupid comment I made as a joke?" he asked, clearly exasperated.

"Yes."

"Well, listen to this, then," he said heatedly, grasping her shoulders and pulling her close, then claiming her mouth with a ferocity that sucked the breath right out of her lungs.

Only after what seemed like an eternity did the kiss gentle before ending on a sigh. His. Maybe hers.

He gazed deep into her eyes. "Did you hear what I was saying then?"

Shaken, she nodded. She hadn't needed words to get that particular message.

"What? Say it, so I can be sure we're on the same page about that much at least."

"That you want me."

He shoved a hand through his hair. "And that's all?" he asked with evident frustration. "You just felt the wanting?"

She nodded.

"Not the love?"

Oh, how she wanted to believe in the love, but she couldn't let herself. "No," she said softly. "Not the love."

Pete regarded her wearily. "Then, darlin', I think you might want to consider the possibility that you're tone-deaf, if all you can hear is what might tear us apart, instead of the one thing that will keep us together."

He stood up, called to Davey, then gave her another of those weary looks. "I'll take you home now. Give you some time to think."

Jo nodded. "That's probably best," she said, though being home alone with her thoughts was the last thing she really wanted.

When Davey came up, he studied them both worriedly. "Are you guys fighting?"

Jo forced a smile. "No."

"Yes," Pete said, then ruffled his son's hair. "But we'll settle it. That's a promise."

"I hope so," Davey said, his gaze on Jo. "'Cause I want you to spend time with me and Dad next time I come."

"If I'm here, it's a date," Jo promised.

But if she had even half a grain of sense left in her head, she'd make sure to be long gone.

For the first time in the two years that he and his son had been separated, Pete regretted the boy's presence. He wanted to settle this thing with Jo before it got all blown out of proportion and she did something they'd both regret. But he knew he simply had to back-burner that conversation until he got back from Richmond on Monday. It made the rest of Sunday and the trip down to Kelsey's drag out like water torture.

They were halfway down there when Davey announced, "Dad, I've been thinking."

"About?"

"Jo."

He glanced over at his son. "Oh?"

"I think she's mad at us."

"Not us, kiddo. Me."

"How come?"

"I'm not entirely sure, but I'll straighten it out."

"And she'll be there when I come back?"

"Yes," Pete said. She would be there, no matter what he had to do to guarantee it. "You really liked her, didn't you?"

"Uh huh."

"What did you like about her?" he asked curiously. Pete knew what *he* loved—her strength, her humor, her gentleness—but those weren't the things that would appeal to a six-year-old.

Davey's expression turned thoughtful. "Well, she's pretty and all that, but I liked it best that she didn't care about getting all messed up. She played with me and just had fun. Mom's always worried about her hair and stuff."

Pete sighed. He didn't want Davey to start making this kind of comparison. "There's nothing wrong with your mom wanting to look nice."

"I know," Davey replied. "But there's nothing wrong with having fun, either."

"No," Pete agreed. "No, there's not."

He was still thinking about that when he got back home that night. Jo had brought fun back into both their lives. He wasn't going to let that go without a fight, especially not over some silly argument he didn't entirely understand. Underlying truths be damned, he thought viciously. He intended to talk to her in plain English until she got how much he loved her.

But before he could call her, he noticed that the answering machine light was blinking like crazy. He pressed the button for messages as he took off his jacket.

"We need to talk," Kelsey announced, her tone petulant. "Who is this woman that Davey was going on and on about? Call me the minute you get in."

Pete sighed. He'd anticipated this. Kelsey hated him interfering in her social life, but she had no such qualms about involving herself in his. And it went without saying that Davey would inadvertently get her all riled up with his glowing remarks about the new woman in Pete's life.

Up till now, there hadn't been many opportunities for her to ask questions. The few women he'd dated since the divorce had merely been passing through. Because of that, he'd kept them away from his son. He hadn't wanted Davey to go through some perpetual cycle of attachment and loss the way he had as a boy.

He'd broken that rule with Jo. Though she was still cautious with him—more than cautious, if yesterday was anything to go by—*he* knew she was in his life to stay. He wanted her and his son to get to know each other and to get along.

Until this moment, listening to his ex-wife's tone, he'd been ecstatic at how well the weekend had gone. Jo and Davey had taken to each other at once. It had never occurred to Pete to tell Davey not to mention Jo to his mother. Even if it had, he wouldn't have done it. Teaching a kid to keep secrets from one parent or another just to keep the peace was flat-out wrong.

Based on the six messages that were more of the

same and because he knew his ex-wife would only keep calling until she got the answers she wanted, he grabbed a bottle of beer from the fridge and called her back.

"What's up?" he asked, as if she hadn't already made that plain in her message.

"Who's Jo?"

"A friend."

"I thought you said you weren't going to parade your women in front of Davey."

He bit back a sharp retort about her parade of men through their son's life. "For starters, I don't have a lot of women in my life, so there's never going to be a parade."

She hesitated, then asked, "What's different about this one?"

Before he could answer, she gasped. "Oh, my God, Jo—she's the one, isn't she? Jo's the reason our marriage fell apart. Jo, what was her name? Something Italian. D'Angelo? That's it. Is that who you were with this weekend? The woman who broke up our marriage?"

Pete was stunned by the totally unfounded accusation. "What the hell are you talking about, Kelsey? Our marriage fell apart because you were unhappy. You didn't want to stay here, and I wouldn't move."

"I didn't want to stay there because I knew you were still in love with someone else and that everything in that stupid place was a reminder of her. The whole town knew I was your second choice."

Pete clamped a tight lid on his temper. "You're revising history, Kelsey. I did everything I could think of to make our marriage work. I never once threw some other woman in your face."

"But she was there just the same," she insisted stubbornly. "Don't you think I knew all about your sweet little summer romance with that girl from Boston? The whole county knew about it. Even when we made love, I knew she was in your head. You couldn't stop talking about her. The two of you were sickening."

"And yet you couldn't wait to sleep with me," he reminded her.

"I wasn't in that bed alone, hot stuff," she reminded him. "You didn't put up much of a fight."

Pete sighed. He hated it, but there was no denying what she said. Rehashing it again wasn't going to get them anywhere. "Kelsey, all of that happened a long time ago. It doesn't matter now."

"It does if she's the woman you introduced to our son. I won't have it, Pete," she said heatedly. "I won't allow you to humiliate me like that. It was bad enough that everyone in town knew about her, that they knew you'd only married me because of the baby."

"How am I humiliating you?" he asked, genuinely baffled by her spin on his relationship with Jo. "We've been divorced for a couple of years now. How many men have you introduced into Davey's life? Have I ever suggested that you're doing it to humiliate me? My only complaint is when you neglect him while you're courting your latest conquest."

"This is different," she insisted. "This Jo is the woman who came between us."

"I think you have that backward," he said. "The truth is that you're the woman who came between me and Jo. That was my fault, and I took responsibility for it. When you got pregnant, I married you."

"Only out of obligation," she repeated.

"Yes," he said, seeing little point in sugarcoating the truth when they both knew it. "But I wanted it to work, Kelsey. I gave it my all. You can't possibly deny that."

"Really? How many times were you thinking of her when we made love? Don't you think I knew that? You'd get this faraway, sad look in your eyes, and I always knew you wished I was her."

The conversation was spinning wildly out of control, and Pete was tired of it. She wouldn't believe anything he said anyway, not when she was in this bitter, accusatory mood.

"I've got to go," he said. "We'll discuss this some other time."

"I won't let you see Davey if you insist on having her around," she threatened.

It was the last straw. His temper snapped. "Don't you dare try to use that boy as a weapon," Pete retorted furiously. "Two can play at that game, Kelsey, and trust me, if I play, I'll play to win."

He hung up before she could reply to that, then threw the half-empty beer bottle across the room. It shattered against the wall, sending glass and golden liquid raining down.

"Pete?"

He turned to find Jo staring at him, her eyes wide with shock.

"I'm sorry," he said tightly. "I didn't know you were there."

"I just got here. I knocked, but when you didn't answer, I came on in. I hope that's okay."

"Yeah, sure," he said, raking a hand through his hair. "Why are you here?"

She regarded him hesitantly. "I came over because I thought we ought to talk, but if this is a bad time, that can wait. What on earth happened just now? Who were you yelling at?"

"Just a little chat with my ex-wife," he said, forcing a light note into his voice. "She knows how to push my buttons."

"Want to talk about it?"

"Absolutely not," he said flatly. "Now come here and kiss me."

She gave him a skeptical look. "Don't you think we should clean up the mess first?" She gestured toward the puddle of beer and broken glass. "That one, and the mess I made of things yesterday morning?"

He glanced at the glass and liquid on the floor. It could wait. So could the conversation, if her being here meant she was reconsidering that stupid underlying truth garbage. There was one way to find out.

"We could mop up the mess," he agreed. "Or we could go upstairs and make love. You tell me which sounds like more fun."

"Going upstairs, definitely," she said, but she still didn't move. Nor did she accept his outstretched hand. "But I think we should talk first. About what happened yesterday morning and about what happened just now. Something tells me the latter is even more important."

"Why?"

"Because it's real life, Pete. You can't protect me

from the bad stuff. And I know you're still angry about what happened yesterday. Let's get it all out in the open. We can't heal things and move on if we don't face them."

"I'm not trying to protect you from anything," he said defensively.

She gave him a disbelieving look. "Do you honestly think I don't see that you're determined not to ever let anything hurt me again? You're trying to make up for what happened seven years ago. You want to push all of that into some hole and bury it, pretend it never happened."

"So what if I am? What's wrong with wanting you to be happy?"

"Nothing. I love you for trying, but unfortunately life simply can't be all smooth sailing. We have to be able to weather all of it."

"We're not making love, are we?" he asked, resigned.

She grinned at him. "Not just yet. You pick up the glass, and I'll get some soapy water to clean up the mess."

"You know that's the symptom, not the issue, don't you?"

"Of course, but you can tell me all about it while we work."

He laughed at the idea that he could explain it all so easily. "It's not that big a mess. It won't take that long to clean it up."

She studied him quizzically. "Is it such a big issue, then?"

He snagged her hand and pulled her into his arms, then rested his chin on her head. "It could be, if we let it turn into one."

"Then we won't let it," she said simply.

He gazed into her eyes, surprised. Her doubts of the day before seemed to have vanished. "Easy as that?"

"If we face it together," she said at once. "That's what I was going to tell you. That's the conclusion I reached."

And seeing the confidence and love shining in her eyes, Pete was almost able to convince himself that she was right. And so he sat down, pulled her onto his lap and told her about his fight with Kelsey.

Jo had never let herself think that much about Pete's ex-wife. She hadn't wanted to think about the woman who'd stolen him away from her. Not that Pete was blameless. They'd acknowledged that and moved on.

But Kelsey Prescott Catlett was some faceless woman who was no longer a part of his life, beyond her role as the mother of his child. That's the way Jo wanted to keep it. She could see, after listening to Pete, that it wasn't going to be that easy.

"She sounds jealous," she said when he was through.

"Don't be ridiculous."

"What do you think is behind her reaction?" she asked.

He considered the question, his expression thoughtful, then shrugged. "Okay, she's jealous, but that's absurd. She wanted the divorce. She's been dating ever since she got to Richmond. Why, all of a sudden, is she all bent out of shape about me having someone in my life."

"Because it's me," she said simply. "I suppose I can't really blame her. It's another one of those reality checks like the one that got to me on Sunday. We have to deal with them, Pete. They're not going to go away."

He gave her a questioning look. "But I thought you were."

"A momentary panic attack," she said.

"How'd you get over it?"

"I tried to imagine my life without you in it. I couldn't." Saying that made her vulnerable, which terrified her, but it was the truth. He needed to know it.

"Make me a promise, darlin'."

"Anything."

"If you ever feel one of these panic attacks coming on again, talk to me. Don't ever just turn tail and run."

Jo nodded. It was an easy promise to make, because she'd made it to herself only a few days ago. Somehow, on Sunday morning she'd lost track of that. It wouldn't happen again.

"Come here and kiss me," she said, fisting her hand in his shirt and dragging him toward her. "That'll help me remember the promise, if we seal it with a kiss."

He grinned. "Always happy to oblige, when it involves kissing you. Do you think you'll need reminding often?"

She chuckled at his hopeful expression. "Only about a hundred times a day."

He grinned. "It's going to be damn hard getting any work done at that rate, but I'll give it my best."

"You always do," Jo said right before his lips met hers and the world went spinning.

14

Jo couldn't seem to shake the image of walking into Pete's and hearing him on the phone in such a bitter argument with his ex-wife over her. She'd gone over there figuring she owed him a conversation about the whole incident on Sunday. She'd even had what she was going to say all planned out, but she hadn't expected to face a whole new quandary that seemed to turn her temporary moment of insanity into little more than a minor tempest.

She'd gotten scared, that was all. She'd let all her old fears and insecurities resurface in the blink of an eye, blown it all out of proportion and started an argument she hadn't known how to end. If she hadn't realized how stupid it was on her own, then walking in on Pete's argument with his ex-wife had shown her.

Those two had real issues, hurtful issues that could come between Jo and Pete, if they weren't very careful, if they weren't united. Ironically, having that common goal made their relationship stronger than ever. Jo doubted that Kelsey had considered that outcome before calling Pete to throw down the gauntlet.

Jo smiled as she thought of just how united she and Pete had been during the night. They'd definitely been in tune then. All their differences had been put behind them.

She'd awakened in his arms this morning, bounced out of his bed and gone happily off with a kiss to do more research for his landscaping projects. She wanted to finalize those plans with him soon, then talk to the local nursery owner about ordering the plants so they'd be in at the optimum time for planting in the spring.

Today it was even possible to believe that spring might be right around the corner. The sun had warmed things up to nearly sixty. The last of the snow had melted and she'd even spotted a couple of crocuses coming up in the garden at Rose Cottage. Daffodils were bound to be close behind. Perhaps that's why she was suddenly feeling so optimistic—maybe it was the natural exuberance of someone attuned to spring's symbolic evidence of rebirth and renewal. In her profession, the seasonal changes were something to be watched with appreciation and respect.

She came inside from her tour of Rose Cottage's garden feeling lighthearted. Maybe she'd even call Mike this afternoon and set up an appointment to talk about that partnership. It was time. She might as well admit that despite that little incident of self-doubt on Sunday, she wasn't going anywhere. Her future was here, hopefully with Pete, but if not, she knew she could be happy right here in Rose Cottage, which held so many joyous memories.

When the phone rang, Jo answered with a cheery greeting, only to have someone launch a venomous harangue that had her reaching for a chair to sit down. Her knees went weak and heat rose in her cheeks as she was called a litany of uncomplimentary names.

Kelsey, no doubt, she realized when her brain cells recovered from the initial shock of being verbally attacked and focused on the female voice, rather than the hateful words.

"I won't listen to this," she said quietly, interrupting the steady flow of venom. She hung up.

Naturally, the phone immediately rang again. She debated not answering, then decided to make at least one effort to turn it into a civilized, rational conversation. It was doubtful, but she couldn't ignore the opportunity to try to mend a few fences.

"Hello, Kelsey," she said, her voice as calm as she could make it when her nerves were a jittery mess. She was proud of the maturity and restraint she was capable of under these circumstances.

Apparently her recognition of the caller gave Kelsey pause. She was greeted with silence.

"If you want to talk about this calmly, that's one thing," Jo said, seizing the advantage she'd gained by catching the woman off guard. "But I won't listen to you spew all that garbage at me."

"You think you're so damn high and mighty, don't you?" Kelsey said heatedly. "You're nothing but a two-bit—"

Jo cut her off. "There you go again. I told you I wouldn't listen to that and I won't. Now, do we keep it civilized and try to work this out for your son's sake, or do I hang up again?"

"Don't you dare say a word about my son," Kelsey

shouted. "You don't have the right. He's mine and I won't have you in his life, do you understand that?"

"I understand why you might prefer that, but you don't get your way on this one, Kelsey. If I'm with Pete, I will be spending time with Davey. He's a wonderful boy," she said, determined to take the high road until it fell off the edge of a probably inevitable cliff. "You've done an amazing job with him."

Kelsey was silent, probably grappling with how to react to hearing such a compliment from a woman she evidently despised. "I don't want you around my son," she said eventually.

"I can understand why you'd be concerned about that, but I promise you I won't do anything to interfere in your relationship. You're his mom, period."

"Aren't you hearing me? I said I don't want you anywhere near him. And stay away from Pete, too," Kelsey said. "You ruined our marriage, and I won't let you have him now."

"It's not up to you," Jo said patiently.

"Oh, really?" Kelsey replied with a bitter laugh. "Sweetheart, I'm holding all the cards. You had what? A couple of months with Pete when you were just a kid? I was with him for five years, as his *wife*."

"And yet you still don't know him," Jo retorted with quiet confidence.

"I know him well enough," Kelsey corrected. "I know he will never do anything that might cost him his son."

"Of course not," Jo agreed.

"You could be the one who costs him Davey," Kelsey said coldly. "Which of you do you think he'll choose?"

Jo felt sick. How could this woman use her own child to threaten his father? But it was plain she wasn't above doing just that and turning all of the joy Jo and Pete had found into something ugly that could only tear them apart.

"I hope it won't come to that," Jo told her quietly. "I hope you care enough about your son that you'd never use him in that way. Davey loves both of you. Don't make *him* choose. It could backfire on you."

"Don't you dare suggest that you know more about my child than I do," Kelsey said furiously. "I hope you enjoyed that cozy little time you all spent together, because, trust me, it's going to have to last you forever."

This time, Kelsey was the one who hung up, leaving Jo shaking. Tears welled up in her eyes and streamed down her cheeks, because she knew that if push came to shove, she would walk away from Pete before she'd let that wonderful boy of his be hurt because of her.

And if that happened—*when* it happened, she thought fatalistically—it was going to break her heart.

Jo was still sitting at the kitchen table, her head aching from all the tears but her cheeks dry at last, when her sisters came through the door. Their timing couldn't have been any worse. One look at her and the fussing started.

"What did he do? What did that son of a bitch do to you?" Ashley demanded, bringing her an unwanted glass of water, then pulling a chair right up beside her.

"It wasn't Pete," Jo told her emphatically. "At least not directly."

"I don't care if it was directly or indirectly, I won't let him get away with hurting you," Ashley declared. "I warned him. Heck, we all did."

Melanie placed a hand on Ashley's shoulder. "Maybe we should let Jo talk."

"Good idea," Maggie said, settling into a chair on Jo's other side.

"I don't know where to start," Jo told them. For them to understand, she needed to go all the way back to the beginning. She supposed it was way past time for her to do that.

"Take your time," Melanie said. "How about some soup first? Have you eaten?"

"I don't think so." She'd lost track of time, lost track of everything in the misery that had swamped her after Kelsey's threatening call. "But I'm not hungry."

"You need food." Melanie shot a warning look at Ashley. "Let's put the conversation on hold until you've eaten something."

Ashley frowned at her, but didn't argue, which Jo figured was testament to how awful she must look.

Everybody sat in silence and watched as she sipped the hot, homemade vegetable soup that Melanie had defrosted from one of the containers Maggie had left in the freezer.

"This is delicious," Jo said, wanting to end the awkward silence. "Will you teach me how to make it, Maggie?"

"Sure," Maggie said at once. "It's best if you use

fresh vegetables, but you can make it in no time if you use the packages of frozen vegetables."

"Are you finished yet?" Ashley demanded impatiently. "We're not here to swap recipes."

"Do you want some more?" Melanie inquired, giving Ashley another of those daunting looks that effectively silenced her, at least temporarily.

"No, I'm finished," Jo said with some regret. If she could have forced down another bite, she would have been able to postpone this conversation.

"Your color's better," Ashley noted.

"But there's still no sparkle in your eyes," Maggie commented. "What happened here today?"

"I got a call from Pete's ex-wife. Let's just say she's not happy with me and leave it at that."

"Where the hell does she get off calling you?" Ashley demanded. "If she has a problem, she needs to take it up with Pete."

"I couldn't agree more," Jo said. "And, believe me, she's made her unhappiness known to him, too."

"What did he have to say?"

"Last night, he told her to butt out. He doesn't know about what happened today. He doesn't know that she warned me she'll use Davey to come between us. She wants to force Pete to choose between his son and me."

To her relief, all three of her sisters looked totally scandalized by that.

"She doesn't stand a prayer in court," Ashley said. "If Pete needs help fighting her, tell him to come to me."

Jo regarded her with surprise. "You'd go to bat for him?"

"On something like that? Of course." She frowned. "Unless you don't want me to."

"No, of course not. I think it would be great. I just don't want it to come to that. It'll be better for everyone if they can work this out between the two of them without involving lawyers and a judge."

"Why is his ex-wife all of a sudden focusing on you?" Maggie asked.

"I guess Davey went home and told her about me and she went all weird and jealous." She debated not getting into the rest—into the past—but knew she'd feel better once the whole story was out there. "I almost think I understand some of what she's feeling."

Her sisters stared at her blankly. "You're sympathizing with her?"

"No," Jo said at once. "Not sympathizing, exactly." She sighed. "It's a long story."

"How long can it be?" Maggie asked. "You haven't known the man that long."

"Actually I have," Jo admitted. "I've known Pete for over seven years."

"Oh, my God," Melanie whispered softly, her eyes filled with sudden understanding. "He's the one."

"The one what?" Maggie asked.

"The one she was always hiding out from when she came down here while each of us was staying at Rose Cottage," Melanie said. She looked at Jo. "I'm right, aren't I? He's the person you were avoiding?"

Jo nodded. "I've been involved with Pete since I was eighteen years old," she finally admitted. "Or rather, I was involved with him that summer, and have been regretting it ever since because of how things turned out."

All three sisters stared at her as if she'd started babbling in some incomprehensible language.

"How?" Ashley asked.

"When?" Maggie chimed in.

Melanie frowned. "Wasn't he married?"

Jo scowled at her. "Of course he wasn't married when we met," she said. "But then he was, and that put an end to things."

By the time she'd explained it all, her sisters were staring at her with stunned expressions.

"And you never said a word," Ashley said. "I don't believe you could keep something this huge from us. Your first big romance and we never suspected a thing."

"You were all caught up in your own lives by then. And the whole pregnancy and marriage thing came up so soon after I got back to Boston that there was hardly any time to mention that I'd fallen in love before I would have had to say that he'd broken my heart."

"And then I had to go and hire him," Ashley said, her expression grim. "No wonder you were so furious with me."

"You didn't know," Jo said. "And it turns out that it was the best thing that could have happened. We've moved past all that, or past most of it, anyway."

"Then you've forgiven him? You trust him to do right by you now?" Maggie asked.

Jo nodded slowly. "Yes," she said quietly. "I think I do. But I can't be the kind of woman who gets between a man and his son, no matter how much I want a future with Pete. I could never have done it back then, even if he'd given me a choice, and I can't do it now."

Ashley gave her a look filled with resolve. "Then we won't let it happen that way. Tell Pete about his ex-wife's call—and I mean every single vicious word of it—then tell him to come and see me if his wife doesn't start to see reason. I'm sure I can put a legal spin on things that will wake her up."

"Then you think there's still a chance for us to work this out?" Jo asked Ashley.

"Absolutely," her sisters said, obviously in total accord.

"If he's the one you want, then he's the one you should have," Melanie said. "And just to lock it in, I think I'll send Mike over here first thing in the morning to work out that business partnership."

"Maybe now's not the right time to do that," Jo protested. "Don't get me wrong. I want to do it and I want to stay here, but if things don't work out for me and Pete…"

"They will," Ashley assured her. "Have you ever known any of us not to get what we want when we fight for it together?"

A grin slowly spread across Jo's face. For the first time all afternoon, her heart felt lighter. "Now that you mention it, no."

"Then let's not even consider the possibility of ruining that track record," Ashley said, giving her an encouraging smile. "Deal?"

"Deal."

When Pete checked his messages at midafternoon, he had three from the D'Angelo sisters—one each from

Ashley, Maggie and Melanie. But none from Jo. That alone told him that where he needed to be was Rose Cottage, and he didn't need any one of them telling him that. Something had happened, and the sisters were on the warpath. Even his answering service had gotten that much. Each message had been marked *URGENT*.

Pete called his secretary and had her reschedule the rest of his appointments and drove straight to Rose Cottage. When he knocked on the door, he wasn't sure what sort of response he expected, but it wasn't a woman who looked as if she'd spent most of the day crying and the rest trying to cover up the evidence.

"You're here," she said, looking surprised. "Who called you?"

"Ashley, Maggie and Melanie, in that order. They left messages. Since it had to be about you, I came here instead. What's going on?"

"I went a few rounds with Kelsey this morning," she said succinctly. "She called and shared her displeasure about our relationship."

Pete felt his blood begin to boil. "She did *what?*"

Jo summed up their conversation. "My sisters thought you ought to know what she's threatening. Ashley says she'll be happy to give you legal advice, if you want it. I'm still hoping it won't come to that." She lifted her gaze to meet his. "I'm so sorry. This is all my fault."

"How the hell is it your fault?" he asked heatedly. "This is Kelsey, start to finish. I'll handle her." He pressed a hard kiss to her lips. "You okay?"

She nodded, though he couldn't help thinking she still looked wounded. The only way to wipe that expression from her eyes, though, was to settle this with Kelsey once and for all. The urgency of that was the only thing that could have gotten him to leave Jo alone right now.

"Then I'm going to get this straightened out," he said with grim determination.

She regarded him with worry. "What are you going to do? You're not going down there and have some huge fight in front of your son, are you?"

Since that was precisely what Pete had intended, he faltered at the warning note in her voice. "No," he said retreating. "But I have to get through to her."

"Then make her come here. Tell her you need to talk and to get someone to look after Davey. Maybe he can stay with a friend tonight."

"I don't want her here," Pete countered. "I don't want her anywhere near you."

"She's not going to come near me, not when she has a chance to be with you. Come on, Pete. It's the only way."

"I suppose," he said skeptically. "Maybe we should have this meeting in your sister's office. That way Kelsey won't be able to misinterpret every word out of my mouth."

"Having a lawyer there, at least this first time, will only put her on the defensive. You have to try to work it out on your own."

Pete understood her logic, but the thought of actually inviting Kelsey to come here to talk made him nervous. He knew better than anyone just how easily she could misinterpret the overture.

But what could happen, really? It wasn't as if she could make something happen between them, not the way she'd managed to when he was twenty. He could control this meeting.

He tucked a finger under Jo's chin. "I'll call her," he said. "And I swear to you I will get this resolved tonight. Then you and I have a date, okay?"

"Let's not make any kind of plans just yet," she pleaded. "Just keep all your focus on making this okay so you won't lose Davey."

"I'm not going to lose Davey," he said with finality.

Jo grinned at his conviction. "Then tomorrow morning we'll celebrate that," she promised.

"Eight o'clock? My place for pancakes?"

She slid into his embrace and held on tight. "My favorite way to start the day," she told him, her words muffled against his chest.

"Next to making love, mine, too," he said, smiling as he heard her chuckle.

"That goes without saying," she agreed, then lifted her gaze to his. "Make this work, Pete, please."

"I'll do my best, darlin'. That's a promise."

Even as he said it, though, he wondered if his promises meant a damn thing to her. He couldn't blame her if they didn't. So far, his track record wasn't exactly stellar.

15

Pete paced through the house he'd once shared with Kelsey, debating for the thousandth time if he'd made the right decision by asking her to come here. Too late now, though. She was on her way.

Instead of regretting the invitation, he needed to be planning what he was going to say to make her see reason. Unfortunately, he doubted there were sufficient words in the English language to make his ex-wife see past her own self-interest. He'd always known how self-absorbed she was, but her threats this morning only proved it.

It was nearly seven by the time he saw her headlights swing into the driveway. The knot in his gut twisted even tighter. He went and opened the door to avoid the awkward moment when she'd have to decide whether to ring the bell or walk right in. He was pretty sure he knew which she'd choose, if only to make a point that she still had a right to be here. Since she didn't make a habit of showing up, he'd never bothered to change the locks. Maybe he should do that just to make his own point.

"You made good time," he said when she got to the door.

"Rush-hour traffic wasn't too bad, for a change."

"You have any trouble finding someone to stay with Davey?"

"He's doing a sleepover next door," she said defensively. "You can call if you don't believe me."

Oh, how he was tempted to do just that, but someone had to start the mutual respect and trust needed here, and it might as well be him.

"I believe you," he said, drawing a look of surprise.

"You do?"

"You're not going to lie to me about something you know I can check out for myself, Kelsey. I want to trust you. I always have."

"Yeah, right." She walked into the living room and tossed her fake fur jacket over the back of a chair, then looked around. "You haven't changed much."

Pete shrugged. "I didn't see any point to it. It's okay."

She frowned at that. "Just *okay* was always good enough for you, wasn't it?"

"And it was never good enough for you," he replied, regret, rather than accusation, in his voice. But even if he'd built his dream house while they were still together, it wouldn't have been enough. All she'd ever cared about was leaving for a more exciting life.

"I suppose that's true," she said. "Do you have any wine in the house? I could use a glass."

"You can't drink and then drive back to Richmond," he said.

She gave him a seductive smile. "Then I'll just have to crash here, won't I?"

"Kelsey!"

"Oh, don't go all weird on me, Pete. It's not as if we haven't slept under the same roof and in the same bed before. Maybe we should do that tonight, for old time's sake."

"I don't think so. What we had is over, Kelsey. Surely you know that by now. Hell, it was your idea to end it."

She ran a polished red nail down his cheek, then sashayed toward the kitchen. "Maybe I've changed my mind," she called over her shoulder as she apparently went in search of the wine she wanted.

Pete bit back a sigh. He was not going to let these seductive games of hers get in the way of the discussion they needed to have. If he overreacted and got her angry, they would wind up settling nothing. Besides, she was mostly talk.

She came back from the kitchen with two glasses of white wine and handed one to him. He set it aside.

"Let's talk about making peace," he said quietly. "For our son's sake."

Her expression brightened. "That's exactly what I'd hoped you'd say."

"You did?"

"It's time to put the past couple of years behind us, Pete. We can start over, make a home for our son." A smile touched the corners of her lips. "Maybe give him a baby brother or sister."

Pete stared at her. His mouth had gone dry, but he managed to squeak out one word. "What?"

"Don't look so shocked, sweetheart. We both know this is for the best. You believe in family. I've had my taste of freedom. It's past time for us to get back together and be the family Davey wants."

Pete shook off the panic crawling up his spine. "What exactly are you suggesting, Kelsey?"

"Darling, isn't it obvious? I want to move back home."

"You mean here, to town," he said, hoping he'd gotten it all wrong, though she was expressing herself pretty clearly for once.

She regarded him with tolerant amusement. "No, of course not. I mean right here, with you. This is our home, after all. Maybe we can even have that big wedding we missed out on the first time around."

The words hung in the air, leaving Pete speechless.

She put aside her own glass of wine and twined her arms around his neck, her breasts pressed against him. "Isn't that the news you've been waiting for all this time?" she asked, her face radiating confidence. "Davey and I are coming back to you."

Jo was going just a little stir-crazy waiting to hear from Pete. She knew they'd made plans for breakfast, but she wasn't sure she could wait till morning to find out what had happened when he saw Kelsey.

She sat at the kitchen table and watched the minutes tick off the clock. Each one felt as if it took an hour to pass. Surely the stupid clock was broken.

Since she didn't dare call Pete's and risk throwing a monkey wrench into whatever delicate negotiations were happening there, she called Ashley and announced, "I'm going out of my mind."

"Why? What's happened?" her sister asked at once. "Do you need me to come over?"

"No, I just need you to talk me down."

"Down from what?"

"This lonely limb I'm sitting on."

"You're talking in riddles. Stop it right this instant or I *will* come over."

Jo laughed. "I'm not literally on some limb."

"Thank God."

"Pete called Kelsey. She's supposed to be here now, so they can try to work out this mess."

"That's a good thing, isn't it?"

"It should be, assuming she'll listen to reason. I'm not convinced she will."

"I'm sure Pete can handle her," Ashley soothed. "He was married to her, after all. And if he can't, he has me as legal backup. Based on what you've told me about her neglect, he has more than ample grounds to reopen the custody arrangement and file for permanent custody."

"He won't do that unless he has to," Jo reminded her.

"But it is a nice piece of leverage to have, don't you think?"

"I suppose. I just hate anything that turns Davey into a pawn between them."

"Which just proves that you're a better woman than his own mother."

"You're biased."

"Not about this," Ashley insisted. "The evidence

speaks for itself. You're putting the child's needs before your own. And just so you know, now that I understand the whole story, I have to admire Pete for doing the same thing seven years ago, even though it cost both of you very dearly."

"I know," Jo said softly. "Me, too. He's a good man, Ashley. I don't want to be the reason he or Davey gets hurt."

"Not you, sweetie. Kelsey will get full credit for that one, if she doesn't see reason. You didn't break them up. That happened long before you even came back to town."

"I suppose."

"Look, if you're so worried about what went on over there tonight, why don't you go on over?" Ashley suggested. "Pete probably figures you've crawled into bed by now and he doesn't want to wake you. There's no need to wait till morning."

Jo thought about that. "I suppose it wouldn't hurt. She'll be gone, so it's not as if I'll get her all stirred up again. If she's not gone, I'll turn around and leave. She'll never even know I was there."

"Sounds like a plan to me," Ashley enthused. "I hope Pete has good news for you when you get there."

"Me, too," Jo said with heartfelt yearning. "Me, too."

Pete stared at his ex-wife as if she'd suddenly grown two heads. "You want to move back home?" he echoed. "And get married again?"

Kelsey nodded. "Moving away, leaving you…" She shrugged. "It was a mistake, Pete. I want to try again.

We belong together. We have a history. We have a son. I know this is what you want, too. You fought so hard to keep me from going. I finally get it now. You were right. What we have is too important to throw it all away."

"*You* threw it away, Kelsey. You can't just decide out of the blue that you want it all back. It's too late."

"It's never too late," she said, still clinging to him, her breath whispering against his cheek.

And then her mouth was on his, hot and urgent and demanding. Once the greediness of her kiss would have turned him on, but not now, not since he'd rediscovered what it was to like to be kissed with real love and passion, not just lust and convenience.

He tried to push her away, but she was determined. She cupped his head with her hands, ground her mouth against his until he tasted blood.

"Enough," he said, lifting her and setting her aside just as he heard a faint whisper of sound and a gasp. He whirled around just in time to see Jo's horrified expression before she took off at a run.

"Dammit to hell," he muttered, tearing after her, Kelsey and her ridiculous request forgotten. He would deal with her later. He wasn't going to allow her to ruin his one chance at happiness for a second time.

He caught up with Jo as she made the turn onto the main road. She was on foot, which must be why he hadn't heard her arrival. He fell into step beside her, but that only made her pick up her pace. She obviously wasn't going to make this easy, wasn't going to wait for explanations.

Finally he latched onto her arm. "Whoa, sweetheart, where are you going?"

Tears were streaking down her cheeks. "Home," she said fiercely. "Back to Boston." She frowned at him, then added bitterly, "Again."

"Why?" he asked, though he knew perfectly well that she was running because of what she'd heard Kelsey saying back at his house, what she'd seen. He couldn't be sure how much she'd heard, but it had evidently been enough. Too much, in fact.

"Because I won't stand between you and your family," she said, her voice cracking on a sob. She gave him a look filled with heartbreak. "We were so close this time, Pete, but I don't blame you for choosing them. It's what you have to do. They obviously need you."

He wanted to shake her gently, make her listen, but first he had to find the right words. Filled with desperation, he searched his heart.

Holding tight to her shoulders so she couldn't break away and run again, he said, "Look at me, Jo."

When she continued staring at the ground, he repeated, "Look at me. Please."

She finally lifted her gaze.

"Now listen to me," he pleaded. "Really listen, Jo."

He waited until she nodded, then said, "What I need is you," he said quietly, his gaze locked on hers. He couldn't get this wrong. He had to find the words to convince her to ignore whatever she'd seen and heard and listen to his heart. "It's you I need, Jo. Not Kelsey. It's always been you. I thought I was doing the honorable thing seven years ago, but all I did was make a bunch of people miserable. I won't do that again."

"But your son," she protested. "I know how much

you love him. Kelsey's right. You should be a family, if at all possible."

"Davey will always be important to me. I'll never abandon him, not for anyone, but it's over between me and Kelsey. Hell, it was over before it really began."

He brushed a wayward tear from her too-pale cheek. "You're the family I need, Jo. And we'll make a place for Davey, too, on whatever terms I can work out with Kelsey, but I won't give in to her emotional blackmail. I want to do things right this time. I want to marry you, if you'll have me. Maybe, depending on how things work out, Davey can spend more time with us, if you're willing, but Kelsey's out of the picture. She's my son's mother, but she is not the woman I love. Please," he whispered, "you have to listen to me. You have to *hear* me. Nothing I've ever said to you before was this important."

She was silent for so long, he thought he'd lost, but then a sigh shuddered through her and her eyes shimmered with a fresh batch of tears.

"Don't cry," he pleaded.

"Happy tears," she said, swiping at them impatiently. "Are you sure? Really sure?"

"That I want to marry you?"

She nodded.

He dug in his pocket and came out with several crumpled pieces of notepaper and a small velvet box. He tossed the notes on the ground, then flipped open the box to reveal a simple diamond set in platinum. "I bought this after I left your place earlier today. I'd planned on asking you in the morning, and I'd hoped to do it someplace a bit more romantic than a ditch by the highway," he said.

A smile trembled on her lips. "This is the most romantic place ever," she insisted. "The stars and moon are out, and I can hear the waves on the bay. What could be more amazing than that?"

He smiled. "I'm glad it's working for you. Do I get an answer?"

"I should make you wait," she said thoughtfully. Her eyes sparkled mischievously. "But I can't. I've been waiting way too long to hear those words cross your lips. Yes, Pete. Yes, I'll marry you."

He whooped, then spun her around until they were both half-dizzy. "You know, years ago, I thought maybe Rose Cottage was enchanted and that what happened with us there was some kind of dream, but it wasn't, was it?"

Jo shook her head and looked at the winking diamond on her finger. "No, the feelings were as real and lasting as it gets. It was only the humans who got it wrong for just a little while. Maybe we didn't believe hard enough. Something tells me, though, that the magic will be waiting when the next generation comes along."

"Darlin', there's no magic involved," Pete insisted. "I'm sure of that now. It's all about love. That old house has always been filled to bursting with it. A little bit was bound to rub off on anyone who passed through."

She gave him a sly grin. "Maybe I should loan it to Kelsey for a while. She needs to find a man of her own."

Pete laughed. "Something tells me she won't welcome any help from us."

Jo's expression sobered. "You need to go back and tell her, Pete."

He sighed. "I know, but can't I stay here for a couple more minutes and hold you?"

"A few more minutes," she agreed. "That's it. Then you have to go inside and make things right for your son. After that, you and I will have the rest of our lives to hold on to each other."

"That won't be nearly long enough for me," he said. "I'm holding out for eternity." He pressed a kiss against her lips. "Did you walk over here?"

"At this time of night? No way." She regarded him with chagrin. "I got so upset, I forgot all about my car."

"I'll walk you back to your car. Then I want you to go home and start a fire. Give me an hour and I'll join you. We have a lot to celebrate and we have a wedding to plan."

"Is it too much to hope that there will be more?" she asked wistfully.

Pete glanced at the house and knew the conversation awaiting him wouldn't be as easy as he wished it would be. "I hope so. She's not a bad person. She's just a little lost."

"Then show her the way," Jo said. She touched his cheek, her eyes shining. "And then come home to me."

"Ah, so you're thinking of Rose Cottage as home?"

Jo laughed and this time the sound was filled with mischief and joy. "Only till that house of yours is finished. And then I'm moving in before you change your mind and sell it to someone else."

"Never happen," Pete promised. "It was meant for you from the day I nailed the first boards into place."

"No," she said. "It was meant for *us*."

Epilogue

Jo's mother finally had time to plan a proper wedding. Jo and Pete had set the date for June in Boston and, to her mother's delight, in church, as Pete had gotten a religious annulment of his first marriage along with the divorce. Colleen D'Angelo was in her element making all the details come together. Jo hardly had to lift a finger, which was just as well since she was swamped with work in her new partnership with Mike. She'd been lucky to squeeze out a three-day weekend for the wedding and one night for a honeymoon. The real thing was going to have to be postponed for a while till things slowed down in both their lives.

She looked around the table at her family, all of whom had gathered for the rehearsal dinner, and felt contentment steal through her. Maybe it had always been meant to be this way. Maybe she and Pete had needed to endure a separation in order to know just how important this moment was.

She felt a tug on her arm and looked down at Davey. "What's up, sweet pea?" she asked.

He made a face. "Don't call me that."

She regarded him with exaggerated dismay. "Something's wrong with calling my new stepson sweet pea?"

"It's *dumb*," he said emphatically. "It's what you'd call a girl."

"Oh?" she said, giving that serious thought. "Okay, then, want me to call you macho man?"

Davey's eyes lit up. "That's a good one. Yeah, you can call me that, but what do I call you?"

She heard genuine concern in his voice, which told her to take the question very seriously. "You've been calling me Jo. Do you think that should change?"

"I don't know. You're sort of going to be my mom now, so it seems like it should."

"I'm only going to be your mom some of the time," she reminded him. "Nothing changes between you and your real mom. She will always be the most important mom you have, and you're going to be living with her, same as always, just spending a little more time with your dad and me."

In fact, the visitation arrangements were only slightly more liberal than they had been before. Pete and Kelsey had worked out a revised plan, but at least Kelsey was sticking to them. Once she had finally accepted that Pete was going to marry Jo, she'd grasped the positive benefits of having a few more weekends to herself so she could make a new life, hopefully with a new man. Right now, though, she was using the extra time to take some college classes. She'd finally made peace with Pete's decision and started to think about what she could have, if only she worked for it. Maybe she'd eventually find that exciting life she'd always longed for.

"Still, you need a special name," Davey insisted, then grinned impishly.

That expression reminded Jo why she'd fallen in love with his father and with him. With the two of them there would always be unexpected surprises.

Davey gave her a triumphant look. "Maybe I'll call you sweet pea."

"I don't think so," she said, laughing. "Try again."

"But I can't think of anything," he complained, but then his expression brightened. "How about Mama Jo? Could I call you that?"

Tears stung Jo's eyes. "Nothing would make me happier," she told him, giving him a squeeze. "I love you, kiddo. I can't wait for tomorrow to marry your dad."

"Me, either," Pete said, leaning in to steal a kiss. "It's going to be the best wedding ever."

Jo met his gaze. "It's going to be my *only* wedding ever."

He stroked a finger down her cheek and regarded her solemnly. "Guaranteed, darlin'. Guaranteed."

The wedding was everything Jo had always dreamed about, everything she and Pete had talked about all those years ago. They were surrounded by her family and even Pete's uncle, who'd insisted on coming despite the arthritis that made it increasingly difficult for him to get around.

"Glad to see the two of you together finally," he told Jo right before the ceremony, when she paused to give him a kiss on her way to the altar. "It was too long coming. I knew way back that you were the best thing that could happen to this boy."

"I knew it, too," Pete said, giving him a wink right before he turned to stand by Jo's side in front of the priest.

When it came Jo's turn to say her vows, she looked deep into Pete's eyes and saw all the love that had been shining there when she'd first met him years ago. It had only deepened and matured thanks to everything they'd been through.

She touched his cheek. "I promise in front of our families and friends and in the sight of God to love you all the days of my life. I know that my grandmother Lindsey is looking down on us today, and like your uncle, she's saying, 'It's about time.'"

"Past time," Pete said. He glanced heavenward. "I promise you that I will never let Jo down the way I did before." His gaze sought Jo's. "I make that same vow to you, to love you the way you deserve for all the rest of our days, to make a home with you, to share the joy of my son with you and to create a family of our own. I love you, Jo. Always have. Always will."

Jo's eyes stung with tears. There it was, the promise of eternity. And this time, she knew they wouldn't let anything tear them apart.

"Keep your eyes closed," Pete commanded.

"I've had 'em closed for what seems like hours. You blindfolded me in the car for the last two hours of the drive, which, I might add, you'll never get away with again. Where are we?" Jo grumbled.

"In a minute," he said. "Hold your horses."

She grinned. "Is that the way it's going to be now that we're married? You're going to be all bossy?"

He laughed. "Exactly how long do you think I'd get away with that?"

"Not long," she confirmed. "So when can I open my eyes?"

"When everything's ready."

"It's a hotel room. How much has to be done?"

To her increasing frustration, he ignored the question. She stood right where he'd set her down after carrying her across some threshold or another and waited, tapping her foot with mounting impatience.

"There," Pete said at last. "You can open your eyes now."

She scowled at him before she did. "It's a real tribute to my love for you that I have not peeked even once."

"It's a tribute to my faith in you that I knew you wouldn't," he retorted. "Do you want to discuss trust issues right now?"

"No," she said, then slowly opened her eyes to a room lit with candles and filled with bouquets of white flowers. French doors were opened to a sea breeze and the familiar sound of the bay gently splashing on the sandy beach. Delight washed over her. "It's our house. You brought us home. I had no idea it was ready."

"Didn't you wonder why I had you working so hard all over town? Mike and I taxed ourselves to come up with enough assignments that would keep you away from here. I didn't want you to know about this."

"I just thought Mike had made too many commitments and was really, really swamped," she said, moving slowly around the room in disbelief. He'd accomplished so much, and it was all exactly right. "It's beautiful, Pete. It's exactly the way I imagined it."

"I know you're not supposed to do a honeymoon quite like this, but I figured our first night together ought to be the place we were going to spend the rest of our lives. We'll make this house ours tonight."

He studied her intently. "I didn't do all the decorating. I just brought in enough furniture so we wouldn't be sitting or sleeping on the floor tonight. You can change it all, if you want."

"I'm not going to change a thing," she told him firmly. "We'll just add to it together, like the layers that come with time in a marriage."

He reached for her then. "I love you, Jo."

"And I love you." She met his gaze. "You know, I realized something while we were in Boston."

"What's that?"

"That this was the way it was meant to be. All the time apart was a blessing, because now we know how much being together really matters."

"That's one of the things I love most about you," he told her. "You've always been able to turn things around and find the blessings."

Jo wound her arms around his neck and rested her cheek against his. "And from now on, I won't have to look far."

He slid his arms around her. "You talking about the view?"

"That, and your face," she said quietly. "Being able to wake up and look into your eyes is the greatest gift I've ever been given."

"Same here, darlin', and I'll never, ever take it for granted."

And like the tides changing just a few hundred feet away, Jo knew what they were feeling right now would go on forever, steady and reliable and powerful.

* * * * *

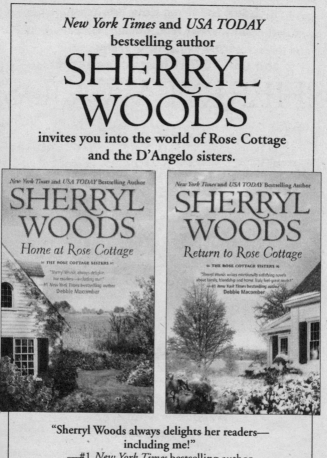

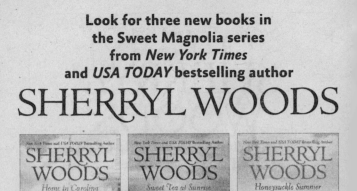

REQUEST YOUR
FREE BOOKS!

2 FREE NOVELS
FROM THE ROMANCE COLLECTION
PLUS 2 FREE GIFTS!

YES! Please send me 2 FREE novels from the Romance Collection and my 2 FREE gifts (gifts are worth about $10). After receiving them, if I don't wish to receive any more books, I can return the shipping statement marked "cancel." If I don't cancel, I will receive 4 brand-new novels every month and be billed just $5.74 per book in the U.S. or $6.24 per book in Canada. That's a saving of at least 28% off the cover price. It's quite a bargain! Shipping and handling is just 50¢ per book.* I understand that accepting the 2 free books and gifts places me under no obligation to buy anything. I can always return a shipment and cancel at any time. Even if I never buy another book, the two free books and gifts are mine to keep forever.

194/394 MDN E7NZ

Name _____ (PLEASE PRINT) _____

Address _____ Apt. #

City _____ State/Prov. _____ Zip/Postal Code

Signature (if under 18, a parent or guardian must sign)

Mail to **The Reader Service:**
IN U.S.A.: P.O. Box 1867, Buffalo, NY 14240-1867
IN CANADA: P.O. Box 609, Fort Erie, Ontario L2A 5X3

Not valid for current subscribers to the Romance Collection
or the Romance/Suspense Collection.

Want to try two free books from another line?
Call 1-800-873-8635 or visit www.morefreebooks.com.

* Terms and prices subject to change without notice. Prices do not include applicable taxes. N.Y. residents add applicable sales tax. Canadian residents will be charged applicable provincial taxes and GST. Offer not valid in Quebec. This offer is limited to one order per household. All orders subject to approval. Credit or debit balances in a customer's account(s) may be offset by any other outstanding balance owed by or to the customer. Please allow 4 to 6 weeks for delivery. Offer available while quantities last.

Your Privacy: Harlequin Books is committed to protecting your privacy. Our Privacy Policy is available online at www.eHarlequin.com or upon request from the Reader Service. From time to time we make our lists of customers available to reputable third parties who may have a product or service of interest to you. If you would prefer we not share your name and address, please check here. ☐

Help us get it right—We strive for accurate, respectful and relevant communications. To clarify or modify your communication preferences, visit us at www.ReaderService.com/consumerschoice.

MROM10

Try these Healthy and Delicious Spring Rolls!

INGREDIENTS

2 packages rice-paper spring roll wrappers (20 wrappers)

1 cup grated carrot

¼ cup bean sprouts

1 cucumber, julienned

1 red bell pepper, without stem and seeds, julienned

4 green onions finely chopped— use only the green part

DIRECTIONS

1. Soak one rice-paper wrapper in a large bowl of hot water until softened.

2. Place a pinch each of carrots, sprouts, cucumber, bell pepper and green onion on the wrapper toward the bottom third of the rice paper.

3. Fold ends in and roll tightly to enclose filling.

4. Repeat with remaining wrappers. Chill before serving.

Find this and many more delectable recipes including the perfect dipping sauce in

SHERRYL WOODS

MIRA®

www.MIRABooks.com

MSW1010BL